SPILT
MILK

SPILT MILK

AMY BEASHEL

Harper
North

HarperNorth
Windmill Green
Mount Street
Manchester M2 3NX

A division of
HarperCollinsPublishers
1 London Bridge Street
London SE1 9GF

www.harpercollins.co.uk

HarperCollins*Publishers*
Macken House, 39/40 Mayor Street Upper
Dublin1, D01 C9W8, Ireland

First published by HarperNorth in 2023
1 3 5 7 9 10 8 6 4 2

A catalogue record for this book
is available from the British Library

HB ISBN: 978-0-00-852643-6
TPB ISBN: 978-0-00-854194-1

Printed and bound in the UK using 100% renewable
electricity at CPI Group (UK) Ltd

This book is produced from independently certified FSC™ paper
to ensure responsible forest management.

For more information visit: www.harpercollins.co.uk/green

Dolly

Babar and I have a longstanding joke that I'm obsessed with books about women finding their own self-worth. Truth is, the obsession stands in real life too. Especially when that woman, or girl, is you.

And so this one, my darling, is – and was *always* – for you.

Because I want your opinions to be respected, your choices to be honoured, and your relationships to be equal.

And because I love you.

I love you.

I love you.

(No buts.)

AFTER

I love you, Mabel, honestly I do, but…

Your hands, your lovely hands. We have a picture of one of them, your tiny new-born fingers gripping on to my thumb. There's nothing original in its composition. I've seen enough versions of that photo with different babies, different mothers. The kind of mothers who don't come with a "but".

Craig told us he couldn't stop looking at the picture when he was at work. It was one of those first evenings after his week's paternity leave, and he'd appeared home around six, scooping you from your Moses basket and saying, in this sing-song voice I'd not heard before, how much he'd missed you. He risked glancing up from your eyes for just a second, 'You too, Bea.'

I joked about being his after-thought. And when he kissed me then, with those lips of his that were more gentle, or less reaching, or something I couldn't quite articulate, I yearned for the me my husband had kissed with a heat.

Was that old Bea still in there somewhere? Sleeping away the shock between my rips and bruises? Even then, I didn't think so. Because there was this flash of Craig in the delivery room, with you curled into his chest as the midwives held onto my shoulders, urging me to push. There was more to come, they said, it's not just the baby you have to birth, they told me. And I know they were talking about the placenta, but I remember thinking how maybe other parts of me had dropped into the bowl as I watched him holding you.

I love your hands. I love looking at the lines on them, imagining myself as a fairground fortune-teller, who runs her tips across the creases and wonders at your brilliant future. How picky in love? How strong-willed? How bound to convention? Maybe I love them because they're a fresh start, a clean sheet without certainty.

Or regret.

These are the hush hush thoughts I feared would spill into your mouth through my milk as you fed during those nights we spent together in the dark. You would latch on and stare into my eyes as if you knew, instinctively, what you should expect from me. I got it, then, why secrets are things we call skeletons in our closets. Because what I thought I could never say out loud crept further from my lips into my bones, where it nestled. Silent. Gnawing.

But secrets are brittle, Mabel. Like exhausted bones and exhausted mothers, they snap.

I spoke them.

And when I did, my words – like your birth – changed everything.

BEFORE

SUNDAY 31ST MARCH

CHAPTER ONE

It's gone nine when I wake, playing chicken with my wrecked pelvic floor as I roll on to my tummy to reach for my book, not risking the loo in case you or Craig hear me and come running, come needing, come breaking the almost but not quite silence that comes with earplugs on this Mother's Day morning.

Craig had swept you from your cot at just gone six with the promise of pancakes. 'A Daddy special,' he'd whispered, swiftly changing key into 'the runaway train came down the track and she blew.' You joined in with the woo-oo-oos as he carried you down the stairs, closing the door to the kitchen, to the noise, to the hands, to the constant stream of it so I might turn back into the pillow and sleep sleep sleep.

I can't hold it though. I have to go, allowing myself the gift of locking the bathroom door for three minutes of inane celebrity gossip on my phone, which is shallow, maybe, but what it is too, Mabel, is sanctuary.

A former *Love Island* contestant is making headlines for carrying his daughter in a sling while doing his weekly shop in Tesco. All the more noteworthy because his girlfriend was snapped on the same day "flaunting her incredible post-baby body" while drinking cocktails in a beachside bar in Marbella.

I inch my unslippered feet away from your potty, which sits pink and full on the blue and black tiles. They'd been a statement when we laid them. Different. Bold. Maybe we didn't treat them properly because they're stained now.

Emptying the potty into the bowl before I flush, I make a mental note to have you pick out a sticker for your chart before we leave for lunch with Grandma.

I wipe the speckled toothpaste from the mid-century mirror with the cuff of my pyjama sleeve – *Jesus, my fringe* – then turn the tap hotter before splashing my face and then my bed-head hair, unsure why dishevelled in my thirties isn't sexy like dishevelled in my twenties. Maybe it's the roots: arid grey forging into fraudulent brown. Or the lines. Or maybe it goes deeper than that because didn't Mum always say how negative thinking leads to more negative thinking.

'You have to be so careful, Beatrice,' she said. 'Or else it can become a vicious circle.'

I promised her then that even my thoughts would be good.

Look at me though.

Two years into mothering, and I am *not* good, Mabel.

My right thumb slides the bolt back open, as my phone flashes with a call: Kim.

But before I can answer: 'Mummy!'

You are a megaphone. Your voice scales the stairs, like brash and boisterous smoke that seeps through every tiny gap to reach me.

'Mummy's just sorting the washing.' I re-bolt, lifting the lid on the laundry bin, which is actually an American style trash-can that clatters against those marked tiles on the floor. I swipe to answer the call with my free hand.

'Hey,' I whisper, separating darks from whites, unsure if it's even necessary these days but doing it anyway because isn't that what we've always been told to do. 'Excuse the wailing. I reckon Mabel's about to jump the stairgate. You alright?'

'Oh, Bea.' Kim's tone is weary. 'I'm falling to *peaches*.' Since she ranted in one of her *Edible* Insta posts about her loathing of food puns, the two of us have made a running gag of them. 'Peaches? Pieces?'

As someone well used to making dire situations sound appealing for both my teenage students *and* my own website, *Tonight Will Bea Fine*, I hear how Kim's usual post-pun laugh falls a nanosecond too late. 'What's up?'

She heaves a sigh so heavy the weight of it pulls me down to the floor. 'Adam slept with someone.'

'Okaaaay.' My back presses against the wall, and I nudge Craig's pants further into the pile with my big toe. With any other friend, this kind of revelation about her relationship would likely mean her marriage is game over. But Kim is not like any other friend. And her relationship is not like any other marriage. Not any other marriage I know, anyway. 'I thought you were...'

The word Kim used a few months ago when she told me about this new development on our weekly Facetime was "open".

'You know, non-monogamous,' she'd clarified when my silence then had betrayed the distance between us. Not only the one-hundred-and-seventy-eight miles from me in Shrewsbury to her in Shoreditch but that other gap, the bohemian freedom that's possible, maybe, when you're child-free. *I* barely have time or head space for sex with my husband let alone adding another body pawing at my body to the mix.

When I close my eyes, there's a flash of the box I hid beneath three unread books in my bedside drawer yesterday.

'We are,' Kim says now. 'So, I know, I know, I should be alright with this, but...'

When I was trying to get my head around the non-monogamy, I'd asked her point blank if she was worried about jealousy.

'I don't think so.' She'd looked right at the camera, persuasively holding my gaze. 'Adam and I are still committed. Romantically. Domestically. All that life-building stuff we talked about when we decided to get married, that remains our priority. And if we're secure in that, if we know our *home* is with each other, then another person can't pose a genuine threat.'

Her soft crying this morning though suggests differently.

'Is this the first time he's been with someone else since you —'

'No.' It's blunt. And her frustration sounds not like it's with Adam but with *me*. 'Sorry,' she says, gentle this time. 'Only, it's not what you're thinking. The problem isn't that Adam had *sex* with someone else.'

'Oh.'

'It's that he had brunch with her.'

'*Brunch*?' I say the word slowly and with too much of an uprise to sound like I'm taking it seriously. But of all the possible pitfalls I'd imagined when Kim told me she and Adam were going to sleep with other people, *brunch* hadn't once figured on my list.

'It's not funny, Bea.' Even so, there's a smile in Kim's voice too.

'I wasn't laughing.'

'No, but your amusement was audible. You *do* know you can't hide anything from me, right?'

I wonder if that's true.

'Mummy!' Your scream is a vuvuzela.

'Is that Mabel?' Kim asks.

'Yeah.' Because when isn't it you, Mabel? 'But I have a few minutes so tell —'

'Don't worry.' There's a familiar resignation in my friend's tone. When it comes to the hierarchy of relationships, everyone knows who holds the trump card. 'It's Mother's Day. Speaking of which, I should probably call my own.'

'Nah ah ah. You are *not* hanging up, Kimberley. I refuse to be one of *those* friends who always has to —'

'MUMMY!'

'It's cool.' Kim's voice is warm. 'Your resistance is futile.'

She's right, Mabel.

'Fine. But I'll ring you this evening. Once she's in bed. Promise. We'll have a proper talk then, yeah?

'I'll hold you to it.' And she's saying goodbye when, 'Bea?'

'Hmm?'

'Thank Mabel for me, yeah?'

'*Thank* her?'

'If it wasn't for that unfortunate incident with her nappy, I might never have met you.'

It's true, of course. After a blog post I wrote about inadvertently eating actual baby faeces I'd mistaken for egg yolk on your baby grow went viral, Kim contacted me about collaborating on a job she was running for a Hoxton bakery, where all the edible goods would be based on emojis. Somehow, in the space of a few days and through the medium of text and email, we established a friendship. One that, weirdly given its beginnings, a year-in feels very grown-up. And for all our chat about London life, very separate, Mabel, from you.

When I come out of the bathroom, you're standing, thrilled and naked, behind the gate at the foot of the stairs. A sudden panic rises in your sweet face, pushing you onto your toes as you run back to where you left Craig on the sofa. He smiles at me through a yawn as I enter the sitting room, his finger pressing the remote, switching the TV from the Grand Prix to Heart radio. There's that Spice Girls' song *Mama*, as you ask him, 'card, Daddy?' snatching and holding it up for me to admire. On the front is your hand, or an outline of it, in a plant pot, your fingers and thumb each forming a stem for a bright pink flower.

'Wow, Mabel!' I crouch to take it and kiss your fat tacky cheek. 'Did *you* make this?'

'Nursery.' You nod, eyes wide and so pleased with your effort. 'Diane.'

We all love Diane, her voice pitched perfectly so each child can intuit her mood with no need for shouting.

'It's the most wonderful card I have ever, ever seen.'

'You are not surprised by my conclusion. That toothy smile as broad as your confidence. The happy certainty with which you move through the world.

'Thank you.' Your hair, the colour of conkers, is matted beneath my lips, the luminescent skin of your belly sticky when I pretend to gobble you up as greedily, as messily, as you would chocolate ice cream. 'Shall we give you a wipe?'

'Nice lie-in?' Craig's sprawled, topless, in just his pyjama bottoms on the sofa. His body is still his body. His muscles flex as he stands. Another yawn.

'Lovely. Thanks.'

He follows us into the kitchen. 'We made you breakfast, babe.'

'Mummy!' You're itching to get down from my arms. But where to, Mabel? The floor and surfaces are thick with two hours of quiet chaos. As if this room isn't tiny enough.

Outside, the sun burns hard and bright.

I pull your scrunched-up bib from the highchair so I might sit you down while I make tea, and a thin trickle of milk runs from the folds of the fabric to the seat, dripping then to the floor.

'Here.' I hold you out to Craig, who play-throws and catches you once, twice, three times as I rinse the bib with Fairy then hang it on the oven rail to dry. 'Drink?'

He points, probably at my Best Mum mug, although the side is so littered with the detriments of this Mother's Day feast, he could just as easily be pointing at blueberries, eggshells, a whisk, a plastic cow, a beaker, a nappy sack bursting with something I'd rather not imagine being in such close proximity to my breakfast. 'I was making you tea.'

'Hold her still a moment, will you.' I take your leg. 'I need to wipe her down. *And* the chair.' I don't mention the floor. 'Did she spill something?' I'm on it with a cloth and spray.

You're proper chuckling as he bounces you in time to the beat of a new song coming from the TV. Every room bleeds into the next here. Everything is always on the verge of closing in.

'You got a teeeeeny bit over excited with your Weetabix while waiting for pancakes, didn't you, Bells?'

'Yup!'

'And *then* what did Daddy have to do?' He tickles your tummy, which is still clinging onto that beautiful baby chub. How easily, needily, we both touch you, Mabel. This constant desire we have to not just see but grasp but the tangible flesh of our creation. 'Daddy had to whip you out of your onesie quick smart, and then you were good to go.' He blows a raspberry on your belly. You howl with delight. 'Honestly, babe, sit down. I'll bring you everything in on a tray.'

Let him do this.

Craig has been keen to point out that not everything has to be perfect. Let the kitchen be a bit messy. What does it matter if we don't brush your hair?

'You want to choose a story, Mabel?'

You come back with four, clamber up and burrow into my lap, an elbow in my boob, three book-spines in my thigh, and my hand on the fleshiness of your bare bum as I hoik you into a less intrusive spot. 'Where are your knick-knocks?'

'No now. No knick-knocks,' you say. 'Room Broom.'

When I imagined motherhood, this is pretty much it. My child curled into me, my chin resting on her skull, our fingers perhaps looped as we turn pages and repeat words, trace the lines of pictures and guess what might happen next.

You open it at the first page. Not even the title but a wordless illustration of the witch's hat, bow, wand and broom, all her distinguishable markers tumbling down from the sky.

'Happy Mother's Day!' Craig balances on one foot, prodding you playfully with his big toe so you crawl to my side to make space for my pancakes, tea and a single daffodil, which you take and press to my nose.

'Thank you.' My lips catch on the petals. 'This all looks amazing.'

'I'll run you a bath, yeah?'

'Me bath too —'

'I'm not sure we have time, Mabel.'

Craig looks at me like, what's the rush?

'Lunch? With your mum. Twelve?' Didn't we talk about this last night?

'Again! Again!' Your legs fly out behind you as Daddy lifts you from beneath your armpits and spins.

'I sent you a calendar invite.' I shape my voice into something that's not an accusation. 'It should all be in your phone.'

'More! More!' You stomp your foot into the carpet when he puts you down.

'Sorry, Bells. Mummy needs me to listen.'

What I need is for him to take note of this shit. 'We're getting the train? Remember? We thought it'd be fun? For Mabel?'

He looks at you open mouthed, like, can you believe your luck? 'The runaway train came down the track and she blew!'

'Woo-oo-oo!'

The pair of you chug around the living room as I eat my pancakes, honestly not thinking about the pregnancy test I swore to myself I'd take this morning, or the mark your bare bottom has left on my thigh.

CHAPTER TWO

I could write it as an Insta post. List all the wonderful things Craig's done this morning. The lie-in. The pancakes. The bath. It all happened. None of it's a lie. Though neither is it telling the full story. Real life's less charming than that. More bitter. More outraged. More irate.

But those kinds of feelings are not becoming of an Insta-mother. Of a woman who – curated – has it all.

I pee on the test then run the bath water so hot that it's steaming. Anything to make these wicked thoughts clean.

Craig and I used to take baths every Sunday. Together. He'd massage my head and, brace yourself, Mabel, because this sounds so pompous, but I'd read him a poem I'd discovered or, yes, even written, that week, topping up the hot water so we'd languish for an hour, maybe more. If we were feeling particularly decadent, we'd mix a couple of Happy Ever After cocktails and prop them within arm's reach on a stool.

I liked how our voices echoed in bathrooms. How condensation ran in thin streams down steamy windows. How it might be daylight, but I could still feel the prophecy of stars, which whispered in uncomplicated language that Craig and I were meant to be. And I get it, Mabel, how make-believe it sounds. But I stand by the fact of our mythical romance, which turned me into Nike, not the infamous swoosh but the goddess of victory. For I reckoned, there in our cast iron ocean, your father and I were a new fucking order.

Today's bath though is perfunctory. It's a wash with a ripped whale-shaped sponge I rush across my limbs, careful not to drag it near my breasts, where a tenderness has settled.

'Mummy?' Your call is changed. Less demanding, more uncertain, wanting to be sure, perhaps, that even though there is a door between us I am still here.

Where I should be.

Standing now to stretch for a towel, my yellow-white, raw-pink reflection glares back at me like a sweaty motorway-services ham sandwich. Beneath the mirror, lying on the basin between your toothbrush and my phone is the test, placed purposefully out of reach so I might boil in the bath, ignorant of whether the one thing Craig believes is missing from our family is on its way.

The writer in me, the one who shares close-to-the-bone takes on motherhood (always immediately there-there'd with a reminder of how there is nothing that compares – is there? – to this), appreciates the potential narrative of this perfect timing. Is there a better Mother's Day gift than two blue lines confirming in a matter of months we will have twice the joy?

The mother in me burns for a different outcome to the story.

The secondary-school teacher in me reprimands I should have been more careful.

I *was* though. I *have been* so quietly careful.

The water lowers around my ankles, a gurgle in the pipes as the last of it drains away.

It's simple. All I need to do is step over the side of the bath and look.

'Bea?' It's Craig this time.

'Coming.' And I am. One foot on the bathmat already, the other mid-air, my eyes darting from floor to ceiling, looking anywhere but there.

'You mind if I go for a ride with Stu this evening?' I can hear how his cheek is pressed against the door.

The bathroom is small. There's only so long you can avoid any part of it.

'It's not ideal going out in the dark. But he can't go any earlier; he's got a swim session this afternoon.'

I'm pretty sure Stu's swim session won't be Puddle Ducks with his toddler in the local pool.

'I know we're riding tomorrow after work too, but it's only a week 'til we go away. If I don't get in some practice, six days on the mountains are going to be torture.'

If I were to describe torture, Mabel, it wouldn't be that.

When I stretch for my phone to check my calendar, my knuckles catch your toothbrush and the test, which both fall to the marked tiles below.

My chest rises with a deep inhale. My eyes, though, despite every other inch of me refusing the inevitable, look down.

The wand lands face up.

My future now is as tiny as that twice-lined window.

'No. No,' I say.

'No?'

'Not you, Craig.'

I pick up the test.

'It's…' But how do I tell him? What would I say?

'Well? Stu's waiting, babe.'

I steady myself with my free hand on the knob of the locked door. 'Sure, you go if you want to.'

If only someone would say the same to me.

* * *

Heart and mind scrambling, I scroll through Instagram as I head to the bedroom, checking for comments on last night's post about the abundant joys of toddler poo. Through the wall, I hear the pair of you giggling.

I've an email from a potential sponsor offering me an ergonomically approved potty.

The thought of a second round of toilet-training.

A second round of everything.

I politely decline.

'Here she is, Bells.'

'I just need to dry my hair then we'll go, yeah?' But when I pull the neck of my jumper down over my head, I see this isn't possible. And I know, I know, there are far worse problems and I've had that lie-in and those pancakes and that bath, which should mean I'm relaxed.

But.

'She's not even dressed.'

Craig looks at me, like, *chill*. 'We were doing a puzzle.'

That you are in his arms, albeit straining for mine, is the only reason I say nothing of the *news*.

The curdling doubt in whether I can be someone else's mother is as irrelevant as its sibling: curdling shame.

He throws you onto the bed, where you immediately tunnel into the unmade covers, your feet kicking scatter cushions on to Craig's discarded jeans and Coldplay T-shirt abandoned two nights ago in a creased wad on the floor.

'Tent, Mummy!'

I untwine you from the sheet, the same white as the toilet paper in which I'd bound the test before concealing it in an old wash bag at the back of the bathroom cupboard.

'Spin! Spin!'

But I'm not as fun as Daddy. Not now anyway. 'I'm sorry, Mabel, no. We need to get you some clothes.'

We negotiate a dress. I insist on either a jumper or a coat, I don't care which, but it's too cold for neither and, no, it's not the right season for sandals but, yes, OK, it doesn't look like rain so if you wear tights, whatever, the sandals will do.

'Did you get a bag ready?' I will a voice different to the one in my head.

'Sure did.' Craig disappears downstairs and is waiting by the door, his eyes all, *what took you so long*, as I untwine the band from my wrist, pulling my hair up into a wet bun, smearing some Vaseline on my lips.

'Gorgeous, babe.'

'Where's the bag?'

'Here.' He holds up the Occitane gift bag I got for his mother.

'The *change* bag?'

'But she's potty trained.'

'Barely.'

It's a risky business, leaving the house. Spare knickers. Spare tights. Chocolate buttons – thankfully, you're well-tuned to a bribe.

'Why don't you two go?' This doesn't matter, Mabel. There was the lie-in, the breakfast, the bath. Honestly, everything's fine. 'I'll catch up. It's going to take you a while to walk anyway since she'll no longer sit in the buggy.'

I go to your room for the spare knickers and tights, to the kitchen for the chocolate buttons and a bottle of water. I look for what I need and try not to see the filth and clutter. I think of the pancakes. Of the card. Of the daffodil. Of the extra time in bed and the soak. Anything anything anything but the two blue lines.

* * *

The rucksack smacks against the small of my back as I run for a train to a lunch I booked for my mother-in-law's Mother's Day celebration.

I arrive at the station a hot sweaty mess.

'Look, Mabel, it's Mummy!' Craig holds you out so I might take you, but I need a fan, not a child with her hands all over my neck and chest.

'Can I just have a minute, *please*.'

'I got the tickets,' he says.

'Thank you.' I catch my breath, surprised by how much I want to cry. 'Then it looks like we're good to go.'

Fifteen minutes later, I message Kim from the train.

```
FFS. Don't ever underestimate baby
admin. Muggins here was stuck gath-
ering essentials and had to sprint
to the station, while Craig got to
saunter at a snail's pace with M.
```

I send her the video I captured of the two of you as you left the house, a short clip of you entwining pinkies as Daddy sang, 'Just you and me then, Bells.'

Kim's reply is immediate.

```
I wonder how he'd cope if it was. 🫠
```

CHAPTER THREE

'Poo-eee,' you shout from the kitchen.

You were first in through the door when we got home. Craig and I are removing our shoes in the hall.

I smell it too. Sour, not just in my nose but on my tongue.

'Poo-eee!'

I turn on the light to see what's causing the stench and, honestly – the carnage – it could be any number of things. 'You want to start running her bath, and I'll clear up down here?'

'What is that *smell?*' Craig's nose twitches in your curls. Then, playfully, 'Is it *your* bottom, Bells?' He bends over, sniffs the base of your spine. 'Oh, Mabel!' You're hypnotised by his clownish grimace, his wink. 'We said to tell us if you needed a poop!'

'No, Daddy. No poo.' You're laughing though. Until you're not. 'Not me.' Outrageously offended because, well, it's gone your usual bedtime, and you're tired.

'Daddy was joking, Mabel. We know it's not you. It's something in this kitchen.' *Keep your voice light, Bea.*

But you're hungry too.

I did warn you, as I attempted to coax you with roast dinner while mine cooled under the congealing gravy. 'You'll be hungry later,' I'd said. But what's time to a two-year-old? It's like loneliness – or regret – you have no understanding of it.

I butter you some malt loaf. But where there was a dimple, there's already a tear. Your bottom lip's wobbling. Craig and I catch each other's eye, like, *shit*. We have limited time to contain what might be about to explode.

Perhaps the stickers for your potty chart will be sufficient distraction. I pull them from the junk drawer. Out come hairclips, washi

22

tape, a Farrow & Ball paint chart we colour-matched for the bedroom at B&Q.

'Look, Mabel!' You're whimpering, but not enough to block me out. 'Mummy has stickers.' I pass them to Craig so I can hunt down the real cause of the stink. 'I can't see what it could be.'

'Would you like a fairy?'

That bottom lip steadies as you eye up the options Craig dangles at a height so you must stand on your tiptoes to see. It's a good tactic. The physical effort it takes to stay upright pushes aside that hint of your temper.

'A football? A flower? A fish? Oh, did you hear that, Bells? They were all F-words!'

'I've got another F-word.' I look pointedly at Craig, who grins. My fondness for profanity has always made him grin. Daddy's tried to shield you from it, Mabel, but the hard Germanic whip of a good swear is too powerful a release for me to forgo.

'You'll have to excuse, Bea,' he'd say, introducing me to his friends as a muck-spout, which I liked, for that too sounded satisfyingly firm, temptingly dirty. He'd wink as his friends winced at the surprise of a good girl like me coming out with the C-word. I'd apologise as your father poured me more wine, whispering when he was able how he couldn't help but be turned on by my filth. It was a joke, of course. But that humour in itself was arousal. As was our walk home when we'd link fingers, bump hips, going over what such and such had said about so and so. Not bitchy exactly but perhaps a little sharp in our analysis of their relationship, which we never directly compared to ours.

But.

I loved him. So soon after knowing him, I loved Craig with a love that was soft and long and hard and fast and underpinned with a confidence that together we were a new deal.

Precarious on your tiptoes, you snatch the sheet of stickers, asking for paper.

Together we've disposed the bomb.

That *smell* though.

The sides. The highchair. The floor. All clean now but it's still here. Something rotten. A dead mouse? I get down on my knees, nose to the skirting boards.

All those unhoovered crumbs.

When I imagined motherhood, this wasn't it.

'Babe?' Craig shouts from the bathroom. 'You know where Mabel's onesie is?'

I don't. I wasn't the one to take it off.

I go to the bottom of the stairs. There's less chance of me sounding aggro if I don't have to holler. "Where were you when you undress—' I stop mid-sentence because I remember now, even if *he* doesn't.

The Weetabix.

This is Instagram content.

It could be funny in the right tone.

And in retrospect.

The washing machine, where it would make sense to put sodden clothes is empty. Your onesie is on the radiator, Mabel, where Daddy must have tossed it after you got a 'teeeeeny bit overexcited' with your cereal.

Unrinsed, unwashed and uncrumpled, even, the stink of it is baked not only into the fabric but the air.

'Spilt milk,' I mutter, heaving then swallowing the sick risen to my throat like a badly quashed secret.

It reeks.

CHAPTER FOUR

'Don't hate me,' Kim says when I call her after bedtime stories and lullabies. 'But I'm the mother of all millennial cliches right now.'

'Tell me...' I creep downstairs, the vinyl a benign kind of cold against my bare feet when I walk into the kitchen, where the anti-chafing cream Craig slathered on his groin before he went off on his bike to meet Stu sits open on the side.

'Would you believe me if I told you this afternoon I actually Googled "how to have a bath"?'

'Fuck me, this *is* serious. What part of turn-on-the-tap had you forgotten?'

'A *self-care* bath, Bea.' Kim's tone might be full of piss-take, but I know the importance she places on nurturing her emotional and spiritual health.

'Sounds complicated.' The light of the washing machine has been flashing green for the past two hours as a reminder that it's done. 'And lengthy.' Phone wedged between my ear and shoulder, I heave the clothes up onto the kitchen counter. I am never not surprised by the weight of a family's wet load.

'Exactly!' Kim gulps what I imagine is a large glass of red. 'Which is why I'm now lying in sadly tepid water with eucalyptus draped across a bamboo bath caddy while sipping kombucha and supposedly receiving energy from my rose quartz crystal. I mean, thank god, I live in Hackney where forlorn and privileged hipsters like me have easy last-minute access to this type of woowoo shit.'

'I wish I lived closer.' The jeans and T-shirts and onesies are awkwardly entangled from their spin in the drum. 'I'd come squirt essential oils in your tub and burn some incense to purify your aura.'

'I don't think it's my *aura* that needs purifying.' It doesn't take a genius to hear the sadness wound into Kim's laughter. 'And you may think it's bollocks, but I'll have you know, I do feel a tonne better for going through this ritual. When you feel as paralysed as I did earlier, doing something – *anything!* – even if that something or anything is a self-care bath, can be a power move.'

As I tug the airer from where it's wedged between the fridge-freezer and the wall, its bent leg catches the monkey magnet, our one concession in the zoo's gift shop on your last birthday. You'd used it to attach a photo of my mum to the door.

'You there, Bea?'

Her face smiles up at me from the floor.

'Bea?'

'Sorry.' I stick Mum back in place, my fingertip running over the grey-blonde hairs the wind had blown across her eyes that summer's evening. 'Just wondering whether a family of rubber ducks and Grandpa Pig's bath-time boat would enhance or impinge the benefits of Himalayan salts and scented candles?'

Kim sighs. 'All those things *are* moveable, you know. It's entirely possible to create a space of your own.'

Only someone who doesn't have a toddler would say this with such certainty.

Of all the people I could tell about the test though, maybe the fact that she doesn't have, and isn't sure she wants, kids might make Kim less inclined to judge if I'm not exactly elated by the news.

But this call is about her.

How many times have I had to hang up too soon because of you, Mabel? I can't let another possible baby intrude.

'Enough self-care chat.' I shake out a second pair of Craig's cycling shorts, hang them over the thin plastic bars, then smooth out your onesie. Some things are easier than others to get out in a wash. 'What we really need to discuss is the *B*-word.'

'Eugh.' Another swig of kombucha. 'Do we have to?'

'I've never understood brunch anyway. I'm happy to take a stand against it for the rest of my life if that's what you want from me.'

'I appreciate your solidarity, sister, but I actually like brunch. Or at least I did until…'

'Until?' Washing done, I take a clean cloth and wipe it over the radiator. Despite all the disinfectant, there's still a hint of something sour.

'When we first talked about opening up our relationship, Adam and I agreed that we could stay over at someone else's house. But only if we gave each other notice. That way, we wouldn't worry if the other didn't come home.'

'So, what, he didn't tell you?'

'No, he *did* tell me.' Kim inhales. 'I just didn't expect him to be out so long. For breakfast maybe but, I dunno, Saturdays are our day. We buy the paper, go to the market, get lunch. Nothing major, but it's how we unwind, and he was home way later than I expected and too full to eat. I was fuming.'

'Are you sure it's about the brunch?' I rinse and hang the cloth, go to the living room to finally sit down.

'Sure as I can be. I mean how much objectivity do we ever have when it comes to analysing our own emotions. But I didn't have a problem the other times.'

'Have you told Adam?' The daffodil you gave me this morning, Mabel, has bloomed in its vase on the sill. 'How you feel?'

Kim snuffs a sound I think counts as a "no." 'Is it not kind of pathetic to moan about brunch when I genuinely have no issue with the sexual escapades he enjoyed before his eggs bloody benedict?'

'You need to speak with him. Be honest.'

The irony of telling someone to speak and be honest with their husband isn't lost on me, Mabel.

'True.' She pauses then takes a breath. 'But what I also really need is for you to do me a favour.'

'Anything.' I mean it too. We've never met in real life, but this friendship with Kim quickly became as solid as my friendship with Della, who I've known since school. Sometimes it's easier to forge a new self when old baggage isn't out on display. The pithy one-liners I share with Kim almost daily are a reminder of a younger, freer me. And in those thirty minutes every Friday, when I've let you sit in front of the telly, Mabel, so I can have an adult conversation with my friend, I've felt more like myself than I have done in years. Your shit, and my eating it, may have been the thing that brought Kim and me together, but beyond that, she and I rarely speak about motherhood. What we speak about is life. News stories, books and restaurants. And while I may not have seen the stories, read the books or dined at the restaurants, what I *have* done is used the time when you're sleeping and I've been deep in the domestic duties of laundry and cleaning to cram my brain with current-affairs podcasts in the hope that I might at least sound like I have a clue. 'What would you like me to do?'

'My thirtieth.'

That wasn't what I was expecting. 'The party?'

'You always say you fancy ditching teaching for events.'

'Go on…'

'It's only a few weeks away, and I've been swamped with work, and then negotiating all these firsts as Adam and I get to grips with everything.' There's a wash of water. I imagine Kim rising from the bath. 'I've lost focus. The menu's sorted —'

'Obviously.'

'Well, I am kind of a big *dill* in the food world.'

'Smooth.'

'I know, right? But everything else: decorations, music, etc. Nada. The photos you sent of Mabel's birthday party last month. It looked awesome. I was thinking maybe you could… Oh, I dunno, you're busy too. Maybe I should just cancel.'

'You are *not* cancelling.' I run a finger along the spines of all your picture books. So many. And yet you always go back to the same one. 'That party is our IRL meet-cute!' I don't mention it's also the only proper night out I have planned for months. And possibly the last if I have a second baby.

If?

Kim's birthday has been in the calendar since the beginning of the year.

BEA IN LONDON

When Craig insisted that was the only time his mates could all do a week's cycling trip to the Alps, *I* insisted he get Grandma Alice to agree to an overnight with you.

I have a dress. Shoes. More importantly, I have a hotel room and the promise of an entire morning-after when I'll only have to think of, take care of, me. I drop to the sofa.

'Whatever you need, Kim. Just tell me what you want me to do.'

MONDAY 1ST APRIL

CHAPTER FIVE

If I were to caption the pregnancy test on Instagram it would be something like, *how's this for the ultimate April Fool?* I'm not entirely foolish though. If there's ever a lesson worth learning, Mabel, it's to keep clear of socials when emotions are running so high. I swerve Instagram, then, and search *coil failed* instead.

Google fails too, says nothing of fractured hopes or uprooted futures, rather its focus is on how to DIY fix a broken ignition coil on a car.

It's Monday. Always a Mummy-and-Mabel day. A day when I'm not teaching and you're not at nursery. Craig left what already feels like hours ago. 'Pinch, punch, first of the month!' He had play-pinched and play-punched the two of us, as I began prepping this week's dinners and you pointed a menacing finger at the neighbour's cat who appears on our windowsill each morning.

An hour later, and we'd usually be on our way to Honk It music by now. Instead, you're in *Peppa Pig* heaven. You are paying me no attention – your eyes are transfixed by Daddy Pig smashing a giant hole in the wall as he attempts to put up a picture – but I tilt my phone from you anyway, though I'm not sure there's room in this house for any more secrets.

We knew it wasn't big. A two-bed terrace was all we could afford. I would have stayed on living with my parents, but Dad insisted it wasn't right. 'For the baby's sake,' he said, kicking off all that talk of Craig and me moving out. He gestured at the hospital bed in their dining room, the surfaces littered with detriments of late-life care. 'You won't want to bring a baby here, Beatle. You need to make it as easy for yourself as possible when they're little. You should have seen your moth—'

The sound of her coughing, you'd have thought Mum had bronchitis not multiple myeloma.

'All I'm saying,' Dad said a little more quietly, 'is that you should find your own place. Somewhere you can fill with joy.'

On the arm of the sofa, the test looks far bigger and far whiter than it did yesterday. As I'd unravelled it, you tore the tissue into balled-up pieces now scattered like hail stones across the floor.

When does something become a secret? I didn't purposefully not tell Craig. We were out for lunch, we were cleaning, he was on a bike ride, I was on the phone, he was already in bed, shattered from his long ride, and it seemed cruel to wake him.

It's been just twenty-four hours, which is plausible delay perhaps. But I've seen how this goes. A day turns into weeks turns into months turns into two years, though *coil failed* is the punishment maybe for never telling my husband the coil is even there.

'A small gap is great,' Craig said when you were just two weeks old and my mother was two weeks dead. 'Look at me and Alex. Twelve months between us. Always entertained each other. Mum says we made her job easy.'

Her job.

And, anyway, "easy" wasn't a word I could equate with the fortnight since your arrival.

'All I'm saying is why don't we let nature take its course? If we get pregnant again quickly, well…' He nodded at the wedding photo of us taken at the Chapel of Happy Memories. The picture was barely visible among the mingled crowd of congratulations and sympathy cards. 'Another baby would be part of the adventure, right?'

I didn't go to the doctor and ask about the coil, it was offered. At my six-week post-natal check-up, the GP listed my options, and I took one. The appointment was early morning, and by the time Craig arrived home from the salon at almost seven, a million other things had happened, and I was too spent to have *that* conversation, too lost for words to articulate why leaving things to chance, *or nature*, wasn't something I could dare to do. And it wouldn't be for long, I thought. A few months, maybe, until my body and idealism were returned to normal.

It was all just taking a little longer than planned.

You neck your water now like Della and I used to neck vodka. Meanwhile, my tea sits cold on a stack of *Wanderlust* magazines Grandma Alice thought it might be fun for us to cut up for collage. She's taking the piss, right? I mean, there's nothing so symbolic as putting scissors to all those far-flung places now well beyond my reach.

The world is no longer my oyster, Mabel.

I try *coil failed pregnant*.

One in a hundred apparently.

A fellow "one in a hundred" on Mumsnet explained her surprise and then her belief that her unplanned DS (*Dear* Son) was obviously meant to be. And, yes, she replied to the curious women in the forum, her DH (*Dear* Husband) was also delighted (eventually). And her DD (*Dear* Daughter) couldn't wait to be an older sister.

Everything happens for a reason, she wrote.

And I get why people kowtow to optimism, why bad must inevitably lead to good because otherwise how on earth would any of us plough on.

But.

Everything happens for a reason.

Really?

Tell that to the *Dear* Victims of *Dear* Wars, *Dear* Famines and *Dear* Multiple Myeloma …

I don't mean to sound so bitter, but fuck me, does everything about *Dear* Motherhood have to be so twee?

I've done it myself, of course. Tonight Will Bea Fine isn't so different to all the other mummy sites out there. My humour is more caustic maybe, but its punch is always tempered with the reassurance of how much I love you, Mabel, how 'sure this is hard, but —'

'Flumper! Flumper!' You clutch your worn grey rabbit to your chest and point at Daddy Pig, who is surprised to discover the stuffed toy Peppa's shoving into a dress is a boy.

I kiss your shoulder and smoodge you further back into my lap.

Opening Tonight Will Bea Fine, I scroll through all those photos we took of your second birthday party. The digger cake with a construction site made from broken KitKats and rubbled millionaire's shortbread cascading down the two-tiers into Oreo cookie soil. The hard-hat cupcake toppers for the party bags, and a buffet of choco-late-finger logs, Malteser rocks and strawberry-lace tape measures. The yellow plastic cutlery tied in black ribbon with hand-written labels declaring them "tools".

All that effort, Mabel. When I was already so stretched for time.

It was my inner-events wannabe, I wrote, mocking those long-held ambitions to plan product launches, gala dinners and, yeah, I'll admit it, giant weddings with flower walls, photo booths and first dances rehearsed with a professional in secret for months before The Big Day.

'Knock yourself out,' Craig had said, when I suggested the construc-tion theme. His smile was an apology maybe. And his collaboration – physical and financial – compensation perhaps for the conclusion we'd both come to when you were a few months old and I was contemplating my return to work. Given the salon already required him to work evenings and weekends, it wouldn't be feasible for me to quit teaching and launch an events business of my own. Especially one that required hours so unsociable for a new mother.

'Why not let things settle,' Craig had said. 'We're not saying "never". Enjoy Mabel for a bit. She won't always need you as much as she does now.'

We can but hope, I wrote on TWBF.

I was joking, obviously.

I look from the test to my phone.

Try not to panic.

I can work this through.

Della.

She's my go-to, make-a-list, talk-it-out, take-a-breath person.

But so too is my best friend pregnant. And those two babies in her belly are so hard fought for, how could I possibly tell her the apparent ease, the savage dismay, with which I conceived the one in mine.

Peppa and George jump in a muddy puddle. Mummy Pig waits for them with a towel.

What if she was responsible for all that dirty mess in the first place? Would it be as easy for her to wipe them clean?

Would Della agree if I were to tell her what I'm thinking?

She and I have always known what to say to each other.

If we're honest, though, babies have made things less certain, more pussyfooted, between us.

After you were born and Mum died, Mabel, Della came daily and whispered with Craig in the hall. Even though she hates cooking, she brought me three different types of Jamie Oliver stew, not specifying which part of me they were supposed to fix, assuming perhaps that a home-cooked meal might help with the exhaustion no matter its cause. Her hug was as solid as it's been since we were thirteen.

'It must be so strange,' she said, as she watched me feeding you. And it could have been a way into a conversation, I suppose, about you, about Mum, about that unkind, unnatural thought born in the middle of the night that your birth was a trigger. That I am a gun.

Your protection, maybe, but potentially dangerous too. 'So confusing,' Della said.

But *she* must also have felt it, a similar but different confusion, seeing me with a baby she and Nisha had been trying but failing to conceive in their two rounds of IVF. They had delayed the third. They needed a break from the grief, she said.

What she'd said at sixteen was, 'Imagine, yeah.' Della was good at imagining, at sitting in that pretzel-legged way she'd always sit on my bedroom floor, French kissing a strawberry-cream Chupa Chups lolly. 'Imagine, yeah,' she'd said, 'when we're each other's babies' godmothers. I think we should live a bit before we settle down though. Twenty-six? Twenty-seven? That way we'll have travelled and had love affairs with men and women, and my girlfriend'll come from Paris, but I'll insist she moves to London cos' of you.'

'Cheers, Del,' I said.

'You'll owe me though, cos' Nicole'll probably bear a grudge which'll eat away at our relationship. She'll miss her dad's boulangerie. But one day, you'll cycle across London to a cake shop, where the chef was trained at some Michelin-starred bakery near the Seine, and arrive on our doorstep with a basket of *the* best *chausson aux pommes* outside of Paris.'

'*Chausson aux pommes*?'

'Basically an apple puff, Bea Bea. But don't worry, you'll know all this when I've been with Nicole a few years. She'll bang on about French shit all the time. Anyway, she'll be so chuffed you went all that way just for her, she'll realise exactly how awesome you are and, in a grand turnaround of events, it'll be Nicole who suggests you for godmother.'

'Does it matter that I'm an atheist?'

'Nah, just don't tell Nicole. She's Catholic. Though obviously she's gay, which might cause some problems with her family. But, god, when they see how cute Florence is, they —'

'*Florence*? You said you were having Edith and Arthur.'

'Too Eeeeeeenglish,' Della said in an overwrought French accent like the sexually charged waitress in that sitcom Mum and Dad loved so much. 'Imagine, yeah, how Florence and – who are you having again?'

'Angelina.' Because I was obsessed with Jolie.

'So imagine, yeah, how Florence and Angelina will be as ace friends as us.'

'Amazing,' I said. Because it would be.

So, when Della came over with chicken, pork and beef but no Florence, Edith or Arthur, 'I'm just so grateful to have her,' seemed like the right thing for me to say to her about you, Mabel. And stroking your head as I said it seemed like the right thing to do.

The *right* thing to do.

Only I keep thinking the opposite.

Now, I mean.

Not the *right* thing.

Not the *good* thing.

But something else.

Would Della judge me?

She's been in my position, of course. Later wondering on those nights in the long aftermath of her and Nisha's failed IVF whether her body's refusal to conceive was punishment for her twenty-one-year-old self's decision to have an abortion.

'Maybe that was my only chance,' she said once, like it was a matter of fact. 'You know, I *could* have had that baby.'

'With Bradley? You *do* remember Bradley, don't you?'

'OK, so *without* him then.' Della's voice was heavy against my chest. 'People raise kids in worse circumstances.'

And that's the crux of it now, right? *My* circumstances.

Married.

Financially stable.
Mother of one.
Those are not the credentials of women who…
I *could* do this.
Be a mother, I mean.
I *am* doing it.
With you, Mabel.
But.

CHAPTER SIX

Craig arrives home from his ride when you're bathed and read to. He creeps in, raining shampoo-scented drops onto your forehead when he kisses you goodnight.

As I come downstairs a few minutes later, the microwave pings with his casserole. He pours me a glass of red.

'Thanks.' I don't drink it, just run my finger around its rim.

I can do this.

I can tell him.

I can be a mother of two. I can be more efficient with my life, with my love, with my time. 'Craig, I—'

A whimpering erupts through the monitor.

He looks at the dinner he's spooning into his bowl, like, *I'm kind of busy here.*

'Please.' It's an effort not to sound like I'm begging. 'I've been with her all day.'

The whimpering swells into a wail.

'Babe, I've been on my feet for hours at the salon. Don't make me climb the stairs.' Craig buckles his knees in exaggerated weariness. 'And my thighs! Stu insisted on a monster of a hill.'

Up in your room, I pull Flumper from beneath the bottom of your sleeping bag. 'He's here, Bells. He'd just slipped down the cot, that's all.'

Your chin pressed into his ears, you close your eyes and are almost immediately sleeping.

'No, no,' Craig says when I come downstairs and go to open the dishwasher. 'I've just put that on.'

I rinse out a mug of cold tea I'd forgotten to drink while giving you your bath.

'Good day off then?' Craig's voice carries over the telly he's just put on in the other room.

We baked, didn't we, Mabel? On the floor. With bowls that doubled as drums and music that doubled as hope. The kitchen was warm from the oven, your cheeks were red with the joy. We sang Pat-a-Cake, clapping hands and laughing. You napped, and I posted pictures of our chocolate muffins on *Tonight Will Bea Fine*, bent eight minutes of yoga and made a start on the Year Nine *Jane Eyre* essays before the washing machine tinkled the tune at the end of its cycle. I hung out some clothes, folded others and, just now, up in the bathroom when I remembered that mug, I picked up sweaty cycling shorts from the floor. I'll finish the marking once he's in bed.

'Not sure I'd call it a day off.' I plomp down next to Craig on the sofa.

'Sitting around watching *Peppa Pig* all day?' He laughs. 'Sounds like a day off to me.'

MONDAY 8TH APRIL

CHAPTER SEVEN

'Nanna!' You've pulled my mother, Gloria Steinham, Rosa Parks and Malala Yousafzai from the freezer door while I've been on the phone with a supplier for Kim's party confirming delivery of a wooden three and zero. They'll be four-foot tall and illuminated, framed by a cascade of pastel-and-gold-coloured balloons of various size.

You shove Nanna and the monkey in between Cleopatra and Hillary Clinton in the line-up you've made on the floor.

The Little Feminists magnet-set was a baby gift from Della and Nisha. 'Never too early,' Nisha said, her eyes fixed on her wife, who was cradling you, her lips resting softly on the downy chestnut tufts of your hair.

'Back,' you say now, slamming Mum behind a roulette-wheel magnet I bought in Vegas as a wedding gift for Craig.

Higher up is the fridge calendar. *Go with the flow*, it says, its botanical illustrations suggesting March should have been a month imbued with calm. The page scrunches easily into a ball. This puts us, officially a week late, in April.

Craig left for France this morning to do the thing most men his age seem to be doing in Lycra.

'Love you, girls,' he said, as he strapped his bike to the back of Stu's car, kissing you then, Mabel, once on each cheek. '*Commes les francais*,' he said in an accent I've always found ridiculously sexy. Though whatever buzz I got from hearing his foreign tongue drained as you and I headed inside, where the rooms are still clutching onto the dark of winter, as the sky refuses to concede to spring.

I message Kim to let her know the decorations are on their way to being sorted.

44

Her reply is a thumbs up, then:

```
Fingers  crossed  soon  my  marriage
will  be  too.  You  were  right,  Adam
and  I  need  to  talk  ...  I'm  exploiting
a  possible  Edible  sponsor  to  snag
us  a  night  away.
```

Kim's brand, Edible, is huge. What started off as a blog quickly became a lifestyle. Recipes, restaurant reviews, interviews with chefs, and kitchen interiors to die for. It is aspirational and slick. The hush-hush news she's waiting to reveal at her party is that she'll soon be starting a weekly food column in *The Guardian*, a kind of *Sex and the City* meets *Saturday Kitchen*, even more of a coup, she said when she gave me the exclusive over Facetime a few weeks back, 'because Black women just don't get offered these kinds of spots. Do you know how white the UK papers are, Bea?'

As Kim held my gaze waiting for me to say something, the elephant in the room twitched with lumbering discomfort.

'I'm sorry,' I said. 'You shouldn't have to point out these things.'

'No.' Kim's brow arched. 'I shouldn't. A friend at the paper said they almost gave it to Sophie Green. You know her?'

'The blonde sommelier who called you the *exotic newcomer* to London's dining scene?'

'Ha, you remember!' Kim said.

'I remember how mad you were.'

'Mad? I was fucking livid. And you know what she said when she heard I got the column?'

'Tell me.'

'That I'm good at what I do but my writing has *limited* appeal. Hardly takes a genius to see through that line.'

'I can't believe people still say this crap.'

'I don't need your disbelief, Bea.' Kim sighed. 'I need your support.'

My point is, Kim doesn't shy away from a difficult conversation, she'll say the truth when it needs to be said.

The truth.

It's seven days now since I took the test. Seven days of not lying exactly, but close to.

'Dead,' you say, hands on your hips, grubbied knees from all that crawling you did this morning in the garden. You're standing now in just your pants because, when we came in for cheese on toast, you fancied removing your clothes. Apparently, lunch is better when you're almost naked.

At the beginnings and ends of our lives, Mabel, we Williams women are so determined and free.

In the middle though?

'Dead,' you repeat, glaring at your grandmother as if her passing was an insult directed at you.

I nod. 'Yes, Mabel. Nanna is dead.' Well and truly. So much for the living memory she promised when any other kind of living was officially confirmed by the doctors as short term.

'I've been on the Google,' Mum had said.

And no point, I know, because why does a dying woman need to be corrected but, 'It's just Google, Mum.'

She sighed, and not with the pain. 'I've ordered a special organic mixture I'd like you to combine with my ashes.'

'Jesus.'

'I know you don't want to talk about it, Beatrice, but I need you to listen. Your father will be absolutely useless when the time comes, and your brother's not here, so you're stuck with being in charge of *My Plan*.' She'd got into the habit of verbally proper-nouning everything to do with her death. 'As I was saying,' she paused a moment, face taut as she readjusted herself in the bed. 'You combine it with my ashes, add to soil and plant with some bluebell seeds. Simple.' Her fingers struggled with the lid to her medication. 'I'll pop up to see you every year.'

'Wouldn't putting your urn in a Jack-in-the-Box work the same kind of magic all year round? You'd even have entrance music.'

Unswayed by my alternative, she insisted on coming with me to buy the seeds.

'Couldn't we just order them on *The Google*?' I didn't much fancy trying to shoehorn Mum, a wheelchair and my bump, which was the size of a spacehopper by then, into a Mini.

'Oh, get over yourself, Beatrice. They're my *Last Few Weeks* so let me do what I want with them,' which was fair enough, I suppose. And there was something of the excitement of a day trip as I helped her dress, still having to work hard at an expressionless face when I pulled her nightdress over her head, so childishly freaked out by the texture and colour of her skin.

She chose her clothes, a blanket and music for the journey.

'Oh god, no, not Leonard Cohen, please. I thought this was your *Fun Day Out*.' By then, she'd got me proper-nouning too.

'Just listen.' Several months spent mostly in bed had made her pretty adept at *The* Spotify. 'Every cloud,' she'd said, like multiple myeloma could be silver lined with a better understanding of streaming. 'It's top of my *Funeral Play List*.'

'But today isn't your funeral, Mum. It's your *Fun Day O*—'

She turned up the volume before I could finish.

Tonight Will Be Fine filled the car. It was bleakly optimistic, suggesting things might get tough but so too would there be moments when life would be OK. Mum sang along, hand on my thigh, looking at me, like, *humour me, Beatrice, join in*.

When the song was done, 'It's going to hurt,' she said.

'We'll get you the meds you need, as much pain relief as the doctors allo—'

'I don't mean me, darling, I mean you.'

At least she'd waited until I was parked.

'Listen, it's like Leonard suggests.' She unclicked her seatbelt. 'Nothing is permanent, everything's just a phrase. You'll hurt and then,' she pressed both palms on my bump, 'you'll be fine.'

Later, she asked me to put the packets of bluebell seeds on the dining room table which we'd shunted next to the hospital bed when we'd moved her downstairs all those months ago.

'You can show the flowers to…What is it you're going to call the baby?'

'Nice try. I've told you; you'll find out when we introduce her to you.'

Maybe it was cruel, but you read about people needing something to live for. You were supposed to be her something to live for, Mabel. The baby *Bells*. So we wouldn't need those blue ones in the garden.

The garden is empty though.

More than two years later, no bluebells have grown.

TUESDAY 9TH APRIL

CHAPTER EIGHT

'Bloody Liv Baker. You'd think now she's in Sixth Form she'd be beyond this kind of shit.' Lucy barrels into the staff room in her standard chinos and blazer, her face pinched like yours, Mabel, when I accidentally gave you guacamole with a hint of chilli. 'She might not sign her name on it, but I *know* it's her. Look.' She waves a ripped jotter page in my face. 'Another of her Top Fives pinned to the common room door.'

'She's written it on paper?' I swipe at the sheet. 'How very old-school.'

'Liv might be mean but she's not stupid, Bea. These kids know if you put something incendiary online it can ruin you.'

'So what is it this time? Inspiring Women?' A slice of tomato slips from the last morsel of my chicken sandwich onto my knee. 'Most Romantic Taylor Swift Tracks? No, I've got it, her Favourite Shakespearean Plays?'

Lucy rolls her eyes. 'Liv Baker engaging with Shakespeare would be even more shocking than Barbara Streisand engaging with Andre Agassi in the early Nineties.'

'Top Five Teachers Most in Need of Current Celebrity Reference Points then?'

'Very funny, Ms Straw.' She clocks my open lunchbox. Almost everything is gone. 'You *do* know it's only 10:45.'

I shrug, not daring to mention my permanent hunger in case Lucy's nose for gossip, celebrity or otherwise, sniffs out any inkling why.

'Top Five Members of Staff Most Unlikely to Marry. Ever.' She thrusts the list at me. 'Guess who's number one?'

I don't have to guess. I can see. 'Sorry, mate.'

50

'Sorry?' You don't have to be sorry. Not for my single status anyway. Save your sympathy for Liv's ridiculous assumption that my single status is not only something to be mocked but something to be pitied. It's the twenty-first century. Getting married in the least of my aspirations.'

Here we go. Lucy's passion for literature is surpassed only by her passion for feminist reform.

Her hands go to her hips. 'Do these girls not realise marriage is the graveyard of ambition?'

Wait for it, there'll be a statistic in a mo.

'You do know, don't you, that while we women make up sixty-two per cent of the teaching work force, we only make up thirty-eight per cent of head teachers.' Her palms move, upturned to the air now, like, *can you believe this shit?* 'Not that we should be surprised.' She shakes her head. 'We're setting ourselves up to fail from the off. What's that skipping song? You must have sung it at primary?' Lucy chews her lip. 'First comes love, then comes marriage…'

'…then comes the baby in the carriage.' Forget primary, Della and I sung it all the way up to Year Nine. Even when she came out as bi, our certainty in – and hankering for – that nursery-rhymed path remained true.

That said, Craig and me, we hadn't intended to get married. Because our coupling had felt so different, we'd simply intended to "be".

Whatever that means.

We were thirty when we met, our birthdays exactly one month apart, which seemed something like fate after three different kinds of cocktails and his hands on my back as we swayed into what he called dancing and what I called an admirable teenage-effort first base. There were pressed lips, trodden on toes and mumbles of thanks to Della, who'd been sure we were a "match made in heaven". And despite my declarations that heaven was about as real as the perfect man, she proved at least one of them true when she persuaded us both to her party and made us jointly responsible for the bar.

'Craig, Bea. Bea, Craig.' Della passed me the limes and told me to squeeze. 'Craig gives good bob.' She tossed him the mint. 'Bea loves a well-placed semi-colon. He's your Robert Philip,' she said, not really winking but definitely smirking as she turned to welcome the other guests who were arriving in a blast of December air.

'Good bob?'

'Hairdresser.' And, god, that smile. 'So, who's this Robert Philip?'

Craig was chopping, head down, but I could hear the question was a verge-on piss-take. And I could have killed Della because I already liked him, this man whose hair, which smelt even better than the mint by the way, wasn't too dissimilar from Robert Philip's dark curls.

'My crush.' I tried to own it, the adolescent rumpling my heart was subjected to whenever I watched Robert Philip slowly surrendering to his true love Giselle through the techni-coloured song and dance in my all-time favourite movie. '*Enchanted*,' I told Craig, totally casual yet totally cringing. 'It's a girl-meets-boy movie about a Disney-type princess, Giselle, who falls into a well and ends in up New York where, in the process of trying to find her prince, she meets Robert Phili—'

'Your *crush* Robert Philip.' Craig's quite frankly beautiful eyes were getting wider by the second. So too was his grin.

'Yes, my *crush* Robert Philip.' I was already knee-deep in mortification with nothing to lose from jumping right in. 'I pretend to enjoy the film ironically, but I'm finally ready to admit I love its saccharine optimism. And that's OK,' I told Craig. 'Because Robert Philip is the anti-prince. And yeah, yeah, you'll probably want to tell me that even though he's the anti-prince, he's still tall, dark and handsome, and you'd be right.' Craig made a noise I crossed my fingers wasn't disdain. 'And you might also point out, again correctly, that a thirty-year-old twenty-first feminist like me would surely prefer Giselle find happiness in the strange land of New York without also having to find a man to share it with.' There was that unidentified noise again. 'But for one hundred and seven minutes, I am prepared to forgo my feminist ideals and simmer in the hot bed of silver-lined romance that is *Enchanted* and the obviously overrated unrealistic possibility of happy ever after.'

'Overrated?'

'Yes.'

'Unrealistic?'

'Yes.'

And I was pretty sure about it too because, spurned by several boyfriends, I was a cynic by then. Happy ever after was a line I'd been fed, and I usually choked on it. But then along came your father, who turned it into a peach schnapps, cranberry juice and ginger-ale cocktail, and I knocked it back, slammed my glass on the table and kept on asking for more.

The snap of Lucy plucking the ring on her can of Coke pulls me back into the present, the fizzy release of the drink timed perfectly with her own exhale as she plomps down on the seat next to me.

'Thing is,' she says, 'it's all well and good teaching this lot the benefits of an Oxford comma, but the benefits of teaching the truth about what it means to be a working woman would be far greater.'

I swear even the way she gulps her Coke is angry.

'What these list-making, husband-seeking girls need to understand is that getting this promotion will be statistically far harder for me than it is for Stephen Baldry. Even though, as we all know, Stephen Baldry isn't half as good a —'

Hold on a minute. 'This promotion?'

Lucy looks at me, like, *get with the program.* 'You haven't heard? Paula's gone on sick leave, Bea. Emergency hysterectomy. She's booked in next week. Jake Flanagan – you know in Physics – plays Warhammer with Paula's husband, who reckons she won't be back until September earliest. They'll need cover for Deputy Head of Department for at least the summer term, and whoever bagsies *that* job…'

Lucy gives me the nod. At the Christmas party, Jackie, our Head of English went a bit too wild on the Pinot Grigiot and let slip she's hankering for early retirement next year. Any management experience we could get in the interim would put us in better stead for her role.

The bell rings for class.

'I think I'm in with a decent chance.' Lucy gets to her feet, smooths her sharp-fringed bob with her palm. She might be small, but there's something formidable in the way she holds herself. 'I mean, let's face it, Stephen Baldry aside, there's hardly much competition. And given he had to see the head last term after that parent complained, I could be a shoe-in.'

I stand, straightening my back. Surely, I can be equally imposing. 'Er, *hello*? What about *me*?'

'*You*?' Lucy checks herself then, realising she probably shouldn't sound quite so sceptical. 'Sorry,' she says. 'I didn't mean…I just had you down as a working-mum type rather than a career-type, you know?'

I *know*, Mabel.

But.

Lucy's attention is already shifting from me to the Head of Drama, who's suddenly centre stage in front of us, shaking a Tupperware that rattles with pathetic scraps of change.

'We're doing a collection.' Mary delivers all her news with the glorious ebullience of Miriam Margoyles. 'For Paula. Because of the…' She points to her genitals and mouths, 'op-er-a-tion.'

'Sure.' I grab my purse. Your photo stares at me from between my credit and library cards.

'That your little one?' Mary asks.

I nod.

'What a cracker!'

This is not unusual, Mabel. People – friends, strangers, even – tell me you're beautiful. 'Thanks,' I say, like it's all down to me, to some talent I have for making babies.

I asked a woman in Sainsbury's once if she thought your eyes, which she'd said were "dazzling", were nature's trick to make me fall in love with you.

'Oh, they don't need no tricks.' She brushed your cheek with her finger. 'It's instinctive, innit?' And I nodded because, well, even nature's a mother, isn't she? And who am I to think I can argue with biology? With the universal truth of a mother's love.

I swear I *do* love you, Mabel.

But.

It's been a process. And I get how mundane that sounds. But when my father looked up from his armchair, where he held you while you slept so peacefully at three weeks old, and told me you'd be a heart-breaker one day, there was no way he could have known you'd already broken mine. But that's not fair. Because it's not you who broke it exactly. You're brilliant, and I mean that, Mabel. It's not you, it's me. Or more, it's the permanence of our attachment, the way the umbil-ical cord, despite the scissors Craig took to it, retains these invisible threads that bind us so I'm never just Bea now.

I'm Bea wrapped in motherhood.

I'm Bea forever tethered to you.

'Bea!' The clatter of Mary's tub brings me back into the room.

'Here you go.' I'm out of coins. My ten-pound note sits on top of all that noisy change.

'Jeez!' Lucy baulks at the money. 'It's almost worth having a hysterectomy if everyone gives as generously as that.'

I can think of other benefits.

I picture the two blue lines.

Another tether.

Another thing to stop me moving forward.

Another long mat leave in the house with a baby and all these riddled thoughts and feelings, which surely aren't only noxious for me Mabel.

Are they not equally noxious for you?

CHAPTER NINE

Bang on six-thirty, Craig calls, fulfilling his promise to phone from France each evening so we can Facetime our reading of *Room on the Boom*. It's been your favourite for months. You laugh every time at the wailing witch and the spitting cat, flying after the blown-off hat.

'Hat,' you'll say. 'Cat,' you'll say. Then, 'dog,' you'll say, when a dog appears, hat in mouth, and is welcomed onto the broomstick, which begins to look a little crowded, a little precarious, under the weight of a third living breathing creature. 'Woosh,' you'll say, so thrilled with the onomatopoeic thrust of the word.

I never fail to envy the ease of your happiness, your satisfaction. Your ability to find joy in the Groundhog Day of this life the three of us live.

So, Craig calls. Sure he does. Always a man of his word.

Back in the beginning, he was the first to arrive whenever and wherever we were meeting. He was reliable, see. Not in a slippers and cardigan kind of way. Rather he was respectful. Unlike those other guys, who'd bail by text last minute when I was already at the bar with a glass of red to finish on my own. I'd style it out, the leaving that likely no one else even noticed but felt so spot-lit, so look-at-me: sadly-not-good-enough-again. Your father's difference was apparent even on that first Morning After, which had all the potential to be awkward but was made easy by him saying, 'It might be too much, so tell me if it's weird, but do you fancy coming to mine? I'd just need some time to tidy.' He cocked his brow. 'Give me an hour?'

In exchange, he gave me his address, where I arrived, right on 2.00 p.m., with an accelerated heart, which felt a little adolescent, yes, but with an edge of grown-up sophistication because this seemed symbolic, this second date. Hurried but not desperate. Sexy but not just sex. For as well as tidying, he'd bought the ingredients for a curry. An invitation, then, to dinner, which we made together in a kitchen he shared with two other guys, banished for the next three hours but returning to eat with us. 'If that's OK?' Which it was, because Craig was the same Craig when his flatmates came home, still moving me when I didn't necessarily need moving by placing his hands on my waist and gently pulling or pushing me just so. And that touch, in the company of others, felt as intimate as his touch before they'd appeared, when we'd washed our hands clean of the spices and he'd given me a tour, ending in his room, made cold by the open window, then warmer, in not too long, by us.

Us.

We didn't talk about it, the consolidation of two people into something more together than separate. But it was already apparent when we lay beneath the covers and took it in turn to ask each other questions from a list – *One-Hundred Questions to Ask Your New Lover* – that Della had sent me that morning when I'd messaged her aubergine and smiley-faced emojis.

'Coldplay,' he answered. 'Going over the handlebars of my bike when I rode it down a slide.' 'You.'

'Mint choc chop,' I told him. 'My mum.' 'What kind of cheese do you use to hide a horse?' He shook his head. 'Mask-a-pony.' Groaned.

'Last one. What's something you've always wanted to achieve but never have?'

'A world record,' I said.

'In what?' His finger traced the line of my thigh beneath the duvet.

'Dunno.' I reciprocated with my hand on his shoulder, which was broad but not gym-honed. What I mean is, Craig felt like a man who wasn't trying to become anything he wasn't. As if he really knew himself and was already the kind of man he wanted to be. 'It would just be cool to the best at something.'

'Other than sex?'

'I'm the best at sex?'

He'd worked his way up to my chin. 'On the evidence I've accrued thus far, I'd say so.'

'Well then, yeah. I'd like to be the best at something other than sex.'

We ditched the questions, scoured the Guinness website for feasible and less feasible challenges and discovered this guy, Ashrita Furman, who holds the record for holding the most world records. We flipped to his website, then, reading about his efforts in grape-catching, pogo-sticking, land-rowing, often assisted by his mate Bipin, who helped him train.

'I'll be your Bipin,' Craig said. 'But only if I get to choose the record.'

I shrugged like, *whatever*, thinking nothing of it until three weeks later when I arrived at his place to find him holding a stopwatch, a spacehopper and a whip. 'You ready?' he asked, and with him, Mabel, it seemed I was.

Less so now though. Because when Craig calls at six-thirty, you and I are far from ready. What we *are* is lagging. My fault, obviously, because you're two-and-a-bit, and I'm a grown woman who really should have learnt by now that the whole dinner-bath-bed combo cannot be interrupted by Instagramming. Not without consequence anyway. But there you were, in your highchair, singing (of sorts) the words (of sorts) of that song Craig plays on repeat from *The Greatest Showman*.

'…not square to be see, make no apol-lo-bee, Peppa Pig. Peppa Pig. Peppa Pig.'

Your very own mash-up.

'Again, Mabel, again!'

Your cheeks puffed at the praise, mouth already open, shoulders pulled back for your encore.

'Wait. Wait.'

Your fingers were mad for the Fairy-bubbles wisping up from the sink onto your arm when I tossed the dishcloth into the bowl as I ran to snatch my phone from the lounge.

'Again,' I told you. And you strained from your seat across to the basin for more froth but, 'No, the song, Bells. Leave the bubbles. Sing your song.'

I'd always thought three was the magic number, but it took eleven attempts over nine minutes for you to get what I was after. Me singing your version and sticking my thumb in the air when the camera was ready for your turn to copy.

'Go,' I said, when you didn't get the cue. Of course, I cut that bit before I posted it because, well, spontaneity and all that. It wasn't as good as the original. It was funny enough, though. And I laughed as much if not more as I'd done the first-time round, and the multiple takes gave me chance at least to give your tray and face a wipe ready for show time too.

"B-Festival" I called it when I posted it to Tonight Will Bea Fine: a hundred or so words about the joy of music mashed up with the joy of Bells. Apologies for the state of the kid and the house. #TooMuchFunForCleaning

So, we're not in bed, we're on the stairs when Facetime chimes, and you've wedged your fingers into the nook between the tread and the riser, where a spider is emitting magical waves that prevent you from hearing but not from prodding and picking, as I'm telling you, 'Up, Mabel! keep moving! Daddy is waiting!'

The spider curls in on itself, protecting its legs, its life. And I know how it feels to shrink away from you. But you're too big, too curious, too there.

'Now!'

'Bea?' Craig's is the voice of a man who's been cycling in the sunshine with his mates. Probably two beers and a bowl of nuts into his evening. 'Bea?'

'Now, Mabel!' Mine is the voice of a woman trying to sound vaguely like the girl who was all, 'sure, sounds cool,' when Craig proposed in a Vegas casino. 'No fuss though, right?' I was totally chill back then. This evening though, no patience for any more spider-pokery, I scoop you under one arm and hold up the phone with the other.

Finally, we reach the top of the stairs.

'Daddy!' Your pitch is ten times higher. You haul yourself up onto my bed, turn to me, almost face to face with the height you've gained. 'Daddy!' He's snatched from my palm.

'Mabey Baby! Miss you, gorgeous girl,' he says. Your fingers are on his mouth as if you want to catch the words as he speaks them. 'Lemmie see Mummy a moment, Bells.' But, now you have him, you're reluctant to share.

I budge you along the bed so we're both half sitting with our backs pushed against the headboard. 'Phone, please, Mabel.'

'*My* daddy!' There's no venom in it, just fact.

'Pass me over,' Craig says, and you look from him to me and from me to him, like, *as if.* 'How was your day then, Bells?' It didn't take long for him to concede to your need for attention. 'Did you go to the park on the way home?'

You swoop closer to the screen, less interested in the conversation than the wrinkles you can make in your nose. 'Look!' You pull faces: wide-mouthed O's and sucked-in cheeks. These are for your own pleasure, not Craig's, though he's happy to watch as he sips a beer, his whole evening stretched out long and warm ahead of him.

I see mine shrinking, my quiet minutes alone.

'Pass me to Mummy now, Bells.'

Large inhale, and I prise the phone from you.

Spine arching against the pillow, you stretch to your fullest, stiffest self, sliding down across the duvet. You're wounded. Not physically, obviously, but in that other way I'm so scared of whenever I'm with you because fear and guilt weigh me down as much as gravity.

I pull you up and the covers back. The closer the better as far as you're concerned. You soften into my side when I cocoon us beneath the quilt.

'How was work? Good day?' And seeing Craig's face, how totally laid back he is in his greeting, I'm smacked with how deep the changes have dug into us. Time was, your father and I would have joked about the truth of Della's match made in heaven, how separate we were kind of hellish, but together, well, we were something else. We got each other is what I mean. And not just the flow with which we teamed up to make cocktails that first night. It was everything else and every other night too.

'Mine?' I'd suggested, as we were putting our coats on at the end of the party. And I'd meant whose flat we'd head for after, but —

'I think I will be,' Craig said. And it didn't feel cloying or overrated or unrealistic. It felt right.

'Good day?' Craig asks me now. And old me would have been total disclosure. I'd have told him I'm struggling, asked if there's any chance he could come home early.

'Fine,' I say, which should be a giveaway because we all know, don't we, that *fine* is a thin-veiled attempt at wellbeing. But Craig and I are two-and-a-bit years in to this New Us, and *fine* is a word we barely register because *fine* is a word that will do. 'I told you Paula's gone on sick leave?' He nods. 'Well, the head of department made the search for a temporary replacement official…'

'Sure,' Craig says, not to me but to Stu who appears in the background, two cans of Stella in hand. Craig takes one, pulls its ring.

'She sent an email. To all of us, asking if we want to appl—'

'Daddy!' You go for his face on the screen now but hit the *end call* button instead. 'Daaaaaaaaaaaaaaady!' It's my fault apparently. 'Want Daddy.' Your face is a breath-held pout. Your fists turn purple. You exhale only to scream.

'She's lost it,' I tell Craig when he reappears. 'Look, Mabel, it's Daddy. It's Daddy, Mabel. He's back, see. Mabel! Mabel!'

But it's too late, and you're too tired, and I shouldn't have given you the chocolate buttons to keep you quiet while I washed up.

'Never mind.' How could I create time to take on Paula's role when I haven't even got the time to talk about it.

'Hey, guess what?' Craig leans closer toward the camera. 'Stu and I have signed up for a triathlon.'

You're kicking the duvet and rubbing your eyes.

'A what?'

'A triathlon. You know, swim, cycle, run.'

I know what a triathlon is, Mabel.

'We were chatting about it on the flight over.' He brings a hand to his forehead, shielding his eyes from the sun. 'I mean, I love the bike, it's great headspace after work and that. But I need something else, you know. The riding on its own's not really challenging enough.'

Rain smatters against our bedroom window.

'I've joined the local group. Stu's a member, says it's great. Organised rides, coached swims, and track sessions on a Thursday. Signed up for my first event in the summer. With enough training, I reckon I should be OK for it by then.'

Swim.

Cycle.

Run.

Where are you in all of these hours, Mabel?

63

Where is another child?

Where am I?

'I have to go,' I say before I say something else. Before my vocal cords give noise to the thought that's been skulking since I first saw that thin blue line, a thought that comes not from my head or my heart but from my gut, where honesty burns, rooted and crude, at my core.

I, *we*, can't have this baby.

A triathlon might not seem life changing.

But.

As the call ends, the thought pierces through my gut so it's almost tangible. Sharpened by Craig's ability to make such time-consuming decisions without me.

What was it Kim said about taking action when you feel powerless.

We each have to make our own choices, Mabel.

And, sure, there's no use crying over spilt milk but, truth is, I'd rather die than spill any more.

CHAPTER TEN

'As soon as possible, please.'

The voice at the other end of the phone must be used to my kind of desperation and to the tormenting tick of the clock as she checks availability while the caller holds her breath and the line.

'Mummy!' There's an urgency to your voice too as it comes from the lounge where, yes, I shut you in when we'd finished the call to Daddy because you hearing the word "abortion" seemed worse than me actually booking one. 'Mummy!' And again, 'Mummy!' And again. The woman won't be long. And if you're able to shout for me, and there's been no crash, then surely everything is fine behind that closed door, and you're just wondering where I am, Mabel, and how I dared to leave you.

'Hello?' She's back.

'Mummy!'

It's amazing what can happen in another room in what must only be a few seconds. Or, it's amazing what I *imagine* can happen in another room in what must only be a few seconds. The chair you *may* have climbed on near the window I *may* have left open. The man who *may* be lurking outside that possibly open window whose long arms *may* be reaching for you as I listen to the options I have for my consultation.

'We could do Frida—'

'Yes.' I snatch at the appointment. The rush and relief taste like a first glug of wine. Then, barely a breath later. 'How long needs to pass between the consultation and the…' I inhale, exhale. 'How soon after can I get the pills?'

'If you are suitable, we can do it on the same day.'

'Fantastic,' I say, and while I wonder if "fantastic" is a word I shouldn't be using the in context of this kind of appointment, I wonder too whether the police will check my phone records if you have actually been kidnapped through an open window by a man with long arms and, if they do, whether the man with long arms stealing you from the open window will be the guilty one when they see who I was calling at the time of the crime. Just picture the head-lines, Mabel.

'Friday at ten.' I repeat, confident I can get you in for an extra day at nursery. You're usually off with me on Fridays. My finger stops its run down the fridge calendar at Friday 12th. *Shit*. This Friday is not just any normal Friday. It's *the* Friday. *The* Friday with Craig away and Grandma Alice booked to babysit. Kim's thirtieth-birthday Friday, my one night away planned meticulously over the last six weeks. The location. The timing. The dress. The train to London and a night in a hotel room on my own.

'Is there any other day?' I ask.

I open the door a crack to check you've not been stolen.

'Mummy!' That hurt on your face as I snap it shut.

Did the woman hear you? The child I kept.

'Umm, we could possibly do first thing on Thursday,' she says in the same calm voice as if nothing is a problem. As if everything is OK.

I can't have Thursday off. I couldn't bear to sit through the "return to work" interview we have to endure with the head every time we take leave from school. Can you imagine Evans' face, Mabel, as she sits beneath the crucifix on her wall and I confess my deadly sin.

'Otherwise, we're looking at next week.'

And practically, with next week being the school Easter holidays, that would make sense but, now the decision is made, a weekend of waiting would be too long. Too much.

'Friday is good,' I say. 'Friday at ten is good.'

'Are you sure?' The woman asks me.

'Mummy!'

'Absolutely.' I tell her. 'Thank you.'

She must sense the tectonic shift in my tone because when she speaks, though her words are purely admin, they are softened and kind. 'It's confirmed, then, Friday at ten.'

THURSDAY 11TH APRIL

CHAPTER ELEVEN

'You *have* to come. Tomorrow night's not only my birthday, which you've bloody organised, it's also *our* moment.' From her breath, Kim's clearly walking at a Londoner's pace. 'The first time I get to clap eyes *and* actual hands you.' Her words are spilling as fast as her feet are moving to keep in step with the crowd.

'Are you in Bethnal Green? I thought you and Adam had been comp'd a night in Whitstable?'

Kim had hoped sea and conversation would clear the air before tomorrow's party.

'We were. I'm late, as usual, which Adam'll tell me is bad form, but what's worse form, Bea, is you texting me the news that you're not coming. I appreciate we millennials are supposed to be afraid of phone calls, but in certain circumstances…'

She's right, of course. But in the two days since making the appointment, every time I'd thought about how a conversation with Kim about me bailing might go, speaking out loud had felt too dangerous, too vulnerable to the slippery truth of why. And I could hardly tell her, could I? That a party is no place for a mother who will have just aborted her second child.

No, that mother needs to sit in the dark. In shame.

So, while you'll still go for your extra session at nursery in the morning, Mabel, it will be me, not Grandma, who'll pick you up at lunchtime. It will be you, not Kim, with whom I'll spend the afternoon.

'Isn't there someone else who could look after Mabel?' A horn sounds in the background, the London traffic obviously harbouring similar frustrations to Kim. 'I can't believe Craig's mum has let you down.'

'It's not Alice's fault she has shingles.' The fictitious illness I've thrust upon your grandmother is a minor lie in the grand scheme of things. In the version I told Alice, it's me that's unwell. She offered to take you as planned, but it seemed wrong, Mabel, to have someone else look after my child when any pain I suffer will be my own doing.

The skin on my forearm immediately goosebumps with the blast from the open freezer. I pull tomorrow night's dinner – bolognese I made on Monday – from the top shelf. The tray of ice cubes catches my eye.

Just one.

'There must be someone.' Kim's tone isn't too dissimilar from yours when something doesn't quite go your way. 'What about Della? She might want the practice, no?'

'She's shattered.' In reality, Della would jump at the chance to have you over for the night. 'And anyway, Nisha's visiting family. I don't want to ask Del to do it on her own.' The lies pour as easily as the gin into my glass, Mabel. 'I promise you, though, everything will still run like clockwork. I'll call all the suppliers again tomorrow morning.'

Kim's sigh is a kind of retreat.

'And this lovely guy, Dillon, at The Hidden Gem has promised to be on standby to do everything I would have done on the night. I'm so sorry. You know I was as excited about this as you.'

I open my laptop on the kitchen counter, its lid knocking into the Ketchup you insisted on squeezing onto your pasta at dinner. The Premier Inn Hub website gleams on the screen. The room I'd booked is not extravagant. "Compact" is what they call it. But size isn't everything, Mabel. The marketing people obviously don't know how significantly a space expands when it's child free.

'Mummy!'

71

Seriously, what is the point of a monitor? It's not as if we can't hear you. "Compact" is how I'd describe our house too.

'Mabel is screaming.'

Another sigh. And I don't blame her. In Kim's position, I would also have sighed. Because aren't I now exactly the kind of woman I always swore I wouldn't become? And I'm not even talking about the abortion.

'I'm so sorry.' I try not to choke. Is it skewed that it's this – the being a shitty friend rather than being a shitty mother – that's pricking the tears? I wipe them away before they even have the chance to fall. 'Listen, I'll call you in the afternoon once I've checked everything's in place. OK?'

''K.' Kim's voice is warmer now. 'I'm sorry I was short with you. I'm just gutted tha—'

'Mummy!'

And for once I'm grateful for your screams, Mabel, for the excuse they give me to end the call.

* * *

You needed one more cuddle, that's all. Thirty-seconds or so of soothing and you were calm. My head, though, is not so coddled.

I watch you from the doorway to your room, urging myself to go downstairs and crack on with some marking. At the very least, I should turn on the TV, read a book, update Tonight Will Bea Fine, anything but stand and stare at you because in your waking hours, I'm on countdown to these moments of quiet. Of Still. And yet, when they come, the shame of that yearning keeps me locked in close to you, checking the ill of my wishes hasn't weaved some ancient curse upon your lungs to stop you breathing. A mother's love knows no bounds, they say. But what of a mother's regret?

I mean you no harm, Mabel. My regret is a mute one. And while I would undo the tangles of my choices, while I would undo the dragging mundanity and burden of having a child, I would *not* undo *you*. I mean it when I say you are brilliant. When I write of your intelligence, your fun, your joy. When I agree with my friends who are also mothers that, yes, I would die for you, Mabel, every word of that promise is true. I might think *I've got to go*, forty / fifty times a day, but believe me, I'm not actually going anywhere.

I'm here, aren't I?

'I *do* love you.'

'Love you, Mummy.' You voice comes from the dark.

Those friends who are also mothers say this kind of declaration is the pay-off. The time in the day when you realise it's all worthwhile, but.

It's complicated.

'Sweet dreams,' I whisper, edging further from your room and closer to the gin and tonic, to the slice of lemon I'll suck before it goes in the glass because I am a lemony type of mother, maybe. Sharp and bitter. The yellow of cowardice and deceit.

At least on the inside.

On the outside, I am Ms Straw – a respectable teacher – and in my online separate and anonymous from school life, I am @MsTWBF – Instagram popular and Twitter droll. I am 74k-follower successful. Great marriage. A hassled-but-finding-all-this-crap-amusing kind of mum. Alongside the teaching, I make a pittance wage of the jokey misery of motherhood. Of the drudgery of wiping a bum for no money but for the love of a child who has made me complete. Of my mistakes and your misfortune at having a slummy mummy like me. But it is tongue in cheek. It is look at how I can take the piss out of myself and still be a woman who is pretty fucking close to having it all.

I began writing to you when I was pregnant. It was Mum's idea. She wrote to you too, a small bundle of letters putting things to paper that she would never get to say to you in person. And although she didn't exactly frame it like that, she did tell me how sometimes it helps to write your feelings down. Her head had tilted to the side, and she'd laid a hand on my rounded belly, 'Just remember, Beatrice, thoughts don't always do so well if they're left to curdle in your head.'

We talked to you too. Because I read in a book or online how you would come to recognise voices, and I wanted you to know me *and* Mum from the very beginning. I wanted you to know why you were here.

'What would you say to having a baby?' Craig had tossed the question out there, like he was asking how I felt about having toasties for lunch. We'd been married a year, which would, in the normal course of things, be the *right* time to think about children. But when he'd proposed in a casino in Vegas, hadn't he, *we*, proposed something different to the normal course of things. Hadn't the idea been that the two of us were something special. The rush into parenthood made it clear that he didn't think two of us alone were something special enough.

'Do you not think we should wai—'

'I think we should do it now.'

And, of course, Craig had his own reasons, but when your mother is dying, it's easy for everything to acquire a sense of urgency.

'Sure,' I said, trying to sound casual, as if I hadn't just realised how much everything depended on it. So, I came off the pill and calculated dates. Within a few months, I was writing love letters to the baby-shaped carrot I could dangle in front of my mum.

I carried on after your arrival. Mining any moments in the day which could be blown up into something resembling happiness, amplifying the good because, well, fake it 'til you make it, right?

Come 11.00 p.m., I'd sit on the sofa with you crooked in one arm literally sucking the life out of me. As I urged you to ease up on the predawn feeds, I wrote everything for which I was trying to be grateful and listened out for signs of Mum. All while teetering on Leonard's uncharacteristically optimistic slant that Tonight Will Be Fine.

It rarely was, Mabel.

It wasn't you though. As the old saying goes, *it's not you, it's me*. And it was. For even when *you* slept, *I* wouldn't. Rather, I would stare into the dark, reminding myself everything is a phase, wondering just how long this current phase might be.

When Craig read them, those night-time distortions of our days, 'You should write a blog,' he said.

'A *blog*? Are we back in the Noughties?' Time travel was a super-power I longed for as I scrolled through photo after photo of Mum.

'They're still a thing,' Craig said. 'One of my clients, Callie, has one, and she does alright. Call it an *online presence* if that makes it cooler. And you know Stu's wife's a graphic designer, right? I bet she'd knock you up a site.' Stu's wife was also a mother of two who, if she was anything like the other mothers I mixed with, was likely already struggling to complete the paid work alongside parenthood let alone chucking freebie favours for her husband's mates into the mix. 'Truth is, you write way better than Callie does. You're funnier too. *And sexier*.' Craig thew my love letters to you aside so he could pull me closer and, no need to cover your ears, Mabel, because I was still too raw, too lost in the black hole of very early motherhood. Tethered to you. Untethered from Mum.

A bit of extra ice'll weaken the double maybe triple shot of my third glass. A suck of the lemon. A cheers to my reflection in the kitchen window. A scroll through Instagram then Twitter to see how the other mums fare. Like. Comment. Share. Like. Comment. Share. B-Festival's doing alright. They love it when you sing. When there's just a hint of chaos. When the balance between boundless struggle and boundless love is spot on.

Your dad messages to check you went off alright after your meltdown. I send him a picture of you sleeping followed by a picture of my gin. Even though he doesn't ask, 'Just the one,' I tell him. 'To get me through the Year Eleven marking.' Cocktail and sleepy face emojis.

'Miss you,' he says, and I believe him.

It's not the first, second or tenth time I've been to look at the test. When I take it from the wash bag now, it's tacky with something leaked and floral smelling. Back in the kitchen, I rub it with the rind scooped out from my drink. 'It's the acidity.' I hear my mother's voice, the same as it was when I was four and sitting on the loo – seat down – my feet dangling, swinging, as I watched her wipe a lemon around the rim of the bathroom sink. 'One of Nanna Agatha's tricks,' she said. 'Get a bit of this on it first.' She sprinkled some salt into the basin, then beckoning me with one hand, passed the squeezed fruit with the other. 'Scrub,' she mimed to show me how. 'Better than bleach,' she said. 'Cheaper too.'

These were the moments I felt closest to my mum. When she made secrets of this maternal inheritance of cleaning tips and recipes passed through the generations.

They weren't real secrets though, were they?

Silly to put the gin away when the bottle's almost done. Out of lemon now, but the cucumber I got for your nursery sandwiches will do.

The *Shropshire Star* leaves its stories on my fingers as I pass-the-parcel the test before I bin it. The opposite of peeling an onion. Any threat of tears diminishing with each layer I tape. That sting, though. That sting lingers longer than ink.

I should probably keep it. The pregnancy test, I mean. Hang it over my bed like that mobile of white clouds and multi-coloured raindrops dangling above yours. They sway when I blow on them now, the blue one knocking into the green one, the green one into the yellow one and so on and so on like one of those toys your granddad has on his desk.

I'm glad for the rainbow rug on your floor, pat it with gratitude for its softness when I fall. 'Sssshhhh.' But you don't stir. Even with the clink of my glass on the bars of your cot, you sleep on, totally peaceful, face lit by my phone as I tap tap tap at it. Let everything out. The secrets of a generation. Tap tap tap. I pick out the cucumber from my drink because it won't do. I am a lemony type of mother. Tap tap tap. Sharp and bitter. I read it over. Tap tap tap. The yellow of cowardice and deceit. Tap tap tap. On the inside. Tap tap tap. Maybe now on the outside too.

'I love you, Mabel, but. Ssshhhhh.' I repeat, wary of my fingers. Of you.

FRIDAY 12TH APRIL

CHAPTER TWELVE

They are a cliché, these seconds when I am woken by 'Mummy! Mummy! Mummy!' and the smack smack smack of your water bottle against the wall. You are calling out for the immediate start of everything, but when I lift my head to reach for my beeping phone, my brain is syruped with gin and lemon and an invisible hand down my throat wrenching my heart up and over my tongue and through my teeth like the opposite of labour. Like I'm birthing my own death. The test rests on my pillow, half wrapped in *Shropshire Star* headlines – 'chaos' 'library' 'youth' – an origami of all those public-interest stories binding my most personal.

'Fuck.'

A palm on my belly. A flash of my hands taking my test from the bin.

'Mummy!'

A bottle on the bedside table. Half full. Not so bad, I think. And then the flickering truth of the other one: emptied. A glass on the floor. Soaked cucumber on the fireplace. A trail of what? My pilgrimage to Mother's Ruin?

'Mummy!'

'Coming.' Only I don't move. Because what doesn't flash or flicker loiters. Or scratches. Memories like those mice in the first flat I shared with your father. Like them, but before we knew they were mice, when their scuttling sounded like the previous residents' dirty secrets niggling for attention beneath the floorboards.

There's something that needs letting out of my head is what I mean. But I can't reach for it. What memory has slipped?

'Muuuuuuuuuuum-eeeeeee!'

'Coming.'

It's like the morning after Bryony Jackson's eighteenth birthday party when she'd dared me to take a swig from every bottle of her parents' stash of booze. There were flashes, flickers, then too. But it wasn't the lit-up bits – the dancing, laughing, the singing – that were the problem, rather it was the dark bits in between. The gaps Bryony refused to fill, merely relishing how I hadn't been drunk-stupid, I'd been drunk-insane. That smirk of hers, her power in knowing me better than I knew myself. I pretended she wasn't real, this other side of me who smelt of filth and shame. And yet she's here, isn't she? Has always been here, lurking beneath the good girl with her unmotherly wicked thoughts and her unmotherly wicked ways.

Did I call Craig? Tell him about the pregnancy? The appointment? How I feel, Mabel, about mothering you?

But my phone, which has a message only from Della, shows no evidence of drunk-dialling or texting. Unlike my breath and my skull, it's clean.

'Mummy?' Less anger now. More fear. 'Mummy?' That quiet trickly kind of sob when you bite the inside of your lip.

'I'm here, Bells.'

One tear balances on your cheek, which is circus-tent red, burning against my own when I tuck the train of your sleeping bag under the fold in your knees and lift you into me.

'Mummy.' It's half way between accusation and relief. How many times a day do you say it, do you think? *Mummy!* How many times do you remind me of what I am now? I tried counting once but quit when I hit the hundreds,

'We're OK, baby.' I turn my face away so you don't inhale my hangover. 'I promise, we'll be OK.'

* * *

As if it hadn't already caused problem enough, the coil is still working its nefarious magic. I'd offered its failure on the phone to the clinic on Tuesday as some kind of justification for my actions. A this-wasn't-my-mistake. A this-is-science-letting-me-down. An honestly-I'm-not-some-silly-girl-who-should-have-known-better. I *know* the consequences of unprotected sex, I wanted to tell her. But maybe she was trained in hearing the grains of things because she seemed to understand without me saying anything more.

'I'm sorry,' she'd said. 'I appreciate it must have been a shock. It does happen sometimes.'

There was a pause, then, a small inhale of breath on her part and an exhale on mine.

She doesn't hate me, I thought, which is ridiculously high-school, I know. But that was the relief, as heart-stoppingly physical as when Mum brought me up a bowl of tinned tomato soup a few hours after I'd made *that* confession about what I'd done with Adrian Johnson. *She doesn't hate me*, I thought, willing her to sing *Top of the World* as she usually did as a kind of comfort, which was asking too much, maybe. But the soup, at least, was warm hope in my belly.

'It does mean you'll have to visit your GP or sexual health clinic,' the receptionist had said, 'to have the coil removed before we can administer the pills.'

Which is why I was in a rush this morning, Mabel. Why I pushed through the gin fog to neck coffee while serving Weetabix and chop carrots for your nursery snack. Why our morning routine was slick and quick and you were at nursery by eight-thirty so I could be at the GP surgery on the dot of nine, lying on the bed with my jeans and knickers removed.

He didn't say much, the doctor, when I arrived, just tapped at the keyboard with the occasional glance at the ringed finger of my left hand, which I slid – a child caught with contraband sweets – under my thigh.

He'd asked if I'd like a chaperone.

Not wanting any further witnesses, I shook my head.

'No, thank you,' I'd said, pathetically desperate for him to see how polite I was being. How despite what I'd told him, I wasn't a bad woman really.

I watch him approach the end of the bed with the forceps and hate myself for how violently I want him to confirm that all of this – everything I'm doing – is OK.

'Done,' he says, pulling the privacy curtain back around with a methodical swoosh, though we both know, don't we, that it would take more than that to restore my dignity, to sweep away the bare fact of shame.

* * *

'Is there someone here with you?' Sarah, the woman at the clinic, has a voice that is low and kind. 'To take you home?'

'Yes,' I say, 'my mum,' understanding, then, what people mean by the words slipping out. "My mum" slipped like a shucked oyster. Sharp. Salty. I can't tell if it was delicious to say it, or if the feel of it was wrong on my tongue.

Sarah, filling in some paperwork, looks up briefly with a small smile. They all have small smiles here. Genuine but small. Anything broader would be insensitive, I suppose.

'She's waiting for me in Costa.'

My thumbs smears snakes onto the black screen of my phone, veering towards the home button, to the contacts, to Mum, still in my favourites. Would I still be in hers if she knew? If she could, *would* she wait in Costa? Or at home? With a bowl of tinned tomato soup. Or would she be too disappointed?

'I'm not angry, I'm disappointed,' she said, when I confessed to losing my virginity at fifteen. 'I'd have expected this of your brother, Bea, but not you.'

Despite the tray she'd brought to my bedroom, she was quiet for days.

Is that why her two-and-a-bit-year silence, then, Mabel? Because, you know, despite Mum's promises to always be here, there's not even been bluebells. And maybe that's because of her disappointment in how I've felt about you.

It's silly, I get it, to have expected anything else. Ghosts are nonsense. And your Nanna, as you like to tell me, is dead.

I can't help it though, the idea of her holding me, loving me, Mabel, which is stupid because I'm thirty-four, way beyond the age when, even if she were here, she could kiss and make it better.

'I'm just going to call her when I —' When I'm *what*? Done aborting my baby? Craig's baby? 'She's been amazing.' I try one of those small smiles. 'My mum, I mean.'

'I'm glad.' Sarah says it like she believes me, like she means it. A minute or so passes. 'OK, Bea. Are you sure about your decision?'

'Yes.'

Sarah had barely finished the question. Another small smile.

I want to hug her, this woman who is saving my life, because I may have lied about Mum and Costa, but when I tell Sarah that one way or another my life would be over if I had this baby, it is true.

CHAPTER THIRTEEN

'I can't believe it.' Kim's voice is a blister, only a thin layer between discomfort and oozing wet pain.

'Is it the florist? I know there's an issue with the peonies, but they've left me a message and said they're sorting it.' I'd come out of the clinic to a barrage of missed calls. 'Listen, I'm just getting in the car now, and then I'll phone them, OK?'

But the blister has popped. And Kim's crying. Like something totally awful has happened, which it has, I suppose, but it's not as if she could know.

Could she?

'Why not tell me the whole rotten story from the off?' she says, and raging shots of whetted guilt lance my chest and throat and catch my tongue. I am speechless. 'Hasn't he always agreed that honesty's what matters most?'

He?

'Adam?'

'Yes,' she says. 'Adam.'

And despite Kim's obvious heartache, my shoulders drop with relief.

'Hold on a minute, let me get in the car and switch you to speaker.'

The thud of the door closing. I'd felt the same when I took the first pill.

'We were driving to Whitstable last night, and his phone was connected to Car Play so when this WhatsApp came in from that woman he went for brunch with, I heard every word.'

"OK.' I push the clip of the seat belt into its holder, check the time. I need to be at nursery by 12:30. The journey's at least forty minutes. It's already 12:05. 'And what did the message say?' As I pull out of the multi-storey away from the clinic and what I did there, the world turns a little less dark.

Not for Kim though.

'It suggested Adam read the review of their brunch in the Metro online this weekend.'

The sat nav, showing mounting traffic, diverts me from my usual route.

'You know who writes restaurant reviews for the Metro online, Bea?'

I do my best to keep on top of all this shit so I can hold a decent conversation with Kim, but this is a detail too far. 'No.'

'Sophie fucking Green.'

'The sommelier?'

'The *fucking* sommelier,' Kim says.

'Shouldn't she be writing about wine?'

'Seems she's spreading her wings.' Kim's heaved breath is as rankled as the guy in the lane next to me slamming his hand on the horn. 'Not just her wings either.'

'Fuck's sake.'

'My reaction exactly.'

I don't admit I'd been referring to the traffic, which is snarled on this route too.

I take a left. 'Did he know it was her? When he…' What do I even call it?

'When he what? Played at being a couple and took Sophie fucking Green for Oaxaca eggs?' No matter how many times Kim explains it to me, I still struggle to comprehend how that's harder to stomach than the sex.

The sat nav offers me another diversion.

'He says he didn't make the connection until they were in the restaurant, and she said something about how fucking serendipitous it was that they'd got together because she'd been meaning to review the place for a while.'

'What did you say?'

'I said that, yes, we'd agreed to give each other some freedom. But there are almost nine million people in London. It shouldn't be that hard for him to find someone to hook up with who doesn't consistently undermine his wife.'

Kim's crying. The sat nav's directing. My phone's beeping an incessant alert.

'Crap. Craig's on the other line. Ten minutes, and I'll phone you straight back.'

'Sure,' Kim sobs.

I end the call.

'Bea?' Craig's breaking up. 'Can you hear me?'

'In one hundred yards, please turn right.'

'Bea? You there? Bea? The nursery called me.'

'Turn right.'

'Twice. Bea?'

Shit. 'I'm almost there.'

'At the roundabout, take the second exit.'

'Listen, I'm not sure you can hear me. I've sorted it. Mum's going to get Mabel. She'll be there in five.'

'Take the exit.'

'There's no need. I'm nearly —'

'I can't hear you. Call me back, yeah?'

'In two-hundred yards —'

'Fuck's sake, shut up.'

'Bea?'

'Not you, Craig. The sat nav.'

'Did you just tell me to —'

'Fuck.' And I shut them both down.

* * *

You're in Grandma's arms when I pull up outside the nursery.

'Sorry. Sorry. I'm so sorry,' to you, to Grandma, to Diane, who's run out with your bag.

'It's alright. She's calmer now.' Alice, your Grandma, dabs at your face with a hanky. It's a doting, gentle gesture, but I want to snatch it from her anyway. 'These things happen,' she says in that voice she has that suggests she's talking about something else as well as me being late for pick-up. It's a kind voice. But still.

'Mummy!' Your fingers, sticky like the test before I'd wiped it with the lemon, catch my face as you stretch for me. 'Mummy.'

Alice quickly glances at *my* fingers, temporarily ringless because, well, what would Sarah and her colleagues think of a married woman who —

'Sorry.'

If there are other words, I can't find them.

When we've waved goodbye to Mrs Kingdom, Grandma Alice picks up your rucksack from the pavement. 'Have you been somewhere, Bea?' She follows me with your bag to the car. 'I thought you weren't well.' She touches my arm. 'You look shattered. Why don't you let me take Mabel like we planned?'

You are blowing yourself up, breath held ,and limbs expanded in an attempt to Hulk your way out of the straps I'm struggling to buckle on your car seat.

Alice eases me out of the way and takes over. In less than a second you are giggling as if there's nothing you love more than being strapped in. 'Should I come back with you now.'

Jesus. She thinks I'm useless.

'I appreciate the offer—'

My phone vibrates in my pocket.

```
You don't still have that Premier
Inn room do you? I need some space
from Adam. From everyone. I'm
cancelling the party. The mood I'm
in, I think it's better if I spend
my birthday alone.
```

'Everything OK?' Alice asks.

Another beep.

```
If ever I needed you IRL it's now.
```

Ditto, mate. I feel like writing.

But hot footing it to London this afternoon would be madness, right?

What was it Sarah said at the clinic though? 'For now, you can go about life as normal. The bleeding is unlikely to start until after you take the second lot of pills.'

I can't bear the idea of Kim sinking on her birthday.

A five-hour round trip for a few hours in London with Kim *is* madness, but better that than her suffering alone. I could be back just after midnight. No one but Kim need know.

I turn to Alice. 'Actually, I *do* feel awful. Perhaps it *would* be better if Mabel came to you. What do you think, Bells? You want to go sleep at Grandma's?' Your head bobs in a definite nod. 'I'll just take her home, give her some lunch and get her stuff together. You could pick her up at one-thirty, if that's OK?'

'*OK?*' Alice tickles under your chin. 'It's more than OK! It's perfect, isn't it, Mabel. Who wouldn't want to spend as much time as possible with you?'

CHAPTER FOURTEEN

Della: Total eclipse of the toes.
I have to use a selfie stick to see
them. I'm not even kidding.

Me: Give it a few weeks. Toes will
be way down the list of bodily woes.

Della: Cheers, Bea Bea.

I put your lunch on the table, Mabel, open Tonight Will Bea Fine and send Della the link to the piece I wrote on cracked nipples and a leaky pelvic floor.

Della: Fuck.

Me: Breaking news, you won't want
to do that either.

Della: Haha

Della: You're kidding right?

Della: Bea Bea? Tell me you're
kidding.

Me: Er…

Della: Stop it! Tell me it's going
to be ok.

My best mate is thirty weeks pregnant with twins. What option do I have?

Me: It's going to be ok.

'Aunty Della'll be OK, won't she, Mabel?'

'Amdee Della got boys.'

'A few months and she will have. You wanna do a message for Aunty Della? Tell her she'll be OK?'

'Amdee Della got boys in tummy. Me! Me!' You smack your spoon against your bowl and look right at the phone, my Instagram-trained baby. 'Love Amdee Della.' You blow out your cheeks and your belly. 'Amdee Della fat.' Despite all the efforts we've made to speak neutrally about different body shapes, the way you spit the word "fat" is clearly an insult. How to win friends, Mabel.

We go again 'til we get a good clear: 'Love Amdee Della' without the verbal epilogue slap.

'Whaddat?'

'Bolognese. You like Bolognese, remember. Mummy made it last week. Same one. Exactly the same, Mabel.' I place Flumper carefully into the top of your pull-along suitcase, as you toss fusilli at the window.

All the bloody effort with all the bloody meals.

What was it Lucy said? That she had me down as a working mum not someone focused on my career?

And this – a carrot now belligerently dropped to the floor – is my payoff.

Screw that.

As you continue your slow progress, I email Jackie, our Head of Department, offering my sympathies to Paula and suggesting if I were to return full time after Easter, I could assume managerial duties without the disruption to timetabled teaching that might be incurred if other members of the department were to assume Paula's role.

'Who's the career-type now, Lucy?' I sing-song while mopping sauce from the floor. I call the Hidden Gem, fetch you a yoghurt while I'm on hold then, as per, bribe you with chocolate buttons so

I can focus on a whole three minutes of sweet talking bar-manager Dillon in the hope that he'll waive Kim's deposit due to the extenuating circumstances of her husband behaving like a bit of a nob. Thankfully, having recently been ghosted by his boyfriend of seven months, Dillon is totally down with the broken-hearted. He says he'll not only refund the deposit to Kim's debit card but will also personally deal with the florist *and* the balloon supplier *and* give us each a free cocktail when we're next in.

I negotiate all this with Dillon while negotiating with you, Mabel, as you demand a turn on my phone. 'Peppa!'

I'd like to see Stephen Baldry, or even Lucy for that matter, multitask like such a pro.

From my handbag, I pull my hairbrush and a compact mirror. Is eye liner too much? I'd messaged Kim as soon as we got in, told her I'll be her knight in shining armour, with the caveat that I'll actually be in old jeans and a jumper but will still do my utmost to ward off anyone who might dare cause her more pain.

'No way,' she said, livened by the resuscitated plan. 'You'll wear the dress you bought for the party!'

'Is it not a bit overkill for some generic bar at a mainline station?'

'Nothing is overkill for our IRL Meet-Cute, even if I do end up sobbing onto your satin-crepe'd shoulder for the entire three-and-a-half-hours before you need to jump back on the train.'

I pull the brush through my tangles.

'Peppa!'

'If you eat your lunch, you can play some Peppa while I —'

'Peppa!'

Aged fifteen, the thin swishes of black eye pencil made me look older. This afternoon, they make me look, well, old.

'Peppa!'

'After lunch.'

The greyish smears of eyeliner on the facewipe are a reminder, Mabel, of all the tiny ways I've tried to make myself different. All the tiny ways I've failed.

'Peppa!'

'K'sake,' under my breath.

It's quarter past one already, the train leaves at twenty past two. Alice will be here soon. When you and she are gone, I will get changed into my dress and be on my way. Though maybe I should get changed into pyjamas instead and lie on the sofa sobbing my fucking heart out because of what I've done. Not the abortion. What I mean is, not *just* the abortion. All of it. This: the tiny kitchen, the dirty toddler, the New Us, the me who's not me and the Craig who's not Craig.

And yet.

It was what we wanted.

All of it.

This.

It's what we wanted.

> Alice: Sorry. Stuck on a call with the manager at the village shop. Who knew volunteering could be so complicated. On my way. XX

'Here.' Because you're over-tired, maybe? That's why the fuss over something you've eaten no problem before. So, have Peppa Pig on my phone while I check I've got everything sorted for Grandma.

Your eyes widen at the game.

Polly Parrot wants two yellow crackers.

I'll quickly clear up then I'll read you *Room on the Broom*.

Polly Parrot wants one red cracker.

And we'll smile again. Won't we, Mabel?

Polly Parrot wants three red crackers.

'K'sake,' you mutter when, I assume, you've gone for the yellow cracker or only given Polly two. And I know I shouldn't because none of this is funny, but I laugh. 'K'sake.'

'Exactly, Mabel.' And we're smiling already, as you play with my phone, and I tie my hair back – just the hint of a different woman – then clean.

* * *

I need to leave in ten.

But time, like everything else in this three-up two-down, where I can't even find space for the painkillers Sarah gave me without Calpol sticks and plasters falling into the sink, is spilling over. I put two Paracetamol and, should the worst happen, a spare heavy-flow sanitary towel in my handbag.

'Bath!'

'Not now, Mabel. You're going to Grandma's, remember.'

You love the water. Maybe it was those lessons our NCT friends Catherine and Jack recommended, when we'd bob about in that tiny pool and I'd let you go a few feet under, in awe at how you'd make your own way to the surface, at your innate desire to survive.

One of the other mums couldn't do it. Let her baby go, I mean. I'd nodded like everyone else in the group when she held her baby to her chest and told us she was frightened he would sink.

We were lighter in the water. My body felt more like my old body, and you didn't feel like you were dragging me down. We could float, drift, even. And when I let you go, wooshing you away from me towards the instructor, it was a glimmer of how you wouldn't always be my barnacle, that nothing was permanent, how everything will inevitably change.

That's what Tina, who ran the Enjoy Your Baby group, told me at the beginning, when seven ripped-apart women sat on rubber alphabet mats at the children's centre, shifting our bottoms until we found a spot that wasn't a sharp reminder of the needles and stitches, of how we weren't yet healed. Though maybe that was just me.

Tina, our font of knowledge, offered to hold our babies so we could take it in turns to fetch ourselves a tea. I was the last.

'It gets easier,' she said in a voice that was purposefully mellow, purposefully low. 'You want me to keep her for a few minutes? So you can just sit?'

'Please,' I said. Or almost said but couldn't quite because if I'd opened my mouth who knows what would have come out of it. And my eyes were already too close to revealing the wet truth of my failure to enjoy anything, let alone you. You looked up at her too, pupils as wide as they were in the magnifying water of the pool we'd been to that morning. They soon closed, though, when Tina rocked a gentle to and fro, as she spoke to us about baby massage and baby music and baby sign.

Baby.

Baby.

Baby.

I drank my tea

slowly

slowly

slowly

so the last sips were cold but still

slowly

slowly

slowly

until the dregs too were sipped, and Tina said goodbye to the other wounded women and told me she had a few minutes if I wanted to stick around.

'Sure.' I managed the word this time, even holding my arms out to take you. But instead of giving me you, Tina gave me a leaflet about post-natal depression.

'I'm not saying…'

'Thank you.' I wasn't sure I meant it. Half glad someone had noticed. Half scared how nakedly obvious the bare bones of my motherhood must be.

'Everything's just a phase.' Tina propped your head with one hand as she passed you to me. 'The bad bits are just a phase.'

And my heart, well, it didn't exactly sink, it drowned, Mabel, because isn't that exactly what Mum had said only a few months ago, when she played me Cohen and suggested pain was only ever temporary.

'It all is,' Tina said. 'Sadly, the great bits too. And there *will* be great bits, Bea.'

It was all I could do to nod.

'Be kind to yourself.' It was the warmth of Tina's palm on my skin that made me leave.

Your palm now, Mabel, when you clasp mine, is hot. Your other hand holds my phone as we walk to the bedroom.

Come on, Alice. I need to go.

My party dress is laid on the bed in all its ruffled fuchsia glory. I'd ordered it online, felt silly as I stripped from my jeans and t-shirt to try it on in the semi-darkness in front of the bedroom mirror. Who was I kidding, I thought, to believe that this bold and glamorous look could have anything to do with me? But as I slipped it over my neck and down across my body, even with the too-big pants which were visible beneath the satin, the dress was as exciting as sex that first night with Craig. It held the same kind of promise. Of someone not trapped. Someone who could do things – *new* things – and be free.

'Pretty!' You point at the dress and then at me.

My nose wrinkles when you tap it.

Tap?

Not quite a flash but a glimmer of memory sparks in me.

Tap tap tap?

My bone fide smile echoes across your face as we stop in front of the mirror. You squeal and giggle when I bend down and press my cheek to yours.

See, I do love you, Mabel.

Seven minutes until I have to go.

'Rub!' You lie down on the carpet and lift your limbs in turn. When you raise your left arm, your hand unfurls and my phone thuds screen-side-down on the floor. 'Rub,' you say, ready now for the one-potato-two-potato massage we learnt in that first phase: the I'll-do-anything-to-get-out-of-the-house phase, even if it means pouring oil on my baby and rubbing invisible Maris Pipers from her skin.

I threw the PND leaflet Tina had given me away before I got home. Because what if Craig saw it? What if he realised I wasn't the mother we assumed I would be? What then? So there was that. But there was the other fear too. The suspicion that what I was experiencing wasn't depression but was instead the simple understanding that my life had been better before having a baby.

No one says that though, do they?

Do they?

Tap tap tap.

Six minutes until I should leave.

The pad I put in my knickers, just in case, presses against the top inside of my thigh as you give up on the idea of a massage and instead use the fabric of my jeans as leverage to heave yourself onto the tops of my feet. I bend down to you, hands in your armpits and lift you up close to me.

A waft of honey. Mothers like to bury their noses in their children's hair. You see them in adverts and movies, head down and long inhale.

For once, I am no exception. This is one of the rules I've adhered to. Your crown has always smelt delicious, Mabel.

'You know about the fontanelle?' The midwife stroked the soft patches between your skull bones as Craig held you up to his face and kissed you. I was climbing out of the birthing pool. The other midwife, whose name was Claire, had a firm grip on my arm, and I remember staring into the water that was no longer just water but my blood and guts and shit, even, and wondering whether the reason her grip was so tight was because my body didn't now have the strength to hold itself together on its own.

'Fuck!' I couldn't take my eyes off the carnage.

'Bea!' Craig's eyes were on *you* obviously, brows raised because I'd used the F-word in front of our baby within just minutes of your birth.

'Sorry.'

The midwives laughed, and Craig shook his head, like, *seriously, Bea*, and I remember being so mad at him. You know, like women in films who are mid contraction and scream at their husbands to fuck off and never touch them again because *look at this fine mess you got me into*. I swallowed it though, that fury, because everything was different than it had been just minutes before when I could be as much of a muck-spout as I wanted. Because I wasn't yet a mother, because you weren't yet born.

Post-baby, there was a new level of good.

'Don't worry, she won't have heard it,' Claire said, her clutch on my elbow easing a little so I reached out and grasped her. And in this whisper I remember sounding like desperation, I asked her not to let me go. 'I've got you,' she said. 'You've done so well,' she told me, sounding not unlike my mother, as she led me to the shower, where I turned the heat higher and higher and wept.

Because I *did* know about the fontanelle. And I knew about meningitis and sepsis and asthma and leukaemia and paedophiles and the cords for blinds and the branches of high trees and the hardness of the earth beneath them. Only a few minutes into your life, Mabel, and the infinite possibilities of harm and death burrowed into my skin like ticks. And, yes, I knew about Lyme disease too. But mostly I knew about multiple myeloma and the rush we made from the hospital to the hospice, where my mum had somehow kept on living with the cancer so that she might meet you.

'My honey baby,' I murmur into your scalp now. 'Bea's honey baby. Bea's honey baby goes buzzzzzzz.'

And you do. You go buzz too, giggling at the tingle in your lips as we buzz kiss and buzz nuzzle and buzz fly you into the air in front of the mirror, where you flap your arms and 'Whaddat!' you ask me as Grandma Alice's *bump-bump, bump-bump-bump* knocks at the door.

Your left foot stomps at the carpet when I put you down.

'Fuck it.' *My* left foot slides across *Room on the Broom*, which I'd left on the top step ready for you to take to Grandma's. I drop hard onto my arse so I'm thumping down the stairs on my behind like you do.

'Fukkit,' you say from behind the trap of the baby gate.

Midwife Claire wouldn't be so sympathetic now, would she?

'Phone, Mummy! Where Peppa, Mummy? Polly Parrot, Mummy! Crackers, Mummy! Fukkit.'

As I open the door to Grandma, there's the hint of a cramp in my tummy. Sarah had said nothing would happen immediately, that most often, things start the following day. But I swear I feel it. The twinge of my secret. The stirring of guilt.

'MUUUUUMMY!'

Grandma Alice kisses both my cheeks. 'Now where's that gorgeous girl?'

CHAPTER FIFTEEN

Power walking to the station in my swanky dress and my less swanky pumps (and my heels in my bag for later), I am cutting it fine. Those few precious minutes after you and Alice left were mostly spent looking for, and failing to find, a charger. When I'd retrieved my phone from where you'd dropped it, Mabel, it was dead. Not ideal when I'm travelling over a hundred miles away from you with crossed fingers that some kind soul in the bar will charge it for me. Maybe I should turn back, have another look, but there's only a few minutes until my train and —

Bluebells.

Despite the time ticking against me, I stop on the bridge towards St Julian's, my eyes locked on the cluster of violet flowers beneath the trees in the park below.

Her last night before she was transferred to the hospice, Mum made a kind of ceremony of presenting us with the packets of seeds. My brother and his wife, Tanya, had come for the weekend, and she summoned us all in turn to her bedside, nodding at The Death Box on the table, which she and I had filled with her Preparations.

'This obviously isn't our Last Conversation,' she said, her thumb rubbing the back of my hand. Her skin was thinner by then. 'But I wanted to thank you now, while I can.'

'I should be thanking *you*.' It wasn't me who was dying, but it was *my* life that flashed before my eyes. Or at least Mum's role in it. Her delicate fingers balancing a penny on my thigh where she'd brushed aside a bee sting just seconds before. My dad rolling his eyes but knowing not to challenge the magic of her wisdom. Same with the butter she rubbed into my cheek and elbow when I fell from my bike. And the strawberry jam she'd encourage me to lick from the spoon when we were making tarts, not for any medicinal purpose but because she believed its saccharine stickiness sweetened the soul. The apple crumble she'd make on Saturdays because it was my favourite. The canned tomato soup she'd bring me on a tray in front of the telly when I was sick. The Sunday night ritual of star-fishing in the clean sheets she'd put on my bed so I could go fresh into a new week. A packet of pork scratchings on my desk ahead of a long night of revision. A song she'd still sing to me when I should have been old enough not to need it, The Carpenters' *Top of the World*, its chorus on repeat, always a reminder of how much her love for me had raised her to astronomical levels of joy.

She sang it, barely audible, to you too, Mabel. Just those four lines. And as much as I wanted to take in every moment, I had to turn away. The image of her looking down on creation had always made her omnipotent, but all it did on the last full day of her life and the first day of yours was exaggerate the insurmountable distance that would soon separate her from me. From us.

But I'm jumping ahead, because I was by her bedside, she was holding my hands, having given me the bluebell seeds, and I was reliving the millions of other times our palms had pressed, our fingers had intertwined, her gentle grip had guided me on my way.

'I've had a good life,' she said. 'A happy one. Please don't be sad when I'm gone.' And somehow that hadn't seemed impossible. As everyone kept reminding me, I'd been so lucky to be able to move from London to help care for her. I would never regret that extra time, they said, and I'd have the baby, who would bring me happiness and purpose and the knowledge that my mum would be so proud.

In the first few weeks of your life, which were the first few weeks after her death, I'd lay you in your cot, lock the door to the bathroom, toilet lid down, and sit on my right hand until it went numb. It was a trick we heard the boys at school would use for what they called "a stranger", only I didn't want my hand to feel like a stranger's, rather I'd hold it in my other hand and hope it felt like my mum's.

It never did. Obviously.

Now though, it's not so much her physical touch I crave, rather the essence of her always being there, ready to catch or soothe me if I fall.

Have I fallen?

Am I a twenty-first-century fallen woman?

Thing is, I'd do it again. Make the appointment. Take the pill.

There's no penny, butter or jam to undo that ill, is there?

The river rushes hard under the bridge.

If I were to throw myself into it, would it wash me clean?

It's not the bluebells but the church bells that are a sign, chiming twice from across the park.

I need to go. To the station. To London. To Kim.

Surely it's possible – isn't it? – despite what I've done, to be a good friend *and* a good mother. Not everything has to be either / or.

I rush for the train, sending you silent promises, Mabel, that giving up on the idea of a second baby absolutely does not mean I have given up on you.

CHAPTER SIXTEEN

When I arrive in London, a little dazed from sleep on the train, Kim is already in the bar. Barely distinguishable pop music plays at a volume that's meant to be a background to after-work chat. But there's a hint of sway in Kim's hips as she sips a glass of Champagne and smiles at strangers with those wide eyes and white teeth, which look wider and whiter than they do on Instagram even.

Why would Adam want sex – or brunch! – with any other woman when his wife is so fucking beautiful? And I know, I know, because Kim has tried to explain, that their "arrangement" stems from the same need they have for different friends for different parts of them-selves. 'Like, I'd never confess my deepest and darkest to Alyssa,' Kim said a few weeks back when she was working on a potential piece about non-monogamy she'd thought she might pitch to *Cosmopolitan* or *Marie Claire*. 'But if I wanted a night of crude jokes and cocktails, Alyssa would be the first girl I'd call. My point is, one person can't meet your every need in any other aspect of your life so why should it be any different with sex?'

I watch Kim now as she tops up her drink, quickly raising her glass to her lips so as not to waste the bubbles from her generous pour.

She catches sight of me hanging back by the door. Her jumpsuit, antique rose with a cropped cut-out at the waist, is super sexy. My earlier confidence drains, leaving me in the dregs, one hundred per cent "mum".

'Bea!' Kim's voice is birthday-girl squealy as she flings her arms wide in birthday-girl glee. When she holds me, she *really* holds me. Tight. Like if she loosens her grasp around my middle, she may well drop to the floor. 'Bea,' she says again, her voice deeper now. Flatter.

Her chin rests on my shoulder. Her hair, which she had braided earlier this week, falls across her face.

'I'm afraid you're playing catch up.' She tilts her head toward the bar. 'I'm waaaaaaaay ahead of you.' Those wide eyes of hers look a little glassy closer to.

'You heard any more from Adam?'

She shakes her head. 'Didn't want to ruin the good mood you put me in.' Her hand is warm when she leads me to her seat by the bar. 'Not touched my phone since you and I spoke.'

'Speaking of phones…'

But when I ask if I can charge mine, the barmaid isn't playing ball. 'Rules are rules,' she says in a tone not so dissimilar from Bryony Jackson when she was made librarian in Year Six and caught Della and me eating a pack of Rolos in the poetry section in wet break. The barmaid has the same mulishness as Bryony too, no hint of budging when I explain I've left you, my two-year-old daughter, several hundred miles away with a sick relative and how I must be on stand-by in case Grandma needs to call. She shrugs, dismissing your importance with an unconvincing 'Sorry,' which bores into my heart, Mabel. The distance between us is suddenly so visceral, so sore.

'Here.' Kim hands me a glass of Champagne. 'You make a start on this, and I'll work some Edible magic. The thought of my million followers might be paralyzingly grim when I think of having to explain the last-minute cancellation of my party but, on the flipside, the beauty of our sites, Bea, is the way they can so quickly turn a tide.'

Kim's generosity in assuming Tonight Will Bea Fine has the same influential clout as Edible is flattering but untrue.

'TWBF is hobby money,' I'd said when Craig and I were calculating our finances prior to me returning to work, and I'd once again raised the possibility of events management as an alternative to teaching.

'I know teaching's not your dream career, babe, but you can write the blog alongside it. Use your creative powers there. And if you keep pushing at it, who knows, maybe one day, you'll be successful enough to quit the day job. That'd be a win-win, right? Working from home? We'd never have to worry about childcare again.'

I can't hear what Kim says when she leans in closer to the barmaid, whose face softens when she looks at the screen of Kim's phone. Whatever Kim says, it works, *my* phone is soon put on charge.

'An exchange of favours.' Kim winks. 'I'll just tag the bar in on a photo. Smile!' She goes into full selfie mode, leaning in, clinking our glasses and putting her best face on for the camera despite the heart-break I'm here to console. 'Could you grab those seats in the corner while I quickly write this caption?'

By the time she comes over, I've placed a large book on the table.

'What's this?' She runs a finger across the pale blue cover.

'For your birthday. I stole your guestlist and asked everyone to send me something in writing. A favourite poem or song, an extract of fiction or journalism. The form didn't really matter, it just had to be something they either wanted to share with – or that reminded them of – you.'

'Bea! This is so thoughtful.' Kim reaches over, touches my hand.

'I didn't know if I should bring it. Or if I should leave Adam's piece in. In the end, I figured I'd give it to you as is. I hope that's OK?'

'Forget Adam.' Another swig of Champagne. 'The contribution I'm most excited to see is yours.'

'Mine?'

'Yes,' she says. 'I don't think you realise how much our friendship means to me. With all this Adam stuff. I dunno, even though we'd never actually met before tonight, of all my friends, *you* were the one I wanted to speak to. You know I'm all for rituals, and I swear our Friday afternoon call is *the* most uplifting ritual of all.'

'Better than a jade roller or removing your bra as soon as you walk through the door?'

'You mock, girl, but my eyes have never looked less puffy and my tits have never felt so free.'

'Your eyes and tits are as wonderful as the rest of you.' I lean across the table and pull her into me. 'Happy birthday.'

'I can't tell you how buzzed I am that you came. And *this*,' Kim unwinds herself from the hug to open the book. 'Honestly, it's amazing. With everything you have on too. Selfless!'

'I wouldn't go that far.'

I mean, there's that clinic, those pills, the regret.

'Oh, let a drunk birthday girl gush over you, would you.' She tops up her glass. 'And get drinking. You've barely touched yours. Now let me find your piece.'

'It's nothing fancy.' I turn the pages.

I'd not long ago used AA Milne in a vain attempt to steer you from *Room on the Broom*, Mabel. You were not for persuading, but I've continued sometimes, in the sleepless nights on my own.

Kim looks at the illustration of Winnie the Pooh and Piglet that I printed and glued into her book. They are sitting at a table laid with a teapot and a jar of honey. 'When Pooh's on a bit of a downer,' I tell her, 'Piglet promises to bring him tea and honey until he feels like himself again.' Below the sketch, I've written a note –

Thank you, Kim, for the tea and honey on Fridays. Bea

'You know what this picture actually tells me?' Kim's laughing.

'That Pooh – whether it's AA Milne's or Mabel's – will always play a significant part in our connection?'

'Ha! No, that despite your piss-taking, you are also fond of ritua—'

'Excuse me.' The barmaid's face is serious. Though her eyes, the nervousness in them, suggests this is not the job's-worth seriousness of before. 'It's your phone,' she says, handing me my mobile. 'You mentioned you needed it because of your daughter? Well, it hasn't stopped ringing since it came back to life after I put it on charge. I thought I'd better…'

But her voice drifts into the ether when I clock the number of alerts on the screen.

WhatsApps.

Texts.

Missed calls.

Before I have the chance to see who or what or why, it's ringing. The flash of Craig's name is a siren, a reminder that me maintaining my story is a state of emergency. That I must not lose my cool.

'Hey. Everything OK?

'I'm not sure, Bea.' Craig's voice is shrapnel. Tiny fragments of a shell. 'You tell me.'

Does he know?

'Is it Mabel? I wasn't well so she's with your mum, —'

'Then all the better for her. God forbid my daughter was anywhere with you.'

I've no idea what's happened.

'Well?'

No idea what to say.

'Oh, so *now* you have no words. Is that it? Saving them for the blog, are you?'

'I don't know what you're talking about.'

'No? The feeling's mutual, Bea. I mean, why didn't you tell me if things were so awful. So wrong.'

'There's nothing awful. There's nothing wrong.'

'Really? *Nothing*?'

'Nothing.'

'I think your readers would disagree,' he says.

'Craig?'
But the question's too late.
He's gone.

* * *

He doesn't pick up. Sends a text though.

```
Craig:  How  could  you  write  that
stuff?
```

'Bea?' It's Kim. 'What's happened?'
How can I tell her when I don't have a clue?
Write that stuff, Craig said. *Your readers.*
Tonight Will Bea Fine?
Kim, 'Are you OK?'
'Yes.' But the tap tap taps and scuttling rodent feet of secrets itching at my fingers would suggest otherwise. I can barely work my phone for the shaking. I swipe away WhatsApp and Instagram, go straight to the blog.
'Shit.'
LET'S TALK ABOUT REGRET, TWBF says. *I* said, in capitals, like writing it wasn't enough, like this was something worth shouting.
'Sorry,' I say to you. To the thought of you, to the weight of you, to the blood and flesh and bones of you that bind us wherever I go.
'Bea?' Kim's voice is somewhere distant, though her hand is on my arm.
'Sorry.' I read in my head and tell you 'sorry' out loud, Mabel, as if that one word is enough to make up for all these other words I wrote last night as I sat by your cot, necking gin, planning an abortion and airing my dirtiest laundry.

'Bea, why don't you sit down?'

I hadn't realised I was standing.

Jesus.

I'd scour it clean if I could. I'd scrub at every millimetre of the blog and the dirty brain behind it.

I love my daughter, but.

In my head the thoughts were nasty, but on my blog they're an atomic bomb.

We are raised to believe motherhood is the be all and end all for women. That through birthing a child, we will come to know not only our true selves but true love. I call bull shit on that because I love my daughter, but.

It's so public. So permanent. And, I hate to say it... so true. How could I have made it so true?

'Shall I get you some water? Is there someone you'd like me to call?'

'I'm sorry.' I say it to you, and I type it to Craig but delete before sending because it's not enough, is it? A text is not enough. What is though?

I will not be having another child because having my daughter robbed me of a life I can never retrieve from beneath the piles of nappy sacks, chopped up snacks, the sleepless nights I can't get back, a marriage derailed from its perfect track and a body that's wounded and saggy and slack.

I was pissed, I want to tell Craig and the readers by way of explanation for my confession, and for that picture-book poetry too. Because of all the things I know are wrong about this piece, I'm stuck on the come-out-of-nowhere rhyming that makes it all seem so much more, well, inappropriate. As if declaring regret for motherhood isn't inappropriate enough. Seriously, how could I do this?

`Craig: How could you do this?`

His text is the salt in my self-inflicted wounds because even now, in the midst of this clusterfuck, he and I are in some kind of match-made-in-heaven sync. *See*, I want to say to him, *it's still there, the magic is still there, Craig.* But I'm not sure he'd believe me.

'Shall we go to the ladies?' Kim suggests.

But I'm stuck.

Tomorrow, I am having a termination because I love my daughter, but. There is no room in my life for another child. Imagine, yeah, that my life is a bed. My daughter has climbed in between my husband and me and pushed me to the edge. The space where I used to spread my arms and legs is now occupied by her. The cool patches I'd turn to are now taken. There is no inch of it that's just for me. It's stained with milk stains and piss stains and I am

I am what? I don't say because I didn't finish. Because I was absolutely hammered. You can see that, can't you? And Craig will too, hopefully, because the bed/life metaphor is clearly the work of a drunk woman. And I remember now, not in flashes or flickers but in slap-in-the-face 4K quality, I remember sitting in your room and writing this, Mabel. I don't deny that I wrote it, I don't even deny that I think it, but I remember sitting in your room and knowing I should never ever post it. That these are the things I should never say out loud. I shut it down, Mabel. Just like I've tried to with the actual thoughts, I shut it all down and vowed to leave it be.

Polly Parrot wants three red crackers.

'Could you get her some water, please? Bea, I really think you should sit down.'

Polly Parrot wants three red crackers.

And then she didn't, did she? I hadn't noticed at the time because why question the silence when it comes? Why not just enjoy it? But this afternoon. After lunch. Polly Parrot stopped asking for crackers. And you still had my phone.

The dateline of the post is today.

'What did we do, Mabel?'

'What's that, Bea?'

I go to Post Information: 13:23. And I'm at one of our board games nights, the worst kind, when Della would insist on Cluedo: It was Mabel. In the kitchen. With the mobile phone.

CHAPTER SEVENTEEN

'But your birthday. And Adam.'

'Don't worry about my birthday. Or Adam. Honestly, Bea.' There's a waft of Kim's hand cream, as her finger attempts a soft rise of my chin.

The black and white tiles in the ladies' make thin zebra-crossing stripes along the floor. It doesn't feel safe to cross.

'Has something happened?'

Where would I begin though, Mabel? Because where does the story of what I wrote on Tonight Will Bea Fine truly start? Birth? Conception? The suggestion that perhaps we should try? I don't know how far back I'd have to —

'Is it Mabel?'

There are three wooden framed mirrors, designed to look like an antique hand-held looking glass, on the bathroom wall. My face is the same level of distraught in each of them.

'Bea? Has something happened to Mabel?'

There was a picture last summer of a bin lorry sinking into the tarmac of the road on an exceptionally hot day. When Kim says your name, Mabel, I am that bin lorry, like the earth's surface is melting beneath the weight of the rubbish I've spun. It's apocalyptic, like the stench of what I've carried inside is discharging in the strength of the heat. I stink is what I mean.

Kim may have given up on lifting my head to make me look at her, but her voice, her placing one hand on my shoulder, they both suggest – madly, perhaps – that she hasn't quite given up on *me*. 'Do you need to go home? I can check the train times.'

There are eighteen whole tiles in the first row of black.

Nineteen in the first row of white.

'Or call Craig? If you give me his number, I can call him for you?'

A fatalistic snuff of you-have-to-be-kidding puffs from my nose.

'No?'

'No.'

I pass Kim my phone, opened to *that* page. No point holding anything back now. 'I thought I'd deleted it. I was drunk. I never meant to...' But the excuses sound no more persuasive than they did when I offered them to Craig.

If Kim's appalled, she doesn't show it. Her expression isn't one of hate or fury as she reads.

And then, 'Oh.'

My heart plummets at her – at her what? Shock? Disappointment? Disgust? But it's Craig's name, alight on the screen that's surprised her. 'Here,' she presses him gently into my palm. 'I'll give you some privacy.'

It's only tiny, the shake of my head, I mean. But Kim sees it, stays. Her arm lays across my shoulder, against my neck, as I say hi.

'Hi,' I say. *Hi!* But then, how else would I answer? What greeting is suitable for a storm?

'I'm trying to get a flight back this evening.'

There is no suitable greeting, then.

'So we can at least talk about tomorrow's abor—' But he can't say the word. 'I can't believe you arranged it. Without even telling me.'

'It's not tomorrow.'

'Well, that's something, at least.'

'I wrote it last night, Craig, Mabel posted it today but I —'

'What? *Mabel?*'

'I gave her my phone while I was clearing up after lunch.'

The way Kim looks at me is somewhere between agony and disbelief.

'She must have accidentally gone into the app, into drafts and —'

'Mabel posted it?' Craig's voice is a thin wire, the kind that slices even the hardest of cheese.

'By accident, yeah.' It sounds so implausible when I say it aloud. 'I never meant for it to go live, Craig. I was pissed. Ridiculously pissed, not-been-pissed-like-that-since-eighteen kind of pissed.' I can no longer look at Kim. 'I must have written it in some pathetic attempt at catharsis, or, I dunno what, but no one was ever meant to read it.'

'Oh.'

It's not clear from his 'Oh' if this changes things.

'But they have,' he says. '*I've* read it. My *mum* has read it. Your Aunty Pat has read it. And our friends who get alerts when you update your stupid blog, they've all fucking read it. I've already had messages from some of them. Ichiro said Hannah read the whole thing out loud to him. Three times! They read it three times and still couldn't understand how you could say those things. That I didn't even know you're pregnant. That you would book an…an…an… appointment without telling me. And then put it out there for the whole fucking world to see.'

'I was drunk.'

'So you keep saying. And let's not even get into why you thought it was OK to get pissed like you were eighteen again when what you actually are is a mother who was in sole charge of our two-year-old daughter…'

The door to the ladies' swings open. A girl, twenty / twenty-one, glides in, checks her pout in the mirror. Paints it red against her pale white skin.

'…Because while that'd normally be a major fucking issue, Bea, weirdly it seems kind of minor right now, don't you think?'

'O! M! G!' The pout moves in exaggerated incredulity. 'You're Kim Benn, aren't you?'

114

Kim holds the girl's gaze, nodding in my direction like, *we're kind of in the middle of something here.*

'I love love love Edible! My friends won't believe it! Can I?' Her phone is already out of her bag, the pout already perfected. Snap.

'Craig, listen, I'm really sorry but I can't —'

Kim's shaking her head like, *you've got to talk to him.*

'You can't what?' Craig isn't shouting, but his words are big and crashing. 'Where even are you?'

'You got braids!' Does this girl say anything that isn't followed by an exclamation mark?

'Can you not?' Kim takes a step back when the stranger fingers her hair.

'No need to get so antsy! I was only saying how nice it looks!'

'Bea? Are you listening?'

And I am. But I'm also watching. Because Kim has her eyes closed and is taking a deep breath and then saying to the girl, 'Actually, you weren't just saying. You were touching me —'

'Mum told me Mabel's with her because you weren't feeling well —'

'Jesus! Learn to take a compliment already!' The girl flicks her blonde ponytail and leaves.

'Fuck's sake,' Kim says to the back of the closing door.

'Bea!' In Craig's mouth my name is a portent of doom. 'Where are you?'

'I'm…it's…'

'It's what?' He asks.

'Complicated.'

'Complicated?' Craig's echo is spiked with repulsion. 'Sounds ominous. What you trying to say, Bea? Have you met someone?' His tone is both nervous and *I cannot believe this shit.*

And I know it's not the time or the place for *me* to play the wounded party, but really? Is that actually the way he wants to go?

'No, Craig, I haven't met someone.'

A thick gulp as he swallows that line of conversation. Meeker, 'What then? What is so complicated about where you are?'

'I'm with Kim. In London.'

'Mum said you'd cancelled that.'

'I did, but she… forget it. I'm leaving. Now. I'm going back now for Mabel.'

'Don't.' It sounds like a threat. Slightly softer, then, 'Mum can keep her at theirs.'

'I don't need your mum to keep he—'

'She's keeping her, Bea, alrigh*t*.' His t is a pointed arrow. Craig does this, when he's nervous, things get sharper. 'So, when is the appoin*t*men*t*? How long do I have to…' He tapers off, like he's not quite sure what he's hoping to do. Persuade? Coerce? Fight for his unborn daughter or son? In those drunken nights around the dinner table – when we lit candles and felt like real grown-ups because we served three courses and then, wait for it…cheese – Craig had been the only man to say he was a feminist. It's not as if the others were balls-deep in sexism, but there was the usual, 'Is there really a need for feminism in this day and age? I mean, aren't things pretty much fair and square?' But Craig got it. The battle's not done, right? He's the guy who calls out his mates when they send some crass sexist joke in a WhatsApp group. He's the boss who banned a client for speaking inappropriately to the receptionist. And when he later over-heard a stylist commenting that 'the dude didn't actually touch her, you know, so what's the big deal,' he issued a formal warning, held a staff meeting and made it clear that Looks Like Straw was not a place to stand for patriarchy. He read the rush of #MeToo experiences women posted online then asked me about mine. And when it came to abortion, he was the first to say, it's the woman's right to choose.

And yet.

'How long do we have to talk about the possibility of keepi—'

'I told you.' I knew he hadn't understood, but still. I'd hoped not to have to spell it out. 'I wrote the blog last night, Craig.'

'Yeah, I heard you, but…Oh.'

This 'oh' definitely changes things.

'So, the tomorrow in the blog was…'

'Today.' The confirmation extinguishes a flame, and smoke winds itself like an old-fashioned telephone wire between us. Around my neck. 'Craig?'

Was it really my right to make the decision without him?

'I love you, Bea…'

'But.' I say it for him.

'Yeah,' he says. 'But.' The noose tightens. 'I'll see you soon.'

And, that's it, our connection has gone.

CHAPTER EIGHTEEN

'Have you read the comments?'

'Yes.' Della's voice, normally ten-to-the-dozen, is like you, Mabel, when you are faced with the truly unfamiliar. Despite your usual confidence, in those situations, you have never been one of those children who charges right in. Even the 'hello' when Della had answered had been shaky, as she hovered on the perimeter of our conversation wondering, it seemed, if it was safe for her to step inside. 'Not all of them.' Quiet then. Not realising, obviously, how much I need the sound of her to carry me along the train journey home.

Kim had paid the barmaid a tenner for the charger so I wouldn't be plunged into the same dead-battery darkness that earlier allowed me four hours of ignorant bliss. And I should be grateful, but at least if I had no means of communication, Craig's lack of further contact could be put down to something other than hate.

'How many are there now?'

A moment while, I assume, Della refreshes the screen.

'One-hundred-and-thirty-two.'

I could hear the ding of alerts as I was speaking to Craig earlier. And then, well, as I wasn't speaking to Craig.

Maybe it's best he didn't answer when I tried calling him after I left the bar. Maybe he'd say something he couldn't take back and, as I've done that already, maybe the only hope lies in us grasping onto any silence we can. So there's no regret in the heat of a moment.

Ha, no regret? Right.

'No regrets, Mrs Dawson?' Craig asked an hour or so after we left the Vegas Chapel of Happy Memories as Husband and Wife.

'I am *not* Mrs Dawson, Mr Dawson.'

118

Craig knew that obviously. It was number one in the ten rules we'd flippantly concocted so we could commit without the same old same old tying us down.

'No regrets then, Ms Williams?' As he twirled me round. The sequins of my jumpsuit shimmered like mad in the sun.

I'll admit it, I felt full on rock 'n' roll. Sweaty, sure, but one hundred per cent rebel. No parents. No guests. No fuss. Just the two of us doing our thing. Newlywed and strolling hand in hand along The Strip. Yeah, *strolling*. And strolling isn't something we'd normally do, it's not even a word I'd normally use. But our walk was injected with something, I don't know, something romantic, perhaps. It had a honeymoon-that's-not-a-honeymoon swagger to it, is what I mean. Our hands were held in that loose but connected way that was pledged but not needy. Our bodies weren't too close, a couple of feet apart so our arms were a little stretched, and there was a swing in the way we moved that wasn't quite in time with each other, but that was all good because it meant, despite the vows we'd just made, we were still our own people, walking our own path, just holding hands while we did it.

'I've been thinking about that.'

Craig's brow shot up, like, *that's a shock turnaround.*

But, 'Not Mrs Dawson, Craig, I wouldn't go there. But I would go Ms Something Else, if you were Mr Something Else too.'

'Craig Something Else Too.' He did that downturned-mouth and slow-nod thing people do when they're mock thinking. 'Has a nice kind of ring to it, I guess.'

'I'm serious.' I was surprised at how keen I suddenly felt to share a name. 'It'd be kind of cool, right, to both become something new?'

'Dawson-Williams? Williams-Dawson? Willison? Dawlliams?

I shook my head. 'Something unconnected to either of us. Or connected to both of us but not through our names. You know what I mean?' But Craig was halfway into a casino already. Obviously, I *strolled* right in after him.

119

'Slots?'

There was silence when I jangled my purse. 'No can do. All out.'

'No, babe, Slots? Bea and Craig Slots?' He wasn't even joking. 'Or Craps?'

Sure, it'd been our favourite of all the games we'd played since we'd arrived in Vegas, but, 'Doesn't give us the most auspicious start to our marriage.'

'Marriage! Who'd have thought.' He twirled me again and again until I knocked into a little big-haired old lady in wedges and a sun visor clutching a cup full of coins.

'I'm so sorry.' I tipped my head at Craig as if to tell her it was beyond my control.

'We're celebrating our *marriage*,' he explained, that one word as shiny as my sequins. 'And now all my good wife wants is a name.'

'Fool.' The little big-haired old lady in wedges and a sun visor rattled her cup full of coins in disdain.

'I'm sorry?' The two of us said in unison because, well, weren't we a match made in heaven?

'Fool,' she repeated, eyeballing Craig. 'Mrs Fool! 'Cos that's what any woman'd be for marrying you, mister.' Her bony thumb pressed firm against my cheek as she leant in to impart her wisdom. 'And it's not just him, lady. It's all of 'em.' Her face turned from angry to sad as she fingered the sleeve of my jumpsuit. 'They'll all steal your sparkle in the end.'

'Not this one,' I told her, pulling away from her touch and hamming it up with a tiptoed sweep of a kiss with my groom.

Your father, holding me steady, kissing me back, was delighted. 'You have a good day, m'am!' My husband sang, laughing at the nonsense of her prediction, strolling to go order a couple of Happy Ever Afters at the bar.

Craig didn't steal my sparkle, and I didn't regret our marriage, not even when, on seeing the evidence of our runaway wedding, my mum smiled this smile that aroused a guilt I'd not felt since Adrian Johnson. This why-would-you-do-this-to-me. This this-is-not-the-kind-of-woman-I-raised-you-to-be. This did-you-forget-that-I-have-cancer-and-seeing-my-daughter-walk-down-the-aisle-was-on-the-bucket-list-we've-not-yet-discussed-because-we-are-still-pretending-I'll-be-OK.

Mum's sister, Aunty Pat, was not best pleased. 'You're her only daughter, Beatrice. You know seeing her daughter married is a mother's greatest wish.'

'What about seeing her daughter happy?' The rebellion of Vegas was still buzzing, Mabel.

Aunty Pat sucked in her disappointment. 'I'd have expected this of your brother,' she tutted. 'But I had higher hopes for you.'

I wonder if Craig's high hopes for me have been proved a falsehood too.

No regrets, Mr Straw?

The name took us a while. We toyed with Match (together we were one), Strong (together we felt it), Bipin (in honour of us being a team). And then I read this poem, as you do, by Carol Ann Duffy. You see, we'd made that deal, remember? That Sunday mornings, whenever possible, we'd bathe together. For Craig, it must have felt like a kind of busman's holiday, because he'd wash my hair in the way only hairdressers do, those supple fingers pushing with just the right amount of pressure into my scalp as I read aloud from whichever poetry book he plucked at random from the shelves. One morning, as luck would have it, he'd plucked Duffy.

'More, more,' he said, sounding like a child he'd hinted we'd have one day. I'd just finished *Name*, which likens a lover's name to jewels, to rain, to prayer, to something you hear in everything you listen to, and it set us off on the hunt again.

'Duffy?' Craig suggested. And for the first time, I was properly tempted because her collection *Rapture* was so full of everything I felt for your dad. And then I read *Hour*. 'Again, again,' Craig said, his beard tickling my bare soaked shoulder. I read it again, taking the last couple of lines super slow when she reveals how time is the enemy of love, but love, well, love spins gold from straw.

The rest of it was beautiful too, of course, but those last couple of lines summed it up for me. Our love, I mean. Because, you know what, Mabel, I could never get enough of your father. There was never enough time in the day for me to get enough of him, and there really *was* something transformative in what we shared. At the risk of sounding incredibly cheesy, in all those seconds we spent together, we made magic of the mundane and gold of all the straw.

'Craig and Bea Straw.'

'Would Gold not be better?' He had a point. Why be the cheap and dry stuff?

'It's our secret,' I said imagining our marriage was like the eighteenth-birthday time capsule we buried in Bryony Jackson's Garden. 'No one knows what's in it but us.'

'Like superheroes?'

'Huh?'

"We're wearing a very ordinary, some might say bland, suit but it conceals our capes and powers.'

'Our gold.'

'Our super gold.'

'Our super gold,' I said. 'Bea and Craig Straw. Craig and Bea Straw.' I rolled over, slippery in the wet of it, so we were belly to belly and kissed him. 'Let's do it, Mr Straw.' And in every which way, we did.

* * *

'Would… would you like me to… come over? When you're home?' Maybe it was Della's own superpower that sensed a shift in me. Perhaps she heard the sharper intake of breath as I remembered that bath, that decision, that intimacy with Craig. Maybe she understood how much I need her, the physicality of her, I mean. Because, until you, Mabel, Della understood everything about me. Every head tilt, bitten lip, extra sip of gin was a signal in which she'd intuit what lay beneath. It occurs to me that the hesitance in her offer to come over now stems perhaps not from disapproval of my feelings about you but from the invisible palisade they built between us. Each time I didn't tell Della the truth was another stake in the fence that's only now become apparent. And with that giant two-babied bump of hers, she sounds unsure if she wants to jump it, wondering, maybe, if she and *they* are safer on the other side.

'Please.' I give Della no room to retract her offer. No room to hang up the phone and run.

CHAPTER NINETEEN

Almost home. Once I'm there, it'll be just a few minutes' drive to Grandma Alice's where you're safely sleeping under her watchful eye and her uncomplicated love that slots within that one single declaration. *I love you.* Has love always been so easy for her? With your grandpa? With her own children? With you?

Maybe 'I love you' is never the clean slate we imagine it to be.

'I love you, Bea,' Craig had said on the phone when I was still in the bar in London. And it'd been me who added the 'but'. Though Craig had agreed to it. He'd acknowledged it's there, rammed between us like a little big-haired old lady in wedges and a sun visor rattling her cup full of coins at Mr and Mrs Fool. She's not the only one. Everyone has an opinion, they always will. And so they should because free speech and all that, but I've seen how this can go, even with the supposedly innocuous TWBF posts. The ones about breast feeding (too much, not enough, too bare, too concealed). The ones about weaning (too mashed, too hard, too pureed, too sweet). The ones about work (too soon, too selfish, too I'd go fucking crazy if I were a stay-at-home mum). This isn't innocuous. This is the opposite of innocuous. This is in the realms of 'Let's tear this bitch down.'

But they don't, not most of them anyway.

I read the comments as I walk from the station along the final pavements home.

There are some who call me narcissistic, who ask me what did I expect, who declare me a snowflake, a whiner, an ungrateful cow who should stop making money off my daughter if I find her such a drag. But they're the minority. Most of them ask if I'm OK, if I've spoken with a doctor. I don't sound like myself, they say. And they're kind but they're duped, Mabel, because this post has more of myself in it than any other in the history of Tonight Will Bea Fine.

I look for *him* in the comments. For your father, who was my husband before he was your dad, which sounds petty, I know. But I miss the simplicity of that relationship. Here on the blog, he goes by @MrTWBF because, like me when we married, he wanted to be part of something. He wanted to show how we are connected now, husband and wife now, so he's @Mr TWBF to my @MsTWBF. He hovers on the side lines and cheerleaders me on. He did the same with The Hop.

'Don't make me use this,' he'd said that Sunday morning three weeks after we'd first met, when I'd turned up at his place and he announced that together we would clinch me a world record. His eyebrows were raised, his head was cocked, and he offered up the hopper as the only alternative to a lashing.

He was serious. Not about the whipping, Mabel. But the hopping? Well, according to your father, no doubt about it, The Hop was on. 'Twenty minutes,' he said, as if that explained everything, and told me to get changed into the workout gear he'd tricked me into thinking I'd brought for a run. 'I've checked, and you need to do it in twenty minutes.'

'Do *what* for twenty minutes?'

'Hop,' he said. 'For a mile! Your world record!'

'You know I didn't actually mean it.' I was starting to panic by then. No way was I hopping through Victoria Park. 'I was just trying to make myself sound more interesting.' That wasn't quite true though, Mabel. 'Look!' I pointed out the window. 'There's a fucking frost!'

'What there is,' Craig said, 'is a fucking dream.' He kissed me, proper kissed me and, evidence of how hard I'd fallen, my own frosty resistance to his idea was already beginning to thaw. 'And where there's a fucking dream, there's a fucking Bipin helping make that dream come true.' He kissed my forehead. 'Let me be your Bipin.'

He kissed my nose. '*Please.*' He kissed my chin. 'I've done a spreadsheet and everything.'

He had too. He showed me on his laptop, which was ready and waiting in his bedroom. And somehow Excel in his hands was sexy, which sounds as absurd as a mile on a spacehopper, I know, but it was true.

'Date. Distance. Time. Oh, and average heart rate.'

'Mine's way above average after *that*,' I said, because we'd not quite made it to the data before I pointed out that real athletes do a decent warm up prior to vigorous exercise.

'You're game then?' He was out of bed already, pulling on his joggers, and playing with the timer on his phone.

'We're not actually going out there?' It was supposed to be a fact not a question.

'Why'd you say wanted a world record?'

'I told you, I was just trying to mak—'

'The truth, Bea.' When Craig reached out his hand, I took it, and he pulled me up to my knees.

'The truth is somewhat pathetic.' It really was, Mabel. 'And aren't I already exposed enough?' For I was naked, the duvet smushed on the other side of the bed, where our feet had entwined and unravelled and jettisoned anything that wasn't heavily breathing body. I had nowhere to hide. 'And for some reason, probably because I am the best in the world at sex,' Craig nodded, 'you seem to quite like me.' That nod again. 'And I'd rather not ruin that by revealing my most feeble desire.'

'I want to know *all* your desires.' He did this mock sexy, mock serious, mock intense thing with his voice. 'Go on…' Meanwhile, his fingers were attempting a bribe.

'You'll have to stop that if you want me to be able to speak.'

'Done.'

'And I'll need cover.'

'How about I get naked again instead? Then we're even.'

'If it delays getting on a spacehopper by a few minutes, then win-win, right?'

He scooched me across the mattress and buried us beneath the duvet like we were kids in a den. 'Spill.'

I sighed because this was it, wasn't it, the moment when he'd realise what an immature dick I was with my grudge. *Here goes*, I thought. 'My brother played for Shrewsbury Town Football Club Under Eighteens.'

'And?'

'And? That's all Mum and Dad bang on about.' Would I always be thirteen? Always second best to a rebel child who broke every rule bar kicking the odd ball into a goal on a Saturday morning?

'I'm sure that's not true.'

'Believe me,' I said, remembering the christenings, the funerals, the summer barbeques, the Boxing Day drinks which Matthew couldn't be bothered to attend because there were better things for a sixteen-year-old boy to be doing, Mabel, than listening to our parents justify his absence by bigging up his sporting prowess, claiming he needed to rest before a big game because, hadn't they mentioned, he was playing for Shrewsbury Town Under Eighteens. Yes, it really was amazing, they said. What a talent, they agreed, while I stood there, their compliant, hard-working perfectionist daughter and barely got a mention. Getting As and being home on time, not smoking weed or shoplifting fucking hot cross buns wasn't good enough apparently. So, yeah, I harboured ideas of world-wide achievement so maybe I could be a talking point instead of merely being quietly, invisibly there.

'We'll make you a talking point,' Craig promised.

And that very first time I brought him to Shropshire, he did.

Having just broken the news of Mum's cancer, Dad, obviously feeling a change of subject was needed, had asked, 'Who do you support then, Craig?'

'Not massively into it,' Craig said. 'Always enjoyed playing sport more than watching it.'

'Right.' Dad flipped the burgers, asked me to go butter the baps. 'You know Matthew, Beatle's brother, used to captain Shrewsbury Town Under Eighteens.'

And, yeah, I was in shock about Mum's diagnosis, Mabel, but I still managed to roll my eyes in the same way I'd been doing for, what, sixteen, seventeen years. Craig looked at me, like, *don't worry, babe, I've got this.* 'Has Bea told you about her space-hop?'

I swear to god, I nearly choked on my Pimms.

'Her *what*?'

I shook my head, *don't even.*

But on he ploughed. 'Your daughter is going to be the fastest woman in the world over a mile on a spacehopper.'

Dad was laughing for the first time since we'd arrived.

'For charity. Aren't you, Bea?'

'I guess?'

Craig hadn't mentioned The Hop since that afternoon when we'd forsaken the frost and the training for several more hours in bed. But he'd spotted exactly what I needed in that moment with my parents and was my greatest support. 'No guessing. Just yessing,' he said. 'You and me, we'll be the ultimate team.'

So, 'Yes!' I beamed. As did Dad and Mum too when we told her. Not the same kind of pride they had in Matthew but there was, at least, a glimmer of joy in the madness of it. And your father gave them that, Mabel. Or at least he allowed *me* to give them that.

From the off, in the grand moments, Craig was my lynchpin.

My readers have lapped it up even more than my parents did. With all his virtual P.D.A., he's the Athena poster boy times ten, not just holding the baby but praising his wife. And – platinum bonus points! – he can do my hair too. What more I could I want, they've asked me. And they're right. Because what more could I possibly want, Mabel? Don't I have everything I, and they have wished for? Aren't I the girl who has it all?

Maybe not.

Because, 'I love you, Bea,' he'd said.

'But.'

'But.'

I search for him in the comments.

Nothing.

Nothing.

Nothing.

Until he's everything.

Everywhere.

Tagged.

@MrTWBF is tagged in the comments from 5.23 p.m. And after 5.23 p.m. the sympathies change.

SlackBookAir: @MrTWBF wtf? @MsTWBF already had the abortion?

QueenMum: @MrTWBF You didn't know? About the regret? About her being pregnant? None of it? Seriously? Not cool.

LucyJay1979: @MrTWBF game changer

FJL1981: @MrTWBF I'd kick that bitch to the kerb.

LadyLovesCactus: @MrTWBF You need to grab your DD and run.

BirminghamMumOf1: Woah. Why you all hating on @MsTWBF Clearly something's not right with her? Where's the sympathy, ladies?

LadyLovesCactus: @BirminghamMumOf1 @MrTWBF commented but it's been deleted (by @MrTWBF or @

MsTWBF?!) She hadn't told him she was pregnant. She had an abortion WITHOUT EVEN TELLING HER HUSBAND. Who the hell does that?
BirminghamMumOf1: ☹

I could read Craig's deleted comment, of course. He can remove it from the public page, but it will remain in my inbox in the notification I will have received when he posted. Knowing how much I wish I could retract all this shit, though, I wonder if I should allow Craig the courtesy of his withdrawal. If that's the least I can do for him, for this man who now loves me with a "but".

As if I have that kind of willpower. As if I have that kind of grace.

My fingers work quickly. I've seen yours do it too, Mabel, the ease with which they move around my phone when they want something from it. All that desperation in the tips.

I've got it.

Amid all the other notifications, Craig's is there.

But.

I'm home. And I can either read your father's diatribe or come to get you. Something tells me I should put you first.

Weirdly, when I ring the bell and the door opens, it's Alice who's apologetic. Her neck is crooked as she grips her phone between her shoulder and ear.

'Is that her?' I hear Craig's voice in your grandma's phone when she ushers me in with her hand.

'Yes,' she says to your father, who's obviously still taking calls so long as they're not from me. 'I've got to go,' she tells him, shaking her head and, 'Only if she says so, Craig. I am not in the business of kidnapping, dear.'

I should perhaps say hello, or sorry, even. But 'No,' I say when Alice ends the call and asks if I want you to spend the night with her.

'Just one night.' Her eyes scan the length of me, the fuchsia gall of my dress. 'Craig will be home in the morning.'

Like you'll be safe then, Mabel. With Daddy to protect you, I mean.

My mother-in-law smiles, but I can't read her. I can't tell from her mouth or eyes what she makes of me now my wicked truths have been exposed. 'Craig thinks —'

'And what about what *I* think?'

Her palm is a flash of livid fury on my cheek.

I've never been slapped before.

From the look on her face as she clenches her hot fingers into a shrinking fist, Alice is equally stung.

'I'm sorry.' Her hands are all Lady Macbeth with the guilt of it. 'I shouldn't have. It's just I —'

'It's OK.' And it is. Because at least the burn is tangible. At least she's made her position clear.

'Let Mabel stay here, Bea.' As if there wasn't just a moment of violence between us, Alice's voice is level, reasoned, almost painfully kind. 'Just for the night. If nothing else, couldn't you do with the break?'

You were quick to walk. That's what the health visitor told me. And the NCT lot seemed to agree because at eight months, three weeks and two days, you were the first among the babies to teeter between coffee tables and sofas to a round of applause. I was proud. Of course, I was proud. You were so clever, toddling and waddling. Your fat cheeks punctured with a grin.

'Good girl,' I said. And I meant it.

'She's off…' I posted a video of you in action dragging a small bag I'd joked packed with your things.

Readers warned: blink and you'll miss it. Readers said: before you know it, your DD will be gone.

In the harder darker moments, I'd blink. And I'd blink. And I'd blink. But you were still there, Mabel. All I wanted was ten, five, even two minutes. Just one would do. But you were always, resolutely, still there.

The sky is darker than it was in London. The air is closer too.

'I need to see my daughter.' My whisper is desperate. 'To tell her I'm sorry.' To make sure you understand, Mabel, that despite everything, I don't want you to go away.

Alice retreats further into the hallway, leaving room for me to go past her and up the stairs.

In your travel cot in the guest bedroom, you are on your back, mouth open. Peaceful. And so vulnerable too. I'd hug you, curl your limbs toward your middle so you're balled against my chest, and we'd be close again. But it would be selfish to disturb you when you're already hugging Flumper, when you're already sleeping, when your life right here, right now, is content.

'You'll see her tomorrow,' Alice says when I come back down. 'What time would you like me to bring her home? Ten?'

'I was actually going to ask if you wouldn't mind having her for a few hours in the morning. I've got an appointment.' The audacity I have to muster is sickening. 'At the clinic. They insist you go back for the—'

'OK.' Alice's interruption is as benign as her hand on my arm. 'I'll bring her in the afternoon then.' She sees me out, stands by the door to wave me off, which is gracious, Mabel, given all my embarrassment and shame.

CHAPTER TWENTY

'What can I do, Bea?' Della's on the sofa, that ginormous bump of hers behind a cushion she's propped on her knees.

'I dunno. Anything I do, I'm screwed.'

'I meant *me*,' she says. 'Twins!' Neither of us has mentioned her babies since she arrived twenty minutes or so ago. 'You regret *one*. How the fuck am I going to cope with *two*?'

'You'll be great.'

She kicks me. Not hard but enough to make me look at her, which I've not done, not really, because her tummy's too huge to avoid if I look anywhere in her direction. And it's not, obviously, but its protrusion feels like an allegation.

'You will, Del. You'll be a natural.'

'Is there such a thing?' Della says, and she's sad, I know, but there's an incline in her voice, which has the rise of accusation. 'I've been spinning out since the beginning of the second trimester.'

'About what?'

'How to do it. Be a mother.'

I shrug. 'I'm not exactly the best one to say.'

'Nisha keeps reminding me it's something we all have to do our own way.'

'You'll find a way then.' I don't intend to sound so bitter, Mabel. 'Let's hope it's better than mine.' I flip the phone over on my thigh to check for alerts.

'C'mon, Bea. Put it down and talk to me, will you?' Given swift movements haven't been Della's forte for a month or two, she does a good job of snatching it from me. She makes a thing of slipping it into her jacket pocket. 'You've deleted the post now, right?'

'Yeah. Twitter though.'

'Huh?'

'An automated tweet goes out when I post.'

'Surely the link's no longer working?' She's right, but there have been comments anyway. 'Fuck's sake, Bea. Can you stop shrugging your shoulders and pulling faces and talk to me, *please*.'

'I dunno what to say.'

'What are you? Like fifteen? You sound like a teenager who's got caught with an eighth of weed in the padding of her push-up bra.'

'Sorry.' How can two small syllables be so sour?

'For what exactly?'

I can't shrug, can I. Instead, I pick at the lose thread in the seam of the pyjama bottoms I'd put on as soon as I got home.

'I can't help you if you won't talk to me.'

'I'm fine.' I should have gone for another word, of course.

'*Fine*? You are not *fine*. You've announced to the world that you regret having Mabel so much that you've had an abortion without telling your husband. I know I'm no Susie Dent, but that doesn't sound anything like the definition of *fine* to me.'

We love Susie, Della and me. We love, or loved, sitting on the sofa with a bag of wine gums, ideally the reds and blacks, and mugs of gin and tonic we poured from a *Countdown* teapot I bought for Della off eBay apropos of nothing in 2009.

'Holy fucking moly!'

'You like it then?'

She turned the unwrapped teapot in the air. 'Bea Bea, I don't like it…'

'IIIIIIIIIIII LOVE it,' we said in unison, mimicking Simon Cowell because, it's true, Della and I have basically spent a lot of our time together in the glow of easy-viewing TV.

'Are you *crying*?'

'Yes.' She raised her head defiantly, let the tear roll all the way down her cheek until it dripped, unwiped, from her jaw. 'Anyway, you can't talk, you cry at all the dead-gran stories on *X Factor*.'

'Fair enough.'

'And this, Bea Bea,' Della held the teapot as if it were a World Cup, 'is so much better than all the dead-gran stories on *X Factor*.'

I miss her. Or, I miss the her and me were when we could sit on the sofa with our wine gums and gin and watch back-to-back *Countdown* with Della doing alright with the numbers and me doing alright with the words. I miss crushing on Susie Dent in Dictionary Corner. And sure, I follow Susie Dent on Twitter, but Twitter's not real life is it. Watching *Countdown* with Della was. And I miss it. Like I miss not having to plan a dinner or drinks or a phone call around bedtimes and nursery times and not having to stop at the one bottle because any more than that, and your six AM cries would be an air raid siren, and I'd want to take cover.

A baby is a bomb with no shelter, Mabel.

'You've seemed so hap—' Della stops herself. 'You've seemed OK.' She tries not to make it a question. Or a plea.

'I have been.'

My best friend looks at me, like, *c'mon.*

'I've not been *not* OK.' I concede. 'Not all the time anyway. I love Mabel, honestly, I do…'

…

That other word hangs between us.

'Nothing's the same after, that's all. I'm not saying I've not enjoyed any of it, of course I have. Mabel's lovely…'

…

I can't tell her. And I've told Della everything. And I mean *everything*. Like my weirdest fantasy crush (Nigel Havers), the passcode to my phone (her birthday), and the location of both my favourite tweezers *and* all those random spiky black hairs that appear overnight on my chin and neck so that if I ever get Alzheimer's she can take responsibility for the pluck.

I can't tell her *this* though, not now, not with those imminent babies.

'I love Mabel. I love being her mum. Like you will with yours. I'm just not ready for another one. That why…the abortion.'

Maybe it's the light, or my imagination, but she seems to flinch at the fact of it.

'And all that regret stuff, that was just the gin. More than a *Countdown* teapot full. It's no wonder I went off on one. OK?'

'K.' She knows though.

Like when we were twenty and she got off with my boyfriend and I knew, and she knew that I knew, but I told her I'd ended it because he was moving to America to train to be a pilot and, 'god, does he need some training, Del, 'cos that boy has absolutely no fucking clue what to do with his cockpit.' And she'd laughed and said OK, but she knew there was all this stuff *I* wasn't telling. And I knew there was all this stuff *she* wasn't telling. And we both knew we had a better chance of survival if we kept schtum.

Maybe we've not been as open and honest as we've thought then, Mabel.

Maybe all relationships need secrets to survive.

'Here.' I hold out my hands to Della now. 'I'll help you up. 'One, two, three.'

'I'm a walrus.'

'You're a legend.'

'Shit, Bea Bea!' She unlocks my phone.

'What?'

She turns from me, my phone to her bosom, before scrolling and scrolling and, 'Shit,' she repeats. 'Twitter.' Sharp breath. 'It's mental.'

'What do you mean? Let me see.'

'I think you've gone viral.' She hands it over, screen down, eyes down too.

'It can't be that bad.' Twitter's not real life after all.

@LordOfMen75 I need to go fuck @MsTWBF to show her what her cunt's for

It can't be that bad, I'd said.
Oh, but it can.

CHAPTER TWENTY-ONE

I read somewhere recently that the average human will spend just over forty per cent of their life looking at a screen. If you're called a cunt repeatedly on Twitter, are you likely to look less, or more?

I can't keep my eyes off it, thread after thread all topped with the screenshot of my Worst Words.

I will not be having another child because having my daughter robbed me of a life I can never retrieve from beneath the piles of nappy sacks, chopped up snacks, the sleepless nights I can't get back, a marriage derailed from its perfect track and a body that's wounded and saggy and slack.

No matter how long I stare, it doesn't change. Because once Twitter has you pegged, it's stiff and unbendable and you're a monster with no nuance, just that hard solid fact of your secret abortion.

Lord of Men @LordOfMen75
Replying to @MsTWBF
Anyone involved in #feminism needs to read what this cunt did to her husband then go stick a dick in her mouth until she stops talking

I've always made an effort to respond to every tweet, even if it's only to like it. I keep starting a reply. *I'm not saying what I did was right, but…* there's nothing to follow the *but*.

'There's no point.' I know from her voice that Della's rolling her eyes at me. 'Leave it, Bea Bea,' she says. 'If you respond you're only going to make it worse.'

'What about the normal ones then? The ones who aren't going to rape or kill me. Can I respond to them?'

Because they're not all crazies. Though the scary thing is, the not-crazies mostly hate me now too. Or if they don't hate me, they definitely don't "get me". They feel sorry for me, maybe, think I need to see a doctor or a counsellor or take some pills or go running or embrace hygge and slow things down.

'Like a bloody hot chocolate or log-burning fire is what's going to save me. That's what they think. They think they can fix me, Dell.'

'Well, maybe they can. Not with those things exactly but…' When I look at her, Della is biting her nail. 'Have you thought that maybe you're, you know…depressed.?'

'Of course I'm fucking depressed. There's nothing left of me.'

She might heave a sigh that practically calls me a dick but what Della does too is come over to my side of the sofa and hold me.

'It's the day to day to day to day to day mind-numbing crap of it,' I say into her shoulder. 'The never feeling like you're alone, because even when you're not with them, you're doing stuff for them, or worrying about them, or hiding from them in an actual wardrobe because you just want one minute of peace.' Given what else the world now knows about me, Mabel, the fact that I've done that – pulled out shoes and boxes to make room for my tightly curled body – no longer feels so steeped in shame. I pull away from my best friend and for the first time tonight look right at her. 'What's that quote? The one about the pram in the hall being the enemy of art? It's not just art. It's the enemy of time, the enemy of pleasure, it's the enemy of fucking everything.'

'Maybe it's the enemy of grief.'

'Fuck off.' My cheeks burn from the nerve she's hit. As soon as the words spit from my mouth, I want to claw them back. 'I'm sorry,' I say, shaking my head like that might tilt all these nasty thoughts and retorts from my brain.

'I'd like to help you,' she says, voice straight off that hypnobirthing CD she's addicted to. 'But I don't think now is the right time to... It's gone midnight. I suggest you go to bed.'

Stay, I think but can't say.

I want her to sleep over like she used to after a night out when we'd collapse onto the mattress with our shoes on and take it in turns to smear each other's make-up with inefficient wipes. She'd hold my hand, and we'd fall asleep mumbling that nothing would ever beat these days of our lives while harbouring a secret wish that it would.

A vibration. I can't help but glance at my phone.

'Craig?' Della's voice is hopeful.

'No.'

'He likes time,' she says. 'Remember? He was the same with the move.'

The move.

Craig knew it was coming. It wasn't like I'd spring some major life thing on him without talking about it first. Well, not *that* kind of major life thing.

My mum was dying. Had been dying, slowly, remotely, for over a year. And I'd said to Craig when Mum first told us that I didn't think I could stay in London too long because how could I leave Mum to face everything the internet was telling me she'd go through on her own?

'Your Dad will be there.' Craig had said. And it was true. Dad *would* be there, but wasn't it also true that his need for me would be as great as Mum's?

Two to four years, the doctor had told her. And the time seemed both long and short. Long enough for Craig and me not to cancel the trip we'd booked to the States that summer. Short enough for me to run through all the things I'd assumed my mother would share with me but would likely now miss. And obviously it wasn't all about me, Mabel. It was predominantly about her. Or at least it should have been. Because when a woman is diagnosed with multiple myeloma, you'd hope, wouldn't you, that her family would let it be about her. But that's the thing when you're someone's child, and maybe with all the shit that's happening right now, you'll be different, Mabel, but the thing is when you're someone's child, you never stop being someone's child. Your connection to them is always about *you*.

So, when I took Craig to Shropshire so he could meet my parents for the first time, that occasion was totally meant to be about me. Or me and Craig. But when Mum took us into the garden, where Dad was at the barbeque and gave Craig a hug, Mum gave Craig both a beer and this look, like, *sorry love, things might get a little intense here*. And the quick trip to Shropshire that was all about me showing my family, *look, here I am with a proper could-be-very-serious boyfriend*, turned into a quick trip to Shropshire that was all about showing my proper-could-be-very-serious boyfriend how stoic I am in a crisis.

There may have been a few minutes before the stoicism kicked in though, a few minutes when I let my mum hold my face in her hands and apologise.

Apologise! For what exactly?

'I'm sorry for putting you through this.' Her windscreen wiper thumbs swept across my cheeks. 'I wasn't going to tell you, but your father, well, he, *we*, thought you should know.'

'Of course I should. I can't believe you'd even think of not telling me.'

'I said it'd be obvious from the fact she's made me do the cooking.' Dad, not thinking to put down the tongs, came in for an awkward hug. 'But she's already playing the cancer card.' He looked at Mum, like, *too soon for gallows humour?* 'How could I refuse?'

For all his joking, Dad wasn't far wrong. He never cooked. Never really cleaned. Certainly never had any clue how to load a washing machine. And no matter how hard he tried to conceal it behind crass jokes and a conversation with Craig about Matthew's captaincy of Shrewsbury Town Under 18s, his panic was stark.

On the train home, after plotting a training schedule for The Hop, I'd said, 'You know, at some point I'll need to move home.' And Craig had said something like *absolutely*, the Pendolino rocking us side to side like we were babies. And for the first time since being a grown-up, I wished I was. A baby, I mean. I wished the rocking was enough. And if that didn't work, I wished Craig would. I wished Craig would work. His arm around my middle, his palm on my hip, his fingers creeping inside the waist of my jeans. Because for the few months I'd known him, Craig's arm, Craig's palm and Craig's fingers had worked like magic, making everything possible, making everything good. But from the moment we'd left Mum and Dad's, as he'd been Googling *exercises to do with a spacehopper*, I'd been Googling the worst of things to come. And suddenly there was no cure, not only for the multiple myeloma, but no cure for its ripples either, for the rifts it left as it ripped from me every child's assumption that her parents will always be there to watch over her, to make sure everything's OK.

And I get the irony, Mabel. I can hear the keyboard warriors. Their caps lock screaming 'ISN'T THIS EXACTLY WHAT YOU'VE DONE TO YOUR DAUGHTER?' 'WHAT A HYPOCRITE', they'll say. And they're probably right. But I'm telling you all this because when I Googled what was to come for my mother and told Craig there's no way I could leave her to go through its prophecies alone, what he said was something like *absolutely*. And that was enough for me to believe he'd be OK with it when, a year later, after the States and Vegas and marriage and massage and poetry and a World Record Hop and spinning gold from straw, I returned from yet another trip to Shropshire, where my solid eternal mum was shrunk and perished, and told my husband, 'It's time.'

What Craig said then was 'no'. What Craig said was he couldn't possibly. What Craig said was I could go every weekend if I wanted, but 'what about this life we've made in London? What about all those conversations in which we'd sworn off small towns for good? 'We're not homing pigeons,' he said. 'We're spur-of-the-moment Vegas, baby. And yeah, sure, one day we might choose to up sticks, but for somewhere exotic, not the bloody Midlands.' And, anyway, 'What will happen after,' he asked, 'when your mum is…' And he couldn't quite bring himself to say the word. But we both knew what he was getting at. We'd give it all up – our flat, our jobs, our friends, our bars, our games nights, our Sunday mornings in the bath and afternoons in the park – we'd give it all up and then in not too long my mum would be dead and so would our opportunity to come back. Because we'd seen it happen before: how mates left London and couldn't afford to return.

'Are you sure this isn't about Della?'

When they'd started fertility treatment, she and Nisha had moved back to Shrewsbury to be close to Della's mum. She'd joked at the time it wouldn't be long until I followed. And for a guy rarely intimidated by other men, it had been a surprise, this quiet threat Craig felt from my best mate. *From* not quite the right word because that makes it sound like the threat was something she was deliberately casting, which she wasn't. Della really had no clue of her powers of intimidation. Was there nothing I wouldn't tell her, he'd asked me once when I'd spilt one too many secrets in the hope of her advice. And at the time I'd been honest, said probably not, though even that's turned out to be untrue.

'This isn't about Della.' It took everything not to swear. 'This is about my mum.' To keep my voice at a sensible level. 'Who has cancer.' Because this was a sensible decision as well an emotional one. Mum and Dad both needed me. And, yes, I could keep driving up every weekend as Craig had suggested, but I was knackered and becoming less and less help to anyone. 'And I miss you.'

It was true. With lesson planning, meetings, parent's evenings and marking there was no time for Craig in the week and, by Friday, I was on the road again, home late on Sunday when I'd collapse in front of whatever Netflix series Craig had discovered in my absence.

He sighed. Not exactly exasperated. More lost. 'Let's give it a couple of months at least. Before rushing off. See how your mum is in September, have the summer in London. C'mon, Ms Straw, you'll be on holidays then, it'll be easier. Can't we see how it goes?'

'I don't have the luxury of time.'

It wasn't just cancer creating a ticking clock. School required sufficient notice. I'd have to find supply work for the September. We'd need to advise our landlord and potentially find somewhere to rent in Shrewsbury too.

I moved in with Mum and Dad in July.

Craig borrowed money from his parents to cover the rent I could no longer afford in London.

It was three months before he made the move.

'He likes time,' Della said of my husband just now. 'Remember? He was the same with the move.'

I remember alright. All that time Craig wanted? Like Mum, we shrunk and perished in it. We stopped spinning gold and spun lead. Our Happy Ever After turned poisoned apple, and I feared it wouldn't only be Mum that was dead at the end of Craig's precious precarious time.

'Will I see you tomorrow?' When I lean in, I can't tell if it's Della's bump that makes our hug awkward.

'Sure.' Her kiss is polite, and her feet move too quickly to her car.

I draw the curtains then pick up that picture of you and me on your birthday, Mabel.

Mother and daughter.

The holy fucking grail of love.

I proved that once, right? When I galloped from London to Shropshire, from husband to Mum. An utter belief in the healing power of *that* bond. Quit my job. Said I'd supply teach on the days when I wasn't being a good fucking daughter, which wasn't too dissimilar to being a good fucking wife. I get this sounds bitter and twisted, Mabel, but after all the holding, driving, medicating, soothing, cleaning, feeding, washing, practically fucking perfect nursing and house-wife'ing, I even gave her a child.

And what did she do?

Well, she's not here now, is she.

'Nanna dead.' I spit, charging into the kitchen. When I throw it, the monkey magnet clatters against the oven. The Cleopatra magnet slides across the floor. Mum's face acquiesces to my fingers as I tear the photo of her into a hundred pieces, a hundred seeds I scatter in the garden like ashes so I can no longer kid myself that her eyes are following my every move.

SATURDAY 13TH APRIL

CHAPTER TWENTY-TWO

When you go on a cycling holiday and your wife decides she regrets your daughter and has an abortion without telling. Yep, that.

@MrTWBF's comment is the only real reaction of Craig's I've had. And even that was deleted within minutes so maybe it doesn't count. Maybe his real reaction, the one I couldn't see because he was seven-hundred odd miles away and wouldn't answer my calls, maybe the words of that real reaction were fire and fury. But this? Weirdly, this has the tone of Craig's Facebook status from that time Supergran booted him from the bus.

When you try to do the right thing and the elderly lady you offered to help with her bags mistakes you for a mugger and knocks you off the double decker with her shopper. Yep, that.

You see, Mabel? How the sardonic phrasing fits with an OAP / public-transport incident but not with a wife / abortion.

His key is in the lock.

Showtime.

'Hey, you.'

It's what he said to me the morning after that first night when I'd woken and wished it wasn't so cold in my flat because maybe then Craig wouldn't have needed to put his T-shirt back on after we'd... after we'd, what? What *did* we do? With someone else, I might have said we fucked. A good old no-strings-play-with-a-near-enough-stranger kind of fuck when it's drunk and handsy and all about the

148

take. The kind that was fine, almost fun even, in the midst of it, but by the morning, when I was sober, both my body and head were rotten and raw. Meaty, almost. But with Craig, it *was* drunk and it *was* handsy, but it was total body too. Like there wasn't enough of me to give to him, and there wasn't enough of him for me to grab, to lick, to corral. So, it wasn't just fucking. But it wasn't *making love* either. There were no posh White Company candles. No *Dirty Dancing* soundtrack setting the mood. What it felt like was a pact. A slightly awkward, verging on dirty but kind of magnificent pact, which made us laugh at the end of it because, well, I don't know why. Maybe because it's sort of funny when you think about it, how only a couple of hours previously we'd been doing that slow side-step school-disco dance to *Last Christmas*, and then we were at my flat naked. The drift of our clothes on the floor and all this flush of our skin, every pore and mole and hair of it, not exactly sprawled but sort of knotted on my bed. And I swear it felt like the beginning, like what we'd just done was unearth that time capsule I buried in Bryony Jackson's garden. Like Craig had uprooted the crux of me, and all my secrets would spill. Not right then. But soon. Because I knew, I *honestly* knew, I would see him again soon. And not only once or twice but over and over into something we might call a future. And that's why I wished he hadn't needed to put his T-shirt back on because if he hadn't, I would have worn his T-shirt myself. Like in the movies – for a cynic, I sure did want the movies – when, after sex, the new girl wears the new guy's top, and it signals that this is definitely something better, something stronger, than a no-strings-play-with-a-near-enough-stranger kind of fuck.

Instead, I wore my pyjamas to make him coffee and a slice of toast and used the *Atlas of Human Anatomy* Della had given me for my twenty-first birthday as a tray.

'*Get to know yourself*,' she'd written in loopy red scrawl in the card.

'Hey you,' Craig said as I went into the bedroom. He shifted to sit up against the headboard and smiled a smile so hard and true, I knew it didn't matter that I wasn't wearing his T-shirt because he didn't need those movie signals, he already felt it too.

'Hey,' I said back to him then and I say back to him now, the nerves different this morning to that morning because the future of which I'd then been so certain today feels more like that drift of clothes on the floor. Dirty laundry, easily separated. Possibly hung out to dry.

He holds up what I assume are two cappuccinos from our local, House Coffee. 'Walk?'

'Sure'. I am not sure though. Because A Walk means serious. A Walk means what we need to talk about is too big for our tiny house. A Walk means The Walls Won't Take It. A Walk means Craig can look forward and say the harder things without having to face my reaction.

God, you know how it works, Mabel. It's what we do with you when you're on meltdown. We manoeuvre you into all the bumpf that comes with a taking a child outdoors and stomp through the Quarry Park like it'll solve everything, explaining the reasons why you can't bite your father, throw your food, put your literal shit in my shoe, hoping the height of the sky might raise you from your temper.

The kitchen clock ticks. Its hands are almost at nine-fifteen.

'Somewhere you need to be?'

And, yes, there is. But how to say it?

'The clinic?'

He knows, then.

I nod.

'Mum said.' Of course she did. 'She wasn't exactly sure when though, I thought maybe we'd have time to...'

To what?

And just as when we moved from London to Shropshire: 'I'm sorry, Craig. I don't have the luxury of time.'

I *never* have the luxury of time.

I'm grateful for a knock at the door.

'Craig Straw?' A lean and sweaty man calls from the street as he lugs a giant box from the back of his van.

'Here, you want a hand with that?' Craig appears in the hallway, his voice much friendlier than it had been with me.

'What is it?' I ask.

'Quite a tasty bike, I reckon, if the Bianchi branding on the box is anything to go by.' The delivery guy lowers his end of the huge package down on the front step.

'A bike?'

'Ooops. Not dropped you in it, have I?' He winks at Craig, who's signing his name to confirm receipt. 'I think she'd have been on to you though, mate; something this size is hard to keep a secret for long.'

'I was going to tell you last night,' Craig says, as he shunts the box into the sitting room so it's not taking up the entire space of the hall. 'But then,' he shuts the door on his purchase and looks right at me, 'other things felt more important, you know?'

The inside of my lip is tender when I bite it.

He puffs a little noise from his throat that's indicative of something. I'm just not sure what.

'My appointment's at eleven.' Hot coffee burns the tiny fresh cut in my mouth. 'I'm really sorry, I don't have time for a walk.'

'A drive then,' Craig follows me, pulls open the top drawer and takes the keys. 'You'll need someone there with you. It might as well be me.'

* * *

151

He doesn't say anything more until we're in the car. 'You think they're happy?' Craig bucks his head at the couple pushing the buggy along the pavement when we're stopped at the crossing. The woman – the mother – perhaps feel us watching and catches my eye. Does she know? Can she see through my clothes to the pad in my knickers? Or is it the skeleton I let loose from the closet, how it sits, unflinching, between Craig and me as we wait.

It's like when I was pregnant with you, Mabel, before the bump, but I was sure everyone must have known the secret I was carrying inside me. Because couldn't they just tell? Didn't I have this look of a mother and mustn't they have known from that look exactly what kind of mother I'd be. Awesome, right? Because once we'd made the decision, I was totally gung ho. I'd keep journals, do crafts – *fuck it* – I'd even knit a cute little bonnet in an ironic sort of way, and my baby would carry it off no problem because my baby would be part me and part Craig and what could possibly go wrong with that.

I couldn't knit for a start. I tried all these tutorials on YouTube, but my hands weren't made for it. And Craig was no help. Something about me knitting got him all Harlem, he said, a reference to our three days in New York when the heat and art and hum of the city ramped up the honeymooner in us, and it was like we were new again. Proper new. Only-just-made-cocktails and our-anato-mies-were-atlases kind of new. And for some inexplicable reason, something about the knitting, 'maybe it's the click of the needles,' he said, like that would make sense of it, but whatever the reason, it made him turn down his book – my tatty copy of *The Time Traveler's Wife* – and lift the hem of my skirt. 'Or how un-you you look.' The Vegas / Newark boarding pass stub he always used as a bookmark ran a line across my still-flat tummy. 'How old-fashioned motherly you are when you're knitting.'

'Eugh, Freud'd have a field day with that.' But I surrendered the basic-effort bonnet as Craig unravelled the ball of wool, using the string of it to tickle my arms, my neck, my collar bone, my… you get the gist. It wasn't only my basic-effort bonnet that came undone in my teenage bedroom of my parents' house, where Craig had finally agreed to live with me until… We said until you were born, Mabel, but we both knew it was really until the other thing, which I wouldn't even imagine, let alone make real with a name.

We were two and a bit of us then. We're a three now. And even though you're with Alice so the maths theoretically makes us two again, it doesn't matter. For these days, we are always three.

'Who knows,' I say in answer to Craig's question about the family now crossing the road in front of us. 'They look happy enough.'

He inhales deeply, noisily, through his nose and moves the car forward. 'Are you OK, Bea?'

I could cry. Because of his voice and its layers of feeling, and because he reaches – out of habit? Love? Please let it be love – for my hand. Though his fingers are tentative, nervous of this new me, I suppose, like when he let the strands of wool drift down across my thigh and the nail of his thumb edged the lace of my thong and into me, his breath suddenly keener than his fingers, which were held-back and careful and not at all Craig. 'How un-you you feel, how un-Harlem,' I teased, urging him to reach further inside. But we were two and a bit of us then, and Craig was more… I don't know what Craig was. More afraid of hurting you than overcome with ravishing me.

'I'm OK,' I say, which is stupid, I know, because obviously I'm not. Quite clearly, I am not OK, because Craig is driving me to a clinic, where I will swallow the pills that will end this second pregnancy.

And what else, Mabel? Exactly what else will end?

'Bea?' Only our little fingers remain in the hold. 'Please,' he says, the top layer of his voice pared back to bare a trace of, what? Frustration? Despair? It would be easier if he said something.

153

Something more than my name. More than *please*. If he was specific. If he either held my hand properly or let it go.

He lets go.

'Why didn't you tell me?'

'I knew you'd want to keep it. Try to talk me round, and I couldn—'

'Not the baby.' The car quickens. And, yes, it's because we're on the dual carriage way, but there's more to the acceleration. 'Not only that anyway.' His change in gear is an ellipsis. 'Mabel.' There's a crack, then, in those remaining layers of his voice, and I don't know how to fill it. 'Why didn't you tell me about Mabel? How you feel about her? The regret?'

'How could I?'

The words were unspeakable. They *are* unspeakable.

My palm slips with sweat as I grip the car seat, afraid to move because any strand of wool that might ever have tied us has turned to barbed wire, and any attempt at connection could draw blood.

For fortyish minutes, we sit in silence, face forward, our eyes grateful for the distraction of the increasing traffic.

'We were perfect before Mabel,' I whisper eventually, unable to look at Craig because any miniscule change will be a sign. And I'm not sure I want to know.

He risks it though. Craig risks the wire, risks the blood, as his focus shifts back and forth between me and the road.

'We weren't,' he says, while I search for other words, and he brushes my wrist with his thumb before retracting it, as if remembering that easy kind of touch is no longer a given.

'What?'

'We weren't perfect.' Your father, driving at just above seventy, looks right at me, Mabel. Or *into* me. Craig looks right into me, as if really seeing me for the first time since he came home. Or ever, even. The suspicion of this woman he married so clear in the lines of his face. How he's realised what little or no clue he had of me. Until now. He knows now, Mabel. 'We were never perfect.' Eyes to the road then back again. His quiet outrage rewinds me nineteen years to age fifteen when I told my mum I'd had sex with a boy, Adrian Johnson, who was two years older and took me to the cinema three times in as many weeks and didn't that make him my boyfriend, and didn't that make it OK? And I told Mum not because I wanted to but because Bryony Jackson, the same Bryony Jackson who later encouraged me to bury them, had Sharpie'd my secrets on the toilet walls. She denied it was her, but I knew her writing. How she always made a stupid heart of a dot over an i, which made the "in" of "in the Quarry" look so much sweeter than losing my virginity in the Quarry Park had actually been. I was called into the head of year, who told me to tell my mother before he did. And so I told my mum I'd had sex with Adrian Johnson, and even though I didn't mention the Quarry, I began to vanish. Or at least her specific daughter-version of me did. And maybe that doesn't make sense, but what I mean is, Beatrice Williams, the sweetheart daughter of Caroline Williams diminished, and in her place sat someone less perfect, someone less good, someone less loved.

'Do you honestly think things were perfect before we had Mabel?'

I nod, but doubt slips in through the tiny holes his barbed-wire words have pricked into my skin.

'You're wrong,' Craig says, as if he sees it, feels it, the slow puncture of his question. 'I've never lived up to your expectations.'

'Expectations? Of what?'

'Your *Enchanted* version of what we should be.'

'You what?'

'Your perfection driver, or whatever the fuck a shrink would call it. Whatever bit it is in you that wants the movies.'

'I don't want the mov—'

'You say you don't. You pretend to be above it, to be realistic, a little bit snidey even about those who you reckon have been fooled by Hollywood. But when it comes down to it, Bea, you want everything to be ten out of ten.'

It's not that he's wrong exactly, but —

'I'm not saying it to point out your flaws, babe. All I mean is, you're not the only one who…' He drifts.

'Who what?'

'Who's found us hard.'

'Us?' My regret isn't about *us* though. Is it?

'Thing is, it didn't matter to me that we weren't perfect. What family is?' Craig's sigh is so huge the windows could steam with it. 'And that's what I thought we were, Bea. A family.' He takes the slip road.

'We were. We *are*.'

'Well tell that to Mabel. Tell our daughter what a great family we are. And, while you're at it, tell her what a great mother you are too.'

'I'm sorry?'

And maybe Craig's anticipating the other kind of *I'm sorry*. The kind that isn't followed with a question mark of disbelief.

'Are you seriously pissed off at *me* right now, Bea?' His hand comes down heavy on the indicator lever.

A moment in which to deny it. But I don't because, yeah, I *am* pissed off at him. Because, you know what, despite most of the time wishing I could be doing something else, I think I have been a pretty good mum to you, Mabel.

'If I'd asked you yesterday morning whether I was a "great mum", what would you have said, Craig? Would you honestly have said I was shit?'

'No, but —'

'You would have said I'm good. You would have said – you *have* said actually – that I'm superwoman. You're always telling me I don't stop. I need to relax. That I'm too busy doing stuff for Mabel to think about myself. But it's not only Mabel I'm doing stuff for, Craig. It's *you*. Constantly.'

His head cocks, like, *what the* — But all my guilt turns to fury and spills hot and bitter from my mouth, which is as twisted as the rest of me.

'Maybe I couldn't cope with the idea of having another child because I already have two.'

A silence, as slippery as water,

drip

drip

drips

between us.

'Well,' he pulls into a space at the carpark, 'it's a good job we're here then.'

Your father gets a ticket from the machine while I sit scrolling through photos, through picture after picture of you.

* * *

The last time Craig and I were in Birmingham together we were Christmas shopping. It had been a disaster. Since leaving London, we'd become unaccustomed to festive cities, to their crowds, to the pressure, to the half-an-hour queue for coffee and the music that starts off as reminiscent but ends up with a vow to destroy every sodding Christmas bauble and bell. We gave up. On the gifts but not on Birmingham, where we avoided the stores and looked instead for somewhere to eat because, 'we may as well take advantage of the childcare,' Craig said, slipping his hand into mine. That simple act was made so much easier by the fact that neither of us was pushing a buggy.

We ate pizza, and even though it was only just midday, I had a glass of wine. We returned home empty handed but for the mistletoe

I insisted we buy from the street-seller, who said Craig shouldn't need the excuse of foliage to kiss me. 'She's gorgeous,' the salesman said. And even though I'd heard him offering up the same banter to another couple, I chose to believe him. We hung it in the kitchen, lauding the memories it evoked of that night we met at Della's and swearing to obey its romantic demand.

We forgot, of course. Or became distracted. Or perhaps it was simply that once you were home, Mabel, we tended to look down not up. I unpinned its withered stalk from the ceiling months later and tried not to cry when I threw it in the bin.

The pizza had been good though. The company too. We'd laughed, and our feet had played a kind of dance beneath the table, initiating a flirtation that swelled until we were in the car, where the rising fever pushed us from the front seats to the back. We weren't giggling by then, rather we were hard and desperate needing, as the muscle memory of our bodies carried us beyond the exhaustion and familiarity into something like that first night when it wasn't only our hands we couldn't keep from each other. It was quick. It had to be. Too much risk of other shoppers, yes, but it wasn't them I was most afraid of, Mabel. Your car seat was digging into my elbow, and the possibility of my mother's ghost lingered close by.

It's not so different in the carpark this morning. The ghost-induced shame, I mean. The sentiment between Craig and me though? Well, that's totally changed.

'Which way?' He lags a few steps behind as we walk to the clinic. Then, 'This it?' He scans the building when I stop outside.

'What did you expect?'

It *is* fairly innocuous. Red brick with glass doors flanked by coffee shops either side.

'It doesn't seem like the kind of place where…' Craig takes a step back, looking anywhere but the entrance now. 'You said eleven, didn't you? It's only ten-to. Shall we…?' He tilts his head toward Costa.

I shrug.

His feet don't move, but his shoulders twist in that subtle awkward gesture of a teenager with a potentially mortifying question to pose. 'I was reading this thing when I was at the airport this morning. It's an American site, but they work with doctors in the UK too.' Before I have the chance to ask where this is headed, Craig pulls his phone from his pocket and opens the browser to reveal his research.

'Abortion-pill reversal?' I shake my head as I read it aloud.

'Listen,' he says, taking my hand, which I retract because is he actually doing this? 'If you've only taken the first pill, Bea, there's a chance we could make things OK. It's the progesterone or something. They can boost your levels and so long as you don't take the second lot, the baby could survi—'

'Don't call it that.' I stumble as I move away from him.

His face is sorry, 'But…'

'But what?'

'It *is*,' he says, arms reaching, eyes pleading. 'It *is* our baby.'

'Jesus, Craig.' My attempts to keep my voice down clearly aren't working. A guy in a suit double-takes as he walks past. 'You going to pull a placard from your pocket next, are you? Tell me I'm a murderer going to hell?'

'No. I don't think *that*. I —'

'I can't listen to this.' My fingers press hard into my brow. 'Either come in and keep quiet or go.'

I don't wait for him to make a decision. *My* one – the most important one – is already made.

* * *

The lie, when Sarah offers me a seat in reception and asks if someone is here with me, is smaller today than yesterday. At least the person I pretend is waiting outside for me this morning is alive.

Do I blame him? Craig. Could I have expected any different? Any better? Because he's right, isn't he? I mean, this could become our baby. A baby *he* wanted and has been trying to persuade me, long before now, to have.

But we've been there, Mabel, done that. Only his powers of persuasion the last time were infused with my fear of a great big double whammy of loss.

'Bea?' Sarah's waiting for an answer. But I didn't hear the question. I was too adrift in the memory of the dinner Craig took me to in Shoreditch that summer I'd moved away to look after Mum.

'The only time I can really see us living outside of London is when we have kids, babe.'

'Kids?' It's not as if we'd never talked about it. But the conversations were always very loose and the prospect always very distant.

'Did you take the painkillers?' Sarah removes a small white box from a cupboard, as I nod yes. 'And you'll be administering these yourself? Just four of the six, OK?'

We may have been through this once already, but I don't blame her for checking. My attention's clearly elsewhere.

'You insert them —'

'— into the vagina.' I finish, smiling. 'And if I don't start bleeding after three hours, I should have the last two.'

'So you *were* listening,' Sarah says kindly. 'Lie here for ten minutes or so after you've put them in. I'm right outside if you need me.'

But it's not only Sarah who's there when I come out of the room.

Craig stands when he sees me, his face not too dissimilar from in the hospice when I first said the words "Mum's gone".

I never thought I was one for euphemism. I'd always believed that only the very specific language for death would do. But "dead" was too much. Too final.

I don't know how but Craig made himself bigger then. His shoulders were broader, his chest was firmer, and his arms were steady and strong.

He's the same now, Mabel. He takes my rucksack and the bag Sarah's handing me, which she explains contains the extra pills, a leaflet and a pregnancy test for three weeks' time.

Your father holds more than the bags though. He comes closer and closer and does what I thought the last twenty-four hours had made impossible. He holds *me*.

CHAPTER TWENTY-THREE

'You want me to keep you company?' Craig asks when we arrive home. We'd not spoken since we left the clinic.

I might cry if I say yes. And I don't want to cry, Mabel. Tears might be misinterpreted as regret, and there's already been too much of that. So I nod, and Craig comes into the house, where he rummages in the junk cupboard for a hot water bottle, then boils the kettle and asks if I'd like a drink.

Distracted though, 'You already have a bike,' I say, looking towards the sitting room at the hefty box we've just squished ourselves past.

He drops a bag into my cup. 'The new one's different. Lighter. Better group set. Looks a lot nicer too.'

'Can we afford it?' What was it the delivery guy called it? *Tasty?* 'Your other one's fine, isn't it? I'm not sure I understand why you need a second?'

'Apply the same theory to children, do you?' He thrusts the cup at me, my hand scalding pink with the spilt milky tea.

Is this how it's going to be?

'I'm sorry.' He grabs a sheet of kitchen roll and dabs at my fingers and the mug. 'It's just…'

'It's OK, I get it, I —'

'No, *really*. I didn't mean to start anything now. You take that upstairs, and I'll pop out for some bits for lunch.'

Pop. It's such a light word. Carefree even. It's not appropriate in context, but what would be? How are a husband and wife in this situation meant to speak and behave?

When I wake, the house smells of the same mix of spices Craig's hands had smelt of that afternoon after our first night together, when

162

he'd invited me to his for dinner. When *he* made curry, and *we* made love, and world record pacts made *us* a team. This afternoon, there is a tenderness to the gesture of cooking, to the mood of the house, which is so much more still without you in it.

I snatch my phone from the bedside table, ignoring all messages bar those from Della and Kim. When I manoeuvre the pillows so I might sit upright to read them, it's like something's released and the pregnancy begins to slip silently on to the pad.

I breathe a shy sigh of relief.

An hour or so later, 'It's ready.' Craig puts his head around the door. 'You OK to come downstairs?'

I am. The ache is there. The cramps are painful. But I want to move, to show him this hasn't broken me. To hope this hasn't broken us.

'Oh.'

I twist to see what's turned him pale: the bedsheet is stained. Not red but an unbodily, unwomanly brown.

'Your trousers.' He points at my crotch. And I'm fourteen again. The mortifying bleed onto my jeans which meant I had to leave a party early. A couple of boys were jeering. Because it was funny, apparently, how little control I had of my body, how girls couldn't outrun the disgust of menstrual blood.

'Here.' Craig beckons with his upturned palm. 'Give them to me. I can keep the food warm and put a wash on while you have a bath.'

'I'm only allowed a shower.' I hadn't meant to sound ungrateful. And nor do I mean to appear cagey as I slink from the room, but the idea of pulling my trousers and knickers down in front of Craig is too much.

The thought of him seeing those thick clots in the pad.

'Nature calls.' I cringe at the phrase, at my tone, at the solecism. But it's true. Nature does call. Though is it still nature when the cause of all that blood oozing into and through my knickers is man-made. Woman-made. A consequence of a decision made entirely by me.

I might not want Craig to see, but *I* look at the contents of the pad and in the toilet.

There is nothing distinctive in the mess.

I change the pad and my clothes. I wash. I eat a late lunch with my husband, who has asked your grandma if you can stay another night, Mabel.

'It makes sense,' Craig says, as he gets me a glass of water and some Ibuprofen for the pain.

I watch him, surprised. If I'm honest, I hadn't expected such care.

I go to help as he removes the sheets from the washing machine but, 'sit down,' he says. 'Please, Bea, you need to sit down.'

And I do. I sit and read and then we play a game of Scrabble and watch a movie. Craig orders burgers, which are too much after the curry, but we eat them anyway, on the sofa but several inches apart.

The giant unopened box leans precariously against the wall.

At nineish, he brings me in a mint tea.

'Thank you.' Our voices have been quieter than usual. Any conversation has been tentative and slow. 'You didn't need to do all this.'

He kisses my forehead, wonders if I'm hot so takes my temperature. When it reads a little high, he gets me some Paracetamol.

It's not like things are normal. But they are nice. Closer to how they used to be when I had Craig's love and attention.

Does this make me sound jealous, Mabel? Or petty? I guess what I mean is that today has been awful, but what it's been too is a reminder of how it feels to be looked after. Maybe all Craig and I need is time. And maybe that time would have a knock-on effect, and you and I would benefit too because if Craig and I were stronger, maybe I'd be a stronger mother for you.

Maybe.

Maybe.

Maybe.

'How are you feeling?'

'OK.' I pat the cushion next to me. 'A bit sore.'

He doesn't sit down. 'I'll be off to Mum's then.'

I pull my hand closer to me, curl my fingers under my thigh. 'You're not staying?'

Craig looks at the carpet as he tells me no. 'I'll be back tomorrow,' he says. 'And I'll need some space, Bea.' Perhaps his words are coming out wrong because it sounds like he means space away from me. 'You'll have to go somewhere. For a few days, that's all.'

I shake my head like when you get out of a pool and the water in your ears does something funny with your hearing.

'Maybe you can stay with Della.'

'But what about Mab—'

'Don't worry about that.' Craig sounds defeated. 'You won't be trapped with Mabel. My daughter will stay with me.'

SUNDAY 14TH APRIL

CHAPTER TWENTY-FOUR

'It wasn't my decision, Aunty Pat. It was Crai—'

'But you've gone along with it.'

'What other option do I ha—'

'You stay!'

It doesn't sound like an option. It sounds like an order.

'You stay, duckie. You stay and you look after Mabel. Jesus wept, your mother would be— What was that? That bang?'

'Nothin—'

'Was that you shutting the front door? Is that it then? You've left? You're leaving your daughter?'

Even the exhale of her smoke sounds angry.

'I'm *not* leaving her. Not permanently anyway. Craig wants a few days —'

'What about what *Mabel* wants, Bea? There is more to this than you and Craig. This isn't Vegas. You can't only think about yourselves.'

I promise you, Mabel, if you ever decide to get married, the where and how will be entirely your decision, and I shall never hold it against you.

'You have a responsibility.'

'I know that, Aunty Pat, but —'

'But what? Craig says jump and you jump? You let him and everyone else think you're exactly as bad a mother as you came across in that blog?'

'It doesn't matter what everyone else thinks. All that matters is Craig and Mab—'

'Oh! So you *are* thinking about Mabel? She *does* matter? Just not enough to stay?'

I imagine the cigarette, how she'll be grinding it out on her back step with her shoe.

'Breathe,' Annabel, the NCT woman had told us. 'The most important thing you can do is breathe.' She made it sound easy. Like my body alone could do as much with the pain as an epidural. 'This is what your body was made to do.' She held up that life size model of the pelvis alongside that life size model of a new-born. The two looked incompatible, of course, but the ten of us sat in our pairs, cradling bumps, sucking it all up because, hell, yeah, this birthing thing, this motherhood thing, that's what us women of the bump-cradling pairs were made for. I chose to believe it. Hook. Line. Sinker.

'Breathe,' Craig said when the contractions were hard and fast. And I zoned in on my breath and, fuck me, I was one of the lucky ones, because that breath and the water, it wasn't like it turned the pain down to zero, but it was do-able. It made it the kind of pain you see in movies when your hero shifts from crisis to climax and you're pretty damn sure there'll be a happy ever after some time soon. And you were soon, Mabel. You were only seven-hours-of-labour-and-out-you-swam soon because I was one of the lucky ones and hadn't Annabel told us how a natural birth would set you up brilliantly. So hadn't I just given you the perfect start?

Breathe.

'Of course Mabel matters, but Craig said he needs some space and, given what's happened, I think it's fair I do as he asks. A few days he said, and I reall—'

'I've already been on the phone with your dad. And he agrees. Thank god your mum isn't here to witness this.'

The vinegared sting of her words catches in my throat.

'Can I stay with you or not?'

The scratch of Aunty Pat's lighter.

Breathe.

'Oh, duckie. Marriage is compromise and motherhood is putting your child first.'

Breathe.

'So that's a no then?'

'It's me not helping you make the biggest mistake of your life.'

'It's a few days.'

'It's a message,' she says. 'It's a message to your daughter that leaving is something you can do.'

'But Craig —'

'Craig nothing. You are her mother. You stay. You hear me?'

'I hear you.'

Breathe.

* * *

'Bea Straw?'

'Hmm?' It's difficult to see her face from down here on the doorstep, where I'm sitting with the suitcase and my indecision, shielding my eyes from the sun.

'Bea Straw? Tonight Will Bea Fine, isn't it?'

There are two of them, but only the woman is talking. The man? The man is lifting a camera to his eyes. The light is so bright, and I'm halfway to standing to see who they are when, 'Eve Storant, *Daily Mail*,' she says. 'We'd like to talk with you about your blog. One of our interns picked up on the story Friday night on Twitter.'

'I'm sorry?'

'Is that your case?' She turns to David La Chapelle over there, 'get a shot of the case, Tim. Are you leaving then, Bea?'

'Um.' What I should say is "no comment". But do people say that? Real people, I mean.

Or is it like the time I was berated for shouting "bingo" when I scored a line at Gala in Hackney. 'We don't actually shout bingo, love.' This lady with four games on the go shook her head and her personalised dabber in despair. Eve Storant's pen looks even more menacing.

'Because it seems like you probably *are* leaving.' Her hand remains outstretched, inviting me to shake it. I hold on to my phone instead. 'You got one of the front, didn't you, Tim? Might be worth getting one of that too.' She's pointing at your pull-along dog, toppled over, its nose soaked and dirty in a puddle from where you'd dropped it to the right of the door. I must look at them, like, *what the fuck*, because Eve Storant softens her tone, 'Just a quick chat.' And all I can think of is the child catcher in *Chitty Chitty Bang Bang* with his lolly pops, his chocolate and his cage.

You know how narrow the path is, Mabel. How I've struggled with the buggy, so it's not exactly easy getting me and the case around the child catcher and Tim. I may have caught his foot with a wheel. 'Sorry,' I say, which Eve Storant takes as a way in, asking me what exactly I'm apologising for.

'Where will you stay?' She keeps pace. 'Does your husband – Craig, isn't it? – does he know you're going?' The photographer runs a few steps ahead, walking backwards so he can hone his camera in on me as I…as I *what*? What *am* I doing, Mabel? What will Eve Storant call this thing I'm doing as I walk away from our home with a suitcase and no definite plan?

Is it wrong that I think about my make-up? That I put my phone in my pocket so I can run my fingers through my hair and wipe beneath my eyes because maybe there's smeared mascara from last night when Craig told me he needed space. It had felt like a break-up. And, to be sure I got the message, he went and got a suitcase, 'For you not me,' he said, while I sat by your empty cot wishing I could turn back time.

'I understand you might not want to talk now. But it might help.' Eve Storant's hand cradles mine as she presses her business card into my palm. 'Give you a chance to tell everyone your side of the story.'

I toss the card to the ground.

Eve's eyes narrow. 'Did you get that, Tim?'

Tim nods.

I pause, pick up the card from where I thew it because Mum always had a thing about littering.

'Did you get that, Tim?' I ask, and he smiles this smile that's like one of those hammers American judges use to seal the worst kind of criminal's fate.

CHAPTER TWENTY-FIVE

'Bea!'

Scanning the parade of passengers exiting the doors of the station, I hear Kim before I see her and sense a smile in her voice as she calls my name again, louder this time. Closer.

'Over here,' she says, and I clock her, sitting on a bench in the shadow of Shrewsbury castle. My heart shifts, not a leap exactly, but a flit of relief that my friend was, despite all that's happened, prepared to drop everything and travel three hours on a train to see me.

'You're actually here.' For something to do that's not looking directly into Kim's too sympathetic eyes, I reach for the chocolates in my bag. Of all the food she's written about on Edible, Maltesers get the most column inches by far. 'For you.'

'Comfort food?' Her face brightens when she stands and moves into the sun. 'Great minds.' She nods her head at the seat, where her reusable cup, which I see through the sip-hole is filled with tea, stands next to a miniature pot of honey. 'It's a tad literal, I'm afraid.' She takes a hold of, and squeezes, my hand. 'I'm sorry, Bea.'

'*Sorry?*' We sit. 'For what?' I take a sip of the tea.

'For not picking up on what's been going on with you.'

People – utterly, blissfully oblivious people – mooch or scuttle past us up the hill into town.

'I didn't exactly give you many clues. Seriously, you have nothing to be sorry for. I mean, you came all this way because of one pathetic text.' It's true. I'd sent Kim a photo of my packed bag this morning. Within minutes she replied telling me she was on her way.

'Just so you know, this trip ooop north wasn't only for your benefit.' Her left thumb fiddles with the giant diamond of her ring.

'Have you spoken with him yet?'

'Adam?' There's resignation in the way Kim says her husband's name. She shakes her head. 'We saw each other briefly this morning but, honestly, not to make light of your shitstorm, mate, but if ever there was the perfect time for me to have an altruistic excuse to leave London…'

'So, we're two sad girls about town then?' I attempt a laugh as she edges closer to me. 'I hope you used those long hours on the train to plot the perfect escapes from our respective dramas?'

'If only. I guess we just have to trust ourselves to do the right thing.'

It's not Kim's wisdom that moves me. Or it's not *only* her wisdom but the combination of those words and her hand which, as she talks, comes down heavy and decisive on my thigh. It's that multisensory double whammy, then, that spins me back in time to that Fun Day Out when Mum was still here to answer those Big Life questions about what, in a moment of freezing panic, is the right thing to do.

'Should I eat it or not?' I'd asked her.

Despite her exhaustion, on the day we purchased the bluebell seeds, Mum had insisted we stop at the garden-centre café for lunch. She ordered a salad she wouldn't eat. Revenge, she said, for all those barely touched meals she and Dad bought for Matthew and me at service stations when we were kids. On her plate that afternoon were three slices of untouched brie.

I love brie.

'Well? Mum? Should I eat it?'

She pushed the plate towards me on the table. 'It's cheese, love, how much damage can it do?'

God knows what the official line is now, Mabel, but back then soft cheese – like wine and running – was not considered safe for a woman with child.

'The midwife said —'

'Oh, for goodness sake. I've had two pieces, Beatrice. It hasn't killed *me*, and the cancer growing in my body probably makes me as vulnerable as your baby. I say, if you want the cheese, having the fucking cheese.'

'Mum!' Unlike *your* mother, Mabel, *my* mother was not usually one for swearing.

She shrugged. 'It's the cancer.' That phrase had become her stock response for any words or actions that fell outside the realms of her usual conformist behaviour.

'The *fucking* cancer, you mean.'

'Yes, love. Precisely. It's the *fucking* cancer.' Her fingers were in the leaves of the uneaten salad by then, pulling at the cheese. 'Open wide!' She was laughing. No, she was giggling, which is different. More childish. More fun. She wedged one slice of murderous brie onto the end of her fork, which she swooped in a loop-the-loop across the table. 'Nnnnneeeeeeeeeeeeaaaaaaaaawwww! Coming into land.'

It was infectious, that childish fun giggle. And her instruction impossible to ignore. That brie, perilously gooey, stuck in delicious rebellion to my tongue.

'There. That's sorted.' Mum's smile carried sixty-four years of wisdom. 'There will be millions of decisions, love, you just have to make them.'

'But what if I make the wrong one?'

'Ha! Not *if*, Beatrice. There is no *if*. As a mother, no doubt about it, the majority of decisions you make will, according to at least one bystander, if not several, be wrong. But it doesn't matter because even when your decision *is* wrong, most of the time, it will do. Motherhood isn't an exam. Though sometimes you will feel like you're utterly failing.'

'Is that how you felt when I lost my virginity to Adrian Johnson?'

I'd expected her to bristle, but Mum kept smiling and shook her head. 'There were harder times than than that.' She swept invisible crumbs from the table. 'I'm sorry, I don't want to bring the mood

175

down. All I'm trying to say is that there is no grade for perfection.' The reassurance, then, of her hand upon my thigh. 'You'll need to trust yourself, love.'

And I did. Sort of.

Until none of my decisions would do.

Was Aunty Pat right? Should I have stayed?

I could go home, tell Craig there is no way that I'm leaving.

Or I could run for the Shropshire Hills.

Though there is a third option.

We may have joked my dad's girlfriend was only volunteering in the hospice to nab herself a widower but, in truth, it always looks like Dad gets a lot more out of the relationship than Connie.

Case in point, he's been practically shacked up at her place for well over a year.

Tell me, Mabel, what is a respectable amount of time to pass before a widower bunks up with his late wife's carer? Six months, you reckon? Try three. Though it's hard to be mad when you genuinely have no clue how he'd cope without her. Have you seen your granddad trying to fry an egg?

In the wake of Mum's death, we rolled our eyes about inept men and the dawn of ready meals, and I arranged a cleaner and talked with Dad about the benefits of an online shop. My sister-in-law Tanya and I laughed about the probability of us or the grandkids ever receiving a birthday card or Christmas present from Dad again, not because he didn't love us but because he'd lived blissfully unaware of all that backstage work that goes into running a family.

Behind every great man, Mabel.

It's a generational thing, I'd say and invite Dad as often as possible for dinner. He wouldn't want to encroach, and we'd tell him he wasn't, that we liked having him over, and sometimes he'd come, sometimes he wouldn't. And on those times he didn't, either Craig or I would pop by with two-portion Tupperware I'd prepared to see him through. Only it turns out it wasn't just me ensuring he had his fill.

I'd caught them one evening when I'd run over with some chilli and rice and seen Connie at the bedroom window, a pair of hands appearing around her middle, a little too eager on the buttons of her polka-dot blouse as she drew the curtains against the light.

'He's screwing Connie!'

But what was a tabloid headline for me was apparently unnewsworthy for Craig. 'I thought you knew.' He at least had the courtesy to frown, to bite his lip, like, *shit, babe, I would have told you.*

Dad took me aside a few weeks later. 'Beatle, you know how much I loved your mum. I'll never love anyone like her.'

But.

He waited 'til she was dead, I suppose. That's something.

And, honestly, I don't begrudge him, Mabel. I'd rather see him fed and happy than starved and grieving. But it did mean I hardly saw much of him alone after that. There was no space in which to talk freely about Mum. And maybe I wouldn't have done anyway.

But.

Dad's always with Connie is what I mean. His and Mum's place sits mostly empty. Might it, then, be somewhere Kim and I could hide out? Where she could decide what to do about her husband, while I wait for mine to decide what to do about me?

* * *

I hadn't worked out exactly what I was going to say to Dad. Enquiries about the functionality of a tap or whether I've cleared the gutters aside, he's never been one for questions. It was possible, then, that I could reference "small private matters", and he'd simply tell me to knock myself out, stay as long as I like, and hand over a full set of keys.

But when I called him from the bench I was sharing with Kim at Shrewsbury station and asked if he'd mind me kipping at his for a few nights, Connie insisted the pair of them come over and help me settle in. When Kim and I arrive, it's Connie who seems settled. She's "sorting" the kitchen while Dad sits on the sofa scrolling through Twitter and Instagram, downloaded to his phone for the sole purpose of ascertaining exactly how accurate Aunty Pat was in using the word "vilified".

'Oh, Beatle,' Dad says.

I can't resist looking over his shoulder.

There's:

@MsTWBF is everything that's wrong with mum bloggers. Narcissistic, opinionated and under the false impression that anyone gives an actual shit about her life #someoneshutthiswomanup

There's:

If only @MsTWBF's mother had aborted her #abortMsTWBF

Each comment or tweet is a link in the chain of a gathering mob. Their circle is drawing in.

'Who *are* these people?' Connie's still stocking the fridge with "essential supplies" though her voice carries through to the sitting room. Like her, it's always big and full of life, which is a good thing obviously. It's what Dad needed when he'd been so hollowed by death. But right now, I could do without her fervour. 'Do you know them?' She appears with a tray full of biscuits and cups of tea.

Mum's tray.

Mum's cups.

She rests a hand on Dad's arm.

Mum's husband.

I know, I know. Who am I to be so judgey?

Kim takes a cookie. 'Depends what you consider as knowing them.'

She's right. I mean, how well do you know somebody you follow on socials. You may learn, via character-limited thought bursts and well-placed gifs, their views on Trump, #MeToo and puppies. You may even have shared the odd DM about how best to ignore the screams of / entertain your child on a long car journey, or which offers of help from your mother-in-law stem from a genuine desire to make your life easier versus those which are likely a subtle dig. But have you ever actually met these people? Shaken their hand or kissed their cheek? Clinked a glass together or known their name without an @ before it?

'I suppose what I'm really asking is, do they matter?' Connie's not even being facetious.

What she's suggesting, isn't she, is that they don't.

My honest answer, though, would be yes. They *do* matter. Because it's down to them that I have sponsors, Mabel, that we've had a few weekends away, some complimentary babywear, an invitation to write for a decent magazine about life as a twenty-first century mother. They've made me feel like I have something to say, something worth listening to and that – before this obviously – I was no worse at mothering than anyone else. They've said I'm funny and creative and lucky to have a daughter like you and a husband like Craig, all stuff I've needed to read when I've felt like running. They matter because, yes, as narcissistic as it sounds, they've unknowingly built me up with their likes and their comments when my instinct has been to knock myself down.

@MsTWBF is a #fraud

And there's nothing worse than being a fraud, right, when your social-media success relies on being authentic.

I sit down next to Dad on the sofa. And although he smiles and pats my knee, I can't read him, can't tell if under that soft untroubled exterior, he's brewing embarrassment, disappointment or fear.

At least the keyboard warriors are clear in their feelings.

'Leave them, Bea.' Kim's right, of course. But it's not so easy to close the apps and let the conversation die down without me. 'It's only Craig and Mabel's thoughts that matter.'

Trouble is, unlike Twitter, Craig is one for silence. He needs it, he said, has always said when it's come to our quarrels, which haven't been many but have occasionally reached a mute ferocity that's far worse than the few times we've full-on shouted or collapsed in a bundle of screams and tears. Not only mine. Because Craig isn't one of those pent-up men. He will let his feelings be known. But when the stakes are high, he mulls things over, returning later with his considered response so we can 'discuss what's happened like we actually love each other. Because *that*,' he'd said last night, waving his hand loosely at my laptop, or at the Tonight Will Bea Fine logo stuck to its lid, 'that did not read like we actually love each other, Bea. It read like we're kaput.'

Kaput.

It isn't a word I'd heard him use before.

But then, neither has he heard me use the word regret.

Not in that context anyway.

At least the suitcase Craig had fetched me from the attic, the one now sitting in the living room at Mum and Dad's, at least that's the smallest of the set of three, which suggests Craig meant it when he said, 'a few days'.

'It's a few days to think,' he'd said into my hair, his lips never quite a kiss on my crown. His voice had been kind, though less so a few minutes later. 'It's like the move from London all over again.' His keys clattered against the door handle as he turned in that way people who are leaving but still have something to say do, 'The way you just did it. Without so much as a fucking consultation.'

He might have revelled in me being a muck spout, Mabel, but your father's swearing last night was different. His *fucking* had no comedic or sexual intention. It was born of pure frustration. With me.

You and he will be home from Grandma Alice's now. What did she say to him, do you think? When Craig went there last night having cared for the woman who aborted her grandchild? Did she tell him about The Slap? How he deserves better and isn't it lucky she and Jim moved up here after Mum died because, well, at least there will be someone to help him look after you, Mabel, now that I've upped and left. I'm ad-libbing obviously.

'You know you can stay here for as long as you like, love.' Dad's voice hasn't altered since I confirmed the gory details about the abortion, the gin, Peppa Pig, Polly Parrot and her crackers. I don't mention the failure of contraception to protect a woman from nature's will and no one else mentions how three men on Twitter are now debating whether a foot, fist or dick in my mouth is the best way to shut me up.

'Do you need any painkillers?' Connie's already rummaging in her bag.

'The cramps aren't so bad now.' It's true. They've been too brief, I think, wishing the aches and stabs more painful and the bleeding more profuse. I wish too that I could rewind. Not the two and a bit years I usually wish for because just a few weeks would do. If I could rewind to the night I conceived our second child, there'd be a chance I could work things out. That you and me, Mabel, would be OK.

I was trying.

In the face of Craig's desires – not for me exactly, rather for a second you – I was working on damage limitation, erecting defences in the shape of a coil in the hope that if we could survive the next few years with no further demands made of me or my body maybe the existing demands might soften.

My point is, I have not been irresponsible. I recognised the thin ice on which I was dancing and took precautions, attempted to protect us from any additional weight. I'd seen how the witch struggled to keep a hold of everything on her broomstick and knew how easily she dropped things. I didn't want any of us to fall. But the coil failed and the burden was too heavy, cracking the thin ice and plunging us into the freezing water in which we are now all drowning.

'Thank you, Dad.' I'm not sure he understands what this means to me. A place where I can hide out. A place where I can bleed and drink tea. And, maybe, a place still enough for me to lift my head above the water to breathe.

Once they've left, I pull out my phone.

Lord of Men @LordOfMen75
@MsTWBF needs hunting. Show her what it truly feels like to regret

I bolt the front door. Is this really a safe house? It might be made of bricks and mortar, but with a way-in via Insta and Twitter, it may as well be made of straw. And not the gold kind. If anyone comes hunting, they could easily blow it down.

CHAPTER TWENTY-SIX

'They'll write it either way, you know.' Kim pauses as she bangs the tray of ice on the kitchen side to release a few cubes. They whisper, like Eve Storant's possible story, as she drops them into the glasses. Mine is filled only with tonic. I've too many reasons to be nervous of gin.

'Here, make yourself useful,' she says, passing me a lime and nodding at the knife block. 'If you *are* going to talk to her, you need to think very carefully about what you want to say, how your words might be twisted.'

'Surely she can't make my words any worse than I made them already.'

Kim gives me this look, like, *I wouldn't bank on it.*

I said no when she suggested a gin. Not only because the leaflet Sarah had given me warned against it, but the idea felt like a kick in your teeth, Mabel. Or like a party, which is ridiculous, really, but there's something so fun, so frivolous, about spirits at five. I'd usually wait until eight, right? When you're sleeping. When it feels like reward. But at five, the prospect of a cocktail felt like the one night Craig and I have had together without you. The trip we'd planned with Della and Nisha to London. Like old times: a games night with Hannah and her boyfriend, Ichiro, who'd we'd not yet met but was big-deal enough that she'd moved into his place in Balham. So much for those malibu-fuelled rants about people who lived south of the river. We never know, I suppose, who we'll love, or what we'll do for them. What we won't. Thing is, Della got some stomach bug, and I knew, I *knew* when I told Craig she and Nisha weren't going, it'd be enough for him to pull out too.

'We'll make a night of it here instead,' he said. And I'd have told him how old Craig would have been desperate to go, reminded him how opposed he'd been to leaving London but being shattered wasn't conducive to being persuasive. So we stayed home and waved goodbye to you from the doorstep as Grandma Alice strapped you into her car. Before we'd even stepped back inside, Craig was suggesting a Happy Ever After.

Spirits at five? It was a party. For two. We were free.

Only we weren't. Because you were everywhere. Your stuff and your smell and, of course, your *Mummy Mummy Mummy*, which had washed itself into the walls of the house like the sound of the sea in a shell.

I remember closing my eyes, Craig asking, 'Tired, babe?' And me telling him *yes, yes*, and wondering if maybe this was the time I might dare mention it, what exactly I was tired of and how I love you, Mabel, but.

By 5.30, though, Craig had mentioned a second baby four, five times, all with a wink and a nudge and a 'maybe we could practise, eh?' And even though I said things like *not yet* and *let's enjoy Mabel before we rush into another*, even though I suggested we wait a few months until you were settled at nursery and I felt more like myself again, even though I kept closing my eyes, he assumed it was merely the usual kind of mother's exhaustion.

I willed him to ask me – genuinely ask me – if I was OK.

Thing is, if he had, would I - knowing my out-of-kilter feelings might screw things up between us – have dared to say no?

As it was, he asked nothing, so I said nothing, and we drank and laid down together in the quiet obligation of a night alone. Not much of a party – or freedom – after all.

Kim doesn't raise her glass. Out of respect, I think, to you, Mabel, to the situation, which is not a celebration, even though this is what

I've yearned for, isn't it? An evening without the clock-watching over dinner and bath and story and bed.

You'll be in the kitchen now, your pesto-patched limbs stretching from your highchair for the knives, for the hob, for anything we keep at a safe distance because, despite our warnings, you wilfully strive for the dangerous or unobtainable. Daddy will be praising you for your persistence, your sass.

Craig likes your sass. He told me once, as I checked the cupboard for what we did and didn't need in the online food shop, that he takes your moxie as a sign that we're raising a girl who won't be constrained by stereotype.

I hope he's right.

'Maybe you should try writing down what exactly you'd say if you *do* speak with this Storant woman.' Kim puts a pen and notepad on the table, pulls me out a chair.

The words won't come though, not the grown-up ones I'd need for Storant, because it's almost time for the witch's hat and her ginger plait. Will you giggle like you usually do when Daddy reads the lines? Will you call for *Mummy Mummy Mummy* to do 'witch witch'? I must be convincing as that witch, Mabel. And yet she is so resilient. She suffers a loss – a hat, a wand, a bow – and gathers up the pieces, takes on more – a dog, a cat, a bird – carries on flying regardless. What would Craig say? About my likeness to the witch? Or if you ask him where I am? Or why I'm gone?

'Do you think he'll be kind about me?'

'Pardon?' Kim's head appears from behind her magazine. The monthly food supplement from the weekend broadsheets she bought to read on the train. The sort we stopped buying, Craig telling his mother the decision was environmental, which maybe it was, because there's nothing more wasteful than untouched papers ditched in the bin.

'Don't worry,' I say, because what do I expect? Of Craig, I mean. Do I really expect – or deserve – kindness? From him? Or from Eve Storant and her story? Or from you, Mabel? Not now necessarily, but when you're older and all this is relayed to you, or you put our names into Google and…

Your bath water will be running. The hot tap to a three-quarters turn, the cold to half. Four-minutes-thirty on the clock. Precision since Daddy left it too long, and I slipped on the overflowed foamy wet of the floor, screeching 'Shiiiiiii…bbles.' 'Shibbles,' I said because, despite accusations to the contrary, I *have* tried to stop myself from cursing. And what I have tried too is to turn the shit into something like fun. It was catching. *Shibbles* became the word for all things gone awry. When I drew you that rabbit that looked like a sick dog: shibbles. When we were so close to making our train I touched it as it pulled away from the station: shibbles. When you didn't wait for the potty and took a crap in my shoe: 'Double shibbles, Mabel! Triple, quadruple mega shibbles!' 'Shibbles,' we sang, as we thanked god for the solidity of your poo, for its tip-ability into the loo. And for wet wipes. Because I love them, Mabel. Literally. And I love shibbles too. How it sounds. How it feels in my mouth. How your eyes squint when you say it. How you relish it. How it's become this thing among the three of us like the straw and gold was for me and Craig. I love how it gives me hope because I coined it, and it's happy and ours and, unlike so many other things, I wouldn't change it, Mabel, not one bit.

'You alright?' Kim puts her magazines with the others – a neat pile – on the table and looks at the empty sheet of paper in front of me.

'It's bath time,' is my only explanation. She nods, that's all. Like she doesn't think this is a contradiction, this missing you, this wondering if you're shouting 'splash' or 'duck' or – Craig'll hate me even more if you do – 'K'sake'.

'You could go home,' she says. The same line from Aunty Pat would be laced with judgement, brushed with an intent to shame. But from Kim it's mere suggestion. A reminder that my options are still open. That, unlike the abortion, other things – my (in)ability to mother you, perhaps – are not yet set in stone.

'Tomorrow maybe. Craig needs time,' which is true. But what's as true as that and as true as me missing you is the appeal of a long hot shower without being on call, the sleep on my own terms, the liberty to leave a room without explanation or a toddler at my tail. I am sorry, Mabel, for this. This un-mother part of me and how, for the moment, at least, she wins. 'I'll Facetime though.'

I stand at my teenage-bedroom window and hit call. Two men with a pug walk hand-in-hand up next door's driveway. They kiss on the doorstep. One of them crouches to further rumple the dog's wrinkled face in goodbye. The other guy's hands are already reaching for him when he stands, the lead slack as the pug sits patiently while they kiss again. A full on kiss this time. A kind of missing-you-already.

God, those kisses. That longing. The reluctance but necessity of letting go.

'I love you,' I say to the answerphone, not meaning to pause where that other word would have followed, though it sits there anyway, right where it's always been.

My phone beeps with an alert.

Lord of Men @LordOfMen75
Bitches like @MsTWBF need taming

Irritated now, the pug pulls this way and that as its master keeps his eyes on his boyfriend until he turns the bend in the road.

My neighbour and his dog head inside, apparently unruffled by a lone hooded figure standing on the corner. But it's not them the figure was staring at.

It was me.

* * *

'Na ah ah!' I snatch a can of beans from Kim as I come into the kitchen, persuaded by common sense that the person outside was an innocent passer-by because my life might be all sorts of messy, but I am not in a crime drama. @LordOfMen75 and his ilk are unlikely to take their abuse beyond the insults online. 'Let *me* do that. It's the least I can do.' A small kiss on Kim's cheek. 'A thank you for coming all the way up here in my hour of need.'

'Tit for tat, innit?' She pulls a bunch of fresh basil from her canvas tote, 'You came to London for me, remember?' and deep inhales the herbal waft as she tears the leaves with her fingertips.

'Barely.'

Kim nods her head from the cannellini beans to the colander on the side and then to the pan already slippery hot with oil. 'Rinse the beans first.' Her gently assertive tone is reminiscent of my mother who had issued similar instructions from exactly the same position by this stove.

It's nice to be told what to do, to feel the comfort of being in safe and tender hands.

When I tip the can, the beans tumble into the heat, and there is a hiss and a cloud of steam.

Kim can't resist stirring them with a wooden spoon she pulls from the drawer. 'Let them crisp a little.' Our hips bump as we stand side by side at the counter, Kim demonstrating how to slice the jarred red peppers as thin as those ribbons you love me to tie in your hair. 'As good as sex,' she says, licking her thumb tip, raising her brow.

'Speaking of…' I reach into the cupboard for another pan, which Kim places on the ring. She turns on the heat as I add more oil, in quiet wonder at how easily the two of us move around and with each other, how with so few words we've created not just dinner but a team. 'Are we going to talk about Adam?'

The peppers sizzle.

'I know you struggle to get your head around the non-monogamy, Bea, but it's really not the sex that's the problem. The problem isn't even that Adam had sex with *Sophie Green*.' The way Kim says the sommelier's name though... 'OK,' she concedes when I give her some wide-eye, 'I'd rather it hadn't been Sophie Green, but it's very feasible Adam genuinely didn't realise exactly who she was until the sex part was done.' She tips in the basil and, as the leaves begin to darken, adds the beans from the other pan, carefully mixing everything together before dishing it out onto the two plates I've put on the side. 'The burrata,' Kim says and then, while I'm cutting the bag, draining the liquid, 'My issue's with how on the Saturday morning, he didn't think beyond the moment to what *we* usually do together on a weekend. Instead, he just went with *her* flow.'

I place cutlery and glasses of water on the table as she breaks up the cheese. 'Isn't that kind of the point of opening up though? So that you can do these things with other people if you want?'

She sighs as she sits down. 'It's not meant to be a free for all. I know how it looks to the outside, like anything's fair game, but there are limits, rules, even, in what we're trying to do.' Kim dips her head, not embarrassed exactly, but less of her usual pluck. 'I dunno. Maybe there's something to be said for just doing "normal".' She makes air quotes with her fingers then shrugs. 'I mean, we took a vow, didn't we? Promised to forsake all others.' Her eyes pop as if in legitimate fear of being struck down. 'My grandmother was there when we made those promises, and she's scarier than any fucking god.' As she loads her cutlery with food, Kim shrugs, and a pepper slides from her fork to her shirt. 'Crap.'

I go grab the Fairy Liquid and some kitchen roll, start dabbing at the stain on her top.

'It's oil good,' she says, visibly cringing.

'You know, a counsellor might suggest you punning at inopportune moments is a form of deflection.'

She arches her brow. 'And the same counsellor might draw a similar conclusion about you and Tonight Will Bea Fine.'

'Touché, Kimberly, touché!'

She drops her head into her hands. 'Jesus. The state of us. When you were a kid, did you ever think adults were this screwed?'

'God, no. My parents, Mum especially, were the epitome of even keel.' It comes out as fact, but I wonder now if it's entirely true. There were tears sometimes. Hushed conversations. A flash of concern in Dad's face on the rare occasions Mum would ask for some peace or some time.

'What I wouldn't give for straightforward.'

'Hey, you know what I do with Mabel when things start to spiral?'

Kim lifts her head to look at me, like, *go on*.

'The park.'

'The park?'

'Yep.' I grab Kim's coat from the hall. 'You need to take advantage of this Shropshire air, mate. Not too long and you'll be back in London with all its NO2 in your nostrils, wishing you'd made more of your opportunity to properly breathe.'

I hold my own breath as, a few minutes later, we approach the corner of the road. Release it only when it's clear that no one is there.

'I can see why you moved back here,' Kim says, when after quarter of an hour's serious striding, we reach the Quarry. 'It's beautiful.'

She's right, Mabel. In the fading light, the river is the colour of Mum's Christmas silver, and the broad expanse of grass on which you've so often tried to turn cartwheels echoes the stretch and freedom of the great American plains.

These aren't what brought me home though.

I haven't told Kim about Mum. About her cancer. About her dying. Because just as our friendship has reminded me of the person I was before motherhood, so too has it reminded me of the person I was before loss.

'You think *this* is nice,' I loop my arm through Kim's, 'you should see the Dingle.'

'The *what*?'

It's closed, of course. The gates to the sunken gardens are always shut long before dusk.

'We can come back in the morning?' Kim suggests as I poke ineffectively at the lock.

'Fuck it.' A rush of abandon incited perhaps by our location. These ancient trees had been witnesses to the loss of my virginity, to that visceral need I felt for the first time beneath their canopy. No matter how momentary, there was freedom here then. And until the graffitied scrawl in the girls' loos, there'd been a lack of shame too. 'Let's climb over.'

'No way! These are one-hundred-and-fifty quid jeans!'

'And our need for relief from the shitstorms of our lives is priceless.' I drop to one of my knees. 'Here, I'll give you a shove up.'

'This is ridiculous.' But Kim's doing it anyway. Hands on the top of the gate, her left foot in my palm, and I'm about to propel her when, 'Hold it,' Kim says. 'You know if we get caught, it'll be me that takes the flack. Out-of-Town Black Woman Breaks into Local Park.'

'Better than the headlines Eve Storant's got in store for me.'

'About that,' Kim says.

'Not now,' I tell her. And before I can fully calculate just how much trouble I'll be in with the head at school if someone *does* catch us, she's up and over and in.

'Storant could actually help, you know.' Kim says, when I've also scaled the defences and we're making our way down beside the sloped flower beds towards the pond. 'I get that how your regret was made public is...' Her smile as she searches for the right word is like Baby-Group Tina's: subtle and kind and sorry. 'Well, it wasn't the best. But I wonder if it was delivered in a different way whether it wouldn't be so much of a bombshell.'

'I wouldn't bet on it.' A voice as creeping as the night cuts in.

'What the —' Kim spins on the heels of her boots.

'Shit.' I pull her clenched fists down with my hand, which is as clammy as it was the last time I saw the face now staring at me, hard and bitter, through the dark.

* * *

'You?'

'You know this woman?' Kim's body may no longer look battle ready, but her tone suggests she's still primed for repelling a foe.

'We're old friends.' Bryony Jackson's eyes scorch as hot as the Bunsen burner in our year-eight science lab when she joked about setting fire to my hair.

'*Friends?*' And I wonder, then, should I relay to Kim the rumours Bryony spread about me and Adrian Johnson, about the pleasure she took in watching me squirm. No need though, I imagine. Surely she's about to witness first hand a resurrection of my *old friend's* devastating verbal blow. How with a few words she can shrink me to the size of the gum she used to pluck from her mouth and flick with her thumb and finger to the floor.

It was inevitable, I suppose, that she'd return to torment me now.

Kim's unfurled fingers capture mine in their grasp.

Bryony pulls her phone from her bag. And I get that breaking into the Dingle probably pales in comparison to my other recent sins, but if she's about to expose us for this too then —

'Your blog,' she says.

Here we go. I brace myself for the insults, the accusations, the jibes. What I'm not ready for is Class-A-bitch Bryony Jackson's tears.

'Bryony?' I let go of Kim and move closer to this grown-up version of the girl from whom I'd so frequently hidden in the graffitied loos, unsure now if I dare put an arm around her shoulder because twenty-odd years ago, woe betide anyone who insinuated Bryony was anything but solid as stone.

'I'm sorry.' In a bid for an ounce of dignity, she smears her nose on her sleeve. 'I read the post and…went to your old house…wanted to talk to you, but…' Any control she gained of her voice is gone again as her body curls in on itself, the way mine used to when she was so sharp with her tongue.

Kim offers her a tissue and a bottle of water from her bag. 'You're OK,' she says, even though we all know from her uncatchable breath that she isn't.

Bryony lifts her head. 'I was there ages. Waiting. And then I saw you leaving the house, but…I couldn't figure out what I wanted to say. And it's fucked up. I *know* it's fucked up, but I hid and then…I followed you.' Her voice is on fast-forward now, rushing through how she trailed us. 'Like I was in *CSI Shrewsbury* or something.' Her eyes catch mine. 'I didn't expect you to jump the gate though!' She laughs, and I see it, then, a glint of the girl I knew in school.

A moment passes, and Bryony gestures to a bench, where she turns, her face severe again, and tells me: 'I know.'

In another tone it might have been ominous. The same way it was all those years ago when her knowledge was power underscored by a threat to tell. This time though, the way Bryony says it is recognition blotted with a crude, almost helpless shame.

I sit down next to her.

On her phone is the screenshot of the blogpost that fair-gamed me on Twitter. 'What you said, about how your daughter robbed you.' From her bag she takes her purse and from her purse she takes a photo. Two dark-haired children in one of those posed pictures shot by a professional in a studio. The white background gleaming against the bright yellow fabric of their matching plaid shirts.

Normally, I'd say, 'cute,' because that's what normal mothers want to hear, don't they? But I get the sense Bryony's not a normal mother. I get the sense, Mable, that Bryony is a mother like me.

Something scuttles in the bushes behind us. Animals, maybe, who feel safer to come out now it's dark.

'Teddy.' She points at the younger of her sons, whose two front teeth are missing. He's grinning regardless. 'He won't stop crying. He's almost three. I thought this phase would be over by now.' She rubs a thumb across his cheek. 'He's up every night from two 'til four just screaming screaming screaming. And Nick, my husband, he works in York three nights a week.' Bryony sighs as she slides the photo back into its pocket. 'Is it awful that I wish he'd take Teddy with him?'

I shake my head because, *no.* Wouldn't anyone, no matter how good, how natural, have their limit?

'I'll give you two a minute,' Kim says, shining the torch app on her phone and heading in the direction of the pond.

'Was that you?' I ask Bryony. 'Earlier? Outside the house?'

She nods. 'I didn't dare knock. Didn't know what the fuck I'd say. Because once you say it…'

'You can't take it back.'

'Exactly.' Bryony heaves a giant exhale. 'I got in the car once,' she whispers, 'when Oscar was sleeping, and Teddy was doing his usual. I got in the car. Nick was away. But I got in the car and drove.'

I wouldn't wish this feeling on anyone, Mabel. But listening to Bryony is relief. And knowing I'm not the only one stings like the prick of a needle sewing a single stitch in a wound.

CHAPTER TWENTY-SEVEN

'Her husband was furious when she told him.' A few hours later, Kim and I are brushing our teeth in the bathroom. 'And I get why. I mean, they were tiny, there's no way Bryony should have left those kids on their own, but sometimes…' I stop brushing so Kim might actually understand me. 'Sometimes it's not rational.'

'He didn't get it then? Her husband?'

'Course he didn't. He was off three nights a week. Didn't have to do the day in and day out of it but instead came back all excited to see them.'

'Absence makes the heart and all that.' Kim points at our reflections in the mirror. 'We're like an old married couple.'

'You joke but living with you might be easier than living with Craig and Mabel.'

'I have my habits too, mate. Living with other people is hardly ever straightforward, is it?'

'I guess not.' I picture that flat on Fremont Street. The excitement as Craig and I made our first joint trip to Ikea. We barely knew each other, and yet there we were, thankfully with similar taste in cheap art and unnecessary storage solutions. We were still playing then though, or at least that's how it feels with hindsight. Giant kids with spacehoppers bouncing through Victoria Park. By the time my mother was sick, and I'd returned to Shropshire, Fremont Street seemed like a pretend sort of grown-up. 'You should have seen us when we were both living with my parents. Now that was a lesson in living with other people.' I remember Mum still so chatty in the bed we'd moved into the dining room. 'And dying with them.'

'*Dying* with them?'

Shit.

'My mum died. A couple of years ago.'

'Oh. Bea. I'm sorry.' And I'd rather Kim just left it there, but. 'Was she able to meet Mabel? Before she passed?'

'Once.' Even I'm surprised by the bite of it.

I spit out the foam and open the cabinet looking for facewash. A bottle of Lancôme Trésor sits on the shelf.

My heart is a jackhammer.

'You OK?'

'Speak of the devil.' The angular bottle is almost full of amber liquid that sets off a panic even greater than the gin. 'It's Mum.'

'It's your mum's?' Kim's use of the possessive is right, of course, because it is Mum's, but the perfume *is* Mum too. Until those last few days in the hospice, I never knew her with a different smell. It's the smell of school-drop-offs and goodnight kisses. It's parties and elevenses and a nip to the corner shop. It's worry and joy and 'for god's sake, will you *please* just turn that music down.' It's a matinee of Les Miserables in London and a nurse's visit at home. It's fruit and vanilla. It's shepherd's pie and peas. It's sitting in a car with a promise that things will be fine. It's watching an old Victoria Wood show on VHS and crying with laughter at The Ballad of Barry and Freda. It's listening to *The Archers* and sobbing when Nigel fell off the roof. It's the beach in France when she squeezed lemon into my hair to make it blonder. It's the ballet lesson in Shrewsbury when I wouldn't let go of her skirt. It's books, hugs, bikes and baths and singing Alanis Morrisette in the kitchen. It's every moment I ever spent with her, and it's here, *she* is here, in the palm of my hand.

'Bea?'

All I have to do is spray it.

But.

Despite how gentle I am returning it to the cupboard, the glass bottle clatters against the shelf.

'You heard anything more from Adam?'

Kim's eyes are all, *that's it then, is it? We're done talking about your dead mum?*

I try to make my eyes all, *yes*.

'A voicemail.' Her fingertips rub her face cream in circles across her cheeks. 'He's asked if I'll go home tomorrow.'

'And?'

'*And* I'm staying here with you for a few days so *no es posible para me ahora.*'

'You speak Spanish?'

'Honestly, what you just heard is the full extent of my Spanish.'

I splash my face with water.

'Maybe I could take a Spanish lover and learn how to say "adios" to Adam.'

'Or…' I turn away from the mirror to face her head on. 'You could learn how to say, "let's hammer out the details of how exactly we can best get weird".'

She pulls this face, like, *I don't get it*, and pads in her slippers to the landing.

I follow. 'You saw what Adam put in your guestbook for your birthday? That Alain de Botton quote?'

Kim nods.

"Intimacy is the capacity to be rather weird with someone – and finding that's OK with them."

I want to be forever weird with you, Adam wrote.

'Come here.' I hold out my hand, take her into my room where we slip under the covers, clutching pillows on our laps like two lovelorn teens at a slumber party.

Kim tips her head back against the headboard, as if she might find answers to her woes on the ceiling. 'I dunno, Bea. Maybe Adam and I should never have got married.'

'Maybe. Or maybe you need to focus on the fact that you were never going to do marriage the way the rest of us do it. Remember what you told me when you first mentioned opening up?'

Kim shrugs.

'You said one of the exciting things was that you were getting to write a new script. That it was forcing you to really think about your boundaries.' I ditch the pillow, twist my body round to properly look at her. 'When we got back from the park, while you were in the bath, I did some listening.'

'Listening?' She kicks the duvet off with her feet. 'I thought you were marking those essays on Frankenstein or some other Gothic shit.'

'Busted.' I hold up my hands. 'But as Craig wants me to stay away for a few days, I won't have Mabel tomorrow, which means I can do some marking then.' Got to grab those silver linings where I can.

'So what were you listening to?'

'A podcast. About non-monogamy.'

'OK.' Kim's brow shoots up. 'Now you have my attention.'

'Honestly? It made me think about why I felt so odd about it when you first told me. This woman was saying how perhaps people find the whole concept threatening because a lot of us have entered into monogamous marriage without ever really questioning whether it's what we actually want. Like, we do it because that's what historically people have done.'

Kim wide-eyes me, like, *well duh, isn't this exactly what I've been telling you.*

'But you and Adam, you've dared to think beyond that. You've dared to find something that works for you, and just because there's a glitch doesn't mean you were wrong to try it. Maybe it just means you need to keep reassessing those rules.'

The radiator gurgles as the heating kicks on with the timer. I'd meant to change the settings. The house is already unbearably hot.

'It's like when Della met Maxine, her first girlfriend. She said how different it was sleeping with a woman than a man because it made her question what sex really is. Like, for straight people, it's so easy to think about it in terms of penis plus vagina equals sex. We know the story, right? How it *should* go. But suddenly Della was, I dunno… she and Maxine were asking – like *really* asking – what each other was in to. It wasn't just a case of that same end goal. She was forced to think about what it was she liked and wanted. It's different but…'

Kim releases her bottom lip from between her teeth. 'No,' she says. 'I see what you mean. I suppose Adam and I never specifically agreed what time we'd come home if we slept over. And while we did say we wouldn't have sex with friends, we didn't think about those broader circles of connections and how easily boundaries might be blurred.'

'So, maybe despite having a modern marriage, what you need now is an old-fashioned conversation.'

We sit for a minute or so in the near dark.

'Are you laughing?' Kim prods my arm.

'Just thinking about what my Aunty Pat barked at me this morning about marriage being a compromise.' I remember her pursed mouth all those years ago when Della told her she was bi. 'She's not exactly open to unconventional. I can just imagine her reaction if she thought the compromise of marriage might be sleeping with someone else!'

'And *her* marriage was perfect, was it?' Kim cocks her brow.

'Let's just say rumour's rife that my cousin Nikki isn't my Uncle Andrew's only child.'

'But your aunty stayed with him?'

'Til death did them part.'

Kim looks at me, like, *you see*. 'So, consensual non-monogamy is a no-go but if your husband does it behind your back, then just plod on.'

'Yep. Though she *was* glad to be shot of him. I swear, there was a new Pat that rose from her husband's ashes before we'd even left the crem. I hadn't seen her grin like that in years!'

'Good for her.' Kim toys with the ends of her hair and looks right at me. 'You're right, Bea. Just because we entered the institution, doesn't mean we have to play a rigid game.'

Kim's words don't leave the room with her. Rather, when she goes to bed, that sentiment of rebellion lingers. Because isn't that considered anarchy exactly the deal your father and I made in Vegas? Not about sleeping with other people, but in vowing that in our marriage we'd never be slaves to its old-fashioned rules?

In the two days after our wedding, we saw maybe six, seven other couples in similar throes of honeymoon bliss. Neither of us acknowledged them, fearful perhaps, that they were evidence of our alliance not being so unique after all.

I told myself, it's not how it starts, it's how it progresses. I told myself our particularity will be in how we act day to day. I told myself we will not conform to cliché. And yet when Craig asked me why I couldn't bear to have a second child yesterday, I told him it was because I already have two.

He's not a child. Not really. But for all my faults and failures, Mabel, who assumes the bulk of the grown-up responsibilities? The caring, the cooking, the cleaning, the necessary 360 thinking of getting things done. I suppose, my point is, as I – by all accounts a good old-fashioned mother and a good old-fashioned wife – look after you and your father, is there anyone within the confines of this institution of our marriage truly looking after me?

We thought we had it sussed. But our habit of rushing headlong into life-changing decisions without truly considering the consequences didn't begin when we chose to have you, Mabel. It was like Della said about sex and relationships, we know the story, right? How it *should* go.

Should.

Marriage. Babies. They're the *done* things. And sure, Craig and I talked the talk about doing them differently, but there was never any real discussion about how. Turns out people do discuss it though, Mabel. My Google search re non-monogamy proved it. Couples *do* actually ask each other more than the obvious questions about sex and fidelity and kids. Couples *do* actually ask each other about what they *could* do, rather than simply accepting what they should.

MONDAY 15TH APRIL

CHAPTER TWENTY-EIGHT

'You might want this.' The warmth from the cup Kim passes me could be your hands in the morning, Mabel, when they reach over the bars of your cot and the heat of you on my neck is sticky and instant. Though the caffeinated sip's a subtler hit than your face in my face and the first *Mummy Mummy Mummy* of the day.

I do miss you, Mabel.

I miss your morning smile, which normally comes no matter what, delayed a few seconds or minutes maybe if I've kept you waiting or Flumper has fallen to the floor in the night and is, I've thought when I've seen you stretch for him, like The Old Me, slightly beyond reach. I pass him to you and, just like that, you're happy. Simple really, those needs of yours. Or so they seem from a distance.

'Look that bad, do I?'

'Not at all, I just —'

'Takes two cups usually.' My voice fades as I catch Kim's fingers agitating her phone. 'To make me function, I mean. Two cups or I can't even think abo—'

'Storant's written the article, Bea.'

'What? But I haven't even…' I wanted to talk about it with Craig. But when I tried again last night, he was still refusing to take my calls. I hadn't realised I was fighting a ticking clock.

'Seems she couldn't wait.' Despite the grumble of the coffee machine as it grinds my second cup, I hear Kim's disappointment, see it too when she passes me the evidence, and I catch the photo of me in Ibiza 2003, post A-levels and pre-uni when I went loco in San Antonio with Della and Lisa. It was a different time, Mabel. A different time and a different place, where I would have looked perverse if I *hadn't* been wearing a union jack bikini, fag in one hand, WKD in the other, eyes as blurred as the three, four, five nights before.

My thumb flicks and there are other *me*'s there too. The early-London me, mini-skirted and high-heeled and headed to our Christmas drinks after-party when someone suggested pole dancing on the tube. There's Pride-with-Della me, dressed as a rainbow pirate and kissing my best friend who, the night before, had come out to her nan. Granny Barton had been cool with it, by the way. Hence the arms in the air and our peck-on-the-lips elation. There's blogger me, sitting on the loo with my mobile phone as my baby chews on a cake-battered spatula she's clearly just picked up from the floor. There's space-hopper me, astride my bouncy hopper, grinning like a deranged fool. There's yesterday's door-stepped me, panicked and running from the house, which will read as running away from my daughter. And, finally, there is *Mummy-Mummy-Mummy* me, arms held out for you, Mabel, as you run towards me after your first morning at nursery. My grin is as big as your grin. And I remember my heart leaping as high as your heart because it was such a relief – yes, I mean it – to hold you after your few hours away.

A picture speaks a thousand words, they say. But which one speaks the loudest? Which of these carefully selected pictures in the national press is the best description of this woman, Bea Straw, who "wishes away her daughter despite making a living from being her mum"? It's not exactly true what Storant has written. Yes, I've wished away the suffocating nature of motherhood, but did I ever wish away you? She's exaggerating. Not just the wishes but the money too. I couldn't live on what I make from Tonight Will Bea Fine.

Though it *was* beginning to pay off. There'd been an invite to appear on a podcast, a request to write an article, a hint that I could even be up for an award. And all thanks to you, Mabel.

Storant suggests you're material. My Material Girl, she calls you. Harsh? Perhaps not? Whatever, it fits the tone, which is reproachful because I am not only a blogger, I am a teacher too. Professionally charged with the care and development of children. Am I really the kind of woman, Storant implicitly asks, we want influencing our young? She quotes my blog and its readers, a nod to the sponsors too. There are words like hypocrisy, questionable and shame, and vaguely recognisable names from my school days proffering "close-friend" opinions on why things / I may have turned out this way.

The conclusion of the piece is more tempered, more, *I don't expect you to like this mother, but it's possible she's not the only one.* Storant cites a book and a poll and some stats on post-natal depression. There are comments, but Kim insists I swap her phone for that second coffee, tells me, 'you don't need to read it now,' meaning, *it's not going anywhere*, meaning, *neither are you.*

'That's that then.'

But Kim shakes her head, all, *not necessarily* and *let's not jump the gun.*

'Craig's going to kill me.'

'Craig will do nothing of the sort.' She looks at me as if of all the things I've said, this is the most stupid. 'You didn't even give the woman a comment. Craig'll see that.'

'Will he? Or will he see me looking like a pissed-up runaway lesbian sex fiend who loves to surf social media while having a poo?'

'I think your husband knows you better than that.'

'Right now, my husband thinks he doesn't know me at all.'

She puts a bowl of yoghurt, berries and granola on the table in front of me. 'I hope you don't mind, I rooted around in the fridge and cupboard.'

I shake my head. Any other day, this would be bliss.

'Eat.' There's comfort in the lack of choice Kim gives me, how she presses the spoon into my hand and her palm against my shoulder either to keep me seated or to assure me things will be OK. 'They really scraped the barrel with that picture of you sitting on the loo.'

'I wasn't actually doing a poo.' Obviously, Kim gets the artificiality of a blog post, but I still feel the need to explain. 'Craig and I staged it for this piece I'd written on how parenthood reminded me of double maths when I was fourteen, and I'd use my period as an excuse to embarrass Mr Hayes. Seriously, one flash of a prettily wrapped tampon and he'd recoil and let me flee to the loo.'

'I hear your pain, sister!'

'I said we should have called Mabel Algebra. Because sometimes she made me want to hide in a small dark place, only unlike Mr Hayes, Mabel – once she was moving – would always come to find me.'

Kim sits opposite me, turns our phones face down on the table. 'So you *have* talked about your struggle then?'

'You've seen TWBF. I joke about it if that's what you mean. I make light of the dark and then sign off posts with a wouldn't-change-things-for-the-world barrage of yellow faces with exploding brains, hearts for eyes and angelic yellow babies with wings and a bloody halo. Craig always says many a true word is said in jest, but no one assumes you really mean this shit, especially when you cap it all off with emojis.'

'So, Tonight Will Bea Fine… Do you think it was…' The bottom of Kim's front right tooth is stained her trademark lipstick red as she bites down on her lip then smiles, wincing almost. '…A cry for help? I apologise for the cliché, Bea, really I do. I wish I could think of a less armchair-therapist way to say it, but it's quite difficult to form any kind of eloquent sentence with that image of you on the toilet burnt into my brain.'

I pick at the berries. 'They've certainly been very specific in their picture selection. Nothing like Facebook to regurgitate your past and pinpoint the worst of you.'

'The one of you and Mabel is very sweet.'

'Yeah.' It's a consolation, but it's also too far behind the other photos. First impressions and all that.

'And how about...' Kim's eyebrows rise into an apologetic hint at her persistence. 'You know, my cry-for-help theory?'

'I dunno. It's a nice twist on it but, honestly, the blog was just something to do that wasn't changing nappies or weeping slash swearing into a pillow.' Or thinking about my mum and that one time she got to hold you, Mabel. Or how she left me to cope with all of this on my own.

Because no matter how many people gathered around me, it *did* feel like I was on my own.

We sit.

It occurs to me how very good Kim is at not fussing with the gaps, how so often our need to make things better means wadding the conversation with anything to show you're listening, to show you understand. Kim doesn't wad. She waits.

'Writing it *did* help sometimes, I suppose. To make me see the funny side, I mean. Because I promise, despite what I said, it's not all doom and gloom. I *do* love Mabel.'

Another untampered pause.

'I do, Kim. I swear my life on it. It's just en masse, the whole motherhood thing is... I don't know how to explain it. It sounds stupid, but I always think it must be like when my granddad fell from his bike and hit his head on the pavement. And after that, he had this constant ringing in his hear.'

'Tinnitus?'

'That's it, yeah. Some days it wasn't so bad, but others he'd go mad with it. As I say, it's not always awful, but the endlessness of it is what gets me, the lack of control. How every morning I wake up and feel powerless because it's always going to be there. And I do love her. I do have times when I think if I can just get through this next phase, to nursery, to school, to the age when she doesn't need me quite so much, then maybe I'll stop thinking about what could have been.'

'There's no parallel universe though, mate. Believe me, if there was, I'd be taking a peek and seeing how things are working out for the Kim who stood up to Mrs Hogarth, my year nine form tutor who put me – and *only* me – in detention almost every time there was a disagreement in class.'

'What were you? The class rebel?'

'No. The class Black Girl. The school Black Girl really. The one Black face in a sea of white. And Mrs Hogarth was the school racist. Or one of them. Anyway, for a whole heap of reasons beyond my thirteen-year-old self's control, I decided it wasn't worth me battling it out with Mrs Hogarth or any of the other bigots back then. And I've no choice but to work out how best to move on.'

'I'm sorry you had to go through that.'

Kim shrugs. 'I either dwell on what *could* have been or I focus on what *can* be done. These days, I call things out. What you need is to figure out a way to live with what's happened that is more than just looking back with regret.'

Thing is, I don't need to look back. I just need to look at my phone. While Kim makes herself another coffee, I Google my name plus "mother" plus "regret" and it's right there. Storant's piece. A complete fucking disaster. How do I best live with that? There are suggestions in the comments, of course. *Suck it up. Keep your mouth shut. Crack on.* But there, in the midst of the cries of selfish snowflake claptrap, there are kinder ones too. *Seek counselling. Keep talking. Be strong.* There is also one admission of similar feelings.

'You're not a monster,' "Old Friend" has written. 'You are not alone.'

CHAPTER TWENTY-NINE

Craig's leaning with one foot on the pavement, the other propped against the café wall, eyes glued to his phone. Blue jeans. Grey T-shirt. Hair messy but styled to be so. Dress, casual. Face, serious.

If this were the first time I'd seen him, would I fancy him?

Do I fancy him now?

I *love* him, Mabel, because he's my husband, and he's funny and kind.

But.

People talk about baggage, about what we bring with us when we come to a relationship. We are never new, never fresh. We are always a little hurt, a little chipped away at our edges. But what of the weight, the scuffs we craft together? In a marriage – a traditional one – everything is pressed into everything else. The subsidence of passion coaxing a gentle imbalance, in turn coaxing hairline cracks, which may, of course, be nothing of concern.

But.

Would the cracks be the same or different without you?

'Hey, you.' Craig's stance is suddenly awkward. No longer leaning but upright, with his stiff and uncertain limbs. 'Must be the fifth time I've read it.' He flips the phone so I can see the Daily Mail piece glaring from the screen.

'Doesn't get any better.' And I'd know. I've read it at least ten times over.

He shrugs his shoulders, like, *funny that*.

'You know I had nothing to do with it.'

'That's not quite true.' There's this quick snuff of air through his nose before his eyes up and down me. 'It's dominoes, Bea. You tipped the first one.'

'I guess.'

I think I would, you know. Stripped of our self-inflicted damages, I think I would fancy your father. I would want him.

'I thought – *hoped* – Mabel might be with you?'

'And yet you still came?' Paddington's hard stare is nothing by comparison to Craig's. 'Despite the possibility of having to behave like a mother?'

I've no right to be riled, but. 'That's not fair, Craig. When we spoke earlier, when you said you'd come, I said then that I wanted to see her.'

He has this look like, *who the hell do you think you are*, and I wonder when exactly it was that I lost him. Because it's not just this, right now in the door of our go-to café, where they make our favourite coffee in town. It's not just his face which is puffy and unshaven and his mouth which is open as if wanting, but not quite able, to tell me to go, to not come back, to get the fuck out of his life so he can renew his search for his Happy Ever After. It's been happening for a while, hasn't it? The straw in which we bound ourselves has slowly been coated with oil, and we didn't notice the slip, the coming undone of us.

'Where is she?' I play it down.

'With Mum.'

'Perhaps we could pick her up, and I could come home. Even if it's just for an hour or so.' *Keep the tone light, Bea.* 'Or I could come later? Put her to bed? Read her *Room on the Broom*? I could leave after? Unless you wanted me to—?'

'I've told her you've gone away for the week.'

'A week?'

Craig doesn't say anything, just pushes the café door, which I catch as it swings back toward me, suddenly aware of how mightily such a small gesture can roar.

I manage a smile at our usual waiter, 'Two lattes, please,' and take a slice of the lemon and almond cake, Craig's favourite. I put it between us when I sit down, sliding it left then right, forward then back, until it's dead centre. 'Two forks.' It doesn't pass me by how absurd I must seem as I wave one at Craig.

When she was over the shock of it, Mum had said it wasn't that she wasn't there for the wedding that bothered her, not really. 'You need to know someone before you get married,' she said. 'It's only been nine months. Is that really enough to know?'

'I *know*,' I said. And I did, Mabel. My love for your father wasn't like God or magic or something else that requires a sense of jump-in-the-dark belief. It was a fact as tangible as rock. 'You don't need to worry,' I told her. 'When have I ever been one to fail? You're looking at the fastest woman in the world on a spacehopper, remember?'

We'd done it. And it was *we*. It wouldn't have happened if it wasn't for Craig. Pushing me out of bed in the early mornings. Timing my laps around the park. Sticking pictures of Ashrita Furman and Bipin to the bathroom mirror so I'd be reminded at least twice daily of my – *our* – goal.

And it wasn't only the physical effort. There was admin too. Independent adjudicators, timekeepers, witnesses, an officially measured track and an un-adapted readily available spacehopper. One Saturday in August, I hopped a mile in front of a crowd of friends, family and intrigued bystanders, who actually whooped and chanted as I bounced by. That was the me I first became with Craig. Less afraid of exhibition. And it wasn't that I'd been a quiet child exactly, but I'd definitely blended. A gangling chameleon adolescent who'd stand back rather than jump in and risk everything, anything, for fun or love or a moment of mad-as-a-hatter-glee. What I'm trying to say is there was a security in being with your father that set me a little bit free.

Evidence gathered, verified and submitted for approval by the World Record authorities at Guinness, I was, by the time of our return from Vegas, declared officially victorious. And I don't know, Mabel, if it nudged me up the rankings of Mum and Dad's proudest parental moments, but what I do know is that it felt fucking amazing to have found this man who got me, who had my back, who pushed me when I needed pushing and was there in an inflatable spacehopper costume to mop my red and sweaty brow. It was cheesy as hell, but I felt it, how there's no I in team.

When Craig doesn't take it, I place his fork by his hands, which are clasped, his right thumb rubbing up and down his left, his gaze headed out of the window, where a couple walks by, their arms looped, her belly protruding through her jacket, their smiles so confident, so naïve.

You wait, I think. *You'll see.*

I don't know what to do but eat. I wish I'd not bought it though. Cake is obviously too sweet for this meeting, which would be better served with…I don't know what. Chillies? Sliced. Red. Raw.

'I'm your husband, Bea. You *do* remember Vegas?'

'Of course I remember Vegas.' A flash of our held hands, the rings we swore we wouldn't buy but did anyway. 'Cheap. Tongue-in-cheek,' we'd said. Oh and the thrill when he slid it on my finger! Another piece of the puzzle clicked.

I cut a second wedge from the slice because what else to do with my unheld hands but use them for eating cake.

'I know it was supposed to be all unorthodox and everything.'

I smart at the irony of it. When, aside from that first year with Craig, have I or we been anything but orthodox?

A few months after we returned from Vegas, we "upgraded" the tacky plastic rings for white gold.

'But it was still a wedding,' Craig says. 'We still made promises. And I still assumed that marriage made us a team.'

'It did. It does.' Though, he's nailed it, hasn't he? What we were. What we're not. And yet it sounds like he thinks I'm the one who dismantled our merry band of two. Crumbs spill down my chin. In another time, he'd have caught them.

But.

'Liar,' he says. Not loud but somehow still screaming.

The curd would temper the bitter lemon, but I can't bring myself to dip the cake in it.

'Liar.' It's a whisper this time, but the repetition is a root, puncturing the core of us, writhing itself in.

'Please,' I say without really knowing what I'm asking.

Another mouthful.

'The regret is one thing, Bea. That's something we could have talked about. Something I could have helped you with. Something I'm sure we coul— For god's sake, will you stop with the fucking cake?'

'Sorry.' I mean it too, though the cake is all but gone.

'The regret we could have dealt with.' Craig snatches the plate. Then, as if reminding himself to be calmer, places it gently on an empty table. 'But the baby. *Our* baby.'

'You came to the clinic though. I thought you —'

'Let's not pretend you hadn't already made the decision, hadn't already taken the first pill.' He looks across at me, his silent wet mourning seeping through the fractures of his hard stare.

It's *my* body, I think. But there's no way of saying it because any way I try will sound like I'm sure he's wrong, which I'm not. There's no way I could have had the baby, no way he could have talked me round, and it *is* my body, and in theory it *is* my choice, but.

'I was…' What was I though? A thesaurus of panic and nerves?

'You were what? Drunk? Again. Sorry? Again. What was that word you used the last time, Bea? That was it, *compelled*.' And where there was seeping sadness, there is now volcanic gall.

'The last time? What do you mean the las—?'

'You have form is what I mean. Of acting alone. Of making life-changing decisions without me.'

My silence, my confusion, my I-don't-know-what nudges the tectonic plates of his fury so he can no longer say the words but must spit them. 'When you left London, remember?'

'I didn't keep that a secret. I told you.'

'Exactly. You *told* me. There was no talking about it, no possibility of another way. It was *your* wa—'

'My mum had cancer, Craig. I neede—'

'I know your mum had cancer. I was there. Because I came, didn't I?'

'Eventually.' It surprises me how quickly the rage I thought was drowned now floods my bloodstream.

'Your two lattes. Let me get that sugar from over there if you need it.' The waiter, this guy Rich who knows us well enough for this to be even more awkward, is already bringing it over when I tell him it's fine.

'Thank you, but we're fine.' I repeat.

'You reckon?' Craig tilts his head to Rich like, *can you believe this shit?*

The noise Rich makes as he collects the empty plate isn't even an er or an um but an embarrassed swallow as his eyes flit anywhere but the two of us. 'Give me a shout if you need anything.' He attempts a smile, which I'm about to reflect, but Craig's bolstered suddenly, all chin up, shoulders back, hands pressed flat on the table.

'You know what, Bea, I'm not sure you feeling *compelled* to leave London was even about your mum.' If he's waiting for me to challenge him, I'm not doing it. This isn't what we're here for. 'It was about *you*,' he says. A pause, a moment of goading, but I won't allow myself to bite. 'About you being seen to do the right thing. About being the martyr who gave up everything to go nurse her dying mother, when, in reality, you hated it.'

'I didn't hate it.'

I hate it, I'd said, down the phone and then again when I saw Craig in person. I said it, I know, but it was the cancer I hated. The way it was stealing my mum. That was what I hated, wasn't it? 'I didn't hate looking after her. I may have complained about it when I came home to see you, but you know how hard it was, what it was like.'

'Yeah, woe is you, right?'

Who is he, this man that is shaped like my husband but using words like sharpened pencils to rewrite our history in spite?

'Little Miss Perfect doing all that nursing while your brother carried on like normal, swanning in with chocolates and beer and the occasional tear over how awful it was seeing your mum like that. I know the story, Bea. I heard it over and ov—'

'I tried so hard to keep things normal. I came almost every weeke—'

'Sure, but you were disinterested.'

'I wasn't disinterested. I was knackered. There's a difference.'

He's less venomous now. Sadder and maybe sorry for what he's saying but bowling on and saying it anyway. 'All you talked about was your mum and dad. It was as if my life, *our* life, the one you always claimed was the most important was suddenly bottom of the pile.'

'Apologies for being preoccupied. For not being the doting wife you wanted.'

'What I wanted was for us to be together. What I wanted was for us to be like we were.'

'That was impossible.'

'And I realised that. That's why I suggested a baby.'

'You didn't *suggest* a baby, Craig, you *demanded* one. You told me you'd only move to Shropshire if we could turn it into our next adventure. A new life, you said.' And not in a metaphorical sense, Mabel, nothing as simple as a change in career or scene. The new life your father had made me promise to create was you.

216

'I should never have agreed to it. My energy was already spent on Mum.' And *you*, I want to tell him. Because when I'd begged him to come to Shrewsbury, it was with the hope that when he did, life would be easier, that I wouldn't feel so torn in two. But he wasn't a help, Mabel. If anything, it was harder. Because rather than lessening the load, he made it bigger. Another mouth to feed. Another person's working hours to accommodate. Another human demanding so much of my support and my time.

'I was breaking.' I'm determined that my voice doesn't break now too. 'I am not an endless bank of...' I don't know what to call it, whatever energy it takes to care. 'I have limited resources, Craig. My decision to leave London was about being better able to look after my mother, and my decision to have an abortion was about being better able to look after Mabel. And me. And you.'

'Me?'

He doesn't see it, does he.

The screech of the chair as I stand cuts through the silence of the café like your cries in the night, Mabel.

'That's it, leave,' Craig says behind me. 'It's what you're best at.'

And maybe he's on to something, because there's a crack of relief in my chest when I do.

CHAPTER THIRTY

Bottom of the pile, my arse. It was eleven weeks I was in Shropshire without him. And I went back to London seven, eight times. I would have gone more but – and I know Craig made it sound like it was some kind of excuse – I was on my own up here. I'd been right, it wasn't just Mum that needed me. Dad, who'd been so scared but calm at the point of diagnosis, had convinced himself that Mum was falling for this man, Robert, from her Myeloma support group in Wolverhampton.

'She's obsessed!' The ice cubes in what looked suspiciously like an Old Fashioned clattered with the glass as Dad swallowed heavily. I resisted the urge to point out how he'd better watch it, Mum had not long ago given me a lecture on afternoon drinking. 'According to Caroline, even this man's myeloma is smouldering.'

'That's the medical term for it, Dad. Mum wasn't implying Robert's cancer is sexy.'

'I know it's the medical term, Beatle. I was being facetious. I think the stress allows me the right to be facetious from time to time, don't you?' The stress was allowing all three of us to be a little unlike ourselves. 'I just wonder if your mother doesn't want a bit of excitement after all these years.'

'Dad, please!' Though Mum *had* made some hint of it, not about Robert – I mean, Christ, that didn't bear thinking about – but a smudge of regret for all the time she'd wasted. Though when I pushed her for more detail, she just smiled and thanked me again for everything I was doing.

'You're a good girl,' she said, igniting that pinch of familiar uneasy pleasure that comes with doing the right thing.

And the right thing then was working as a supply teacher a few days a week and, on the other days, food shopping, batch cooking, cleaning and washing to give Mum the rest she so obviously needed and Dad the ability to taxi her to and from appointments without the added anxiety of taking on all these new jobs I'm not even sure he was aware existed. In the evenings, I made calls to Mum's friends and your Uncle Matthew, who I asked to visit on the weekends I was back in London, not because I didn't want to see him, Mabel, but because he'd made it clear how busy he was with his work and his wife and his two kids and so it made sense, right, that he should make the journey only when it was necessary.

Oh, but when he made that journey.

I came back once to find him breaking down takeaway boxes for the recycling. There was a bucket list on the kitchen side.

'Cool, eh?' Matthew caught me reading it just as I got to "Kālua". 'What's this?'

'Go big or go home, I reckon.' He was laughing, 'It's a Hawaiian thing; Mum and I saw it last night on YouTube. They roast a pig in a pit they dig outside.'

'I meant the list.'

'Oh, my bad. I suggested Mum write it. Figured we need to do something super special for her, yeah?'

'That's what I've been trying to do.' And it sounded so whiny, I know, but bollocks to the grand gestures because I was in the thick of it and, yeah, it would be awesome to dig a pit in a Hawaiian garden and shove in a pig if that was Mum's dying wish, but someone had to cook the regular meals in the meantime and that someone was never fucking Matthew, was it.

'Glory hunter,' I muttered.

Thing is, while there wasn't much glory in the day to day grind of the caring, there was reward in it. A simple one really: I got to know my mum.

And I liked her. I *really really* liked her.

My point is, I did my best for Mum, for Dad *and* for Craig, who came to Shrewsbury only twice by the way. And the second time was mainly to offer up his "plan".

'I always said I wouldn't raise a kid in London. So give me the reason to leave London, babe.' Craig was grinning, excited. Blissfully unaware that looking after me while I looked after my mother should have been reason enough.

CHAPTER THIRTY-ONE

'Del, it's me. I just met with Craig and…I know this is totally fucked up, and I'm really sorry. For not talking more to you about all this. But…Did you see the thing in the *Daily Mail*? Today? With that photo of us at Pride? You never did like that picture. Good job they pixelated your face, eh? Anyway…Can we talk? Shit, I've gotta go. Aunty Pat's on the other line. Will you call me…? Please?'

I let it ring a couple of times, pretend like I've actually got it in me to ignore Aunty Pat's call.

The mattress gives perfectly beneath my weight so I am slightly cocooned when I answer.

Aunty Pat's voice kicks in to the quiet of my teenage bedroom, which Dad has said is mine as long as I need it.

I wonder if a lifetime would do.

'Well, that's not done you any favours, has it, duckie?'

'Ugh, so you've seen it then?' The duvet comes down soft and dark on my face, the faint peony, jasmine, or summer breeze of a long-ago wash pressing against my nose, the cotton cover rising and falling with each breath, which becomes warmer in the shadows of my den.

'Of course I've seen it. Jeannie from 15a was over with her copy of the *Daily Mail* and a packet of Bakewells before I'd even finished doing my Davina.'

'Your Davina?'

'McCall, Bea. My workout. Anyway, besides the point. It's dreadful. The article. I know you wrote some terrible things in that blog of yours, but the picture that woman paints of you is awful. Awful!'

No matter how tight I pull the covers over my head, daylight seeps through.

'Kim didn't think it read too badly'

'Kim?' Her name's a question. 'The *coloured* girl?'

Coloured? And, *Jesus*, the way Aunty Pat lowers her voice when she says it.

'That *influencer* friend of yours? Well, I'm not sure she should be *influencing* you, Bea. When Connie mentioned this Kim would be staying with you at your mum's house, I looked her up. Have you seen her latest instalment?'

'Funnily enough, I haven't had time.'

'Well, thank god the *Daily Mail* hasn't cottoned on to the fact that you've moved in a with a swinger.'

'She's *not* a swinger.'

'She certainly comes across as very spicy. The press would have a field day with that.' A sigh. 'All this would make your mother so sad.'

I remember what Kim said, about calling things out. 'And what about her sister being a tad racist.' Can you even be a *tad* racist? 'Would that make Mum sad too?'

'*Racist*? Me? Don't be ridiculous, Bea. I'm always very nice to Mrs Chopra. It's your recent behaviour that would have your mother turning in her grave.'

I can picture her. Mum. Eyes closed, mulling it over. It's what she used to do in my teenage years when Matthew would scream how much he hated her. Every inch of her skin and bones. She would close her eyes as if the darkness would black out his spite, or at least allow her to rise, weightless, like an astronaut above it, and the words that would follow would be as unhurried and temperate as an astronaut's walk through space.

'Caroline was such a wonderful mother to you. She'd have wanted you to be the same for Mabel. She would want you to go home, duckie.'

'That may be, but I can't. Not yet. And if you're only calling to tell me that and how dreadful and terrible and awful my mothering is compared to my mum's, then there's no need. I already know.' It's the bluntest I've ever been with her.

The silence that falls between us is a kind of stand-off. Like the staring competitions Matthew and I used to have in the back of the car as kids. It was me who'd blink first, not because my eyes couldn't take it, rather my nerves couldn't stand the building tension.

'All I was trying to say is that Kim thinks some parts of the article are quite sympathetic.'

'Mmmm. The post-natal depression bit maybe. At least that suggests you're not evil. Just mentally ill.'

'*Evil*? Why would you even use the word? And I am *not* mentally ill?'

'Your drunken ramblings suggest otherwise.' Another sigh, this time a cumulonimbus, dense with an unleashed storm. She slow inhales, maybe smoking or maybe counting to five in her head like I do, Mabel, when my brain is a shriek needing calm calm calm. I try to match it, her long breath out, try to find some common ground in the air.

'I realise you'll probably say no.' Aunty Pat is measured now. 'But your best plan is to see the doctor, get some anti-depressants and go home.'

'I don't want anti-depressants. I'm not depressed. Not like that anyway. And I keep telling you. I can't go home. Craig doesn't want me there.'

'Don't be silly. Of course he does. A man can't cope on his own with a child. And despite everything you've said, you're still Mabel's mother. She needs you.'

'I don't know if I can—'

'You don't know if you can what exactly? What is it you find unbearable?' There's no pause for breath for me to answer though. Aunty Pat ploughs right on. 'I'm not saying motherhood is easy, duckie. It isn't. But you love Mabel, you said so in that blog. And when you love someone, you make whatever sacrifices necessary. That's what being a mother means.'

'Sacrifice?'

'Yes, sacrifice. You only had to look at how long I put up with your Uncle Andrew. I didn't stay because I loved him. I stayed because I loved Nikki. Because of all the many things that make being a mum worthwhile.'

'And what about how worthwhile it is being a wife?'

'A *wife*? What's that got to do with this? You need to stay focused, Bea. Stay focused on Mabel and all will be well.' Aunty Pat is in her stride now. 'I'm sure of it. You'll go home. Everything will return to normal.' And her words, which she clearly believed would sound like magic, instead sound like the finality of a slammed prison door.

When I end the call, there's a message.

Craig: I wish it hadn't gone like that. I'm sorry. I'm doing my best. I wonder if we should talk to someone?

If we did though, Mabel, what on earth would we say?

* * *

It's the path, I think. That's what I should have said to Aunty Pat when she asked what it is I find so unbearable. Because for a while it had seemed so unique, so removed from what everyone expected of me. I was raised in a mould, see. And don't get me wrong, Mabel, I got a buzz from growing so perfectly into it. I liked the smiles my well-ordered behaviour and ambition would garner, how it felt to have a plan. College. Uni. Teaching position. Management. Headship.

Marriage. Two kids. A house with three bedrooms, maybe four if we moved out of London. It wasn't extraordinary. But then I met your father and, well, your father was. Extraordinary, I mean.

Craig was a different kind of rhythm.

We met we fucked we loved we travelled we hopped we gambled we wed we danced we bathed we gave we took we soared we looked. And the world was open wide.

And what it was, I think, is that we were so unlike anything either of us had experienced before that we assumed what we had wasn't only different from our own previous experiences but from everyone else's too. Something in our mix cracked the mould. It made me think we, *I*, could be more.

There was no need to prove it, of course, but wouldn't it be wild, we thought, as we gambled in Vegas, to do it for laughs, for irony. So, our stretch-limo drive through the Chapel of Happy Memories was a self-assured middle finger to all those other fools who thought they knew what they were doing but were so much more likely than us to come apart. We were a new fucking breed. We were smug is what I mean.

But no matter how much Craig and I believed our relationship was something out of the ordinary, the relationship enabled the marriage and the marriage enabled the baby. And the baby...

We would be different kinds of parents, we'd said. Well, I got that nailed, didn't I, Mabel?

'I'll move up here, Bea,' Craig's lips pressed the decision into my collarbone as I listened out for Mum's quiet cries from below, 'if we have a baby.' There was something in his tone. That fuck-it, let's be spur-of-the-moment crazy abandon we'd shared in Vegas, as if what he was offering was steeped in untamed romantic jeopardy, as if the seed hadn't already been sewn during a dinner in Shoreditch and over long-distance telephone calls in which I'd fretted as much about what was left of our relationship as about what was left of Mum. His proposal had so much future in it that I lapped it up.

Because elsewhere, time was closing in, the nurse had said so. Months, maybe a year, if we were very lucky.

Craig's was a future-filled solution and so I breathed again, saturated in the relief of one tragedy averted. I thought, when I imagined a child, our Happy Ever After would be OK.

* * *

'Well, it allows you some thinking time,' which is basically Kim's way of silver-lining the fact that I've been told to steer clear of school. It's not only my family that's ashamed of me. Though what Evans actually said in her email is 'following discussions with both HR and the Governors about your recent blog post and the subsequent article in the national press, we have agreed it best that you take a leave of absence from school while we investigate the matter further. As you know, we ask all our staff to maintain a consistently high standard of personal and professional conduct. We are, at present, not fully confident in your ability to meet this requirement.' She'll be in touch, she says.

There's nothing from Jackie, Head of English, in response to the email I sent last weekend about covering for Paula.

The irony's not lost on me, Mabel. That one of the reasons I didn't want a baby was because of how much I wanted the job.

I withhold from replying to Evans, one hundred per cent certain the words pummelling my skull right now would contravene her guidelines on appropriate language.

TUESDAY 16TH APRIL

CHAPTER THIRTY-TWO

The number's withheld, the caller posh and confident. When she asks whether I might be interested in appearing on *Sunrise* to discuss my recent blog post about regretting motherhood, her tone assumes that of course I will be because it's television. Even her pauses are exclamation marks.

'You've created quite a stir, Bea.' And I wonder whether this girl, who introduced herself as Polly from Sit Up and Smile Productions, uses everyone's first names, if it's some trick in her practiced art of persuasion. 'We'd love to hear how you feel about the backlash.' She holds her quiet intake of breath like an ellipsis. 'Not that you haven't received a lot of support too obviously. And what we at Sit Up would really like is to give you the opportunity to explain to your critics —'

'My *critics*?'

'Oh. No. There won't *be* critics. Not here. What I meant was...' Her self-assuredness is suddenly as rustled as her notes. I can hear her slightly panicked scramble through the pages but, when she speaks again, she's as cocksure as before. 'What we're thinking at the moment is you'll be on the sofa with Peter and Emma.'

'Peter and Emma? As in Peter Mason?' It's not like I have time to watch *Sunrise* but, even so, I'm not oblivious to Peter Mason's bullish reputation.

'Yes!' She says, like, *I know right! Peter Mason! What an honour!*

I try to imagine it. Me on the sofa with Peter Mason.

Polly's elongated and enthusiastic 'Soooooooooo,' is a *well, that's sorted then.* 'I'll get Felix, our researcher, to call you back, shall I?' But before I can answer, 'He'll run through exactly what we have in mind and how we'll handle your travel etc. OK then, Bea, great to chat with you. Thanks for your interest.'

Interest?

'I'm not sure I even showed any interest,' I say to Kim who, mouthful of the butternut and chilli soup we made together this morning, opens her eyes wide, like, *go on*. 'I mean, why would I? Craig would never forgive me. Aunty Pat though…' I imagine her face if I do it. 'Let's just say while Peter Mason's views get most sane people hot under the collar, that ruddy-faced gammon gets Aunty Pat hot elsewhere.'

'Yeah, that doesn't surprise me.' Kim's perfectly manicured brow is arched to its peak. 'She's quite something, your Aunty Pat.'

'Huh?'

'I've picked up a new reader.' Kim passes me her phone. 'Check out the comments.'

'Oh god, she didn't actually write that.' But she did. Aunty Pat, on seeing a photo Kim had posted from a café in town this morning, suggested Kim might want to try Birmingham on her way home. *You'll find it has more of your kind of food.* I wince. 'I'm sorry. A naïve part of me wants to believe she was trying to be helpful.'

'And you think she was trying to be helpful when she wrote how eloquent I am?'

'Well, you *are* eloquent.'

'Too right, I am. But look at the exclamation marks. She was surprised, Bea. Do people – *white* people – make a big deal of your eloquence on Tonight Will Bea Fine?'

'I don't think the quality of the writing matters when you've been cancelled.'

'Perhaps. But you can be damn sure that the Aunty Pats of this world would be far more willing to give you a second chance than they would me.' Kim takes her phone, Googles Peter Mason. Links to his opinion pieces on Meghan Markle, woke politics and Trump. 'I'm still not sure I'd trust Mason to give even you a fair trial though.'

'Trial? It's a TV show not a court,' I counter, but Kim doesn't look so sure. 'And isn't it like what you said about the Storant article? Before she went ahead and did it without me? It's a platform, isn't it? Somewhere I could say how I feel without it being edited.'

'Well, yeah, but —'

'All anyone can currently see of me, of my thoughts, is a snapshot of that unfinished pissed blog post with no context. Only social media and what Storant's chosen to put out there.'

'If you were to ju—'

'It's like when I said to Craig how awful it was playing nurse. There *was* satisfaction in being there for Mum. It's the same with motherhood. It's nuanced. Not as easy as Mabel being my be-all-and-end-all while everything else falls apart.'

'Everything else falls apart?' Kim puts down her spoon, her bread. Her eyes fix on mine, like, *do you want to expand on that?* But I don't know what to say, Mabel, because, well, where would I even begin.

'This is delicious.' It's true. The soup is thick and spicy and something you would never eat, Mabel.

'You really need to think about the consequences of TV for you though, Bea. *And* the consequences for Mabel. Craig too, obviously.'

I nod, taking another slice of bread, focusing on the butter, on spreading it neatly to the very edges of the crust.

'The exposure.' She pours herself a glass of sparkling water. 'It can be intense.'

'You think I don't know that?'

'TV might make it worse though. Especially TV with *him*. Mr Misogennui's reputa—'

''Mr What?'

'Mr Misogennui…Peter Mason. His reputation isn't exactly built on empathy, and whatever spectacle he makes of you may be difficult to undo. People latch onto hate. You've had it hard enough already, but you need to understand the potential for vitriol is far more widespread than Twitter. '

'But it could be a chance to tell people how I truly feel.'

'Do you really know though? How you feel. Have you honestly figured that out? You've said the regret is about motherhood but…'

'But what?'

'I've just been wondering about the timing, that's all.'

'Of the blog?'

'Of Mabel.'

When I told Della, who was about to undertake a second round of IVF, about Craig's suggestion that we try for a baby, she was elated by the idea of us being "bump buddies". But it was Mum's eyes who shone the brightest with the news.

You read about people needing something to live for.

We all wanted you, Mabel. Don't ever think that's not true.

There were so many things you were born to fix though. And I'm sorry because on even the broadest shoulders those kinds of expectations would be too much to bear.

Craig and I were living with Mum and Dad when I took the tests. Three to be sure. I sat on the loo and watched six lines appear across three windows. We both grinned as he gathered up the discarded packaging, neither of us acknowledging the box of Mum's cancer medication he'd inadvertently knocked to the floor.

And any doubt I had that the pregnancy wasn't perfect timing? I buried it. Though maybe only as successfully as we buried the Hawaiian pig in the pit, which was not successful at all. Matthew soon realised it wasn't as simple as a hole and a body. We needed canvas, chicken wire, chain and rocks. With my mother dying, all that was too much to contend with. So we compromised with pork belly, which was much more conventional. But we made do.

Because that's what happens, isn't it. We take the conventional, and we make do.

'Leave them,' Kim says, as I start clearing the table. The bowls clatter irritably in my hand. 'We can sort them later.' She tops up my glass with water. 'Tell me about your mum?'

'I don't see what this has to do with *Sunrise*.'

If Kim finds my words sharp, she doesn't look pricked by them. 'I only mention it, Bea, because if you go head-to-head with that nob, he's likely to go hard on you.' She wraps an arm around my shoulders. 'I wouldn't want you facing something other than your feelings about Mabel, perhaps for the first time, under that much pressure.' I resist it, the warmth in Kim's voice, in her hold, and she withdraws a little, just enough. 'To be fair, he probably won't even let you speak.' She plays a short clip of Peter Mason mouthing off about vegan sausage rolls. 'Listen to him, constantly talking over his co-presenter.' She flips her phone screen-side down on the table. 'The thing is though, *he* isn't even my main concern. It's the fallout. Yesterday, I wrote a short piece about tapas. I'll admit, it wasn't my finest – my most *eloquent* – writing. But does turning sharing dishes into a crass metaphor for non-monogamy really warrant people calling me a greedy slut? I'm not saying you shouldn't do the interview.' Kim's sigh is as heavy as her boots, which she swings up onto the footstool when we move from the kitchen into the lounge and sit down. 'But you have to know that it doesn't always go down well with the public when women go against the grain. They take it personally.'

She has a point.

I think about my own initial reaction to Kim and Adam's decision to sleep with other people. And that one occasion when I dared to deviate with a Vegas wedding, and how it sent our families into a spin.

In my pocket, my phone sings its cheery ring.

A number I don't recognise.

'Leave it.'

'But what if it's him? The researcher?'

'Then he can wait. You need time to think about this.'

What I actually need is an ounce of control.

'Bea?' A man. Unfamiliar. Smiling. I can hear it in the way he says my name.

'Yes.'

'This is Felix?' There's a pause. As if I should know. 'From *Sunrise*? You spoke with my colleague? Polly? About coming on the show?' Another pause. 'Bea? I *can* call you Bea?'

'I've been called much worse in the past few days.'

'Ah. Yes.'

Ha, the only thing Felix has said that doesn't have the uprise of a question is his confirmation of how badly the public thinks of me.

'Polly says you're keen to joi—'

'I wouldn't say *keen* necessarily.'

'Interested, then? Would it be fair to say you're interested? Because, if so, it might be useful for me to explain how we're thinking your segment will run?' He doesn't wait for an answer. 'Would it help to know there will be another guest? I've been speaking this afternoon with a family counsellor, who was eager to tell me you're not the only one to feel this way, Bea. Are you following the threads on Twitter?'

'Yes.' My tone's a little more razored than I'd intended, but what does he expect? 'Yes, Felix, I'm following the threads. Though, I think maybe what *I'd* call them is annihilations.'

'Ah. Well. Hmmm. There has certainly been some backlash. But there's support there too.' Felix must interpret the quiet noise I make as scepticism because, 'Honestly, Bea. There *are* others. Who feel like you? And *I* think if you speak out in an environment in which you're given a chance to better explain, I do believe that it might help not only you, but other mothers like you.'

Even though he can't see my nod, it's there. Sombre but certain because, well, because last Sunday night in the Dingle, Bryony Jackson held me longer than expected, longer than comfortable even, and thanked me for helping her realise she wasn't alone.

Kim's taken a notebook and pen from her bag.

Call him back.

'It might be that you could speak with the counsellor off air too?' Isn't that what Craig wanted?

'We really would like to support you, Bea.'

Don't make a rash decision, Kim scribbles.

'But I've never been on TV. What if I say something and instead of helping me or anyone else, it just makes everything worse?'

'Listen,' Felix says, in this way that makes sure that I do. 'Let me speak with the producer and see if we can do it as a pre-record. That way, we might be able to fix anything you're unhappy about in the edit.'

Speak with Craig first?

'I'm not sure. My husband —'

'How *are* things with Craig?' It's so strange, how Felix talks like he knows me. Knows *us*. Knows how it's all come apart. 'Bea?'

'I'm not sure they can get much worse really.'

'Well then,' Felix says, 'this is a great way to reach out to *him* too.'

Kim goes again with the pencil: *What questions will they ask you?*

'I was just wondering…What kind of questions would Emma and Peter ask me?'

'We don't have them written yet, darling, but don't worry, there shouldn't be anything you can't answer. I'll see if I can get the producer to let me know so I can send them over in an email along with details of the hotel in London.'

'So I'd need to come to Londo—'

Kim's pencil clatters against the table and she snatches the phone from my hand.

'Felix – it is Felix, isn't it? – Bea would like time to — Yes, I appreciate you need to make arrangements but — Sure.' Kim raises her eyebrows, like, *if you would just let me finish.* 'Thirty minutes max. And this number here,' she checks the screen, 'is the one on which we can reach you when *Bea is ready?*' Pointed look in my direction. 'Excellent.' She doesn't bother to say goodbye.

Her face is all, *And that is how you handle people like Felix.* But, as she places the phone back in my hand, Kim's confidence is punctured by the beeps and flashing alert after alert after alert on Twitter.

'Fuck's sake. What now?' She attempts to take it back. 'How would you feel about deleting them? I'm serious. Not only those notifications but the apps too? I'm not usually one to advocate ignorance but, in this instance, I do wonder if it might be for the best.'

Knowledge is power though, right?

@AWoman4Life
Check out @MsTWBF dressed for a party and necking champagne a few hours after aborting her baby #notimetoparty #regrettingmotherhood #shameonyou #abortMsTWBF

'Fuck.' My heart is one of those tiny planes – a Cessna? – in turbulence. 'It's from Friday night. In the bar in London. When you…'

Too late now, I do as Kim suggested and pass her my mobile bearing the photo someone has found and shared online.

'Shit,' Kim says. 'Insta. I didn't think…'

I'm smiling. Celebrating. And, yes, invisibly yet undeniably aborting.

'It was a dig at Adam.' Kim's shaking her head at the caption. *This is what freedom looks like.*

Fuck.

'I'm so sorry.'

'I didn't drink a drop.'

'I know.'

'I would never have gone out; I didn't want to let you down.'

'I know.'

'I wasn't celebrating having an abortion, I was trying to be a good friend to you.'

'I know.'

'*You* might know, Kim, but look!' The smear my finger leaves on the picture when I jab at my phone is so spot on I could scream. 'You see how this looks. Like I couldn't give a shit. Like I got rid of one baby, posted on a blog about how much I hate the other, then fucked off to the bar and started knocking back the booze. And there I was panicking about some ancient photo of me attempting to pole-dance on the tube. At least that could be written off as history. This,' Kim winces as I snatch my phone, 'this is *now*, Kim. This is how the world sees me *now*.'

A thud as it falls to the floor.

I had a boyfriend once, in uni, who would punch walls when he was angry. Until this moment, I never understood why.

My bitten nails pierce my palms as I clench fists, bumping them against my temples. But they're too gentle, so harder and harder in time with the rocking until Kim breaks the punched beat with her whole-body hold of me from behind.

'Bea? We'll sort it.' But her voice, which is usually reassurance, is so clearly riven with tears that it, this, everything, is helpless. 'We'll find a way,' she says.

'I already have one,' I tell her, jolting when my phone alights with a call from Della that I decline because there's only one person I need to speak with right now.

I search for the previous received call and hit dial, shaking with the fear and fury of my conviction when I tell Felix, 'I'll do it. I'll come on your show.'

'I'm so pleased, Bea.' And he can't possibly have heard the flare in my voice because he's so ridiculously, so childishly, upbeat. 'I really think this could see a change in how you're perceived. You'll need to come into town this evening. I have your email address from the contact page on the blog so if you're still receiving those…?'

'Yep.' I stare at Kim, willing her to understand this is my only hope of control.

'Fantastic. Take the train, and we'll reimburse you tomorrow. Keep any tickets etc. I'll send you the details of the hotel. It won't be anything fancy, but it's near the studio so you'll only have a short cab ride in the morning. How are you with early starts?'

'I —'

'I suppose you're used to those with Mabel, aren't you?'

'Yes, but I —'

'Fabulous. How does all that sound?'

I imagine Craig when he sees that photo.

'Great,' I say, doing my utmost to sound sure.

CHAPTER THIRTY-THREE

'Aunty Pat.' I whisper into the phone, but there's still a tut. This is the quiet carriage. A furious glance is thrown at me from across the aisle.

'Where *are* you, Bea?'

Shit, I should have let it ring out.

She comes again, 'Are you on a train?'

'Yes.'

'Are you on a train, I said.'

'And I said "yes", Aunty Pat. I *am* on a train.'

I wasn't going to tell her or Dad or Della about the train. Or London. Or *Sunrise*. Because I'd tried calling Craig to tell *him*, but he refused to answer, and it wouldn't be right if he wasn't the first to know.

'What a shame,' Aunty Pat says. 'I was going to pop over. I thought we could Facetime with your brother. Congratulate him on his new job.'

'New jo—?'

'A promotion! He'll be based between London and New York. They'll be flying him business class. Twice a month! I told him about the *Daily Mail* article. You should ring him. He's been quite worried about you.'

I don't comment. If he's been that worried, shouldn't it be him who rings me?

'I think it's hard for him, you know. Ever since he and Tanya separated, he doesn't really have anyone to share his good news with. I do worry about him in that flat on his own.'

'He's not on his own though, is he?'

'He's not living with Helen, duckie. They're just dating. And anyway, it's Tuesday. He has the kids after school on a Tuesday so she won't be there. Not tonight. He likes to keep things separate. So the children don't get confused.' Aunty Pat pauses as if this is the point at which I might like to pitch in with a congratulatory note to my brother for bearing his kids in mind when it comes to how he spends time with them since leaving their mum. 'You'll ring him, then, will you?'

'Yes. Yes. Once I get to London.' *Crap.*

'London? Why are you going to London? If you're going anywhere, it should be home. To see Mabel. I know it's probably not my place to say, Bea, but we're all worried. We all want you to be where *should* be. With your daughter.' An inhale. An exhale. A gap I don't know how to fill. 'Can you hear me?'

I can hear how you don't even mention how Matthew's kids figure – or don't figure – in his new jet-setting equation.

'Sorry. You're breaking up. Can you —' I cover the phone with my palm for a second, try not to show too much relief as I end the call.

A few minutes later, I hit the red button on another incoming from Della. 'I'll message her,' I tell Kim, who shrugs, like, *none of my business*, like, *all of this is completely up to you.*

*   *   *

I'm sitting on the bed in the Premier Inn pretending to read, trying not to think of Peter Mason or the YouTube clip I stupidly watched earlier of him getting into a petulant grump about a mother still breastfeeding her four-year-old child.

Surprisingly, Kim had insisted I watch the video to its end. 'I thought this was about you clawing back some control.' She'd taken my phone when I hit pause. 'And while I wouldn't normally encourage anyone to watch this pale, stale, male berate women for his own entertainment, you need to know what you're up against.' She pressed play. 'See how he asks a question but doesn't really allow the guest to answer before jumping back in and offering another of his bygone opinions. You must keep going. Whatever you do, Bea, don't let him talk you down.'

I put my book aside, check for that list of questions the researcher, Felix, said he'd get from the producer but weren't included with the email he sent about the hotel and timings for the morning. Still nothing.

There is a text though, and my heart fires when I see it's from Craig. Maybe he's heard about *Sunrise*. Maybe he misses me. Maybe he's decided we're done.

> Craig: Mum said something about a flag? For nursery?

No greeting. No kiss. No acknowledgement of my numerous calls.

It's European Day tomorrow. You're to dress in the colours of a flag of your choice, Mabel. Take confectionery (no nuts) typical of your chosen country. Know the word for *hello*. Perhaps even decorate a picture of an iconic landmark. We'd talked about France. I'd kept aside your blue jeans, your red cardigan, your white T-shirt. You'd made clear your preference for pain au chocolat over croissants. We'd practised the word *bonjour* and searched on Google for a colouring-in sheet of the Eiffel Tower.

I tap out a reply. The location of the clothes. The pack of pain au chocolat in the freezer. How you'd attempted to copy my handwritten *bonjour* on your pad we keep in the kitchen drawer. The crayoned Eiffel Tower is in your bag already, I tell Craig, reminding him too that he'll need to get you there early; you always freak out on dress-up days if everyone else is there before you.

```
Craig:        Thanks
```

'Fuck's sake.'

Kim looks up from her laptop. 'Mabel?'

'Yes. Well, no. Not really. Craig.' Because it's not you, is it, Mabel? I mean, it's *your* outfit for *your* European Day at *your* nursery, but surely *your* father could have this in hand. 'I get that he's flying solo at the moment, but it's like he can only manage one thing at a time. So he'll do the basics. You know, food – probably something I've cooked and frozen, mind – and bath and a story, but beyond that…I dunno, there's no broader scope for what needs doing other than the minimum to keep Mabel clean, fed and alive.'

Kim tilts her head, like, *that's something*.

'I'm sorry.' I toss my phone on the duvet. 'I know things aren't perfect between you and Adam but at least your problems have something sexy about them. There is nothing sexy about parental labour. Seriously, don't have kids. Even your issues become dull.'

'Adding it to my list.' Her finger runs across the mousepad.

'Your list?'

'Pros and cons. Re having kids.' I shuffle across the double bed we're sharing so I can see what Kim's up to.

'Jesus. You have a spreadsheet!?'

'Yup. I have a spreadsheet for everything else.' She catches my gawped surprise. 'You seriously telling me my tax return, food budget and menu generator are more important than whether or not I want to take on the biggest responsibility of my life?'

I remember the spreadsheet Craig made for The Hop. How could it not have occurred to either of us that a baby might require at least the equivalent contemplation and planning?

'When you look at the data, mate, you can see why I'm still on the fence.'

She's not kidding. There are different tabs. A baby-cost calculator which, Kim tells me, is linked to her regular budget to predict how much additional income she'd need to be making if she wants to maintain her current outlay on entertainment, holidays and clothes.

'Obviously I have to take into account the probable drop in income because of mat leave, and then there's the risk of a reduction in work when I do decide to return because, well, when I got married, some brands felt it their duty to let me know they're not into the whole "mummy vibe".'

'This is unbelievable.'

There's a time calculator too.

'It started off as a bit of a joke.' Kim stretches to the bedside table, grabs herself a can of Coke. 'When I say joke, what I actually mean is a bugbear. You parents don't half bang on about time.'

She's not wrong. I'm gagging for it. 'Honestly? I lust after time like I lusted after a Furby in the Nineties. You remember them, right? Those furry little hamster robot things. Everyone else had them, but when Mum went to get me one for Christmas, Argos had sold out. I cannot express the envy.'

'Oh, I've seen that envy.' Kim closes the lid of her computer. 'You mothers seem to think anyone without a kid has nothing but rolling hours of free time. And that our greatest responsibility is planning our next wild holiday or determining which restaurant is most likely to allow us a table for an entire afternoon of leisurely food and booze.'

'And it's not?' I'm only half kidding.

'How easy for you were the two years before Mabel was born?'

It's tempting to imagine myself pre-motherhood as a bloom of calm and content.

But.

'And god forbid, I ever make the mistake of mentioning a lie-in, you lot'd glare at me then like I just waved a limited edition Furby in your face.'

I bury my head in the pillow. 'Maybe it's because it's late, but I think I'm losing the thread of the metaphor here.'

'Then you need to sleep, mate.'

She's right.

When I turn off the light, I think of how Mum would have talked about tomorrow. How her proper-nouning would have marked its significance. Its potential for danger. Or change. How she would have told me to rest and ready myself for my Very Big Day.

WEDNESDAY 17TH APRIL

CHAPTER THIRTY-FOUR

The little clock in the corner of the TV live-screening *Sunrise* says 7.23 a.m. You'll be up already, Mabel. Downstairs at the table making mess with a Weetabix and spoon. The radio will be playing, and the cat you call Broom Cat will appear at the window.

'Broom,' you'll say, frowning when Daddy tells him to shoo. 'Cat!'

Daddy will sigh. He's not fond of cats, is he? Especially not that one. Because that one hisses and snarls whenever Daddy makes his way to his bike. And anyway, 'Dogs are better. More loyal,' he might say because that's what he says most mornings when Broom Cat trips off to some other window at some other house, where he's more likely to score affection or food.

Daddy likes loyal.

I'm sorry, Mabel, that I'm not there. With you. This morning. With Daddy. I'm sorry that Broom Cat too will leave you, and that at two-and-a-bit, you'll come to understand the opposite of loyal.

I'm sorry.

'I'm sorry,' I say to the soundman attaching my mic, even though it's his elbow that jabs me in the chin.

'Look at Peter and Emma, not the monitor, OK?' It's someone else talking now, the floor-manager maybe. I can't keep track of the job titles in this space I was brought into by the ... runner?

I should run perhaps. Back to Kim who, when I was leaving the green room, whispered, 'Break a leg! Or his neck if the opportunity arises.'

My laugh had stuck in my throat.

'You'll be fine.' Kim said, all the right words but not quite the right level of conviction.

The maybe-floor-manager smiles as she adjusts my position on the sofa, something about me being camera-left of Peter before, 'This is Karen,' she says as a woman sits down beside me, the soundman at *her* chest now.

'Bea.' I reach out a hand. 'Are you the family counsellor?' I ask, but none of the too bright faces is listening, not to me anyway. What they *are* listening to is the counting backwards from ten, which begins when Peter and Emma walk back on set, and I ask, at nine, when will I get to see edits, and at seven what time will the piece run. At five Emma leans over and asks with these eyes that look almost like kindness, 'Did no one explain this is live?'

* * *

Emma looks away from me to the camera, her smile disappeared into a face that means this is serious. A posture that means – for the audience at home – *prepare yourself, you might not like what you're about to hear.*

'We all know parenting can be tough. We might think about our lives pre-children and reminisce about unbroken sleep and wild nights out with friends. But, for the majority at least, these losses are more than compensated by the gains. The kisses and cuddles and rewards of seeing your child grow into someone of whom you're proud.'

'Not so our next guest.' Louder than Emma, it's Peter at the helm now. 'Bea Straw, a mum blogger, took to her own website, Tonight Will Bea Fine, just a few days ago to announce to the world that she regrets having her daughter to such an extent that she aborted her second child without telling her husband she was pregnant.'

My heart is a woodpecker coming at me sharp and erratic, no rhythm to its attack on my chest, which contracts with the hail of words and those hands of Peter Mason's, which are raised in the air, open and wide, as he turns to me and asks exactly how I think my daughter must feel knowing her mother wishes she hadn't been born.

'I... didn't... say that.' I'm not even sure my words are words. That they're not mere sounds like you made, Mabel, before you had the vocabulary and the wherewithal to make sense of your tongue. 'I never said I wished Mabel hadn't been born.'

'It's just semantics though, isn't it.' Peter isn't asking a question. He's stating facts. 'You might not have used that exact phrase, but the sentiment was there for sure. So, let's try again, shall we?' He quirks his brow to the camera. 'How do you think Mabel feels about what you've done?'

'She doesn't know. She's two-and-a-bit,' I say, or think I say, my pitch high, my breath jagged, my regret now turning from mother-hood to the moment I stupidly said yes to that researcher.

'Maybe I'm wrong,' Peter says to the people at home, then with his attention back to me, 'but if your daughter is only a little over two years old, I don't see what she can possibly have done that's so awful you would willingly undo her as you did your unborn child.'

'Hold on a second, Peter.' Emma cuts in. 'Even for you, you're going too fa—'

'Am I the only normal one left around here? Those watching, can you let me know – though I already have a good idea of your thoughts – tell me via Twitter if you think Bea here has played fair to her child *and* to her husband in revealing her feelings not to them but to her readers and, now here too, to the nation.'

'To be fair, from what I understand, I don't think Bea intended the blog to go live, let alone go viral. And as for coming on here, *we* did invite her onto the show.' Emma turns from her co-host to the camera, rolling her eyes, like, *here he goes again*. And it hits me how, nice as Emma is, this is just momentary circus for her and Peter and their crew. 'And as such, I think we need to give her the opportunity to speak —'

'We did and we will,' he says. 'But I also have to ask myself —'

'Well, actually, I think we need to ask Bea some questions before you ask yourself anythi—'

'If you'd been listening, you'd have noticed, I *did* ask her a question.'

'Can I please just do what I'm paid to do and speak to our guest without you constantly interrupting?'

'Of course you can,' Peter says, like there was never any doubt. It's his turn with the comedy eyes now. The am-dram folded arms. And the legs spreading ever so slightly further apart on the sofa.

'I'm sorry, Bea.' Emma's apology is, I think, quite genuine. I try to smile a thanks but nothing's working properly, and the eyeballing I'm getting from her left is as thick and heavy as the glass of those old-fashioned snow globes, sucking out my breath as it bears down on me, shaking things up so I can't see or hear or think anything but the smothering white blanket of his glare.

'You wrote, didn't you, that you love your daughter, Mabel, but you've found motherhood very difficult, that —'

'She didn't just say she found it difficult, Emma. What she said...' Peter picks up his notes in one hand, jabs his pen at the space between us with the other, 'And I quote *she* – and this is her own daughter she's talking about – *robbed me of a life I can never retrieve*. As you just said, Bea, your little girl is only two years old and the way you talk about her in this blog, you make her sound like a monster.'

'I didn't mean *her* exactly. What I meant was motherho—'

'Ah, so it's not little Mabel who, and I quote again, *pushed me to the edge*, and yet it *is* poor little Mabel who bears the brunt of your lack of foresight, is it not?'

'I'm sorry?'

'I suppose what I'm getting at, Bea, is…What did you expect? When you decided, you and your husband – the same husband you failed to tell about the baby you aborted only a few days ago – when you and your husband decided to try for a child, did you not think about the consequences of bringing another life into this world?'

'I thought I had, but what I —'

'Or were you just thinking that perhaps it would provide you with good material for a blog that might garner you some sponsorship and, what was the paid partnership you did a few months ago? A weekend away for you and your family? Including, I must add, the very two-year-old daughter who's apparently caused you so much grief you felt able to wish the undoing of her on your blog. You can't tell me you don't see the irony there, Bea.'

'I do see it, yes.'

'And yet you did it anyway.'

My woodpecker heart, while still thrumming, still painful, at least has a consistent beat now. A red hot angry one that just about allows me to breathe.

'I did. And I regret how it all came out. But as Emma said, I didn't intend for it to be published. I wrote it when I was drunk, whe—'

'Ah, yes. Drunk!' Peter's head slowly shakes and his hands fall to his knees, like, *doesn't that tell us everything we need to know.* 'And this is what I heard, ladies and gentlemen, that Bea Straw, a parent blogger, admired by – how many is it? – over seventy thousand people?' He looks at me for confirmation, but I'm no longer playing ball. 'Clearly she doesn't want to say, but I think it's about seventy thousand followers. So fair to say she is – or was – lauded by her fans as an example of a good mum. And what I heard is that you were blind drunk while pregnant and in sole charge of your toddler. And that's your excuse for saying the things you said.'

'I don't see it as an excuse. Mabel was in bed asleep but, even so, I shouldn't have been drinking. I admit that. But I panicked. I was pregnant and knew there was no way I could cope with a second child.'

Emma nods, as in, *continue*, and for once Peter Mason is quiet.

Looking at her, ignoring him, I press on. 'I love my daughter, honestly I do, but motherhood isn't…' I try to be careful. 'It isn't what I expected it to be.'

From the corner of my eye, I see his finger point, his incessant mouth open to talk, but Kim told me not to allow Peter Mason to shut me down.

'I thought I *had* considered the implications of motherhood. But it's abstract, isn't it, when you talk about having a baby? All those preconceptions. None of it's real until they're with you twenty-four hours a day. It's only then that you can properly comprehend how much they take.'

'But what about everything having a child can *add* to your life? Doesn't that make up for the losses?' Emma's question seems real, less like a trap than anything that's come from him.

'I love my daughter,' I repeat. 'But I miss my old life. The old me.'

'Let me just pick you up on that.' He's back. 'Because surely you have no choice but to suck it up, like the rest of us do. To accept your responsibility and duty as a mother. But instead, you've moved out, haven't you? Though I might add that in between aborting your baby and walking out on your family, you found time to go to a party.'

I know I was told to look at Peter and Emma rather than the monitor, but I can hardly ignore the Instagram picture of Kim and me now up on the screen.

'I wasn't at a party. I was with a friend. And yes, it was her birthday, and I *had* arranged a party for her, but we had to cancel. Unexpectedly. And she felt awful so I wante—'

'Awful? She doesn't look *awful*. I'd say she looks elated. With the Prosecco, is it? Or Champagne? You both look extremely happy. Because you were celebrating, weren't you? The caption says so.' He pauses to allow the camera to zoom in. '*This is what freedom looks like.*'

'I can expl—'

'Let's get back to the question, shall we, because my esteemed colleague here accused me only a few moments ago of something like deviation.'

'Deviation. Narcissism.' Emma shrugs comically to the camera. 'One of the two.'

Peter shakes his head, like, *what's a man supposed to do*. 'So, to clarify, Bea, you're not living with your husband and daughter at the moment?'

'No, but I —'

'You've run away? Decided motherhood's too hard and scarpered?' It's not a question he's willing to let me answer. His gaze has already shifted to my right, he's moved on. 'Let's bring in Karen here. Karen Riley is also a mum blogger.'

A mum blogger? What about the counsellor? 'But I was tol—'

'Please.' The word is good manners, but Peter's tone is anything but. 'You'll have a chance to talk again in a moment, Bea.'

Karen shifts next to me, quietly swallowing a cough as she prepares herself to speak. 'Hi,' she says, and I wonder what they told *her* about this interview. Whether she was in on the joke.

Emma's attention also moves to my fellow guest. 'Your blog, Karen, Attachment Family, it came about after you, like Bea, found the first few months of parenthood difficult. You look at how your focus on the mother-child bond allowed you to come through that and enjoy a more positive experience. Is that right?' In the time it takes for Emma to ask this question, the runner has brought in a child I assume is Karen's and placed him on her lap.

'Yes, when Elijah was a new-born, he struggled to sleep, which meant I also struggled to sleep, which in turn meant I found being a mum very draining.' Karen flits a glance at me, but in the light I can't see the shade of her feelings. She strokes her son's head with her thumb as she talks. He sits as doe-eyed and perfect as his mother. 'And a friend suggested baby-wearing —'

'I'm sorry! Baby what?'

'Oh for god's sake, Peter.' Emma bats him with her notes. 'Do you have to be such a parody of yourself?' Peter feigns offence. 'You know very well what baby wearing is. We talked about it right here on this sofa not so long ago.'

'Ah, yes,' he says. 'The reams of cloth and a sling —'

'Please ignore him, Karen,' then to camera, Emma shakes her head in pantomime despair, 'as we all probably should. You were saying…'

'Yes, my friend suggested baby-wearing, which, as Peter said, involves having your baby or toddler in a sling and keeping them close to you as much of the time as is feasible. It has worked beautifully for the both of us. It feels incredibly natural and has allowed me to do lots of things I couldn't manage when Elijah was screaming or wanted to be picked up. The pressure just lifted, and I found we enjoyed each other a lot more.'

'So, what you're saying, Karen,' it's *her* name he uses, but Peter is looking at me, much like a teacher making an example of a better pupil, 'is that it's through *more* time, *more* contact with your child, not less, that you were able to achieve a happier relationship.'

'Mmmm,' Karen says, eyes flitting from the child to Peter to Emma to me. 'I guess so, yes.' And she seems perfectly nice, perfectly kind, perfectly perfect, but bully for you, Karen, bully for you.

'And you sleep in the same bed, is that right?'

'Yes,' she says, and I close my eyes, breathe in through my nose, out through my mouth, hoping the camera's not on me but the better of

253

the two of us mothers. 'We find it helps all of us, even Elijah's father and me. It helps all of us sleep better because each of us knows the others are safe. And it's quite beautiful to wake up in the morning when the first thing you see is the two people you love most in the world.'

I'm pleased for you, Karen, really I am, but.

'Bea.' When I open my eyes, Emma's looking right at me, expression like, *ta-da*, like maybe she's found the answer to my woes. 'Is this something you feel could help you?'

'No.' A little too quick? A little too hard?

Emma's head jolts at the speed and the certainty, and where there was a smile there is now pity. Like the woodpecker, it chips at my heart.

Peter though, Peter's face isn't pity. Peter's face is…what? It looks to me like his face is joy in this moment that for him is television gold. 'So would you say, Karen, that the crux of it is, I think, how much, as a mother, you're prepared to give up for your child?'

'And what about as a father?' I didn't mean to. I hadn't thought. I wasn't even.

But.

'I'm sorry?' Peter is bigger suddenly, broader.

'What about how much, as a *father*, you're prepared to give up for your child? Because you seem very interested in the fact that I'm not currently living with my daughter but if I were a man I —'

'Oh, so this is men's fault, is it? It didn't take long, did it? To switch it around and somehow make your behaviour, which I find quite disturbing by the way, the fault of men. And here's my problem, and I *am* a feminist, but we're here talking about why *you* have walked away from *your* child after aborting another baby, and you're now determined to make it about fathers.'

'I'm not determined to make it about fathers. My point was that if I *were* a father, would you have the same issue with me not currently living with my child?'

'That's not what we are —'

'I'm not saying I'm behaving well, or that I'm the world's best mother because, as Karen here has clearly proved, there are much better mothers out there than me. But, despite the huge mistakes I've made, I am trying my best. And it was actually my husband who asked me to leave.'

Peter's right hand is raised to stop me, but *fuck you*, Peter's right hand.

I am surprisingly calm. 'And so I left because he deserves some space, and maybe I do too. And you're not the only one to think that's awful. God knows my Aunty Pat was mad when I told her. But you know what? My brother left his wife and kids a year or so ago, and I wonder did Aunty Pat tell *him* he couldn't possibly leave? Did she tell *him* how it was the worst possible message he could give his children?'

Both Peter's hands are up now. He draws a breath to speak, but don't even thinking about interrupting me, Peter Mason.

'Did she make *him* feel like he'd failed at something that should be the most natural thing in the world? Did she tell *him* his mother would be turning in her grave? No, she didn't. Because just as my Aunty Pat isn't aware of her racist biases, neither is she aware of her gendered ones. And let's face it, I may be failing to reach the standard I should meet as a mother, but I don't doubt I've still done more for my daughter than I'd need to do to exceed the expectations placed upon fathers by comparison.' I hadn't realised how fierce my voice had become until I stop talking.

Peter shakes his head to the camera, baulking at the nerve of me. 'So, I was right, then, you *are* turning your drunken admission into an excuse to have a go at men?'

'I'm not turning it into anything. I'm just exhausted.' I laugh a laugh that's not a laugh at all. It's a you're-never-going-to-get-this-but-I'll-plough-on-anyway. 'Do you know what it's like to have a constant stream of multiple to-do lists in your head?'

'Of course. We all do, Bea.' He's direct to the camera then, eyebrows raised. 'Is that not just the by-product of being an adult?'

'Not only the physical jobs but the mental ones too? The incessant negotiating, not only with your child but with your partner who, like you, Peter, declares himself a feminist, a believer in equality, but when I'm not there, when he himself has asked me to leave because I am so terrible a mother, has to message me to get details of a celebration at the nursery because it is always always *always* me who sorts and keeps on top these things.'

Peter and Emma are looking at each other like I've gone bat shit mental. But I can't control how it spills. Though spills isn't quite the right word. It's more ferocious than that. It's eruption. Rage.

'For some reason, dressing up and pain au chocolats and learning the French word for *hello* and packed lunches and play dates and birthday presents and reading about developmental milestones and sorting childcare and booking doctor's appointments for immunisations and ensuring we have the right snacks and perfectly timed meals and a spare pair of knickers —'

'Yes, we get the idea, Bea.'

Fuuuuuuuuuck. Just the way he says my name.

'I'm sorry if the list is boring to listen to, *Peter*. Just imagine how boring it is to work your way through it knowing that it will never all be done. Because I've not even mentioned the clothes shopping, the parties, the laundry, the holidays and the million other things still quietly believed to be women's work. And if, for one moment, it *is*, taken on by my husband, then it's help. Help! And you know what, I don't want help. What I want is for it not to be *my* job by dint of the fact that I'm her mother. So, yeah, *Peter*, you're right, maybe this *is* a feminist issue because this isn't what I signed up for. So in response to the question Emma asked me earlier if what I've gained from having a daughter makes up for the losses, then, honestly, the answer is no. Because my biggest losses in all of this are the faith

I had in my choices, and the faith I had in my husband and me to do or be something different to the norm.'

Shit.

'I'm sorry,' I tell them. Because I'm leaving, pulling at the mic, which doesn't want to budge from my shirt, and stomping past Karen, whose eyes are fixed on the top of her son's head, clamped in blissful ignorance to her breast.

'I did that, you know.' It's Peter I'm telling, like he actually gives a toss. 'You wouldn't think it, would you, but I breastfed my daughter. Fourteen months and everyone said I was queen of bloody queens for lasting that long. I did that *and* the singing *and* the signing *and* the swimming *and* the weaning *and* the soothing. I did it and, despite having just lost my mother, I tried to smile through it all. I have not been bad for Mabel,' I say. But from the look on their faces as I leave them, I don't think anyone in the studio believes for a second that is true.

CHAPTER THIRTY-FIVE

I ring Della from the toilets, leave her a message, ask her to call.

CHAPTER THIRTY-SIX

'You certainly didn't let him talk you down.' Kim's waited until we're outside the studio to say anything other than 'Are you OK, Bea?' a question I ignored each of the three times she asked it as we left the green room and made our way downstairs. 'You really stood your ground in there.'

'That *is* a good thing, isn't it?' If it is, then surely I should be feeling victorious. And yet, I can barely lift my head as we make our way to the tube.

'You definitely made your point.' It's diplomatic, her answer.

'But what? My point was wrong?'

'I don't know that it was wrong. I don't have that much insight into your marriage. But that disappointment in your choices is going to come as a bit of a shock to Craig if you've not discussed it with him before.'

I've raised it in part.

I'd not long been back at work, a decision I ached over. Not because I couldn't bear to leave you, Mabel, but because in pregnancy, in theory, I was sure I'd be able to establish a work-from-home business while being a stay-at-home mum with you until you started school. I'd imagined the halcyon days of your childhood and knew I wouldn't trade those hours, minutes, seconds with you for anything, let alone crap pay for time with other people's far less adorable children. And when I say *I knew*, I mean it. I absolutely knew what kind of mother I'd be. And my own mum confirmed it. 'You will be wonderful,' she'd said. 'Please don't waste your energy being sad about me, use every ounce for enjoying your daughter.'

I was less sure about this. Less certain I could lose my mother and not fall off the edge of the world. But there was the promise of you, Mabel, and 'I will be there in the bluebells,' Mum had said. It hadn't seemed stupid to believe her.

You were born and she died in the March. By May, I was already drafting emails to my head, Stephanie Evans, about returning to school. And though teaching wasn't ideal, it would at least legitimise me wanting to leave the house, Mabel. To leave you, a tiny baby who inhabited every inch of me and yet was never enough to curb the vertiginous thoughts of Mum. But when I suggested the drop to statutory maternity pay might make things difficult, that maybe I should go back to school earlier than we'd initially planned, Dad said he'd top up my income.

'It's important you don't overload yourself, Beatle. There was a time when your moth—' His voice was quashed beneath Craig's burst of thank-yous. Neither of them understood that school would have been a break.

At home, a break was impossible.

Busy busy busy.

I was living two long lives. One by day, one by night. It meant every difficult part of motherhood – those times Mum and Tina had promised would be a phase – were doubled in length as I lay listening to you and Craig sleeping until it was too much of an insult to hear how far away you both were from me.

In your first September, sleep remained as absent as Mum's ghost, which I still hunted, creeping around the house and into the garden in the dark. One night, I slipped outside at 3.00 a.m. with an urn and a bowl an observer may easily have mistaken for a cauldron. I folded my mother's ashes into the bluebell seeds and the magic mix she'd promised would ensure her resurrection.

I tried talking to her, but it was her body I wanted. I wanted her weight and her arms wrapped around me. I wanted her lips messing my hair as she whispered that everything would be OK. I wanted her wrists and the way the charms on her bracelets jangled whenever she moved. I wanted her thumb making circles in my palm when I was six and she would sing about teddy bears in gardens and tickle my chin or my belly and I would laugh so hard because nothing mattered at all.

These were the parts of her I wanted.

But all I had was an urn, Mabel. And instructions.

'Be happy,' she'd said in the hospice. To you first. And then to me. 'Be happy.'

I promise, I have tried so hard.

There was too much of her for one bowl. I used only a few handfuls, letting her run through my fingers into the mix, which I scattered into tiny holes I'd dug beneath the tree, willing her, like some madwoman who actually put her faith in these things, to rise up through the earth and tell me what it was I was doing so badly.

I lay down in bed as the sun began to rise, my hands and nails hard with the cauldron blend I couldn't bear to wash away with water. When I woke at seven, Craig was clattering what sounded like cups and spoons in the kitchen. You were still sleeping, possibly your longest stretch yet. When your dad brought me coffee and asked how our night had been, I told him of your milestone. We both stared at you and agreed how amazing you were, Mabel, how your propensity for sleep and feeding had made this parenthood thing a breeze.

'Be happy,' she said. So I lifted you from the cot, fed you and said nothing of the games the night was playing with me either then or when I went downstairs for breakfast and saw the cauldron scrubbed and turned upside down to dry on the side.

'What have you done?'

Craig looked at me, like, *what?*

The bowl was so clean I could see my fury reflected in its silver surface.

'I found it by the back door,' he said. 'I was trying to help.'

'Be happy,' she'd said.

So I didn't weep for the dust of her swilled down the sink with the remains of Craig's Cornflakes. Instead, I put the bowl back in the cupboard and told him, thanks. I kissed him goodbye and wrote a few words for TWBF about the time I inadvertently sprayed the bathroom mirror with breastmilk.

'Be happy,' she'd said.

And I was, Mabel.

In the blog.

On the surface.

I was everything she wanted me to be.

'Sit down,' Craig would say in the evenings when I was happy happy happy busy busy busy. Washing or cooking or planning what might be good for you, Mabel, to wear or to eat or to do.

'I don't have time to sit,' which was true because by the new year, I had happy'd and busy'd my way through full mat leave and was teaching three days a week, reminded by Evans to watch my language on the blog, like I was one of her sodding pupils graffitiing about the size of his dick on the wall.

'She hasn't said you can't write TWBF then?' Craig asked when I called him on the way home from my first day back at work.

'No, just that I have to be careful. She's been keeping a close eye on it apparently; thinks I tend to *err on the side of depravity.*'

'I suppose what makes you a good lay doesn't necessarily make you a good teacher!'

'Craig! *Mabel!*'

'It's fine, she's mainlining *Shaun the Sheep* in the other room. What time you home anyway?'

I was later than planned. It's not that I'd forgotten my school day rarely finishes when the students leave, but I'd not accounted for a broken photocopier and a call from Tom Haddon's mother. Given he'd fallen asleep in class that afternoon, I thought she was wanting to discuss scaling down his daily 5.00 a.m. training sessions at the pool. What I hadn't expected was a demand for more homework because didn't I know Tom's uncle suggested he had Oxbridge potential and wouldn't it make sense to really begin ramping up those core English skills now in readiness for his application. Tom Haddon was in year seven, Mabel.

'Ten minutes. I'm just turning off the A5. Can you heat that lasagne from the weekend?'

'Oh. Mabel and I ate that for our lunch.'

'Why were you having lunch with Mabel? You weren't due to pick her up until late-afternoon?'

'She was a bit cranky at drop off. Maybe she sensed some change with you going back to work. You *were* a bit tetchy this morning.'

Tetchy? Yeah, I was tetchy. I had to leave at seven, and Craig wasn't even out of bed until five-to, despite you screaming blue bloody murder for ten minutes because I wouldn't let you come in the shower.

'I shifted some clients around so I could pick her up early. Thought it'd be nice. But we ate the lasagne.'

———

'Sorry,' he said. 'But you're right by Sainsbury's now, aren't you? I'd pop to the Co-op, but we're in our pyjamas already.'

Pyjamas? At least he'd done your bath.

Only he hadn't. Though it's not as if he'd done nothing.

'We planned a surprise for Mummy, didn't we, Bells?' Craig took the shopping bag from my hand when I arrived home and lead me up the stairs. 'Ta-da.' He swept his arm at the impressively neat bed. 'Smell it.' His smile was so broad I could help but smile too. 'Thought you might be a bit knackered after your first day as a working-mum and, given how much you love a clean sheet…'

I collapsed on the duvet and inhaled its fresh scent.

'I hoovered for you too.'

For me?

It was a kind thought. And after we'd eaten pizza, and I'd washed your hair and put you back into your pyjamas, after we sat, the three of us together, and read your stories, after I'd checked your nursery bag for notes about permission slips or dress-up days or invitations to parties, after I'd packed your lunchbox and your wellies because it was Wednesday tomorrow, so forest school, after I checked my lesson plans for the morning, 'Sit down,' Craig said, clearing your books from my side of the sofa. But I was hoping the added busy busy busy of work work work would do the trick and I'd actually sleep sleep sleep, so I kissed him goodnight and thanked him for the gesture because he was right, I do love a clean sheet.

I closed my eyes and laid there not sleeping until gone three. The sheet didn't smell so fresh by then, and in the morning the same old same old began anew.

Only the sheets were a one off.

I asked Craig about it a few months later, raising it as a joke, like, *remember that time when you worked out how to change the bedding.* He rolled his eyes, and I insisted I was only kidding, but 'many a true word…' he said. I shrugged my shoulders, pouring a glass of wine because, well, it had been a long day bookended with meetings and punctured with an hour spent entering marks into spreadsheets we all knew were pointless but…

'Alright for you,' Craig said, 'knocking back the vino 'cos you don't have to go to work in the morning.'

I wanted to tell him *you* were work, Mabel. To remind him that on the days I was off school, there would still be marking and planning while also catching up on the domestic shit I'd skipped on the days I was teaching. It was a slick routine is what I mean. Easier to stick to it than to delegate. Easier to seethe than to nag.

'Be happy,' Mum said, so I smiled and served the stew I'd batch cooked on a day when I wasn't at work. And, later, I thanked him for giving you a bath while I cleared away downstairs.

I was happy happy happy busy busy busy as I took the conventional and made do.

CHAPTER THIRTY-SEVEN

I phone Della, leave her a message, ask her to call.

CHAPTER THIRTY-EIGHT

When we come out from the tube at Euston, there's nothing from Della, but there is a voicemail from Craig asking me, when I'm back in Shrewsbury, to meet him by the river.

Maybe he's planning on throwing me in it.

'It'll be OK.' We've already said goodbye, but Kim's keeping hold of my hand, this look on her face like she's worried what will happen when she lets go.

'Did you say that your PR too?'

She rolls her eyes, like, *ignore that shit*. Her PR woman had been on the phone before I even stormed off set, suggesting it might be a good time for Kim to distance herself and Edible from my increasingly precarious position. The photo of the two of us has garnered a fair amount of negative attention.

Kim points at the departures board. 'You've got to go.'

A glance at my watch. Seven minutes. 'What time's your lunch with Adam?'

'Twelve-thirty.' Kim raises the handle of her pull-along suitcase as if she's about to leave. Pauses then though. Sighs. 'My mum read the non-monogamy piece on Edible.' Her face scrunches with an awkward childish shame. 'She called while you were in make-up this morning.'

'That was, like, six-forty?!'

'When your daughter is a wanton hussy, it's never too early to rant. She wanted to remind me about the time she took me and my sister to Barcelona, and I swore I hated tapas more than I hated Trump.'

'My god. That's a pretty bad rap for tapas.'

'I know, right?' Kim shakes her head, smiles. 'Apparently, the whole time we were away all I did was whine that with too many people

267

around the table, I never got enough gambas al ajillo. It was my favourite. *My* dish. I'd sulk if anyone dared take any. In the end I ordered four portions of it all for myself because – and this is the killer – I was adamant I couldn't handle sharing.'

'Ah.'

'Exactly. She said when I met Adam I swore to her that he was *the one.*'

'Maybe you're a French chef.'

Kim looks at me, like, *you what?*

'Why did the French chef have two eggs for breakfast?'

'Really? You have a few minutes until your train and you're doing this now?'

'Because *the one* was never un oeuf.'

She cracks. 'Is this what happens when you have too much time on your hands? Because if so...'

'After seeing your spreadsheet last night, I won't dare mention time to you ever again.'

'To be serious for a second.' Kim lets go of the suitcase handle, draws her lipstick from her bag and paints her lips that killer red. 'I'm not trying to undermine that extensive to-do list you so eloquently described to Mr Misogennui this morning, but I wouldn't want for you to believe that without Mabel time would be entirely your own.' She looks at me dead on. 'Even if it were only you and Craig, there would still be other commitments and other compromises.' She pauses. 'And other losses too. Isn't that the necessary consequence of love?'

An announcement comes across the Tannoy about my train.

'Go!' She says, waving. 'Before you run out of precious time.'

CHAPTER THIRTY-NINE

From the train loo, I try Della, leave a message, beg her to call.

CHAPTER FORTY

There are many things I've always loved about this river. It's bends. How it stretches far beyond what I can see. How it will have begun as one thing and forged its way through rock to become something new.

Della and I would come to the Quarry all the time when we were kids but didn't think we were. When we were thirteen, fourteen, fifteen and knew everything bar the fact that we knew nothing at all. We went to the park with the other girls and sometimes the boys, but the river we saved for the two of us. It's where we walked and talked and swore repeatedly that we'd always tell each other everything. There would be nothing we couldn't share.

It was here that I told her about Adrian Johnson and the sex I'd had with him in the Dingle. The sex which Bryony Jackson had spied on then written about on the wall of the girls' bathroom at school. The sex I'd had to confess to my mother, who told me, obviously, I was too young and asked me what was I thinking because hadn't I seen how Matthew's escapades were enough to contend with and she didn't know how she'd cope with anymore.

What I told Della but didn't tell my mum was that I'd enjoyed it. In the moment, that is. In the few minutes, five, six, maybe, I was in this new kind of space in which I wanted Adrian Johnson to do what he was doing and then some. It was me who said we should go further, unclear what to call it, but he knew. Because it was me who pulled at his belt and his jeans and who said 'yes' when he asked if I was sure. Eyes wide and mouth open, he couldn't believe it, he said, as he licked my neck and bit my lip, that goody-two-shoes Bea was up for a fuck. Even that word didn't stop me. If anything, it spurred me on. The contradiction of me and it and the 'don't stop'

270

I didn't even whisper but drilled as bold as Bryony Jackson. Nothing like goody-two-shoes me.

'Don't stop.'

I said it over and over, as if I knew any momentary snap in what was happening would bring the other me back, disgusted and telling Adrian Johnson I was sorry and telling myself I was rotten to the core.

I promised Mum it wouldn't happen again. And it didn't. Not with him. Not with any other boys from school. And only one in sixth form, Hugo, who waited four months until I was ready. He was kind and gentle and loved me so sincerely he wanted to follow me to uni and set up home.

I came to the river then too. With Hugo. To tell him, kindly, gently, that we were done.

And *we* came, your father and I, when I first learnt about Mum's cancer, and then again when we'd returned from the States as husband and wife, when we'd been to my parents' house to show them the ring and the photos. Of Craig in shorts and me in my sequinned jumpsuit. Of the stretch limo at the window of the drive thru. Of the bouquet I'd refused but the woman behind the desk had insisted I hold because it was part of the package, and I should have the flowers because it was tradition, she said. And although it was tradition we were trying to avoid, I held them, briefly, in that one photo, goody-two-shoes Bea just peeping through.

We returned to the river when I discovered I was pregnant, Mabel. Your dad and I walked beside it and imagined ourselves with a buggy. Tucked inside, a tiny baby we'd made in the months before Mum's death so there would be happiness in the sadness because the Circle of Life was a Happy Ever After for sure.

They walk alongside us now, our own ghosts, or the shadows of all their expectations.

'The weather is wrong,' I say to Craig, who kisses me, but on the cheek, when we meet by Porthill Bridge. We begin walking, one foot in front of the other, his hands in his pockets as I keep mine hanging, optimistic that he might hold one, because the situation is screwed but this place, well, this place has the possibility of change in its bends.

'Huh?'

How's it this warm in April? It's too hot to feel this sad.' And I'm not sure what I mean really, but my feet feel like they should be plodding through the weight of a night's incessant snowfall. My heart feels like it should be buried beneath a woollen jumper and waterproof coat. Instead, I had to change into an ancient vest and skirt I'd pulled from my old wardrobe at Dad's house. As if enough of me hasn't already been exposed. I point at Craig's flip flops. 'They're the not the right shoes for this time of year.' Or this kind of conversation.

'You know what gets me most,' Craig says.

'I take it it's not the flip flops?'

'You made me agree with Peter bloody Mason. I never thought I'd agree with him about anything.'

'I'm sorry.'

'I'm not sure that changes anything.' He sighs. 'You're not giving me a chance to get my head around one thing before you throw some other spanner in the works.'

'I can think of worse things to call Peter Mason than a spanner.'

'He's a twat.' At least we agree on that. But then Craig stops for a fraction, as if he can no longer walk *and* try to comprehend simultaneously. 'What on earth were you thinking?'

'I don't know.' I wish I was on the opposite riverbank, where the long thin branches of the weeping willows would give me somewhere to hide.

'Bloody hell, Bea, is there anything you *do* know?' He stops completely this time. 'Apart from the obvious.' Only a few feet away, a dog-walker bends, bag in hand to collect his golden-retriever's shit. 'That said, you did sound pretty certain on TV this morning. About your disappointment in me. Your regret in our daughter.'

It stinks.

'I do love —'

'Yeah yeah, I know you love her. Or at least you keep saying you do, but if that's true, how could say about the regret out loud? The first time, in the blog, when you were drunk, that's one thing, but to *Peter Mason*? What did you think you had to gain?'

'They said it might help other women.' The second I say it, I'm not sure that *is* why I did it. I think the real answer to what I had to gain might simply be me. 'You saw the photo on Twitter?'

'Of course I saw the photo on Twitter. Who didn't?'

'I didn't want that to be the last impression people had of me.'

We walk on in silence, turning the bend. A pair of swans sits composed and silent, bonded for life, on the verge. Further off though...

'Look!' I point across the water towards the bridge. Another swan is making its seemingly effortless journey.

'It's black,' Craig says, and it would be stating the obvious if the obvious wasn't such a surprise. 'I didn't know they even existed.'

I take my phone from my bag. The photo doesn't do it justice. 'If I forward it to you, will you show it to Mabel?'

Whatever it was, that moment of curious wonder, ends with the mention of your name.

'How is she? Mabel?' I ask. 'I'd like to see her.'

'She's already seen you,' he says. 'This morning.'

'*Sunrise*?'

'Yeah. At my mum's.'

And my heart, despite the vest and the too-much exposure, is smothered. There's no woodpecker. No thrum. Just a visceral bogging down. A limp pulse in a dead weight guttered with shame.

273

'I couldn't find all the crap she needed for that thing at nursery, and she was already having a meltdown about her cereal, so Mum said she'd have Mabel this morning instead. Seemed easier.'

I suppose it did.

I know full well whether or not you went to European Day isn't the point of meeting up with your father but, seriously, did he not listen – *really* listen – to what I said to Peter Mason?

'Mum was making them toast when Mabel started calling *mummy mummy mummy*, and she goes into the TV room, and you're there on the telly, saying your piece.'

'Did Mabel hear it?'

'Yeah, probably.' He ups his pace, wipes his brow.

This heat.

'And even if she didn't hear it, what about when she's older? When her friends' mums are talking about it, like they're bound to talk about it, and they go all quiet when Mabel comes in the room? Because I've already had messages from the NCT lot. *They* watched it. Everyone watched it.'

Clearly. But it still comes at me like a punch.

'Or when she's doing a family tree or something at school when she's bigger and Googles our names and up pops a video of Mummy telling Peter Mason how she wishes Mabel had never been born.'

'I didn't say that. Have you even seen it, Craig? The interview?'

Aren't these endless circles we're going around in.

I'd prepared the outfit.

'It's motherhood I regret, not Mabel. I wouldn't undo her. I love h—'

'Oh, give it a break. You're her mother.'

Blue jeans.

'Yeah, and I'm also your fucking wife.'

'Keep your voice down.' Craig's eyes flit to the path ahead. A couple with their Dalmatian is heading towards us.

Don't I always keep my voice down.

Red cardigan.

Haven't I, until the last few days, granted, constantly adjusted the volume to keep everything ticking along?

White T-shirt.

'Who am I to you, Craig?'

'What?'

Washed and put aside.

'You heard me. Who am I? To you?'

The dog sniffs Craig's knees, his owner's face tips to the ground as he comes to pull him away.

I taught you to say bonjour.

I do as I'm told, lower my voice until I'm practically mute. 'I thought I was your partner. Do you remember how well we used to work together?'

I found a picture of the Eiffel Tower and helped you colour it in.

'Fastest Woman in the World on a Space Hopper over a mile. *We* did that. You helped me train. Helped me raise over a thousand pounds.'

He looks at me, like, *what's that got to do with any of this?*

'You and me. Together. A *team*. But since we've had Mabel, do you honestly think we've been on equal par?'

Craig moves from the path to the grass of the riverbank. 'I'm doing my best, Bea. I know you bear the brunt of all the house stuff, but I'm working full time and when —'

'It's not only the house stuff.'

I'd printed it. It was in her bag. Everything except the pain au chocolate was ready to go.

'What then?'

But how do I explain it? The marathon of intangible effort.

I stand close to the water and look for stones, yearning for the gentle childish plop that would come with throwing them in.

What was it Kim said about the inevitable complication of living with other people? In my naivety, I'd believed your father and I were above the niggles, but then along came you, Mabel, and...

'I miss you.' It's not what I'd intended to say.

'It's just a few days, Bea.'

'I don't mean that.' And here we go again, this lack of ability to articulate. 'I miss who you used to be. And not just you. Me too. I miss feeling like I'm nice.'

'*Nice*? Of course you're nice.'

'Really? Because the majority of people wouldn't currently agree with you, Craig, and my head's been on their side for years.'

He looks at me, then, like he might actually listen. But how can I tell him? How can I say how I really feel?

'Mabel brings you so much joy.' And that's it, isn't it. You and Craig get to be each other's joy, Mabel.

And me? I am a constant nag.

I sit because if I keep standing, I'll scarper.

'So, what?' He towers above me. 'You're upset because I love my daughter? You're jealous of a two-year-old? You *do* remember that you agreed we should have a baby.'

I look up at him. 'I didn't know what that meant.'

Craig drops to the grass beside me. 'I swear I'm trying, but I don't understand.'

'I miss wanting to be kind to you.'

'You *are* kind to me.'

'You think? I mean, sure, I do all the stuff I've always done, but it's with a bitten tongue.'

'A bitten tongue? You're talking nonsense.'

'Am I? You don't hear the monologue in my head. The words I don't speak. You hear the clean version. The polite version. The let's-not-upset-Craig-or-Mabel-because-it's-not-worth-the-fucking-hassle version.'

'Can you stop swearing at me, please? Talk to me like you actually love me?'

'I *do* love you, Craig. And I love Mabel. But you're a duo. It's you two that are the pair, laughing and playing together while I'm on the sidelines, all *stop that, time for dinner, off to bed, brush your teeth, eat your veg, can you help with this, can you pick up that*, sapping the fun with boring but necessary admin. Parenthood has turned you into Mr Happy and me into Little Miss Moan. And that hurts. Because I used to be happy too.'

Despite everything I do to keep everyone else in order, it's me that's the mess. *My* head. *My* life.

I stand up. 'It honestly wasn't that difficult. All you had to do was defrost the pain au chocolat.'

Well that's thrown him.

Peter Mason was right. About me leaving. About me running away.

CHAPTER FORTY-ONE

```
Nice work, sis. Dragging me into
your clusterfuck. Aunty Pat's going
bat shit. Seriously though, Peter
fucking Mason!!!!😂 U OK?
```

I was so concerned with Craig and Mabel, I'd not even thought about Matthew, what I'd said on *Sunrise* about him leaving Tanya and the kids.

'I've tried, but it's not working,' he told us last year, when he'd driven up from Bedford to break the news. He was sitting in our living room, switching back and forth from appropriate sad face to excitement for the three-bed he was moving into in a few weeks' time. 'If nothing else, it'll be a relief to be off Darren's sofa. *And* there's obviously plenty of room for Joshua and Carrie.'

'How are they doing?' Craig passed my brother another beer.

'They're cool, mate. You know what kids are like. One minute Carrie was crying, the next she was asking for a choc ice. I told them they can choose the colours and furniture for their rooms at my place so they feel involved and that. Obviously, I miss them like crazy, but there was no way Tan and I could carry on as we were.'

I called Tanya when Matthew was gone.

'I dunno, Bea,' she said when I asked if the children were as OK with the changes as Matthew believed them to be. 'I've been online, reading about how best to handle divorce, and the one good thing is they're still so young, which I'd thought would make it worse, but several reports suggested under sevens generally cope pretty well. You know what it's like though, you read one article saying one thing, scroll down and there's another telling you the exact opposite. Sometimes I wonder if I'd be better off with your brother's attitude of storming on regardless and not bothering to read anything at all.'

I try calling him now, but Matthew's phone goes straight to voicemail. No doubt in New York already, strolling down Fifth Avenue without a care in the world.

Don't get me wrong, he's a great guy, a funny guy, the guy everyone wants in the room.

Mum did.

When it came to it, The End, I mean, Mum wanted Matthew in the hospice too and, to his credit, he was there. We all were. Though not exactly in the room. Not when she —

'Let's get coffee,' Matthew had said. 'She's been like this for ages. We need air.' It was true. Mum hadn't woken since you and I had left her sleeping the night before. It seemed wrong to leave her, though, when the nurse had used the words 'any time'.

I'd expected her to shrink, to disappear gradually. Like an iceberg. But she wasn't getting any smaller, which sounds silly, I know. It just would have made sense to me if she had. It's what my grandparents had done. They wrinkled and shrunk, withdrawing bit by bit and in the right order, and when the time was kind of appropriate, they were gone.

Mum was sixty-four, which was fifteen, twenty, twenty-five years too soon. A life lived, sure, but there was this baby on my breast, Mabel, and I had no clue what I'd do. I'd barely even held you, changed a nappy. I'd never gone through a day without calling or texting my mum. I was a thirty-one-year-old child. *Her* child, who phoned to tell, to moan, to seek advice and praise because, yeah, she'd ramped up my perfection driver or whatever it was Craig called it but, *god*, she was good at making me feel like I was her jackpot, at making me feel like I was capable of ruling the world.

You deserve that too, Mabel. You deserve a mother who imbues you with a light that makes you invincible.

'*I'll* stay.' Dad hadn't let go of her hand all morning. If anyone, it was him who was shrinking. And, I don't know, maybe it's just hindsight or personal experience or projection, but I wonder if it was the disintegration of himself, of the Big-I-Am. It wasn't as if he was an old-fashioned her-indoors kind of patriarch, but he'd been the main breadwinner, the one who Mum would use as a threat, a wait-'til-your-dad-gets-home, the come-in-and-put-his-feet-up kind of man, who never saw what went on behind the curtain of – what would he call it? – *woman's work*. Sure, there'd be thanks and the stacking of plates in the dishwasher, but beyond that he didn't have a clue. Until he did. Until the weekends when I went back to Craig, and Mum's exhaustion, her inability to pick up where I'd left off, offered Dad a hint of the previous luxury he'd been granted.

I love him, Mabel.

But.

Until then, Dad had no idea of the cotton wool he'd been wrapped in.

Matthew had gone to the loo while you and I went ahead to the hospice café, where I realised I'd forgotten my purse. We were returning to Mum's room to fetch it.

I saw them through the window of the door. Dad was lying next to her, his head dipped into her neck, his arm around her middle. I'd never seen them so close. Never seen Dad look so much like a child. She'd not said anything for hours and yet, there she was, looking so much like she was saying goodbye.

I wanted to run in and dangle you in front of her. Ask her *does my baby not give you something to live for*. But it had begun to feel like the opposite. Because once she'd held you, once she'd told you and then me to be happy, it was as if her work here was done.

You were supposed to make her stay, Mabel.

'You'll have to pay,' I said to Matthew back in the café.

He shrugged. 'Fair enough. I do kind of owe you.'

I gave a snuffy kind of laugh because it was hardly a debt. I'd heard people talk about the privilege of being with the dying, and I'd not got it, because how could it possibly be anything other than hard depressing labour?

'Finally getting my payback,' she'd joked one afternoon before she was moved to the hospice, when I'd brought soup to her bedside, pulled up one of the dining chairs and offered to spoon feed her. It was more for my own benefit than hers. Her hand wasn't the steadiest, and it was a mammoth task changing the bedding.

'For looking after everyone else all these years?'

She nodded, 'Your turn next,' and tilted her head gently at my belly, in which you lay, Mabel, so small but carrying such vast hope. I wanted her to show me how to mother you. But time gave no quarter to my wishes, to the way I'd imagined my life would roll out, to those pictures I drew of our future in which Mum would be by my side, or at the end of a phone, whispering words of praise, encouragement and wisdom. In this imagined impossible future, she would swoop in after a sleepless night, telling me to 'get some rest, love', and stock my cupboard with treats I'd say I didn't want but for which I'd be grateful because they'd be salt and vinegar crisps and Yorkie bars, Twiglets and pork scratchings, the foods she watched me turn to in my childhood. Like Dad, it was only in seeing her so still that I'd begun to realise all the million tiny things that had kept Mum busy busy busy, how so much of her thought and energy was for me me me.

'If I could change it,' she said, her hands making small gestures at the medical infringement on the room, 'all this'. And although I wanted to give her space to say whatever she needed, I couldn't stand to hear it, that truth of her imminent absence in light of my own imminent motherhood. A staged cough. A gathering of cutlery and china. A promise of something tasty for dessert. 'You will be OK, you know.' Even then, in the pool of her own discomfort, Mum wasn't only treading water, so too was she bearing the weight of the grief I was already suffering. As always, keeping us all afloat.

You'd have loved her, Mabel.

Craig, who'd popped out from the hospice for the most gigantic sanitary pads he could possibly find for my day-one-after-labour bleeding, bumped into us as Matthew and I left the café. He went straight for the swap. You for the towels. I watched him shower your head with kisses, as we turned into the corridor to find Dad stood outside Mum's door. We were what, twenty, twenty-five feet away, but it was clear.

She was still warm when we were invited back into the room. I'd been unsure but Matthew, who'd taken hold of my hand, didn't hesitate. And so it was by accident, I suppose, that I saw her.

We took turns, retreating into a corner to give the one who was with her some semblance of privacy, but it was impossible not to hear their tears.

'It's OK,' I whispered to Mum when it was my turn. I didn't want her to worry anymore. 'We'll be happy. I promise. We'll be OK.'

CHAPTER FORTY-TWO

There's a book I read about an alcoholic detective who would sit each night with a bottle of vodka on the table, hungering for its promised pleasure, trembling with its inevitable pain.

I too sit. At what was Mum's table, twisting the diamond-shaped glass lid of her perfume bottle in my fingers but stopping short of removing it. Because what then? When the smell of Trésor leaks into all those boxed-up words and pictures in my head and heart and blood? What then, Mabel?

It's not only the perfume though. In this house, where she lived and prepared to die, my mum is everywhere. The residue of all that life pressing into the carpet, which is nearing threadbare in the hallway, and into the drawers which are bursting with all these tiny objects she will have touched. The one in the kitchen is the worst. Or the best, maybe. A hundred or so badges she'd made for Matthew and me over the years. Every Christmas and birthday, there'd be a new one, each with a different promise or hope.

Study hard!
Play well!
Be kind!

She used a machine she bought from a catalogue just so she could pin her wishes for us close to our hearts. I rummage through them now, my fingers in all Mum's expectations, pulling out the one I received on my eighteenth as I prepared to leave for uni.

Be fearless!

I thought we'd packed her away. But Mum's still here, Mabel.

We took her clothes to the charity shop, bagged up all those parts of her, tying knots at the tops of sacks, sealing boxes with tape. I was vigilant, making sure everything that was put in its place would stay tucked in.

But Mum was more than her clothes. No wonder Dad so quickly moved in with Connie. Here, it would have been impossible for him, for anyone, to move on.

Her favourite mug – practically a bowl and unsuitable for the dishwasher with its hand-painted flowers and a bright gold handle and rim – is larger than all the others in the cupboard. There's a box of her tea. Three months out of date now. I Google if it's still useable. How can the tea have gone stale, turned weak and lost its flavour when, in the same time passing, my feelings are still so strong?

The doorbell cuts through the rumbling of the kettle. Framed by the window, Grandma Alice stands in the porch laden with Tupperware. Her hair is impossibly shiny in the sunlight. Her cheeks are reddened with the heat. Everything about her looks so alive.

If I am anticipating anything from her, it's another slap for the things I'd said about Craig on television this morning, but Alice's arms are surely too full for violence. And her mouth when I open the door is somewhere between neutral and a nervous smile. Her eyes settle briefly on the *Be fearless* badge I pinned to my chest.

'A few dinners, that's all.' She nods at the tubs as she passes them to me.

'Thank you.'

There's the trill of my phone from the kitchen, and I'm excused from inviting her in.

'I should get that.' I tilt my head in the direction of the ringing. 'It could be Craig.'

'Of course, I just wanted to —'

I shut the door before my mother-in-law can begin the tirade of shock and disappointment in the wicked things I've done to her grandchild(ren) and son.

Della's name flashes. Only it's not Della's voice when I answer. It's Nisha's, and it's a tempest because her words are gone, replaced with these operatic sobs, which my brain patterns into the worst-case scenario.

'Nisha? Tell me.' Still only the crying. 'Is Della alri—'

'Yes.' But then, 'No.' And then, 'Della is OK, Bea. It's the babies. The baby,' she says. And the plural to single is how I know Della will need me. 'One of the babies… We are at the hospital, we…' And the way Nisha can't complete the sentence is why I'm sure I must go.

But.

'No,' she says when I tell her I'm on my way. More certainty in that than in any of the other words she has mustered.

How can I not?

'The amniotic fluid was low,' she stumbles. 'We had a scan late yesterday afternoon. There was no heartbeat. Theo.' Her voice breaks again. 'They keep calling him Baby A.'

'And the oth—' I stop myself. Even if the other baby is fine that doesn't stop his sibling being dead. 'I'm sorry,' I say even though it's nowhere near enough. Though, what *would* be?

'Luca is OK.' Nisha is suddenly measured, detached even, like she has risen above the chaos to breathe. 'But they don't want Della going into labour with him, so they kept her in overnight to monitor her and the, the…' She's dipped back into the terror before pulling herself up again. 'They're monitoring her and Luca.' There's a force in the way she says his name. 'She has to — The baby will — She has to carry both of them to — They can't remove the —'

The only sentence Nisha can finish is the one telling me not to come.

* * *

I've come though, Mabel. I ran to the house to get the car and drove as quickly as I could.

I've not been here since you were born. Since Craig carried you outside and strapped you in your car seat. Travelling was suddenly so much more dangerous. You so tiny in that baby grow, which had looked so small until you were in it and made it look so huge. I sat in the back because how could I sit in the front when only a few hours previously you'd never seen a roof, a window, a sky, a sun, a mother who could now touch you because you were out. You were here. You were breathing. And you screamed so loudly there hasn't been silence since.

I would not undo you, Mabel. I may feel and say these things but know that I would not rewind and leave this hospital without you.

Nisha said they wanted to be left alone to grieve.

```
I couldn't not come.
```

I message Della, and it's true.

```
I'll be quick. Just a few minutes,
Del. I want to give you a hug.
Let me know which ward.
I'll wait.
In the café.
```

I don't imagine she'll appear. And when she does, when I see her for the first time – that huge bump of love and hurt and fractured expectation – I imagine she'll be broken be broken. Not quietly livid or fierce.

'How could you?' Her voice is grief, but her body is war. Wide dogged strides incongruous with her face, which, despite the urgency in her eyes looks adrift of Della's always hopeful soul.

'Della.'

'Go.' If her voice is like anything now it's like the earthy vibration of those grunts as I pushed in labour.

And I should.

I *should* go.

But that 'go', which is longer the second time she says it, hits my skin and soaks into me like panic, too much fright for flight because if I move, there may well be an earthquake, and whatever fault line lies between Della and me could split us forever apart.

'Please.' Desperate and pleading.

'There are televisions here,' she tells me, and my head jerks up and around because I think she means CCTV. Is she warning me? And I don't get it because what does she think? That I'll hurt her? 'In my room,' she says. 'You were on it.'

'There are more important things —' I start.

But if before she sounded like a warning, now she looks like one too. All five-foot-two of her suddenly twenty-feet tall.

'You were on it, Bea,' she repeats. People are looking. 'Telling the world that you regret your child while I was here coming to terms with the fact that I'll never ever know mine.'

'I'm so sorry, Del. About Theo.' And when she doesn't say anything, 'But that other stuff, you knew that already. The regret. The abortion. You read the blog. You came to my house after.' I'm rambling. 'You seemed like you understo—'

'Nisha told you explicitly not to come.'

'But I needed to —'

'Exactly. *You* needed to. What about what *I* needed. Not just now but when I tried calling yesterday and you ignored me? Flouncing down to London so you could sound off to Peter Mason was more important, was it?' Her steps towards me are slower, but maybe everything's slowing down while her disgust sinks in. 'I should have known you'd come. In your own time, on your own terms. Even though we said not to. Isn't that what the blog and this morning was all about? That what Bea Straw wants and needs in any given moment is more important than anything else?'

I thought Della had understood that it was the opposite. That this is the first time in so long I've prioritised me. Only even that's not quite true. For I can't so easily draw a line between what's good for me and good for you, Mabel. And in my own screwed-up way, when I took those pills, it was *us* I was prioritising.

Her face though. Not only that but her body too. Every inch of her slivered with unthinkable, unnameable loss. That she's managing to walk and to talk is a miracle, and it's too much, I realise now, to expect her to comprehend.

The hospital, the patients, the doctors, the noises of the coffee machines and the chat and the ambulances somewhere beyond, they turn to nothing. They or I or we all disappear.

'You have everything.' Della's voice snaps me back to whatever this conversation is turning into. 'You have never had to worry. A white middle class straight woman with a university education and a job that gave you the luxury of six weeks holiday so you could travel with your husband, who got you pregnant pretty much as soon as you asked. You sailed through your pregnancy and labour and had the financial freedom to delay working again so you could stay home with your child and write a blog, which became successful because everything's a success for you, Bea, not least your beautiful clever daughter, who is breathing. One of my babies will not breathe. Not one single breath. But, somehow, you are the one who has it so tough, right?' Della pauses, her face almost softening as she tells me, 'I know it was hard for you when your mum died, I get that. But you had Mabel.' If there *was* a softening, it's calcified. Her breath is hot. It smells of fury. And tea. 'Get. A. Fucking. Grip.'

Her take on me sounds unequivocal.

And yet, I have this visceral urge to hold her. My arms reach like they've done for you, Mabel, when you're falling.

'Go,' she says.

And I should.

I *should*.

I do.

CHAPTER FORTY-THREE

'I'm going home.'

If Kim's surprised, she doesn't sound it. 'Make yourself a coffee first,' she says. 'Sit down for five.' Her voice over Facetime is a balm as I chuck my suitcase on the bed, throwing in everything I've gathered in haste for my departure.

There is no time, though, for sitting down for five, or drinking coffee, or talking, as Kim will no doubt want to do, because every minute is another minute here when I should be there, shouldn't I, with you?

I already wasted too long trying to compose myself outside the hospital, not entirely succeeding so even when I did begin my journey home it was made slower by the clag that comes with the foggy mess of emotion.

It was time, I realised, to put an end to all this. To do what Della and Craig and Aunty Pat and even Peter bloody Mason have been telling me. To quit moaning and get on with everything it was I signed up for when my body worked its miracle to conceive you.

Once I'd decided, that was it. Our future couldn't come quick enough, Mabel. But the traffic didn't seem to agree. And now Kim doesn't either.

'Don't rush,' she says.

'She needs me,' and it's true. I feel it, the tug of those invisible threads of the umbilical cord, which tether you to me, Mabel. And I think how my body made it, that lifeline from me to you, and here I've been wrenching and yanking, fighting biology for the sake of what? What was it I hoped destroying it would do? Make some kind of maternal split-apart?

I will always be your mother, Mabel.

And a mother *should* always be with her child.

'Have you spoken with Craig?' Kim's voice is the equivalent of a tiptoe on eggshells.

There was a reason I didn't bring much when I left on Sunday. Deep down I'd known, hadn't I, that all I needed was a few days to come to my senses, to realise it's a matter of perspective. And I'm not one for believing things happen for a reason, Mabel, especially things like the things that have happened today, but if Della's loss can do something, then let it do this. Let it bring me marching ready and willing, and oh so sorry, to you.

'Bea?' Kim's tone is firmer. 'I really think you need to speak with Craig before you go rushing home.'

It's all just a matter of shibbles, isn't it? A case of turning the shit I've made into something that's acceptable to say out loud.

'Bea, listen to me. You have to sit down. Just for a few minutes. What's happened to Della is terrible, but I honestly think it would be sensible to chill and not rush straight home.'

'I've told you: Mabel needs me.'

'What Mabel needs is for you to go back certain that you can stay.' Kim's voice is a hand on each of my arms, applying pressure like she's trying to take hold. A restrain of some sort. A bid to quell this rush to get to you, Mabel.

'Of course I am certain.' I take a step away from the phone so she can no longer see me. I check the duvet, the bedside tables, the chest of drawers. Then the floor too, and behind the door. Because I won't be coming back. I'll be staying home now, Mabel. I'll be staying with you.

'Bea.' Kim's calm is the same kind of calm we teachers assume with aggro kids about to kick off at school. 'Leave the case for a minute. You're in shock,' she says. And I wonder if I've not been in shock for two-and-a-bit years.

She sits in one of her long pauses.

I stubbornly refuse to concede to it. As always, there's no time.

'I promise you, ten minutes won't make any difference to Mabel.'

But my friend who is so right about so many things is so wrong now. Ten minutes is ten minutes too many, Mabel, when it comes to building my bridge to you.

* * *

'Mummy!'

'Mabel! My lovely lovely girl. Come here.'

Your arms raised and hooked. Your head dipping into that crook between my collar bone and shoulder as I scoop you up to me. Your head making a wet patch on my vest already. Your hair, sticky with yogurt and then feathered with sweat, smelling still of last night's bath as I tip my nose to your crown to breathe in the air, which is so light around you, Mabel. Your feet, toes curled into a clasp on my hips. Your hands too are these mini clamps on my biceps, the nails twitching scratches into my skin. And I'd tell you 'no', Mabel, but the pain is nothing, is it. The pain is gone. Your breath is the clammy life we made for you, and your sweet voice with the *Mummy Mummy Mummy* is the sound I dreamt of, Mabel, when all you were was an idea. The weight of you, your bottom sinking slowly into the bowl I've made of my forearms, shimmying you up every few seconds so as to keep you safe, so as not to let you fall. All of these things a collage of you, my child, of your body colliding with my body. This is us, Mabel, you and me, and I curl you as best I can into that preborn shape when you were small enough to be inside me, and there was no possibility of me leaving you because, for all intents and purposes, for all of those nine months, we were one.

We drop to the front step, the stone slab cool on my thighs as I sing into the bones of your skull, where the fontanelle was once so dangerously soft I kissed you there even more gently than I kissed your belly or your nose, and kept the cold at bay with hats smaller than my hand, which I would rest on your chest at night to check you were breathing. It is closed now, that skull-space, harder when my lips press against it, lullabying promises of a mockingbird, a diamond ring, a looking glass, a Billy goat, a cart and bull, a horse and cart and the sweetest little baby in town, which is you.

I am sorry I ever doubted, Mabel.

It *is* you.

There is another body then. A bigger one. Bigger than you. Bigger than me.

'I'm not leaving, Craig.' It's not a request but a fact as solid as the weight of you against my chest.

If this were a movie, his arms would stretch to hold us both. He would kiss my head while I kiss yours and whisper, 'We'll work it out.' But this isn't the movies. This is life.

When I stand, he moves silently aside, and I carry you into the hallway.

I am home.

CHAPTER FORTY-FOUR

'I'd like to do this without raising our voices.' My husband has made me a hot chocolate. He also made me dinner, a ready-meal curry from the Co-Op, which we ate with you, Mabel, and you told me how you thought I'd moved into the TV. Like when we came in from the doorstep and drew briefly apart. You'd pulled away, eyes scrolling the height of me, and seemed surprised not only by my being here but by my size too, which was larger than when you'd seen me last on the television with that man who made me cross.

'Love you, Mummy,' you said, poking your finger at my cheek. And the fact that you could still love me after everything I've done made my cracked heart cleave to its broken pieces. Some solace, I suppose, that we will have a shot at this. If only I can hold my nerve.

Craig suggests we sit at the table. 'So we're opposite,' he says. 'I dunno, it's something I read online. Maybe we haven't been looking at each other properly.'

I know what he means. 'Like driving.'

He pulls out a chair for me, something he knows I hate strange men doing at parties because I am five foot seven and, even if I was four-foot-two, I am a grown woman and more than capable of sliding a small piece of furniture a foot or so across the floor. His gesture is kind though. There is no power in it, rather a suggestion that we can still be mindful of each other. Isn't it a hint of what I've been wanting? The pulling of chairs, the purchasing of spacehoppers, the running alongside and cheering, raising, ensuring the other is OK. Hearing what they're not saying. Acknowledging when their heart slows to a beat below fine.

'Driving?' He takes a seat on the other side.

I know his face so well, Mabel. If I closed my eyes and thought of him, his limestone skin, tanned by sun and wind and partly concealed by his now carefully combed and clippered beard, would appear like a Polaroid picture.

'You know, when you arrive somewhere and you've obviously driven OK because everyone's safe, but you can't remember flicking the indicator or changing gear. Can't recall any specifics about other cars or pedestrians, what music was on the radio. But everyone's safe so no big deal, right? You know, autopilot?'

He nods.

It's strange to be looked at like this. To have his eyes on me with as much focus as yours when you're colouring, Mabel. All that determination despite your complete disregard for the lines.

Do people actually do this? This *looking*? This seeing into overly familiar Polaroid perfect faces? Couples, I mean. Beyond those first few months of dating? Or the wedding? Or the kids? And what about the distraction of knowing someone too well, a proclivity to assume that the features of faces or bodies no longer need noting.

What does *my* face say? What does Craig see in it when he looks at me like he's not looked at me in years? Can he see into me? Into that darkness? That sadness pooling in layers with shame like oil and water?

Conscious now of my mouth, which is a little open, I close it, try not to look gormless or cross. My eyebrows tend to furrow when I read, to arc when I question. I try to make them neutral, to seem, then, like I am in control of my face as much as I am in control of my feelings, which are returned, I would like him to believe, to normal. I want to look, I suppose, like I can be trusted.

'Are you OK, Bea?' Craig has asked me this countless times in the past two years. He carried you in when we came home from the

295

hospice, where we'd left a body that looked like my mum but was becoming less warm as I held her. Her arms didn't move when I laid my head on her chest. If I'd been on my own, I would have manoeuvred them into some semblance of a hug, but it seemed childish to ask your uncle to do it. And anyway, I could hear you in the corridor, Mabel; it was no longer my place to be so childish. With all your crying, there wasn't the time for me to be Mum's child.

At home, Craig took you from your car seat, cradling your head, unable to take his eyes off you as he asked me, 'Are you OK, Bea?' But your fists clenched, and your eyes screwed tight in shocked and snarling hunger. You pitched an anger so visceral into the room there was no space for anything other than what you felt. What you needed.

'We knew it was coming,' I said.

One-handed, I undid the buttons of my shirt, shifting you to my breast, where you drank the colostrum my body had miraculously made for you. I was done-in. My insides sagging with the lack of you. All the empty bleeding space.

The ache of everything that was gone.

'Are you OK, Bea?' Craig repeats the question now, a slight agitation perhaps in my lack of reply.

'I wasn't,' I say.

'Why?' Your father is meticulous with his tone. Meticulous too clean a word maybe, too contrived. What I mean is, everything is considered, everything is slow.

'The pregnancy.'

'I would have liked to have been told.'

But he hasn't understood, Mabel. Because I didn't mean that one. The recent one. I meant you. I hadn't realised how much I'd made so much of my life – and Mum's – depend on it.

'You should have told me,' Craig says.

It would be too much, wouldn't it, to go back that far? Too stupid to suggest the healing powers I invested in your creation.

'I couldn't.' And it's true. I couldn't have told him. So I concede, instead, to talking about that other baby. The one that wasn't. 'Having a baby was impossible. You would have tried to make it possible.'

'I would,' he says. 'Even so.' His left hand, when it comes down on mine, is warm from its wrap around his mug of hot chocolate. Heat is usually angry or sexy, but like this it's incredibly sad. 'It was my child too.'

'I'm sorry.' I've said sorry to him so many times already, but I wonder if this is the first time I've meant it. 'Maybe some day.' I pull at my hair, sinking into the softening that's come with returning home, with sitting like this with my husband, as if impossible things might be made possible after all.

'There's no need to rush,' Kim had said, and she was talking about heading back here, but not long after, she'd said the same of the promises I might make to you or Craig. 'There'll be a high,' she said, as I closed the door to Dad's house and walked to the car. And she was right, of course, though I didn't tell her I was already on it, that making the decision to return was enough of a jump start to send me soaring.

I put you to bed, Mabel. Craig was with us the whole time, and I couldn't be sure why he was reluctant to leave my side. If it was a need to keep me close or a pressure to keep you safe.

We read *Room on the Broom*, and 'Plait,' you said. 'Long plait.'

And I told you, 'Yes, Mabel, long plait.'

You laughed when the bird fluttered onto the broomstick. The witch, the cat, the dog, the bird. A mismatched and unexpected family. They all looked so happy at their union. It was all so normal, all so nothing-to-dread.

'Love you, Mummy.'

'I love you, Mabel.' The volume of my declaration, usually low at bedtime, was pushed up a notch. Too loud? Too obvious? Craig didn't comment, just came over to where I was standing by your cot, bent down, and whispered something into your neck.

In the dimmed light, your two heads looked like a hairy knot. Your own thing. Tight and intricate. Neat.

'Maybe some day,' I repeat to your father now, as we sit at the table, running through it in my head, how if we were to try in a few months, if I were to fall pregnant within the nine months of that other conception, maybe the birth of a new baby would fade out the memory of the one I aborted.

There is no need to rush.

But.

'I want to help, Bea.' Craig's fingers slide between mine. 'But to do that, first I need to properly understand the problem. Is it Mabel? Is it me?'

You're almost too big for your cot now. I noticed this evening when you laid down in your sleeping bag how much space you occupy in a bed that had once been ginormous.

There was a builder on the telly, probably on *Grand Designs*, who told a couple in their high-vis vests and helmets how the size of a room appears to change during construction. It can seem vast when the foundations are laid, smaller when the walls go up, bigger when it's painted. And so it went on. Maybe parenting's like that, or my capacity for it.

And yet Mum's was always boundless.

I think of how little she complained, even at the end.

She'd blow up sometimes, when we were younger, usually during a Sunday roast, when she'd have spent ages making dinner, and we'd amble to the table in our own time, the veg going cold, and Dad rushing to get his down before the football. But she was happy, I think.

I'd asked her, on one of the afternoons we'd spent watching back-to-back episodes of *Pointless*, if there was anything she'd have done differently.

298

'Less washing,' she said without a nanosecond of thought. I promised her she'd never do another load again. It was a bit late though, because 'I'd have liked to have learnt Italian,' she added. And I thought about those articles you read in the papers sometimes about the number of hours spent doing household chores. Laundry: one-hundred-and-nineteen minutes a week, by the way. I checked, Mabel. Which is practically two hours, which is a decent length Italian lesson, I reckon, don't you?

'Then what the hell are we doing watching Richard Osman if it's Giovanni you're after?' I downloaded *Michel Thomas' Italian* on Audible, and we ditched *Pointless* for an hour practising ordering pizza and beer in Rome.

'*Grazie*,' she said after, and though she was smiling, so too was she tired and wincing with pain. 'It *has* been lovely,' she closed her eyes. 'My life, that is.'

What do I *really* have to complain about, Mabel? If she were here, wouldn't Mum tell me how much easier I have it than her. She said similar to your Aunty Tanya at Joshua's first birthday party when the dads turned up in almost equal number to the mums. 'It's wonderful to see them so involved. I hear Matthew made the sandwiches too.'

She'd be disappointed in me, Mabel.

She said I'd be OK. But how could I be, when she took one look at you and left me do this on my own?

'Mum,' I say to Craig now. But even the word, only whispered, is too much of a tremor to continue. So deeply rooted that if I pull it out who knows what little of me will be left standing.

'The hormones?' I say instead. It comes out as a question, and Craig looks at me like, *I'm gonna need more than that, babe*. 'I'm not saying I've not felt funny about stuff before, but it got worse, much worse when I took the test.'

'I don't understand,' Craig says.

'There's this thing called antenatal depression,' I tell him, punching it into my phone, pulling up the Wikipedia entry, handing it over.

I read about it earlier, in the car, after I'd driven back from the hospital and was sat outside Dad's house trying to work out how I – usually such a good girl, a let's-get-this-perfect girl – could have got things so terribly wrong. I Googled *why was I so upset I was pregnant*. And there it was: a reasonable answer. *Antenatal depression*. Sadness. Pain. Mood swings. Memory changes too.

'So, it's like post-natal depression? But it comes earlier?' Craig is trying – *really* trying – to understand. '*During* the pregnancy rather than after?'

'Exactly.' Is it too emphatic? Too much like *you must believe me*.

It could be true though. Couldn't it? That maybe everything hasn't been as unbearable as I'd thought. That maybe my perception was altered. By hormones. That maybe it's my mind playing tricks on me. Because maybe it was only since that second conception – making the regret sudden not permanent – that everything has felt so wrong.

'OK.' It's not the word itself that's the problem, but the way Craig stretches it, like the longer it gets, the more doubt creeps between its letters. 'But does antenatal depression start that soon? You weren't *that* pregnant, were you? I mean, I've been trying to work it out, and we haven't…not very often…and so it must have been —'

'Yeah, after Mabel's birthday. And I don't know how it can even have happened because —' I stop myself. Does me secretly using a coil contradict my theory of antenatal depression? 'I thought all that alcohol would have ruined any hope of conception.'

'You really think it's ante-natal depression?' Craig's tone is still measured, mature, open.

But.

'I think it *was* ante-natal depression.'

'So, what are you saying?' He lays my phone on the table, though his hands stay over his side, picking the skin around the edges of his nails. 'That all the negative feelings have gone? Because, not being funny, Bea, but it was only this morning that you were on *Sunrise* sounding very much like they were still there.'

It *could* be true. I swear it *could* be.

'I'm not saying they're gone exactly.' Do I sound desperate? 'But what's happened to Della, it's…' It's what? Scared the shit out of me? Made me count my blessings? Woken me up to the possibility that maybe my life's not so bad after all? 'The feelings are, well…less. And anyway, won't it take a while for the pregnancy hormones to completely leave my body. After the a— the pills, I mean?'

'I dunno.' And it's unclear if he's talking about the hormones or my theory as a whole.

Kim had been the same when I'd told her. 'Do you think that perhaps you're looking for an explanation?'

It was a stupid question, really, because of course I was, of course I am. Wouldn't any woman want to know why she feels, *felt*, this unnatural way about her children.

'I suppose what I'm getting at, Bea,' Kim's voice was a tightrope, 'is whether you're trying to theorise your way out of your feelings? To make them belong to something else – such as the pregnancy – and not you?'

'I told you. I had a wake-up call. With Della's twins. It's made me realise, that's all.'

I believed it, Mabel. So much so I had been able to look at Kim properly for the first time in our call. It was then that I noticed she was back in her favourite place: her kitchen. There was a mixing bowl, bottles and boxes, the surfaces were scattered with what looked like a massive amount of food.

'Hungry?'

'I'm making dinner for when Adam and I get home from our first session with the therapist.'

'Therapist? Did lunch not go well then?'

'It went really well actually. I thought about what you said about how maybe what we needed was to keep talking boundaries, so we did. And it was...' She gave me this huge smile. 'It was great, Bea.'

'Why the therapy then?'

'Adam had found someone, booked an appointment on the off chance I'd be up for it, and I am.' For all the chaos on her countertop, Kim was calm. 'I really want this to work, mate. And sometimes you can't figure this stuff out on your own.' When she paused, I knew what was coming. 'Maybe you should talk to someone too?'

My suitcase was packed and ready by Dad's front door. 'The last thing I need is to talk to anyone else about Mabel.'

She shrugged. 'OK. But what about talking about Craig? Or your mum?'

'Mum's gone,' I said with a snuff of *what else is there to say*.

'If you don't want to talk, then perhaps you could it write it down.'

And I must have looked at Kim, like, *write it down? Are you mad?* Because isn't that what sparked this shit storm?

'Not just motherhood,' she said. 'All of it. Everything that came before. All the stuff that's made you confused or sad or angry.'

Your uncle suggested I write the eulogy, Mabel. I found a poem instead. Matthew said it was too generic and wrote something himself, and for once I didn't begrudge him the limelight. It's not like I didn't try. But I couldn't put Mum in the past tense. I couldn't commit *she's gone* to paper. So I took out my laptop and knocked out a few paragraphs about how cartoonish my tits were now that my milk had come in. Writing was where I found it easiest to keep my promise to Mum. To be happy. To convince the world and myself that it wasn't only tonight that would be fine.

Craig is in bed and I'm brushing my teeth when a text beeps from Dad.

> There's always room for you at my
> old house, Beatle.

I won't need it, I type but delete without sending. Not wanting to commit anything to writing until I know for sure that it's true. Another beep.

> I mean it love. Even for the best
> of mums, things can get too tough.
> There's no shame in needing a break.

THURSDAY 18TH APRIL

CHAPTER FORTY-FIVE

'That'll be Mum.' Craig's kissing your head and grabbing his bag as he heads for the door, where there'd been a knock just moments before.

'Your mum?'

'She said she'd come over. To help. I couldn't get cover at the salon so I'm there 'til three.'

'But I'm back.'

'You are,' he says, though I hear him opening the door anyway.

I, *we*, decided to keep you off nursery until after Easter so I could spend some time with you, Mabel. I didn't realise that meant spending time with – being chaperoned by – Grandma Alice too.

She waves with both hands when they come into the kitchen, where we're sitting, you with a pain au chocolat, which I wouldn't normally allow on a weekday, but obviously there was a pack in the freezer so…

'Love you and leave you,' Craig says, kissing Alice's cheek and then yours, Mabel. A pause then before he comes and kisses me.

'Bye,' I call, smiling because it's true, isn't it, that if you say something with a smile it actually sounds happier.

'Bye bye, Daddy, bye bye,' you sing, as the filling squidges between your fingers then drops in a thick slick down your chest, which is bare because you're finding this April too warm to wear clothes. 'Aaaaaaaaaaaaahhhhhhhhhhh!' The chocolate, hot from the oven, streaks a crimson flash amid the brown on your skin. I wipe it clean with my T-shirt because it's the closest material to hand, telling you I'm sorry, telling you I'll get a cold flannel, telling you, 'there there, baby girl, everything will be OK.'

You're laughing, at least, when the patch turns a paler shade of red beneath the mulch of Sudocrem, which also finds its way onto my top.

Grandma Alice dabs at my stains. Though she and I both know, don't we, that they're a lost cause.

'It's fine, Alice, leave it. I've got it sorted.'

She doesn't look so sure.

'We're cool, aren't we, Mabel?' But when I move to lift you from the highchair, the stone of my ring catches on your chin, where a thin white line streaks across your skin. 'Oh, Bells,' I say, straight to you with more kisses, more apologies. But you're crying now, the scalding chocolate was one thing, but this scratch is too much, and I'd forgotten how loud your fists can sound on the tray of your highchair when you want to make clear your rage.

Grandma Alice has laughed off these tantrums before. 'Diva!' she called you once and told me it takes one to breed one. 'Craig's comeuppance, Bea,' she said, so obviously thrilled by your temper. 'He was the same as a toddler. A devil until he turned four.' This morning she says nothing of the kind. This morning she leans against the worktop. Silent. Watching.

'What?' I'd say if she were *my* mother. If I could be so bold. But obviously I say nothing. Neither of us has mentioned The Slap.

'I'll make us some tea, shall I?'

'Sure,' I tell her over your sobbing, which is as angry as the mark on your chest. 'That was an accident, Alice. Mabel's chin.' And I don't even know why I said it because she wouldn't have thought it were anything else.

Would she?

'You look terrible.' She hands me a tea.

'Charming.' It comes out in a playful huff, and I make sure I smile again like I did with Craig's goodbye, same too when I scoop you from under your armpits to the floor, telling, you, 'love you', as I nuzzle my nose to your nose: a quiet thanks for the fact that you've stopped bawling, which I want to point out to Alice, along with the grin you give me when I tell you we have the whole day, Mabel. And you're so obviously delighted, skipping into the sitting room, pulling a jigsaw from a drawer.

See, I want to say, *Mabel is fine, isn't she? Mabel doesn't know anything but this here. This right now. This doing a puzzle and knowing I'm not going anywhere. Knowing I'm home.*

'Did you sleep?'

'Yes.'

I didn't.

The unseasonal heat, maybe. The whirl. The walls. The garden. And then how cool it was when I sat outside in the dark beneath the tree on the ground which has seen no bluebells.

I toyed with my phone, and I know I know, no screens before bedtime.

But.

It filled the gaps, Mabel. Only a quick peek, I told myself, at the *Sunshine* Twitter account that was littered with people questioning why I was given airtime. There was a suggestion I wrap barbed wire around my hand and go fist myself. A heap of the usual shut-your-face-bitch, which is so mild by comparison it barely registers as insulting. But there were longer threads too, two-hundred-and-eighty-character battles of the sexes in which women were stepping up and saying that, yeah, maybe my regret wasn't something to be aired so publicly, but that thing I said about the never-ending to-do list, how the split between Craig and me felt far from even, well, maybe there's something in that. They dared to ignore the baiters, who advised they quit Twitter and get back to ironing shirts, who inserted gif after gif of yawning celebrities, babies and animals, and who said they were just as fucking stupid as me if they thought anyone wanted to listen to all that feminazi crap they were spouting.

Craig, however, had shown some signs of listening. 'I'm sorry you don't feel I pull my weight,' he said last night when we'd persuaded ourselves the bulk of the problem was recent: a hormonal and temporary depression. His tone had changed though, edged slightly from the middle of a seesaw along the arm of defence. 'I try to hel—' He stopped himself. 'To do my share. It's not that I don't want to...' He trailed. 'I'll try.'

And what more could I hope for, given the circumstances of my return. He made a point, I noticed, of asking at breakfast this morning if there was anything I needed him to do. *Look* was what I wanted to say. *See it for yourself.* But what I said instead was, 'You could get something for dinner when you're in town.'

Grandma and I have followed you in, Mabel, sat on the rug, where we are picking out the corner pieces, showing you how it's good to start with a border and take it from there.

'Off and on,' I concede. 'It's hard to sleep in this heat.'

Every window is open. And yet there's still no air. I'd expected the satisfaction of doing the right thing to be soporific. I was wrong.

The top of the castle in the picture of the puzzle begins to take shape.

'Kennilashun,' you say.

'Yes, Mabel, cren-e-ll-a-tion.' I tap the gaps in the roofline of the building. 'For the arrows. Clever girl!' My palm strokes the back of your head. Grandma will see, surely, that I've spent all this time with you, doing this puzzle, teaching you these long words, telling you you're not only clever but wonderful. Aren't these the signs of a mother who loves and does not regret her daughter?

Not that Alice has suggested otherwise, but.

'I tell you what,' she says. 'You go back to bed for a bit. Let *me* have Mabel. I can take her to the park. Give you some time.'

'I've had some time.' *Smile, Bea.*

'It won't hurt to have a bit more.'

'I'm fine.' *Smile.*

'Fine?' She says. 'Really?'

'Really.' We all hear it, the smile that isn't there.

Your back straightens beneath my hand.

'I'm so glad you're home, Bea. I want you to be careful, that's all.'

'Careful?' My tongue slides across the word as a sharpener runs a long a knife. When you turn, your lip is peaked to quiver. 'Let's not do this now, Alice.' I pull you close. 'What do you think, Mabel, shall we read *Room on the Broom*?'

Alice looks at me like, *please, Bea*, but I shake my head, *no*, because what you need is normal, Mabel. What you need is me.

We read the book four times. All those animals climbing onto the witch's broomstick. All that extra weight and responsibility. Of course it snapped in two.

SATURDAY 20TH APRIL

CHAPTER FORTY-SIX

Almost a week after my *thing* as we've come to call it, Jules, one of the NCT mums is hosting an Easter-egg hunt for her daughter Mia's birthday. I've been refusing to go because, well, I imagine it's obvious, Mabel. And yet Craig has somehow persuaded me I am old news.

'Seriously, Bea,' he said. 'How many of our friends do you think have the time or, more importantly, the inclination to watch *Sunrise* in the morning?' which is true. But so too is it true that WhatsApp is the modern girls' toilet wall. And YouTube allows my Peter-Mason phobic mates to watch on their phones what they'd never stoop to watch on TV. Craig had said so himself when we met in the park. '*They* watched it. Everyone watched it,' he said.

He's so sure of their ignorance now though, Mabel. It's astonishing really, the things we can cajole ourselves to believe.

Jules reassured me, when she dropped by with a chicken stew a couple of days ago, that she'd sent all the other mums messages, warning them not to mention the blog or Peter bloody Mason or the four days I left my husband and my child and wondered if I'd be better, happier, alone. I'm ad libbing obviously.

So we're here. You're playing. The sun is burning the back of my neck. And she's not even malicious. The mum who brings it up, I mean. She only asks if Peter Mason is as hot in real life as he looks on the TV.

'No, he isn't. But he is as much of a cunt.'

I laugh. But I've misjudged my audience. It's not even like I'm a massive fan of the word, but Della and I use it sometimes for the sheer joy of the shock of it. And shock is right. From the look on this woman's face you'd think it's worse than saying I regret mother-hood.

All you kids are elsewhere, on your hands and knees in the bushes rummaging for chocolate eggs, or in the floral-bunting-streamed bell tent, pinning a bob tail on one of the ten giant cardboard rabbits Jules roped me into helping her upholster in pastel-shaded gingham a few weeks back. It's an Insta-perfect party is what I'm getting at. Vases stuffed with daffodils, hessian sacks spilling over with real carrots while the kids are encouraged to make fake ones by painting pinecones orange and topping them with a sprig of parsley and a pre-tied bow. I'd sent Jules several craft ideas I found on Pinterest when she asked for activities that would fit with her theme.

I fear your construction-themed extravaganza may have set a prec-edent. And though I'd been proud of my ragged-run efforts at the time, all I can think of now, Mabel, is how when Jules arrived at your second birthday, her face was equal measure awe and despair.

What have I started?

I apologise to Jules' friend, who looks like she might cry.

'It's that word,' she says. And it probably sounds mean, but all I can think is, *aren't there more important things to be offended by?* Like the fact our good friend Jules has more than likely sacrificed an entire week of her life, not to mention a serious amount of cash we all know she can't spare, on this whole spectacle, including an egg-shaped confetti-scattered dancefloor for her precious birthday girl, who at this very moment is mistaking it for a large communal potty. No one but me has noticed, and I would go to stop her, honestly I would, but the way Jules' friend is looking at me makes me feel like I shouldn't be allowed anywhere near my own child, let alone someone else's.

Craig, who'd left me to go inside and get a beer, emerges through the bi-folds to find me stood very much on my own beneath the mint-green and rose-pink balloon arch eating a ham sandwich in the shape of a duck.

'Whassup?'

When I tell him about my inappropriate description of Peter Mason, I swear it's the first time I've seen him laugh since he returned from France. Proper laugh, I mean, like almost hysterical.

'Let's go, he says, waving a bunny-shaped chocolate lolly to tempt you from the bell tent, where you're attempting to roll a plastic egg into the wide-open mouth of a handmade rabbit. He apologises to Jules and Tom for our early departure. 'I need to take my Muck-Spout home and wash her mouth with soap and water.' He winks, turning me as giddy for him now as when we'd walked back to mine after that first Christmas party.

'You dropping the C-word at a kids Easter bash would have been stellar TWBF material,' he says ten minutes later, as you run towards the bandstand in the Quarry park. He laughs again, then takes my hand as if he's not even thinking about it, as if it's instinctive.

That's been the problem, see. For so much of the time, we're thinking too much. About what to say. About how or even whether to touch each other. About what's appropriate, I suppose, given the circumstances, which we have tried to keep talking about, but there's only so many times I can tell my husband I'm OK. That I love you, Mabel. That, yes, I'll talk to a counsellor, but let's just wait until after the Easter holidays, shall we? When you are back at nursery, and we've got things a bit more, well, straight.

It's April. It's not meant to be so hot.

I'm not sure the splash-park fountains are usually on at this time of year, but there you are, running between them, wet and giggling. I remove my sandals and walk over to you, Mabel, buzzing with your look of delight when you see I'm as drenched as you. I can tell from your eyes you've already formed ideas of things to expect of grown-up women. Surrendering themselves to the jets is not one of them.

'Mummy!' You squeal, gazing at me like I am up there with the best of them. And despite the blog and the abortion and the C-bomb at an otherwise perfect children's party, for a few seconds, I believe it can be true, that I can be alright at this, I mean. That things can all be well.

CHAPTER FORTY-SEVEN

What I want to say is, *You'll never believe what I said today.* Though what I actually text is,

Can I come over, Del?

It takes me twenty-three minutes to hit send.

CHAPTER FORTY-EIGHT

'You going to write about it?' Craig doesn't look up from the pancetta he's frying for the carbonara.

I get how he's trying to keep it casual, this not-so-subtle suggestion that Tonight Will Bea Fine isn't a complete no-go.

'Craig.'

Don't sigh, Bea.

Don't roll your eyes.

For all that passion we once had, these days I'm constantly trying to stay neutral.

'I just think, if you're feeling so much better, maybe it would be good to get back online and set the record straight. Some of your followers have been DM'ing me, babe. They want to know you're OK.'

Like *he* does. Your father is desperate to know I'm OK.

My face aches sometimes from all these smiles.

'You could explain?'

My elbow catches his as I whisk the parmesan in with the egg yolk. It's a thick gloopy mess. 'Explain what?' I don't add "exactly" but it's there, and he's heard it.

'I was thinking you could do a piece on the C-bomb. A way into telling everyone you're back. That you're alright. That it was, y'know, antenatal depression.' He says them as statements, but we both know they're questions really.

'I thought you'd never want me to post again.'

'So did I.' He removes the pan of pasta from the hob, and we almost collide when I place the colander in the basin. 'But it'd be nice if people didn't think I was such an arse.'

317

'*You?* What?' There's a blast of steam from the drained spaghetti. 'You're Saint Craig for putting up with all my shit.' Aunty Pat has said as much too.

'That stuff you said to Peter Mason though.'

'What stuff?' I know exactly what stuff. The stuff which means we're cooking this dinner together. The stuff which means he's not been out for quite as many swims and rides and runs.

'About me not being a great husband.' He pours the mixture over the pasta. 'Me not doing my share. It'd be cool if, you know, you could…'

'What?'

'Well, like you said, it was the antenatal depression.'

'Hmmmm.' I take the tongs to it, hoping the egg doesn't scramble.

'Oh,' he says. 'I see.' The plates come down a little hard on the side. He steadies one with his hand. 'So that wasn't really it then? The antenatal stuff was bullshit, was it? A convenient distraction from everything you said about me?'

It's been over three years since my husband's been this observant.

He throws his hands into the air, like, *seriously?* 'So that's why you didn't get my dad a present.'

Last night we were at Grandma and Grandpa's.

'Happy birthday, Dad.' Your Uncle Alex passed Grandma Jim a box.

Alex's girlfriend, Cesca, leant forward, elbows on the table, the fabric of her T-shirt almost catching the remains of the gravy on her plate. 'I hope you like them,' she said. The little parcel was decorated with ribbon and a bow.

Grandpa Jim made a show of unwrapping the gift, sticking the bow to your dress, and we all said how pretty you looked, Mabel, as you waited, desperate for the ribbon too.

'Gloves!' Grandpa held them up for us all to admire.

"Ugh.' You were unimpressed.

'They're for the garden, Mabel.' Grandma Alice looked apologet-
ically at Cesca.

'They're personalised, see.' Cesca pointed out Grandpa Jim's initials
on the suede cuff.

'Here, let me move those out your way.' My mother-in-law began
collecting the dirty plates. 'Almost too good for the garden, aren't
they, love?'

'Splendid.'

The gloves fit him perfectly and made entertaining puppets for a
few minutes while Grandma Alice, Cesca and I cleared the table.

Craig appeared in the kitchen with your bowl of uneaten veg.
'Where's Dad's present, babe? I couldn't see it in the hall.'

I followed him out there while he continued to look. *Don't bother*,
I wanted to tell him. 'Sorry?'

'Dad's present?' He was checking even the tiniest of pockets in
the change bag, as if I might have bought his father something as
small as a diamond ring. 'Mabel wants to give it to him. Though I'm
not sure it'll be a match for the Punch and Judy show he's performing
with the gloves in there!'

'Did you not bring it?' I work hard at sounding surprised.

'No, I thought you—' And then he knew. 'You didn't get him
anything?'

I shook my head, like, *was I supposed to*. And what could he say,
Mabel, because, 'No, sorry, you didn't ask.'

'Oh.' He was unsure what to do with this new information.

'Ready for some pie?' Grandma Alice was making her way through
to the dining room.

'I'll get the ice cream.' I left your father speechless and giftless in
the hall.

'So, we're playing it like that, are we?' Craig says in the kitchen
now.

If I intended to be playing it like anything, it wasn't *that*. It was good mother, good wife. But I'd seen the date on the calendar, Mabel, reminded Craig of the dinner at his parents' and beyond that I couldn't…Well, I suppose I just thought, we'll see.

And we saw, didn't we? The assumption or expectation or whatever you want to call it that underpins my infinite list.

Though maybe that's not fair, because he's here, isn't he? This evening, I mean. Craig's here in the kitchen, doing his part in dinner. He bought the ingredients I asked him to get on his way home. And it was him who suggested we eat later so it could just be the two of us.

'I told you, I forgot,' which was what I said last night too, when he'd asked me about the gift on the way home and implied that perhaps I'd done it on purpose. And, yeah, when he put it like that it sounded petty, Mabel. So, 'I'm sorry,' I said then and repeat now.

'Me too.' Craig puts the plates on the table. 'This looks delicious.'

It does. And it smells and tastes as good as it looks, which goes to show that it doesn't take a lot to make an effort. And I realise how much better things appear to all your senses when you do.

'What a team,' he says.

As we clink glasses and sit down to eat, I remember tomorrow is Easter Sunday. And though I'm not at all religious, I'll take the promise of resurrection. The possibility of starting anew.

TUESDAY 23RD APRIL

CHAPTER FORTY-NINE

'Sounds like things are progressing then? Yes, please, full-fat.' Kim's half talking to me, half talking to the coffee van barista in what I assume is Victoria Park.

'He's trying.' I pour the milk into my own tea, grab one of the fairy cakes you and Grandma baked yesterday. 'We both are, but...' I drop my voice despite stepping into the garden and closing the back door. 'I know I'm the one who's created this mess but... I'm so angry.' My hand runs across the top of the battered outside dining chair, though I won't sit on it. The only place I ever sit down out here is on the flowerless patch beneath the tree. 'It sounds so silly, but it's not only Craig who needs to change. It's *me* his mum calls when she wants to check we're still able to go for dinner and *me* his mum texts to ask if Mabel likes those Percy Pig sweets from M&S. And *me* she looked at utterly aghast when Craig announced there was no birthday present for his dad.'

'Do you normally get the presents?'

'Of course I do.' Isn't that my exact fucking point? 'But not this time, because...why should I? Craig's not an idiot, Kim. He runs his own bloody business, manages to keep everything in line there. Why should I have to take up all the reins at home? So no, I didn't get his dad a present, and you should have seen Craig's face. And the mood he was in when we got in the car. He accused me of embarrassing him. *Me*? Embarrassing *him*. Can you believe it?'

Kim breathes. I mean, obviously she breathes, Mabel, what I'm saying is she does one of those long intakes of breath people do when they're trying to calm themselves or someone else down. 'You didn't tell him you weren't going to buy the present?'

'No, why should I? Why should he get to assume that I would?"
And why is Kim challenging me like this?

'I get what you said before about your issues not being sexy, mate.'
Kim takes a sip of her coffee. 'But just as you said about Adam and
me talking through *our* changing boundaries, aren't things like who
does what simply more rules that need discussing?' Another of those
breaths. 'In the past, you had an arrangement. And if you want to
change that arrangement, that's cool, but you need to talk about it,
no?'

I shrug.

'And maybe just chill? Not everything's a symptom of him not
appreciating you. Sometimes picking up a gift or sorting the laundry
are simply the kinds of things we do for the people we love.'

'*We? We* do these things? Because not being funny, but *I* do all
these things for Craig. And what does *he* do exactly? Sure, he puts
the bins out every Wednesday night, and he might sort the car
insurance and take Mabel to the park so *I* have time to clean, but
aren't *I* supposed to be one of the people *he* loves? Because it didn't
feel like he loved me when he refused to move to Shrewsbury.'

And I know, Mabel, two sides to a story, and Craig says I made
the decision without him, but Mum was dying, and he was supposed
to be here, spinning gold from straw. And instead, he remained
one-hundred-and-sixtyish miles away and set a flame to it.

A thin stream runs down my back.

This fucking sun.

'He wasn't there, Kim. When I most needed him. He only came
when I promised him a baby, when I promised him I'd taken on
even more caring. And when I did that, *even then*, he was never really
there.'

I look up from the lack of bluebells to the clear blue sky, willing
the wash of rain.

* * *

Later that evening, after I've stood, without intrusion, for a whole minute under a cold shower – as recommended by a mental-health influencer on Instagram – you appear naked, climbing onto the closed toilet to wait for me. '*Room Boom*!' You wave the book as if it's a surprise.

'Really? Again?'

'Yes!'

You follow me into the bedroom where, still wrapped in a towel, I sit on the bed and you clamber onto my damp lap, nestle in, pull back the front cover and jab your finger at the first page of the story. 'Now!'

We begin.

There was a witch and her cat, and they were pretty happy, weren't they, when it was just the two of them. But then she went and lost her hat and offered her home to the dog who found it. When a bird retrieved the bow the wind had stolen from her hair, the witch welcomed her too. And maybe she was beginning to feel shaky with all the additional responsibility on that creaky looking broom of hers because the witch dropped the wand then. And yet she couldn't say no to the frog who pulled it from a pond and subsequently asked if she wouldn't mind him joining their party. There was no time for the witch to think about what all this might mean. For her. For the cat. For everyone else in the fine balancing act in the sky. The frog jumped. The broomstick snapped. All the animals fell to the ground while the witch, trying desperately to retain control of the tiny bit of broomstick she had left, flew into the path of a dragon. But the animals, the ones she'd helped, they came together to save her. When she needed them, they were there to stand up to the monster who threatened to overwhelm her. And so, once the dragon had gone,

she didn't mind rebuilding her broomstick around them, accommo-
dating their needs, with seats for the cat and dog, a nest for the bird
and a shower for the frog. You do these kinds of things for the
people you love, Mabel, when you know that if you fly into the
path of a dragon, they will come for you. They will not sit by and
let you burn.

MAY

CHAPTER FIFTY

The emails are still coming. Strangers' thoughts on my misbehaviour, on my mismothering of you. I move them, unopened, to a folder called My Thing. Each marked with a blue spot as a reminder of the unread. The unclean. For they *do* make me feel dirty, Mabel.

I've tried to stop looking. Email. Twitter. Instagram. Refusing the temptation to seek out the vitriol, immersing myself instead in the here, the now. Being present, Della called it back in the days of innocence when the only thing of which I was guilty was an addiction to my phone.

It's *her* name I'm looking for whenever I do allow myself to check messages, living in the hope, naïve perhaps, of forgiveness from my friend.

But it's not her name I see this morning after I've locked the bathroom door, turned on the shower, not washing but sitting instead. In silence. In peace. On the loo.

Scrolling.

There is a name as familiar as Della's though. A name I've known for as long.

Bryony Jackson.

From: Bryony Jackson
To: Bea Straw
Re: Time

You'll never guess how I spent last night... Digging.

I'll explain but first I wanted to thank you. A. for not running a mile when you must have felt I was stalking you that night we met in

328

the park. And B. for sticking around to listen while I confessed "my sins". I came home and wrote Nick a letter, asked him for some time. One evening a week when I can do my own thing.

And last night, I took my "time" and a shovel and went to mum and dad's house, where I dug up that capsule we buried at my 18th. Do you remember?

See attached for a flashback.

Anyway, now I have these free weekly hours, at the risk of sounding like that stalker I denied being, I wondered if maybe sometimes I could spend them with you? Could we meet up? Just for a chat? A Wicked Mothers Meeting? No pressure tho if it's not your bag.

There is a photo of five of us girls, taken by Bryony's mother a few weeks before her eighteenth when Della and I had once again been cajoled into another evening we knew would be spent as the punchline of Bryony's jokes as we drank our way around town. Bryony always suggested we end the night with a sleepover at mine. My room was the only one big enough for all of us, she said. And my Mum made the best cooked breakfast too. I still don't understand why Della and I put ourselves through it.

My grey Skunk Anansie T-shirt suggests rebellion, or at least the hope of it, though I'm not sure who I thought I was rebelling against as I strut into bars, on the tail end of a decade of ladettes who'd paved their drunken way before me. We had it all by then, right? Freedom to study, to drink, to play, to fuck, to do whatever we wanted with the unspoken caveat that the onus was still on us to make sure no one got hurt or pregnant along the way. Hadn't Bryony's mum warned as much as we knocked back vodka and orange in her living room, and she suggested Bryony change her dress for something less revealing.

'You wouldn't want to provoke anything,' she said, not explicitly using the word "men" but we were all vigilant to it, to Bryony's dad whose eyes slid across 'the parade of bodies', as he called us, when we climbed into the back of his Renault Espace.

Della and I would laugh it off later. That too-long stare at her thighs and his thick snort when he spotted my cargo pants. 'You could make more of an effort, Bea,' he said.

Thing is, I was. Not in the way he wanted, but I was trying so hard to become someone I couldn't quite figure how to be. The Skunk Anansie T-shirt was a statement. I was a tall straight white quiet people-pleaser who saw everything she wasn't in the small bi Black rock star who fronted the band. Skin had become Skin through choice.

'She was born Debbie Dyer,' I told Della for what was probably the hundredth time when I made her listen to endless replays of the album *Post Orgasmic Chill*.

My best friend may have rolled her eyes, but she was listening, for when Craig and I arrived at a games night having completed the paperwork to make us officially Mr and Ms Straw, she'd screamed, 'You've done a Skin!' while running her fingers through my hair. I'd not shaved it like Skin, but I had asked Craig to crop it short. A physical representation of this new me and all that possibility that comes with a change of name.

'MUMMY!' Your voice cuts through the past. A reminder of that other name I have now.

'Five minutes, Mabel.' I balance my phone on the basin and pull off my pyjamas.

'Bea?' Grandma Alice is barely audible over the running water. A tentative knock on the door. 'Mabel and I will be leaving soon.'

'Five minutes,' I tell her as I step into the shower.

I wanted to thank you.

The water and Bryony's words rush over me. Not just her gratitude but her ability to work out exactly what she needed to effect change.

I asked him for some time.

The shampoo suds between my fingers as I wash my hair which had returned to its shoulder-length bob by the time you were born.

It's never only one choice, rather a constant stream of choices alongside a constant stream of actions, that determine who and what we are.

* * *

Your eyes droop, your lips quiver, your entire body slumps with exhaustion from whichever adventure Grandma Alice took you on today. I'm sure she said something about alpacas, though I'm not really paying attention because, with a sudden resurgence of energy, you're now clawing at my bag, Mabel, pulling out my notebooks, sanitary towels and purse. I snatch the strap, a little too hard, maybe, because we are all hot and we are all bothered and I shout, 'Stop Mabel. Honestly, can't I have one bag that's mine? One thing you don't ruin with your sticky hands?'

Alice comes in from the kitchen, where she's been making a salad you'll blatantly refuse to eat once she's gone.

'Oh, that's it,' I spit. 'Here comes Grandma Alice, rushing to protect you from angry Mummy, Mabel. That is why you keep coming over, isn't it, Alice? Because you and Craig were worried this might happen? That I might get mad over something that wouldn't bother any normal woman with normal feelings about her kid?'

'Actually, Bea, I think a lot of women *would* get angry about their child emptying their handbag.' How does she remain so fucking calm. 'I think a lot of women *would* shout. It's annoying when children

331

do stuff like this.' She gets down on all fours to pick up my car keys, which she drops in my bag. 'Come on,' she says, 'naughty step.' And you follow her to the hall where you plonk down on your bottom without even making a fuss. 'You're here because you went in Mummy's bag, Mabel.'

My voice, when *I* do this sitting down, this explaining, *my* voice is a knife-edge. But Alice's is a smooth line of behaviour and reper-cussion.

'It's rude to go through other people's things without asking. Two minutes,' she tells you, then closes the sitting room door behind her. 'You need to stop worrying about what *other* women feel or do and focus on what *you* feel, what *you* do. That's all that matters, darling.'

'You've seen what I do. I get cross. So easily.' Even now, even with you shut behind the door, it's rising. 'Isn't that why you keep coming over to look after Mabel?'

Despite my voice and a temper that makes me as much of diva as you, Mabel, Grandma Alice comes a couple of steps closer and holds out her arms. 'It's not Mabel I've been coming to look after, silly. I've been coming to look after *you*.'

* * *

'I could do with your help actually,' Grandma Alice says as she's leaving later that afternoon. And I can hardly say no now, can I, after she's been so incredibly kind. 'It's a bit last minute, I know.' She's almost at the car, picking at one of her manicured nails and babbling at such a rate, I can't get a possible protest in edgeways. 'But could you meet me this evening? Six-thirty? Pitchford Village Hall?' She opens the door to the Fiat 500, avoiding any eye contact with an excessive focus on putting her handbag on the passenger seat, then scrabbling for her seat belt as she clambers awkwardly inside. 'I'm doing a talk for the Women's Institute. And Jim's helped me with a Powerpoint, but I'm getting cold feet. And what with all you've done with your blog, you're far more tech savvy than an old crony like me.'

'Sure.' It's not as if I'm receiving invitations to much else these days. And I can think of worse ways to spend my night than with a bunch of pensioners listening to Alice extol the virtues of perennials, volunteering in your village shop, or baking the perfect Victoria sponge. 'Though isn't your audience likely to have a significant cross-over with *Sunshine*? If so, my presence might not exactly get them on side.'

'Don't concern yourself with that, darling.' Did Alice seriously just wink at me? 'It's not *your* antics we'll be there to discuss.'

I ask Craig to ensure he's back from his workout.

'It's not a workout, babe. It's training.'

He's booked a place in his first triathlon, Mabel, which means, after the slight respite, we're back at full *training* schedule. Almost every day, there's a swim, a ride or a run.

'Whatever it is, can you be done by six, please.'

He is, and by 6.05, I'm in the car with Kim on speaker buzzing from research like a city-boy-banker buzzing from coke.

'You know forty-two percent of UK marriages end in divorce, Bea. Forty-two percent. And yet we keep on doing it. And in those marriages that *do* plod on, a similar percentage of couples admit to being unhappy.'

'That's kind of depressing.' As I pass Lidl then Aldi, I make a mental note to add rice cakes to this week's shop.

'Is it though?' Kim's smile, Kim's excitement, is audible. 'I think it's liberating.'

'Liberating?'

'Yeah, all these naysayers who are questioning our decision to try non-monogamy… the comments and the emails they're sending me, they're so superior. But I honestly think that by trying something different, my marriage might actually stand a better chance than theirs of surviving. It's like Adam said in therapy last week, maybe we were always meant to have this kind of relationship. It's not as if we were ever banal.'

'Banal?'

'Sex wise. I told you about the threesomes, right?'

She did. Kim said how they were fairly frequent before she and Adam got married. But then the officiality or the gravtias or the ceremony of their wedding somehow made them feel the threesomes should stop.

The fields on either side of me extend as far as the horizon. Only a few minutes from town, and everything's no longer hemmed in.

And I hear what she's saying, and I've asked it before, but I can't help myself. 'Isn't it risky though?'

'Maybe, maybe not. It all comes back to that capacity to be weird with someone. Perhaps this is the weird Adam and I need. We both agree we love each other. We don't want to leave each other. I don't think we have any other option but to have faith that something unconventional can work.'

Kim's words stay with me as I pull up outside a black corrugated building and watch Jim helping Alice unload the boot of her bright blue car. There's a laptop bag and a tote, the straps of which are strained with the weight of some hefty-looking books. Mary Berry? Jane Fonda? Monty Don?

'Take these, will you?' The box my father-in-law passes me rattles with a familiar tinny delight.

A woman calls from the kitchen when we go inside. 'Just getting the hot water on the boil,' she says, her voice edging closer. And I'm expecting twin-set and pearls, but when she comes into the main hall and introduces herself, Margaret is the stylish end of M&S Per Una with purple Doc Martens that push her from vanilla to a hint of spice. 'We're expecting a good crowd. Thirty or so have said they'll be coming.'

'You mentioned a projector?' Alice looks up from her laptop. Margaret pulls down a screen on the far wall.

'They *do* know what we're discussing?' Alice chews ever so slightly on her lip. Is she nervous? How raucous can an elderly crowd debating gardens or baking be?

'Absolutely,' Margaret says, handing her the cables, which Alice quickly passes to me. 'You know what you're doing?' Margaret asks me kindly.

I nod. 'Thanks. We have something similar at school.'

Ah, school, Mabel. Mrs Evans has been sending weekly emails, the latest suggests my return to work is as questionable as my mothering. We've agreed I take leave until the end of term. It surprised me how little of a shit I gave when a text from Lucy confirmed the sick cover and thus promotion were both in her hands.

'Here, just put this end of the cable into your laptop…'

When Alice plugs it in, her screen appears huge and… And *what*, Mabel? Shocking. Unrepentant. Bold.

WHY MY OWN ABORTION LED ME TO CAMPAIGN FOR LEGAL ABORTION FOR ALL

I look at Jim, like, *what the hell.*

'What can I say?' He puts an arm around Alice's middle. 'She's a revolutionary.'

'I thought you were a secretary?'

'And I was,' Alice smiles. 'But I've been many other things too. I delivered several abortion talks in the late Sixties.' If she's amused by my dropped jaw, she doesn't show it. 'And I'd hoped, once the laws were changed, that there wouldn't be a need for more speeches, but…'

I am speechless, Mabel, as your grandmother takes my hand. I scramble for words. 'I thought you hated me.'

She shakes her head.

'But the slap?'

'I haven't spoken about this stuff for years. And your blog, well, it roused a lot of guilt in me. Guilt I didn't even realise I had.' She's still smiling, but her eyes are pricked with tears. 'If I'm honest, once I'd had Craig and Alex, it didn't feel appropriate for me to be talking about it in public anymore. But the way you've been treated recently…'

'Thank you.' It's not enough, but it's all I can say.

'It's so easy to forget who you set out to be.' Alice looks at Jim, who's helping Margaret position a few more chairs. 'We're all constantly adapting, aren't we?' She takes a deep breath and adjusts the belt of her dress I've not seen since her seventieth birthday. 'But that *Be fearless* badge you were wearing when I came to see you at your dad's…' she nods at the box. 'Well, it inspired me, Bea. I thought it's about time I start re-spreading the word.'

I put the box on the table and lift its lid. Inside are a heap of badges.

I take one out and pin it to my collar: *My body, my choice*. I hand one to Alice too.

'1966,' she says fifteen minutes later to a bond of hushed women with their eyes flitting between your grandmother as she is now and your grandmother as she was then. An image of Sixties perfection in a yellow-spotted mini dress with white tights and a gamine haircut. She was stood on a stage behind a lectern. A young woman with the world at her feet. 'I was eighteen,' she says, 'when I had an abortion. And I chose to speak about it. Not only to my friends but to the Women's Institute, to journalists to anyone who'd listen. My work was mostly anonymous, though it was still a risk. Because my abortion was a long time ago when it was still illegal. But while I was lucky enough to have the money and access to people who would help me, many women didn't. My doctor explained to me what desperation and secrecy could do to people.' She clicks the slide to reveal one line of text.

Before the 1967 Abortion Act, backstreet abortions were the leading cause of maternal death in England and Wales.

'I wasn't prepared to be complicit in that,' Alice says. 'So, I worked to bring about change. And to do that I had to air my dirty laundry in the most public spaces possible until I felt like it wasn't dirty laundry anymore. It was just my life.'

The audience is silent. A few turn their gaze to the floor.

'The women in the groups I spoke to were so buttoned up. Abortion wasn't something they discussed among themselves. But one by one, in their formal hats and gloves, they'd come up to me after and tell me they or a friend or a sister had been through a similar experience. They'd thank me for giving them the space in which to acknowledge something which wasn't the regret they were led to believe it would be. It was merely a sad but necessary part of their lives.' Alice tucks her long platinum hair behind her ears. 'Abortions are a sad reality for many women. But so too are they crucial. And I would hate for any woman who makes that choice to feel shame.'

One of the floor-watchers lifts her head, wipes away a tear with the back of her hand, pulls her shoulders back, blades protruding through her blouse as if they're wings, and visibly, finally, breathes.

CHAPTER FIFTY-ONE

'Your mum was amazing,' I tell Craig when I get in. 'The women were queuing up at the end to get their badges.'

'That's great,' he says, but his words are scoured with hesitation.

'You don't think it's incredible, what she did for me? What she's done for so many wome—'

'It's not that, Bea, it's jus—'

'Just what? That it's OK when it's any other woman's body, but not your mother's or your wife's?'

'No.' Craig grabs the remote from the arm of the sofa. 'It's nothing to do with that. I'm proud of her.' He turns off the TV. 'Did you hear from Della, babe?'

I shake my head.

'Nisha texted me. She's had the baby.'

Amdee Della has a son, Mabel. Luca Nupur Barton-Patel. He is healthy. He is home. Mother and baby are doing well.

'And Theo?' The baby who —

Craig shakes his head, we both do. All these words but none of them the right thing to say.

* * *

The next day, I send flowers when what I would have sent, if everything were normal, is a weighted pelvic floor exerciser. This is the kind of thing Della and I would have found funny. Though nothing is that normal or that funny anymore.

I'd sent her a card before. After I first came home. *I'm so sorry*, it said. That's all.

CHAPTER FIFTY-TWO

From: Bea Straw
To: Bryony Jackson
Re: Time

Hey

Can you believe we were ever that young? I never understood why you invited me on those nights out. You didn't like me that much.

It was a relief to see you last month though, Bryony. To know I wasn't the only one. And I'd love to meet up some time to chat more. How about an evening walk in the Quarry? No children. Just adults. And coffee. And TIME.

CHAPTER FIFTY-THREE

'Mabel? Come here, please.'

You're singing though. Not an actual song. Rather a string of words and a muddled tune, which may be *Baa Baa Black Sheep*, but could just as easily be *London's Burning* or *A Million Dreams*.

'Now, Mabel. Please?'

In between the sky-high shelves of rollers and masking tape, you've found colour charts.

'We came for Velcro tape, remember? Not paint. Mummy wants to put up those pictures this afternoon.'

You're not for budging. You're for shouting 'red' and 'blue' and 'orange'. You're for tossing the cards to the floor and stamping them with your patent shoe.

'It's a surprise for Daddy, remember?'

You've stopped singing. And, at last, I have your attention.

'NO!'

'I'm going to count to five, Mabel. And then we're leaving. One.'

Your foot stamps hard against the floor.

'Two.'

'NO!'

'Three.'

'NO!'

'Four.'

'NO!'

'Five.'

'Want Daddy!'

I remind myself you don't. Not really. This morning has been a good one. We danced with Grandma Alice. We painted with Aunty

Pat. We baked cookies despite the climbing heat. You don't want Daddy.

Do you?

I concede, come to you. Not just *to* you but down to your level, exactly how I've watched that woman on YouTube do it. I'm doing my homework, see. I remind myself, there is nothing to rush for. I should let you play.

'Shall we get some green ones? We could make a collage when we get home. Use yours too.' I can't prize apart the pinch you have on your three cards. 'Looks like you have some pretty ones there, Mabel. You want to show me?'

'NO!'

I can do this.

As Alice has reminded me, your tantrums aren't evidence of my bad mothering. They're simply a consequence of you being two.

I hold your chin, gently, so that you might look at me when I talk, also gently, to you.

'Shall we make a pattern?' I select five shades of yellow to share with you. 'Look, Mabel.' Make a fan of them. 'Which one is like sunshine?' And this is it, I reckon. I'm doing it. 'Pick a card, any card.' Your fingers hover above Bees Knees and 'Buzzzzzzzz', I go, 'buzzzzzzzz!' My free hand flits around your ear, landing, pretending to sting. And it's working, Mabel, because I've turned your temper round and you laugh.

'Bea?'

I spin at the voice. Familiar but out of context.

'Nisha!' If she's surprised by the force with which I throw myself at her, she conceals it well. 'How's Della? And Luca? Is he feeding OK? Does he sleep? Have you got any photos? Do you think Della might let me — ' I catch my breath. 'I'm sorry. For all the questions. Only I've tried calling, but she... And I'm not blaming her. Not at all. I understand why she doesn't want to see me. But is she —'

'She's OK.'

I've always liked, *loved*, Nisha, but those two words, they sound like me trying to sound like that YouTube woman trying to placate a hysterical child.

'Do you think she'd mind if I —'

'Where's Mabel?' Nisha's eyes aren't on me but behind me, searching.

'She's right ther—'

But you're not.

Nisha is already away, further scattering your colour-chart rainbow across the vast shiny grey tiles as she calls for you. Quietly first. And then louder.

'Mabel?' Your name, or at least the way Nisha shouts it, is a siren, flashing red for danger, red for we need help, so over comes some guy from the colour-match counter, asking are we in trouble, is there anything he can do?

'Mabel!' It should be me talking, but history suggests Nisha is the more responsible grown-up here. 'We're looking for my friend's daughter.'

You are not in the next aisle. Or the one after.

'She only has little legs,' I tell the colour-match guy, who, like Nisha, is rushing, and it's catching because, me too. 'She can't have gone far is what I mean.'

'Mabel!' They say. And I'm sure you'll be fine because you've done this before. You've wandered and I found you and sworn I will pay better attention and yet here we are. And it's awful, I know, that one of my first thoughts is everyone will think I've done this on purpose.

'Mabel!'

A woman, the same black and orange uniform, joins the chorus.

This is silly, I want to tell them, but my heart is clenching, clawing back the words because maybe it's not. Maybe this is the opposite of silly.

'Mabel!'

'Was there anyone else in the aisle?'

It's one of the orange aprons. More of them now, Merging then disbanding like a flock of crows startled by thunder.

'Mabel!'

If there was something. Or some*one*. I didn't see.

'Mabel!'

'Green shorts with white spots.' I say when someone asks what you were wearing. 'A pink T-shirt. There's a rabbit on the front.'

'Mabel!'

We've had a good morning.

'Mabel!'

I may have been a little cross.

'Mabel!'

But I love you.

'Mabel!'

I do.

'Mabel!'

An announcement over the Tannoy. 'Would the manager please come to Customer Services.' Is this for a damaged fence panel someone wants to return, or is this for you?

'MABEL!'

Those who aren't running are taking wide strides and have wide eyes. They're hunting.

'MABEL!'

They become more methodical, working in pairs in the aisles. Nisha scanning the artery running across the width of the store.

'MABEL!'

I'd thought it was them, but it's me. Screaming your name on repeat.

'MABEL!'

'MABEL!'

'MABEL!'

'Mummy!'

It's you.

You're there.

Here.

Behind stacks of large terracotta pots. A hand stuffed in your pocket, totally, *nothing to see here, Mummy, move on.*

'Mabel!'

'She's fine.'

'We've got her'

'She's safe.'

I scoop you up to me, relieved not only at finding you but at the pleasure I have in holding you this close. In this normal reaction. In me being a normal mother with these normal levels of joy.

I feel the eyes of two orange aprons still observing.

'I'm sure she'd said green shorts and pink T-shirt.'

Your polka-dot dress rides up over your bottom as I squeeze you.

'What kind of mother wouldn't rememb—'

I don't look at them as we leave.

* * *

I notice it when we get to the car, my knuckles grazing a lump in your pocket as I drag the seatbelt across your body. 'What's this, Mabel?'

Your chin drops to your chest, eyes lowered, cheeks flushed. 'Nothing,' you say in your guilty voice, not realising our mood can't be tainted because I am as happy and high as you when you first saw the paint counter what can only have been five / ten minutes ago.

I pull what looks like a potato from your pocket. 'It's a bulb, Bells! You thief!' It's a song not an accusation. 'Did you take it from the shop?'

You nod.

'Oops!' I wink. It's a joke between the two of us. 'We'll bury it,' I say, sticking it in my handbag before I get in the car. 'They'll never find it if we do.'

You too are relieved then, the both of us fizzing on our narrow escape.

We sing together all the way home.

CHAPTER FIFTY-FOUR

I was so relieved when we found her, Della. It reiterated how much I love her. Is "reiterated" too formal maybe? I delete. Write "reinforced". But that doesn't say it at all. Though neither does "relieved". Nothing conveys the visceral bliss I had in holding you.

```
Please thank Nisha for me. Love to
you. Hugs to Luca.
```

It conveys nowhere near enough, but I send it anyway.

CHAPTER FIFTY-FIVE

Silence.

JUNE

CHAPTER FIFTY-SIX

From: Bryony Jackson
To: Bea Straw
Re: The Wicked Mothers Meeting

I was too embarrassed to bring this up last night. I never didn't like you, Bea. I liked your mum too much, that's all. She was always really kind to us. My mum's still as judgey as she was back then. It was nice waking up at yours after a night out. Caroline would always be singing and offering to make us tea. I told her once that I was seeing Adrian Johnson. I wasn't. I just wanted to see her face – her disappointment in you – when I mentioned his name. But there wasn't any.

I was a right cow. Sorry.

I really enjoyed talking last night and feel so much lighter this morning. Any chance you fancy doing it again?

From: Bea Straw
To: Bryony Jackson
Re: The Wicked Mothers Meeting

Ha! You *were* a right cow. I'm sure I had my moments too.

I'm sorry your mum is judgey. Silver-lining: she does make a good vodka and orange from what I recall.

Definitely re meeting up again.

I dared to check Insta. DM from a woman who said she didn't enjoy parenting a toddler but loves parenting a teenager. Perhaps

Mum was on to something when she told me everything's a phase.

Maybe marriage isn't so dissimilar in that sense. Babies aren't the only people whose needs change as they grow.

CHAPTER FIFTY-SEVEN

I hadn't expected the circle of support that formed in the weeks after my return, what I'd expected was to be alone. But along came Grandma Alice, who'd called Aunty Pat, who insisted we all need help from time to time. 'Even your mother,' she said. 'That week she was in hospital with an appendicitis when you were just a baby, we all rallied then, Bea. It's what we do.'

It wasn't as clearly defined as one-in, one-out, but between them they had everything pretty much covered. The washing, the hanging, the sorting, the folding, the planning, the shopping, the cooking, the cleaning, the smiling, the playing, the painting, the crafting, the swimming, the soothing, the negotiating, the chastising (surprisingly not of me, Mabel, but you).

'Take your time,' Aunty Pat told me the other morning as she lowered herself to the sitting-room floor, where you were marrying the princess and a postman in the Happy Land Palace she gave you for your second birthday. 'I did contemplate the Fire Station,' she said. 'But when I looked at the different sets online, I saw it didn't have a single female character.' I must have wide-eyed with surprise that she'd even considered the diversity rep, because her chin and her voice dropped as she told me, 'I *am* trying not to be so old fashioned, Bea. I know you think I'm some old dinosaur with antiquated views on sex and race and whatever other things you young people get so mad about, but I promise I *am* trying.' She twisted to watch you play. 'And at least with this set, you can make your princess the boss can't you, Mabel?'

You tossed the postman aside. 'Prince,' you demanded, rummaging in the tub for a more suitable match for what you already believed should be your princess's happy ever after.

The fairy tale starts so young.

'Take your time,' Aunty Pat told me. And I did. I stepped back. I had a shower. I ate breakfast. I looked for a new job, because Evans may say nothing's certain, but I don't think I can face returning to school. Though once any potential employer Googles my name, I'm pretty sure that they won't want me. My CV is nothing compared to what they'll discover online.

With others here to mind you, I've been able to dip out. But when I've dipped in, Mabel, we've had fun. That tinnitus ring of endless thinking fades, not to nothing, but to a volume less intrusive, a volume that allows me to soften, to be.

The NCT lot rallied too. Jules came with that chicken stew. 'I didn't know what else to do,' she said when I opened the door on the Thursday of that first week when word had spread that I was home. 'It's not much really.' She'd put the meals in one of those bags for life, parcelled out into takeaway tubs perfectly portioned for three. 'There should be enough for two dinners. One less thing to think about.'

Kim's called almost daily. She's sent CBD oil and chamomile tea bags. 'Not just for drinking,' she tells me this morning, when you and Daddy are at the shop. 'Soak them and put them under your eyes.'

'Should I be reading anything into this?' I switch my phone to selfie mode, check out my lines. 'Eugh, I swear I've aged about thirty years since having Mabel. That's motherhood for you.'

'Or grief.'

'Don't,' I warn Kim. And yet, it's edging closer.

As all the women have gathered and helped and nurtured, my list – with all its tasks to tick – no longer feels endless. Now I'm not so busy busy busy, what were tiny papercut feelings about Mum have cleaved my heart clean in two.

It's bleeding, Mabel.

You and Daddy arrive home with bread and milk and, 'Alice!' Your grandmother comes too, unexpected through the door behind you. 'Oh!' My breath ripples in my chest as she walks past me into the kitchen. 'Your hair.'

'Blame the badge!' She laughs and runs a hand over her neckline, newly exposed by a severe but elegant crop. 'Be fearless, remember! Rooting through all those photos made me nostalgic for something a bit more…' She searches for the right word. 'Edgy.'

She twirls and smiles at Craig, who shakes his head amused. 'You look beautiful.' When he kisses her cheek, my heart spikes with furious envy that he can still talk to and touch his mum. 'I'll be out the back; I need to fix the gears on my bike.'

'Do I look like Twiggy?' Alice asks, and I nod, yes. But what I'm thinking is *you look like my mum*. Not too much, barely even, and not at all face on, but when she has her back to me, Alice is a similarish enough age, a similarish enough shape, with a similarish enough haircut that when she reaches down for you, it is too easy for me to imagine how things might have been. 'I'm not staying.' She carries you into the sitting room. 'I only popped by to show you.'

I follow behind, watching your head resting on her shoulder. And yes, I could, at a push, mistake her for my own mother, or at least a slither of her ghost. But that's not what finally, totally, rends the wounds.

It's your eyes, Mabel.

They catch mine and, despite your tender age, they recognise the sudden pain I'm feeling and blink that same long blink my mother would blink in a crowded room when she could sense my distress and wanted to secretly tell me she loved me.

It's as if some part of Mum's kindness has been passed on.

I take you, then, clasping you to me as we wave Grandma goodbye. We smile. We close the door, and then I burst. Shocking and long and loud and from the deepest parts of me, the missing-her oozing thick and pungent from my gut.

I'm sorry you have to see it. To hear it. To witness how raw the insides of us can be.

You are two and a bit. It's no wonder you don't know what to do with me. With this yowling creature with her arms wrapped firm around your body. You shout 'tight, Mummy, too tight,' but I can't let go. I need the flesh and the smell of you, even though it's not her flesh or her smell, I need something to hold on to because this groan is as deep as a grave, and I fear it might pull me in.

I don't want to fall in, Mabel. I know how it looks, how people hear the word "termination" and think death, but all I want – all I've *ever* wanted – is life. Mine and yours and Mum's, which is impossible, I know.

'Mummy?' You're scared. And me too. Because whatever is coming out of me isn't making me lighter. What it *is* doing is spreading into every cell. Like those stamps with which you like to make pictures, bearing down into the ink pads and then thudding them on the paper, the keening burns itself into my skin and bones so when the noise stops, my body continues to throb.

* * *

By the time Craig has fixed whatever was wrong with his bike, you and I are up and about again, making a picnic and no longer rocking back and forth on the floor.

We take cheese sandwiches into the garden with a jug of water you like to pour, though our cups are already full.

'Why don't you water the bluebells?' It's what we call the patch under the tree even though there are no bluebells and likely never will be.

You tip the jug over in one big heave and the water is gone.

'Oh!' The toes of your bare feet curl into the sodden grass as you look at me, like, *now what?*

It's a good question, Mabel.

CHAPTER FIFTY-EIGHT

It's hot. Too hot. The days are long and sticky, and you cry in your buggy because the straps rub against your bare skin. You cry in your cot because the air in your room is thick with this strange summer. You cry in the park because the seat of the swing burns against your thighs. You cry in my arms because my heat only makes things worse. I carry muslins to act as buffers, as shade, as an ice pack if dipped in cold water. I blow on your face. I waft you with magazines. I run you cool baths and tell you that in not too long it will be autumn because, like everything, this is just a phase.

Craig too is wilting. 'Bea?' He says, moving in that quiet way he does on these clammy evenings.

I know before I turn to him that he's crying. It's not that he's making any noise. Maybe it's the way he said my name. Or the weight of him in the kitchen. That kind of sadness must weigh heavier than air.

I should go to him. Hold him. Wrap my arms around his body and be a comfort, because that's what wives should do, isn't it? We should not only know to do these things, we should actually do them.

It used to come so easily. So easily it wasn't even movement, it was gravity or breath or all those other things that exist without any effort on my part.

Go to him, I think. The words literally forming in my head, not subconsciously but as a clear and full instruction.

Go to him.
Go to him.
Go.

'I miss wanting to be kind to you,' I'd said a few weeks back in the park.

'You *are* kind to me,' he'd said.

I'd tried to explain how it was no longer instinctive. How the kindness takes effort, which I make as I try not to be a board with him now when I move to hold him. Let me have flex, I think. Let me make noise. Let me not be silent and stiff.

Craig appears not to notice my awkwardness. As much as I am tight, he is loose, leaning into me and down to me, his head resting on the top of my head so I'm bearing the load of all his thoughts, which are pouring now, Mabel, a match for your emptied bath water I can hear flooding the pipes and outside drain.

'I'm trying,' he says. 'To see all the things that you see. I'm doing everything I can to make us that team.'

It's true. I mean, it's not perfect. His vision isn't 360, but whose is? He's cooking three times a week, and we clean the house together on Sundays. We give you a duster and laugh almost harmoniously as you sing joyfully 'me go clean my room'.

His hands move up from my waist to my shoulders. Holding on. His forehead drops to my chest. And I shouldn't think it, not now, but this is the closest his mouth has been to my breasts since the night of your birthday party, when he'd kissed me there and other places too. I feel something, only it's not yearning. It's not even nostalgia. It's a hole where something else used to be.

There's a thin patch I've not previously noticed, right there on the top of his skull. Towards the back. Not huge but definitely the beginning of loss. And it's funny, how it's that, the not quite bald bit of him, that I've no qualms about touching.

It's almost smooth beneath my thumb.

We try to sit together on the sofa. He tries putting his arm around me. I try putting my leg over his. We try narrowing the gap between us, and you'd think we might manage it. Because the gap is only the size of a raspberry. It might be about 1.13 grams heavy. It might be about 1.6 centimetres long.

Is that true though? Is the gap shaped by the embryo I aborted or something else, something less simple? Not that the abortion was simple, Mabel, but it was an act. It was nameable. Whereas this other thing, this other space between us, I'm not sure what we'd call it, what it is.

'You coming?' Craig is at the stairs already when he asks.

'Not yet,' I say, wishing I'd looked away faster, or the room was darker so I couldn't have caught his relief. 'I'm going to read for a bit.'

'OK,' he says, though my book is upstairs, and he knows this because I asked him to take it up there earlier to keep it out of your way, Mabel. But, 'OK.' I wait for the whir of his toothbrush then take out my phone.

```
Who can I talk to?
```

Google says there are therapists. Counsellors. Psychologists. But Google doesn't tell me where I could find the money or time.

There is a number though. Twenty-four hours. Free.

An hour or so later, when I'm sure Craig is sleeping, I step outside, sit under the tree.

'Samaritans. Can I help you?'

Her name is Jill, the woman who answers, the woman who asks if she can help.

'I can't even grow her bluebells.'

'Tell me about them,' she says.

And so I do, Mabel. I tell her about the seeds Mum gave me along with the instructions to combine them with her ashes, the organic mix and the soil. I tell her, Mabel, about Mum wanting me to be happy. I tell her, Mabel, about me trying so hard with the flowers *and* with the happiness, but neither of them seems to be working. Nothing is coming to bloom. I tell her too about the things I've said. The regret. The nursing. And she asks me what kind of nursing I mean? Do I mean looking after my mother or breastfeeding you? Both, I tell her. Because it suddenly, only then, occurs to me how I went from one to the other with no break in between.

'It sounds like you've had a very difficult few years.'

And I wonder how different my *Sunshine* appearance would have been if Jill had been on the sofa instead of Peter Mason. I laugh then.

'Are you OK?' She asks.

And the word *yes* is all ready to go, but the word that comes out is 'No.'

She asks if I want to talk about Mum.

And the word *no* is all ready to go, but the word that comes out is 'Yes.' Then, 'please.' Then all the other words I couldn't put in my failed attempt at a eulogy because they didn't sound important enough, but actually they were everything because they were her. She liked soap operas and those Frankfurter sausages straight from the brine. She played Brittney Spears songs on Spotify when no one was home. She read Chat magazine and Jane Austen with no qualms about enjoying the two. She hated her nose but loved her chin, because it was her own mother's chin, she said. I think *you* might have that chin too, Mabel. When she didn't smell of Lancôme Trésor, she smelt of Body Shop pink grapefruit moisturiser. Or vinegar. She loved so much vinegar on her chips. Her hands were big for her size. She told bad jokes like the kind you'd find crackers and had a mullet in the Eighties and never lived it down. She said, 'Morning, sunshine' without fail when I came into the kitchen for breakfast before school. She sang *Top of the World* whenever I was sad, even when I screamed 'shut up' and slammed the door. She had a terrible voice, but I loved it anyway and would sometimes sit on the other side of the slammed door to see if she carried on to the end because only then could she mean it. And she did, Mabel. She lost her hair during chemo and refused to wear a wig. Apart from the mullet we bought her from the fancy-dress shop in town, with which she humoured us at Christmas, when I made the Yorkshires because she'd never made a decent Yorkshire pudding in her life. And that may well have been her biggest regret. Apart from not learning Italian. So we tried with the Michel Thomas, and I asked Della's cousin's husband, who had once been a tour guide, to come over and take us on a virtual tour of Rome. She ate the pasta I made from scratch even though she felt queasy with the medication. She once set fire to her dress with a cigarette, but even that wasn't enough to make her give up smoking. She hated spiders and loved cats despite being allergic. She waited in a car with me outside Della's house while Della told her parents she was bi. She liked colouring and would have given you a run for your money, Mabel, with your felt tips and staying inside the lines. Aunty Pat could annoy the crap out of her but was the first person she'd call in a crisis. She drank rum and coke, wished her hair had been curly and was the only person I really believed when she told me everything would be fine. 'Eventually,' she'd say. 'It might be hard now, but eventually everything will be fine.'

'I thought it would hurt to talk about her.'

'She sounds like a wonderful woman.' I can hear Jill's smile. 'And from everything you've told me, so do you.'

JULY

CHAPTER FIFTY-NINE

'We're good.'

Craig is thrown, I think, by the certainty of it. He'd been nervous, you see. About leaving me. With you, I mean. What with the last time and how I so quickly came undone.

But ten days' work as a hair stylist at Capture magazine was too good an opportunity for him to turn down, so off he went this morning and, honestly, Mabel, we're good.

It'll be you and me, and then Grandma Alice is going to have you for a few days too.

'Grandma and Mabel time,' she'd said when your eyes rounded at the promise of the zoo.

'Mummy coming?'

'I'll be working, Bells.'

It's true. Me, an events manager. Yes, it's small scale, but it's something. Kim's uni mate, Sandrine, who'd flatly refused to celebrate her thirtieth, had agreed last minute to a girls' weekend in London. She's a book lover apparently. I'm to attempt a literary theme. My fee is minimal, but it's money. It's experience. It's someone putting their faith in the notion that I am reliable, that I can do something well. Of course, it's also a genuine reason, Mabel, to accept Alice's offer to whisk you away.

'It's such a tight deadline,' she justified. 'It'll take the pressure off. And anyway, Mabel and I will have a ball.'

Not quite yet though. For you and I are still in the midst of *Mummy* and Mabel time and, honestly, I could Instagram the shit out of everything we've done that's made us smile. Only I don't; I'm back on a social media embargo.

I have photos, evidence, which I promise to send to Daddy when the three of us are done on the phone.

'We've been to the splash park,' I tell him. 'Along with the rest of the population of Shrewsbury. God this heat. It's baking, isn't it, Bells?'

'I'm really glad things are —' Someone off screen calls his name, and 'Sorry, babe. I've gotta go.' Craig nods at the model in the background.

I can't remember the last time he did my hair.

He left on the train this morning with his packed bag and a cup of coffee and a muffin from the Starbucks at the station. We stood on the platform and waved, stopped off on the way home for our own cake before heading back through the park. No buggy. A ridiculously slow walk, on which you paused to point out dogs, flowers, bins, poo, a wall that you couldn't possibly not climb. I pushed you on the swing until it felt rude not to give it up for another girl, who'd shown surprising patience while you screamed *more more more*.

We were on the bridge when we saw her.

'Amdee Della,' you shouted as I was stunned into silence by the knotted twitch I felt on seeing her face.

She leant her bike against the railings, went as if to kiss me but fiddled instead with her helmet, which looked kind of fancy, more aerodynamic than necessary for a quick trip into town. Like Della was doing what Craig would call 'training'.

'Where's Luca?'

Della stiffened. I recognised that tension, had felt it. And I wanted to kick myself then for the question with its undertones of *why aren't you with your child*.

'With his *other* mum.' The tips of Della's fingers pinkened with the pressure with which she fastened her helmet beneath her chin. She looked only at you. 'Lovely to see you, gorgeous girl.'

And my heart when you reached for her, Mabel.

'Amdee Della come lunch.' Your smile was huge with your plan. 'Toasties,' you offered. 'Kookumber.' And then, more hopefully, 'Icecream?'

'We do have Magnums.'

'Pleeeeeeease,' you said to Della, an amplification of my own internal pleading.

'Another time.' She kissed you, straddled her bike and was gone.

It was true about the ice cream. After we put you to bed last night, Craig offered to go to Sainsbury's so I'd have everything in for at least the first few days of him being away. He checked the cupboards, wrote a list, did the shop, unpacked everything, including the Magnums and a bottle of gin.

'I think you're sorted,' he said.

'Thank you.' I meant it. 'You know, we'll be fine.'

He'd said the same to me when Della and I went away for a night when you were seven months old. Things were strained with Nisha. Another unsuccessful round of IVF, and while Nisha was constantly reassuring Della it was no one's fault, my beautiful best friend blamed her body, which was officially a medical failure, she said. It seemed unkind, then, to express any relief about leaving you. Though I'd wondered in the hours prior to departure if it was worth all the faff. The pumped milk, the hand-written nap-and-feed schedule, the snacks and food I'd prepared because you were weaning – baby led – which meant you'd have a bit of whatever the adult with you at the time was having, and I didn't trust Craig not to offer up your first ever Dominoes. So there was defrosted beef stew and mash potato, chopped veg and a yoghurt for after. The laundry basket was empty because odds on it'd be full by the time I returned. I stuffed the change bag with enough nappies and wipes for a week. Craig watched on from the side, where he was bouncing you on his knee, telling you the names of the Formula One drivers as they droned around the circuit on the TV.

'You do know it's just one night, Bea?' Which was true. But what if something went wrong? What if your father didn't know what to do?

'Sometimes, you didn't always give me the chance to figure it out.' Craig said last week when we were two glasses into a bottle of red, almost but not quite side by side on the sofa while silently watching a repeat of *Have I Got News for You*. 'What to do, I mean. For Mabel. For us. Or how to do it.' His eyes were fixed on Ian Hislop, who was rallying insults with Peter Mason. Will the man forever be a trigger? 'I'm not saying I shouldn't or couldn't have done more, and it's not an excuse, but perhaps it's not as simple as me not wanting to do my share.'

busy busy busy

I took hold of and squeezed his hand.

And this morning, before Craig left, we kissed, with our mouths open, our tongues reaching, for the first time since everything. There was a return of the tenderness albeit spliced with an ache.

This evening, I lay you down in your cot in only your vest and knickers because, even with the window open, the room is a furnace.

'Song, Mummy,' you say a little while later when you spot me spying on you from the doorway. Without even thinking, I begin the song I've not heard since the day you were born, when Mum held you in her arms and whisper-sang how you'd put her on top of the world.

It came up on that call with Jill in the garden at midnight, when I learnt I could say things aloud and still summon the strength to stand.

And your smile when I sing you that song again! And again. And again. The throb I've been feeling since that long howl softens now as I let her in. Mum. Not her ghost exactly. But part of her. The part of her that imprinted itself upon every cell of my body long before grief did the same.

When you're sleeping, I open the gin Craig bought me. I pour. But down the sink, Mabel, because I want to feel it, whatever it is that's happening in my body, it's time to acknowledge it's here.

She doesn't appear to me. There are no unexplained noises or flickering lights. I doubt she'll speak to me in my dreams. And when I sit in the kitchen while you sleep, she is still gone. But. I feel her anyway. And when, tomorrow, I lift you out of your cot and tell you, 'Morning, sunshine,' I'll hear her voice in mine.

Inch by inch she is coming to me as I mother you, Mabel, showing me that you and I will be fine.

In our own way.

Eventually.

You and I *will* be fine.

CHAPTER SIXTY

From: Bea Straw
To: Bryony Jackson
Re: Change of name

As per chat on walk earlier, I've been back on Mumsnet and put some feelers out for the group. The more I think about it, The Wicked Mothers Club as a name feels wrong. We're not wicked, Bryony. We've as much ability to be as wonderful as anyone else out there, so let's not label ourselves – and others like us – as bad. There's a word we use in this house for when things don't quite go to plan. When they seem terrible, but with a bit of time, patience and the spin of a silver lining, they turn out alright. 'Shibbles'. It fits, right? I'm a shibbles kind of mum. And I'm cool with that. You?

CHAPTER SIXTY-ONE

This evening, with Craig in London and you with Grandma Alice, I book the hotel and train tickets for Sandrine's party. I find a walking tour in Bloomsbury and send her the link, along with the cost of a Shakespearean afternoon tea. I call Dad and ask him if it's OK for me to pop round to his house to get the letters Mum wrote to you, Mabel, when I was pregnant and she was dying. In the post-partum blur of the aftermath of her death, I'd given Dad the box, because while I loved the idea of one day reading what she'd written to you, the fact that you'd only ever see her words and not hear them was, back then, too much to bear.

'It's in the bottom bedside drawer,' he says. 'On your mum's side.'

It was the one part of the house Matthew and I had always been banned from touching, the only hint in my childhood that mothers have secrets, a drawer-sized part of their vast lives they weren't prepared to share.

I opened it once before, when I was seven, and the rattle of fallen-out teeth in a small pink pot snapped my take on the world as viciously as my brother had snapped my pencil from Chester Zoo. They were *my* teeth, collected not by the tooth fairy but by my mum, whose word could no longer be taken as truth.

It didn't last though, my scepticism. There was no fun in doubting my mother. Because what was life without a belief in Father Christmas or the Easter Bunny? How could I keep looking forward to a future if I didn't have faith in her promises that everything would be OK?

That pink pot sits now on a stack of two boxes. The top one is the shallow brown A4 box file I'd bought from Paperchase for each of us when Mum said her letters were done. Without even removing it from the drawer, I take off the lid, and there they are, Mabel. All her words – a mix, she'd told me, of fairy tale and real-life escapades – are there.

Touching one of the letters is something for which I must brace myself. Because *her* fingers have touched them too. Just seeing them is enough to chip away at the bricks I laid to keep Mum separate from me when it was too much, even, to think of her. I wonder now if instead of keeping the pain at bay, those bricks kept the grief and its agony in.

'I don't want to feel this way,' I said in my call to Jill.

'Whether or not you want to feel it, it *is* the way you feel.'

'I thought I could push it away.'

'Our feelings tend to wait for us,' she said. 'And our grief.'

Promising myself I will summon the courage to read the letters later, I wriggle the box from the drawer. Beneath it is a second one, older probably, with its dented corners, *1986* written in tiny-pencilled numbers on its lid. I open it.

Downstairs, the front door slams. There are quick and heavy footsteps in the hall.

'Beatle?'

'Up here,' I call, distracted by the wood-smoke smell of old paper and the fact that *Dear Beatrice* is written at the top of every sheet.

'Shit.' Dad's at the bedroom doorway. 'I hoped I'd be here before you.' He's puffed from his scramble up the stairs. 'I wasn't thinking. When I said you could get the letters for Mabel. I'd forgotten…' He looks at the box in my hands. 'They were with the ones your mum wrote to you.' He sits on the grey carpet next to me, his hands open as if expecting me to pass him something, Surely, he can't think I'd pass him these. 'She never meant for you to read them.'

It's too late though. My eyes are already all over the first letter dated 17th April 1986.

'She was shattered, love.' Dad's breath is warm on my shoulder. 'But it was more than that. She wasn't herself.'

I hear the words Dad's saying but only just because the words Mum wrote are louder.

Dear Beatrice, I love you but...

She says how she had to leave me. How she needed to be on her own.

You'll never know, she says. *You're so young. There's no way you'll remember. I'll be back home with you and Matthew soon.*

'The doctor said something about baby blues.' Dad's talking too quickly, the way people do when they're seeking justification. 'But your mum was adamant it couldn't be. Said she'd been fine with Matthew. And how could she be blue when she loved you just as much as she loved your brother. Because she did, Beatle. She loved you so mu—'

'I know Dad. You don't have to worry. I know.'

'Course you do,' he says, smiling, fingering the other letters, telling me she'd returned from a few days in Wales not healed – definitely not healed – but what she called 'a little less weighed down', willing to see a doctor and take some anti-depressants that helped her feel better but were never strong enough to rid her of shame. 'She made me promise not to tell anyone. Lived in fear that one day she would genuinely get the appendicitis I'd told everyone was the reason behind her sudden disappearance.'

'I wish she'd warned me.'

'She didn't want you to feel responsible for her being so down.' Dad's shrug isn't dismissive, it's pained. 'She didn't want you to be afraid either.'

If I'd known though. Not that her experience exactly mirrors mine. I don't think what I had – *have* – is post-natal depression. But it would have reshaped my expectations if I'd known.

'Your mum wanted to protect you.'

And I want to do the same for you, Mabel, but I hope that if any good comes of this shit storm it's that despite how badly I went about it, I will have prepared you for the messiness of motherhood. For the truth that it's not all *dear* sweetness and *dear* light.

I bring both boxes home with me, sit in the kitchen, reading the letters – a mix of fairy tale and real-life escapades – aloud.

'What brilliant luck,' Mum says to you, 'in having Beatrice – your mother, my daughter – as our closest ally. You and I, baby girl,' she whispers, 'have struck gold.'

It's not real, of course, her voice. But. I hear it. And neither is her hand reaching across for mine as I sit at the table. But. I hold it, tracing the line of her finger turning circles in my palms as she sings *Tonight Will Be Fine* and pulls pennies from her pocket to place on the bits of me that sting and scoops butter from a dish to rub into the bits of me that are bruised. And I know, obviously, that the footsteps following behind me on the stairs are as make believe as her laugh when I've changed the sheets and am star-fishing so I might go fresh into a new week, a new life. A life that will be fine.

Eventually.

CHAPTER SIXTY-TWO

'Hey.' I balance my phone against the stack of old clothes on the floor and pull another dress from the wardrobe. 'I reckon we're sorted for the party. You do think Sandrine's happy with the plans, don't you?'

'Screw the book bus and literary cocktails, mate.' Kim's face on my screen is a distraction from the charity-shop haul I've been sorting. 'I want to know how you've been revelling in your orgy of child-and-husband-free time!'

'Oh, it's wild.' I give her a quick three-sixty of the bedroom. There's barely an empty surface. 'I'm culling. Even my bottom bedside drawer has had a sort out. Look what I found…'

'What in holy hell is that?'

'Mabel's umbilical cord stump!'

'In your bedside drawer, Bea? That's the place for lube and vibrators, not rotting flesh. No wonder your sex life has shrivelled.'

'It *is* kind of gross.' It looks like something you'd find clinging to a Q-tip you've pulled from a particularly manky ear.

I remember rolling it between my fingers when it dropped unceremoniously from your belly button. How I couldn't throw it in the bin because once there'd been something almost identical that had tied *my* mother to me.

I tell Kim the last week has been OK. That in the days you and I were on our own, there was something easier about doing the grown-up things by myself, how a mental load was lifted by the lack of expectation of help. How the rooms in this house feel so much bigger on these quieter days and nights alone.

'But, you know what, I miss them too.'

'Good,' Kim says, looking at the camera of her phone but still chopping red peppers on the board in front of her. 'That's how it should be.' She scrapes the pieces into a pan. 'How much longer does Alice have Mabel?'

'Two days, why?'

'Then you should get yourself down to London.' Whatever she's cooking is sizzling. Come to think of it, everything about Kim is sizzling right now. 'You could do a reccy of that bar you booked for Sandrine's drinks. Invite Craig.'

'What, like a date?'

'Exactly. You could role play.' Steam rises from her pan as she ups the heat. 'Strangers in the night.' Her eyes are wide with mischievous glee.

'Is that what you and Adam do?' My brow rises suggestively as I imagine them dressed to kill.

'Sometimes.' She shrugs, like, *it's cool, yeah.* 'Though other times, we meet actual strangers instead.'

'Aw, you guys.' I wrinkle my nose, ramp up the faux sweet charm.

'Don't take the piss.' Kim dips her finger in the sauce then licks it. 'It's great. We've worked hard on setting the boundaries. We know what each other's happy with now. Not being funny, but if you and your husband talked a bit more openly about what you want and need, maybe your relationship wouldn't be as withered as that thing in the jar.'

Ouch.

'Shit, Bea.' Kim's picked up her phone from the kitchen counter. Her free hand presses into her temple. Her top teeth bite her bottom lip. 'That was too much. I —'

'No.' I take in the mess of the bedroom. Everything that was inside now tipped on its head. The bags lined up in the hallway filled with stuff I'd held onto that I've realised needs to go. 'You're right. About that. *And* about London. We should do it.'

I call Craig later. Don't give him an option. I've already booked my train.

CHAPTER SIXTY-THREE

'Hey, you.' Craig hands me a cocktail.

'Happy Ever After?'

He kisses my cheek. 'Overrated? Unrealistic?'

'Probably,' I whisper. Then, taking a sip, smiling. 'Maybe we should give it a new name?'

'What? Muddling Through?'

We clink glasses. Share a nervous quiet laugh. 'Cheers,' we say in unison. 'To muddling through.'

Craig leans in conspiratorially. 'You know, it's probably sacrilege to cast doubt on the Happy Ever After here. The barman just told me the whole place is inspired by fairy tale.'

'Shit, you're right.' I scan the room. At only 4.00 p.m., it's emptyish of people but packed with books. Stacks of them in stylish chaos on the bar. They line the walls too, in floor to ceiling cabinets, which house hundreds if not thousands of tomes alongside bottles and decanters of intricately cut glass. 'Best keep our blasphemous reality check to ourselves then.' The cocktail is as delicious as ever. 'Or else they'll banish us from the booth.'

I take Craig's hand and lead him to the far corner, where there's curved seating, with a privacy screen fashioned from hardbacks piled over six-foot high.

'Are we allowed here?' Craig holds off from sliding into the banquette.

'Sit. I have contacts.' I tap my nose as if VIP access took more than one quick call to Janet in events. 'I've booked it for the party I'm planning.'

My husband sits down, one elbow resting on the table, his fingers toying with the stem of the glass.

'You look handsome.'

He does. He's had a haircut, trimmed his beard. I don't recognise the plain grey T-shirt or the box-fresh trainers, but the difference in him is more significant than his clothes and shoes. The skin of his neck is soft when I run my finger down it.

'This is a nice surprise,' Craig says. Melancholic then, 'I thought you'd enjoy me being away.'

'I have,' I tell him, perhaps too quickly. I lean over and brush my lips against his. 'But maybe it's true what they say about absence's influence on the heart.'

It's the subtle changes I find hope and pleasure in. Like how his thigh presses against mine.

He tells me about the work. The shoot he did on Tuesday at an abandoned holiday camp on the south coast, where two models were styled as grunge musicians, 'very Nineties,' with electric guitars they strummed, unplugged, in a drained and tile-cracked outdoor pool. He tells me about running. The 15k routes through the unpopulated streets in the early mornings, when he's pushed himself harder and faster to dance tunes from the Noughties, which remind him how buzzed he used to feel living in a city that survived fires, revolutions and wars.

'I ran past the Tower of London this morning,' he says. 'It's such a collision. All those old and new buildings.' His head dips, as if he's embarrassed of this sudden passion. But then he necks his drink, looks up at me with these bright eyes. 'C'mon, we're free to do what we want for once, right?' He stands and pulls me up from the banquette. 'You want to see?'

I do, Mabel. And so we walk east, your father and I, along the winding, not wholly logical roads of our old home town to the Victorian Tower Bridge, which spans the Thames to connect a thousand-year-old stone fortress to City Hall, nicknamed the armadillo for its bulbous armour of glass.

'Everything's possible here, don't you think?' Standing in the middle of the bridge, Craig has his feet in two different but intricately woven worlds. 'That's why I didn't want to leave.'

'I'm sorry.' And I am. But. 'I needed you.'

'I should have seen that. I'm sorry too.' He looks up the river towards the Shard and the Gherkin, the column in Paternoster Square. 'I came though, Bea.'

'You did.' The clamour of pedestrians passing behind us urges me against the railing. 'Trouble is, by then, I felt I could no longer lean on you.' My head spins as I look down at the drop into the water. 'By the time you were there with me, I'd already begun to fall.'

We stop for coffee on our walk back to the station. Despite the warmth of the early evening, we sit close, never minding the mingling sweat on our limbs. The silence between us is different to the silence at home.

I watch Craig observing another couple as they come through the door to the café. Her jagged fringe and layered auburn hair frame a narrow face with a stud in her eyebrow and a ring in the end of her nose. His short jaunty dreads fall across his forehead. His tattoos – stars, a rose, indecipherable writing – are as much of a mismatch as their clothes. I follow Craig's eyes to the guy's hand as he reaches for his latte, then to the woman's as she takes her mint tea. They each wear a ring. For all their quirk and alternativity, they vowed to conform.

A little later, 'See you next week.' Craig and I have been standing together on the concourse before I leave for my train. My head is against his chest. His chin is on my crown. This isn't the passion of our early days, Mabel.

But.

CHAPTER SIXTY-FOUR

It's gone ten when I get back into Shrewsbury. Despite the dark, I take the long walk home from the station, not really admitting to myself why until I'm standing outside Della and Nisha's, looking up at the window of the room I helped them turn into a nursery. We spent an entire weekend painting the walls chalky white before applying decals of pine trees, a rabbit, an owl and a fox. We built a wardrobe and two cots. Hung two mobiles to soothe two babies and near enough decided on two beautiful names.

Is she sitting in there now, like I did with you in your bedroom, Mabel, wondering what happens to those who were taken from us, doing her best to love those who weren't?

At Mum's funeral, friends, family, near-strangers called you the Light or the Hope. Wasn't it beautiful, they said, incredible that Mum was able to hold on? To fight for those minutes in which she held you. Mum would have hated that word: fight. For surely, in the wake of her death, it made her sound like a loser.

'I refuse to be in a battle with my own body,' she told me when Aunty Pat left one afternoon, having delivered vitamin water and a series of recipes she found online specifically designed for attacking cancer. 'My body is something I will always love, Bea. It's given me a brilliant life. It gave me your brother and you.'

Craig took you for a few minutes so I could go with Dad and Matthew to thank the celebrant. People's reaction to me was different when they saw me empty-handed, when I was a mourning daughter as opposed to a new mum. There was more physical discomfort is what I mean. When I was holding you, at least they knew where to look.

How has it been for Della? Whose Light and Hope mirrors exactly what she's grieving?

I linger on their street, even though she doesn't answer when I call.

* * *

When I get home, I sit on the sofa with a pen and paper.

What was it Mum said to Dad, about how those days by the sea writing letters hadn't healed her but had allowed her to feel less weighed down? Is that why she suggested we begin writing to you? Because 'Thoughts don't always do so well if they're left to curdle in your head.'

With Tonight Will Bea Fine, I'd been writing most days. And despite what some of my readers have said, I didn't lie. I took the best bits, or the bad bits that I could make into the best stories and wrote the palatable version of us.

Reading it back over, there is a definite absence. Mum. In all the comments – not just from strangers but from those who knew me – no one acknowledged my inability to include her. I don't blame them. It's for the same reason, I imagine, that they found me easier company when I was holding you at the funeral: it is reassuring to see life. To see coping. To see moving on. Because to question otherwise would be to risk what? A collapse? An outpour? An invitation to death to slink its way back in?

I write my story again now. As bare-bones as possible, avoiding any attempt to carve out an appealing bloggable narrative.

Craig didn't come.
I had a baby.
Mum died.

These are not a beginning, a middle and an end. These are not a neat post on Tonight Will Bea Fine. These are facts. But, like the blog, these are only a biggish part of bigger truths I never dared to examine, Mabel, because, like my fellow mourners, it was more reassuring to feel life. To feel coping. To feel moving on.

I must fall asleep on the sofa. When I wake, the notebook and pencil have both dropped to the floor.

Light's dawning when I go into the garden,

Bluebells were fine in theory. When Mum suggested them, it was a beautiful idea, and I could imagine us – you and me, Mabel – running through them, picking them, bringing them inside, and you never tiring of the story of your name, which I chose because, yes, it means loveable, but also because of its ending, its Bells, which would flower and ring for Mum.

'Mum?' It was a question loaded with fear that we were too late because, even though the nurse had said she was doing OK and told me to go on through, when I carried you into the room at the hospice, her eyes were closed, and I couldn't see the up and down of her breathing.

Dad had hold of her hand. 'Caroline.' I was relieved by the lack of uprise, by his confidence that, yes, she would meet you.

'This is Mabel. Bells.' And what I meant was, *we don't want or need the bluebells, Mum*. What I meant was, *what we want and need, Mum, is you.*

But she died.

As did the fairy tale of marriage.

And there are no bluebells.

But.

There is you, Mabel.

'The bluebells.' Jill said, as I sat on the empty grass worrying I'd kept her too long on the call. 'What do you know about how they grow?'

Mum had been specific with her instructions. I assumed she knew what was best. But if I've learnt anything in the last few months, Mabel, it's that mothers – like everyone – are learning as we go.

I tap into Google.
How do I grow bluebells?

The search results begin:
Plant your bulbs...
Plant your bulbs...
Plant your bulbs...

We'd bought seeds, Mabel.

How do I grow bluebells from seed?
You can plant bluebell seeds, but you'll need patience.
It can take years for them to flower.

Five years, one site suggests, it will take for the seeds to turn into flowers.

Five years with an empty garden?

Mum, you and I, Mabel, none of us can wait that long to bloom.

CHAPTER SIXTY-FIVE

After a day making introductory phone calls to hotels and other events venues across the country, I call you to say goodnight. Grandma Alice holds her mobile over the travel cot where, exhausted from a day at the farm, you are already sleeping. You've kicked away your blanket, your hair is slicked with sweat as you lie with your arms tight around Flumper. Has he been better for you than I have? Softer. More permanent. You hold him like you know this, Mabel. Fierce. Grateful.

The house is clean and tidy. You are content and safe.

I realise how easy it would be to run.

So I do.

I pull on an ancient sports bra, leggings and T-shirt and resist the urge to grab my earphones, running instead with only the sound of my heavy breathing. There are my thoughts too, of course, aired now, and less of a guillotine than they were when I'd held them at arm's length, where their immorality was sharpened by forced distance. And dread. I no longer deny them. I have *had* these thoughts, these regrets. Still have them now. And yet. I did and do my best by you. Could it be true, then, that within the parameters of my love and, yes, my regret, I was and am a good mother.

Messy and complicated but good enough.

Could it be the same with Della too? With our friendship. Might I be a good enough friend?

'It was terrible timing.' This is not what I intended to say. But then nor did I intend, when I left the house in search of movement, of air, to run here, to the doorstep where Della now stands with a child in her arm and a look of ambiguity on her grief-and-baby-shattered face.

383

'What was?' And though I can't read her voice, she has already turned, just a fraction, unblocking the barricade her body was making in the doorway.

'Everything?'

She nods. 'Do you remember Maxine?'

'Collins?'

Another nod. And, for a second, I think she might let me in but, for the moment, my oldest friend stays put.

Maxine Collins was Della's first girlfriend. She was nineteen, drove a Mini and made my best friend so happy she gave me hope for a movie kind of love.

'She hit me.' Della's so matter of fact I think I must have misheard her.

'She did what?'

'She hit me. Not just once either. It happened, what, six, seven times.' Della traces her finger back and forth over Luca's crown.

My best friend has a baby I've never held.

'I've been thinking about her a lot. Well, not *her* exactly, but what she did. How she made me feel. Why I didn't tell you.'

Sweat runs in cool trickles down my face, my chest, my back.

And my heat must be obvious because, 'Would you like some water?' Della asks.

'Please.' I don't know if this is an invitation, if I should follow her inside when she disappears.

'Don't just stand there,' Della says when she returns from the kitchen. 'Would you rather sit in here, or the garden?'

If I try to answer, I will cry.

This is almost but not quite normal.

'It's so fucking hot.' Della's eyes widen and she bites her lip. 'If Nisha comes home, do *not* tell her I swore in front of the baby.' She smiles, then, like, *our secret*, and I am a teenager again, when we'd make up after a stupid row. Any sudden movement and my heart will literally burst. 'Let's go out the back.'

'He's beautiful,' I manage. And he is, Mabel. Luca is this beautiful tiny creature who I already love.

I drag a couple of chairs out from under the garden table.

'I looked her up on Facebook. Maxine,' Della clarifies when I quirk my brow. 'You know, I couldn't remember what was true. Whether she could actually have hurt me. Physically, I mean. That's not how the story went. Was it?'

I shake my head, sip my water.

'The more I went on about how awesome she was, the more difficult it was for me to undo it, that version of Maxine and me I'd told you. And some of that *was* true; the candlelit KFC in the park really *was* kind of romantic, and she *did* give me a rose every time we met. And it's probably true that I loved her. So I didn't lie to you. But I didn't tell you everything either.' She wipes away her tear that's fallen on Luca's nose. 'You were so thrilled for me. So happy I was out after all my years of being in the closet. You remember how convinced I was that I'd never sleep with a girl? That I'd still be wanking to that clip of Neve Campbell and Denise Richards in *Wild Things* when I was ninety-five? But then I met Maxine and had everything you and I both thought I wanted, but I was miserable. And ashamed. I'm sorry,' she whispers to Luca, 'I'm drowning you here, buddy.' It's true. Her crying is weeping now. 'I suppose what I'm trying to say is that I think I get it, Bea Bea. I think I get how difficult it might have been for you. Because the longer you keep something a secret, the more shameful it becomes.' She stands. Holds out the baby. 'Would you like a cuddle?'

'Really?' I wasn't sure she'd trust me.

'Really.'

I bring him up to my nose. He still smells so new.

Della goes inside, reappears with a bottle of red.

'Should I not tell Nisha about the wine either?' Luca's hair is so soft, so clean.

'She'd be more surprised if I didn't have one.' Della pours us both a small glass.

'Not for me.' I point at my trainers. 'I have to run home.'

'And I have to breastfeed.' She tips the contents of my glass into hers, compelled, then, to clarify that she'll pump. 'I guess it shifts things that I've now had a taste of motherhood.'

'And?'

'And I love it. But, fucking hell, it's tough. Absolutely brilliant and lovely,' she adds quickly, 'but also absolutely gruelling and hard.'

'I'm sorry about Theo.'

'Me too,' Della says. 'It's awful.'

We sit with the awfulness for a minute.

'When I think about Mum, it makes me want to rip my skin off.' It sounds crazy, I know, Mabel. 'I just think if people could see it – the constant acidic burn – maybe they'd understand the pain. And if it's like that for me, Dell, I can only imagine what it must be like for you.'

Our arms touch as she reclaims Luca. 'There's no hierarchy, Bea Bea.'

And that's true in theory.

But.

'I wish I'd talked to you about it,' she says. 'About your mum, I mean. *And* about Mabel.'

'You want to talk about Theo?'

'I will. But not now.' Her finger runs the length of Luca's nose, then drops and rests on his top lip. 'Nisha's sorting counselling.'

'You two are talking about it then?'

She nods. 'We talk about everything.' It's a statement, sure, but the way Della looks at me, it feels like a question too.

I shrug because I'm not even sure what she's asking.

'All those things you said to that wanker Peter Mason. That list you reeled off. I dunno, when I watched it back on YouTube —'

I shrink into my seat. Because isn't this the moment Della will reiterate how spoilt she thinks I am, that I need to check my privilege, that I've no right to complain?

'— it got me thinking about you being a straight woman —'

Here we go. I close my eyes, heave a deep breath, totally ready to take whatever she throws at me, because she's right.

But Della puts a hand on my knee. 'Look at me, Bea Bea. You *have* had it easier in so many ways, but there's an advantage to my marriage I hadn't anticipated when I first got together with Nisha.' She sips her wine. 'Our practical conversations about parenthood didn't end when we agreed we wanted a baby. We had to work out *how* we would have one, which of us would get pregnant, what we'd do about mat leave. It went on and on. And because we're two women, we were making these decisions outside of all that heteronormative shit that bogs so many of you straight people down.' She sighs. 'It's not that you and Craig aren't capable of talking about this stuff...'

She's right. It's like all those other conversations we didn't have about how we wanted to navigate our marriage; it didn't feel necessary. Not until all those unspoken assumptions about who'd do what had already been fortified by tradition and form.

I Facetime Alice again when I get home so I can just watch you, Mabel. So your grandmother can tell you in the morning that I'm always thinking of you, even when I'm not physically there.

CHAPTER SIXTY-SIX

I watch how you reach for him, your father, who's returned, wired with a job offer, from London.

'What do you think?' His face isn't too dissimilar from the first time he made me a Happy Ever After, when he handed me the glass and asked me 'What do you think?' and I had to concede, Mabel, that it tasted deliciously sweet. He lifts you up into the air, towards the sun, which is still scorching and impossibly bright. 'We keep the salon here – Sienna's more than capable of managing it – and if we rent out the house, it should cover the mortgage. Marco – the editor – says the money won't be brilliant to start off with, but if you're working too, I reckon between your salary and whatever they pay me at Capture we could do it. A new start, Bea. And imagine how much Mabel would get out of growing up in London.'

I picture you in Victoria Park. In the Natural History Museum. Riding your bike along the Regent's Canal. We will meet Hannah and Ichiro for picnics at the City Farm. Kim will lead us to the best kid-friendly restaurants in town. Your grandparents will come to stay, and we'll take an open-top-bus tour around the city. You'll point out the sights because you'll be the kind of kid to remember all the details from the last time you did the same tour when Della and Nisha will have brought Luca for a weekend. Della and I will miss each other terribly but make a pact to meet up regularly in Birmingham, where she will hint that maybe she can persuade her wife of a move back down south. Craig and I will rediscover all the places we used to hang out when we first got together. And there will be new places too, where we will hold hands and plan a cocktail-style life, which will be deliciously sweet for him, for you, for me.

'*Room on the Broom?*' Craig asks later, already with the book in his hand, because life is so predictable, right, Mabel?

'No, Daddy!' You have other ideas. You have *The Highway Rat*, *The Scarecrow's Wedding* and *Tiddler*. You go back to your bookshelf. You take *The Snail and the Whale*, *Stickman* and *Zog*. They are not *Room on the Broom* but the rhymes, the illustrations, they're familiar. They are different stories from the one you were so hung up on. And that's become okay.

Eventually.

* * *

'So?' Craig has a bottle of Champagne; his infamous editor, Marco, gave it to him in celebration of their possible venture. 'What do you think?'

'I think we should sit down.'

And we do. We sit at the kitchen table. Opposite each other like we did on the night I came home when we weren't sure if anything was salvageable.

'Shall I open it though, yeah?' He's so optimistic. And maybe he's right to be, maybe it could be a new start. I run through that Instagrammable version of us in London.

Anything is possible, it's true.

It is easy to curate a future, Mabel. To believe in the story as it should be. To put so much faith in that Happy Ever After that you quietly close a lid on the now.

But.

The now only gets noisier when you attempt to avoid it. A child doesn't stop screaming simply because you put it in another room.

And neither do I.

'I went back to Dad's this morning.' I try not to look away from my husband. Not to look at the fridge, where a new photo of Mum is stuck with that monkey magnet. 'Dead,' you'd said. You have been the only one really to say these things out loud.

'Your Dad'd be fine, Bea. He's got Connie now. And we'll need to come up here every couple of months anyway, to check on the salon, the house.' He's unpeeling the black foil from the top of the bottle. His thumb and forefinger are untwisting the cage around the cork.

'Stop.'

Craig looks up at me, like, *what, babe.*

'Please.' The bottle is cold in my hand when I take it. I hold it against my chest, willing for a break in the heat wave, for the thunderstorm that seems to want never to come. 'I'm not drinking.' I say it like that's sufficient explanation.

'Oh.' He says, like maybe it is.

'I'm trying…' I pause, still figuring it out. What exactly I'm *trying* to do, that is. 'I want a clear head.'

'Fair enough.' Craig looks pleased, like this is progress, which I suppose it is, albeit not the kind of progress he's expecting.

'It's been so…' I thought I had the words.

'So…?'

'I haven't been myself,' is all I can manage.

'The antenatal depression.' Craig announces it as a confirmed diagnosis, as if he's forgotten how, the night after his dad's birthday, he himself suggested it was bullshit. An excuse. He nudges a champagne glass along the table with his finger.

'It wasn't antenatal depression.' It's my turn to sound sure. I place the Champagne on the kitchen side.

He prods the glass another centimetre. 'I don't understand what you're saying.'

I sit back down. 'I'm saying I wish so many things were different to how they've turned out to be.'

'Mabel?'

I shrug. 'My mum getting cancer. You not moving up here. Me not explaining why it was so important to me that you did. Us expecting a baby to solve all our problems. And then, when it became apparent that she hadn't, still not allowing myself to think, let alone talk, about every fucked-up detail of my life, including the bloody bluebells.'

'The bluebells?' Of all the things to have picked up on, he's picked up on this?

'We should have got bulbs. The seeds take years to flower.'

'So give them time,' he says, this look in his eyes, like, *isn't that what all of this needs? Just time.*

'I need a clear head.'

'That's why we didn't open the Champagne.' But we both know alcohol's not the only thing that's been clouding my judgement.

'You didn't come. I had a baby. Mum died.'

When Craig's finger brushes the glass, I don't even try to catch it. There is something right about it smashing. Something important. Loud.

'Maybe I could have coped with one. But all three.'

His hand is warm on my chin, his thumb gentle when he wipes away my tear.

'We didn't talk. And that was me as much as you.' What I mean is, I don't blame him. 'We were so set on our Happy Ever After.'

No juddering shoulders. No violent wails of despair. But Craig is crying now too.

'I think I'm angry.'

'You *think*?'

And I can see his confusion, Mabel, because my voice isn't raised. I'm not swearing or stamping my feet. 'I *am* angry.'

'I should have come.' He says, like that would have changed everything.

'I should have made it clearer that I needed you.'

'I should have done more.'

'I should have asked for help. I should have stopped being busy busy busy in some stupid attempt to block out the pain. I should have known I was drowning. I should have written a blog about grief not motherhood. I should never have agreed to have a baby. Not then. I should have stopped drinking gin. I should have kept my phone away from Mabel. I should have come up with a better compromise with you when I wanted to look after my mum. I should have understood that I couldn't be kind if I was fucking empty.'

But I didn't know, Mabel. I didn't know.

'Thing is, Craig, I can't live with the shoulds anymore. I need to start living with what's actually happened. The choices I actually made. And those I'm trying to make now.'

'Which are?'

'I need a clear head.'

It's all I can think at the moment, Mabel.

'What are you saying?'

'I think I'm sayi—'

'You *think* you're saying, or you *are*?'

'I am.'

The broken glass sits untouched on the floor.

'You *are* saying what, Bea?'

'I asked my dad when I saw him this morning… now that he and Connie have moved in together… I asked him about his and Mum's house.'

Craig's hands now lie flat on the table between us. His chest expands with a huge inhale.

'He said I could…'

He holds his breath.

'I'm going to move there, Craig.'

He closes his eyes. Exhales. 'Bea?' He reaches across for me, and even though our palms are both clammy, I grip on to him. 'You can be honest with me, I won't tell anyone, I promise. Are you sure this isn't about...?'

I know what he's wondering because I've wondered it too. 'Mabel?'

'Yeah. Is this about leaving *her*?'

I shake my head, no.

'I should be relieved.' Craig's shoulders sink. 'But I guess that means it's about me.'

The rattle of the fan cooling the oven from dinner stops, but it's your father's eyes, Mabel, that make me think he might now hear me. 'It's not that I regret having a child so much as I regret what having a child flagged up between us. The gap.'

'The gap?' He looks down at our still-held hands.

I'd always imagined issues in marriage would stem from adultery or something with equal passion and rage but, 'It's so boring.' I dip my head by way of apology. 'Peter Mason said as much, and I realise it just makes me sound like a nag, but the gap, Craig, it's domestic and parental and really fucking dull. But it's there and with everything else, I can't ignore it.'

'Domestic? Like the cleaning and shit? But I've been trying —'

'It's not just domestic. It's...' How can I make it tangible, this 360 thinking I've struggled to put into words? 'The Bianchi,' I say, and Craig furrows his brow because what does a bike have to do with any of this? 'You said I wasn't thinking about you when I made the choice to have an abortion, but when you decided, on your own, to blow almost two grand on a bike, to sign up for a triathlon, to spend hours *training*, not just in one discipline but three, you did not for one second think about Mabel. And you did not for one second think about me.'

'But I've cut back on the training.'

'The training's a symptom.'

'A symptom?'

'For all my flaws – and believe me, the internet has made sure I know there are many – whatever I'm doing, whatever I'm planning, even if what I'm planning is an abortion – Mabel is at the core. We think differently, Craig. And I'm not saying it's your fault. It's both of us. It's what we've learnt. What we've *all* learnt. And maybe, if things hadn't gone so tits up, I'd have lived with it. Moaned about it to Della and Kim, sure, but put up with doing more than my share because *that's men for you*, right?' I roll my eyes. 'But with everything else, the things *I've* said and done and…' We've been over that enough times already. 'Listen, Dad's house isn't far away. And I've been thinking—'

'So it seems.' Craig is that Buckaroo game we played this morning. He could kick off at any time.

'It doesn't have to be the end. Of us. Of our marriage, I mean.' I owe it to you, Mabel, and to Craig and me, to say it, this thought I've had of a familiar but different story. 'We could just do marriage a different way?'

'A different way?' He sits back in his seat, legs spread, arms in the air because he can't believe this shit. And to be honest, neither can I.

'The job Marco offered you, he said it'd be freelance, right? You could be in London two / three days a week. I could live with Mabel at Dad's. You'd then be back here the rest of the time when Mabel would live with you. In this house. And then some nights the three of us could all be together?'

'Together?' Craig's hands slide from the table to his lap as he leans forward. I cling on to the fact that he's not leaning away.

'Yes. Together.' I will him to look right at me. 'Not the way we are now. Definitely together though.' His eyes reveal nothing. 'I love you, Craig, but—'

'And there it is.' His hand slams to the table. 'The infamous "but".'

I glance at the baby monitor, even though we both know if the smack had roused you, we'd have heard your scream.

Kim warned me this would happen. Told me to expect his shock, his anger, or his disbelief. 'You've been the one mulling this over,' she said after I told her what I was thinking. 'But for Craig it's going to be a bolt from the blue.'

I don't rush to say anything. For a minute or so, I let us breathe. The red of the smack disappears from his upturned palm.

'If we each had time on our own with Mabel, maybe the twenty-four-hour responsibility of parenthood would sink in. We'd be equa—'

'So basically this is a lesson?' His eyes reveal fury now.

'No. Yes. Maybe. As crass as it sounds, that probably *is* part of it. But, it's not just that.'

The screech of Craig's chair when he stands is unbearable.

'You looked so happy when I came to see you in London.' He did. He was vibrant with old-Craig vim. 'It got me thinking how it's not only me that's compromised in this marriage. We both have.'

The ring-pull on the can of Bud snaps under the pressure of his finger. 'Course we have. Isn't that just what happens in a relationship?'

'Yes, to an extent.' I stand and carefully gather the larger shards of broken glass. 'But perhaps more than it would if we didn't stick so rigidly to the rules.'

He swallows the lager. 'The *rules*?'

'We're only in our thirties. We've committed ourselves to each other for the rest of our lives. Our marriage, if we can make it work, will be so long.'

He takes another swig.

'That new start in London, even if *I* don't want it, that doesn't mean we can't make it work.' I bend down, use a brush to sweep the tiny pieces into a pan. When I stand again, 'You could have that life, Craig. But also have one, albeit a different one, here with Mabel.

And, if you want to, with me. Separate houses doesn't have to mean separate lives.'

'Don't try to spin this as a favour.' The fridge glows yellow on his cheek when he gets another can. 'Let's not kid ourselves that this is about anything other than you.'

I tip all the remnants into the bin and go to him. This *is* about me, Mabel. But I really believe it is about you too. I want to be a better mother to you. Maybe *this* is the compromise. Maybe *this* is the necessary consequence of love.

'Remember when we were in Vegas? All that good intention we had with our ideas of how we could commit to each other without getting dragged down by the same old same old constraints of marriage?'

Craig nods.

'We made a new name for ourselves. We wanted, or *needed* even, to be different.'

Your father and I are touching now, Mabel. We're still just about holding on.

'But what kind of marriage would it be if we…'

I urge him to feel the hope in my exhale. 'It'd be the City Hall instead of the Tower of London.'

He looks at me like, *I have no idea what you mean.*

'Those old traditional buildings are beautiful, but they don't always work for the way we live our lives now.'

He sighs, draws me into him.

The clock ticks loudly on the kitchen wall.

There's so much uncertainty in his sigh. 'You said in London that you missed me.'

'And I did.'

'But?'

'I liked missing you. It's a much nicer feeling looking forward to seeing you than staring at you while I lie awake at night wondering if things would be better if you were gone.'

'I can't tell if that's a compliment or not.' At least he's laughing, as we move into the sitting room and lie down on the sofa. Closer now than all of the many nights before.

'Isn't it,' he pauses, 'I dunno, a bit indulgent. Two houses. Can we even afford it?'

'We'd need two houses if we were splitting up.'

'I don't know, Bea.' Craig whispers into the back of my head. 'It's not normal.'

I roll over, look him straight in the eyes and smile, 'You're right. But maybe it's us.'

EARLY SEPTEMBER

CHAPTER SIXTY-SEVEN

We've sold the house.

'It wouldn't work,' Craig said. And he'd been right obviously. The idea was outlandish and who did I think I was kidding to seriously believe we could pull it off.

I'd thought I wouldn't cry. The decision, once it was made, had felt like the right one. But this evening, on our last night as a family in our home, I've been crying since we came upstairs. And now still as I climb into bed, and Craig reaches his arm across the mattress, his hand finding the skin between my t-shirt and shorts. It remains too hot for a duvet, but we have the sheet. Thin. Almost but not quite cool.

'Bea?'

I'd rather he didn't look at me. I'm blotchy. Wet. But I lie face to face with him anyway, completely, utterly exposed.

'We don't have to do this.'

Though we both know that we do.

A waft of fabric softener as I scooch myself closer. 'You changed the bedding.'

'I wanted to treat you.'

'Thank you.' I don't begrudge the gratitude because Craig doesn't expect it. He's done it for love, Mabel. For me.

I kiss him. And I'd tell you to close your ears and eyes to this kind of moment, but perhaps it's important for you to see that these decisions we make do not come easily or without confusion. That we are contradictory animals when we love.

It's Craig who takes the condom from the draw.

The what-ifs spiral like ghosts, Mabel.

I enjoy the weight of him on top of me, how I feel pinned to the here and now.

He moves away when we we're done. When we've both come, both crying, both thinking about what we would have done differently given the chance.

For all that we would give to each other, neither of us has the ability to give that.

Things will change for you, Mabel. Despite my best laid plans, from tomorrow, this house will no longer be your home.

I tiptoe, spilling with sorries and expectations, into your room. As always, Flumper, your consistent source of comfort, is clutched to your chest. I kiss him first, then you.

'Who knows what the future brings,' I whisper, 'but always know, Bells, that tonight, at least, will be fine.'

CHAPTER SIXTY-EIGHT

'We're here.'

'Granddad's.'

'Ours,' I tell you. 'Remember?' I lift you from the car seat, ensuring Flumper is in your arms when I put you to the ground, reaching for your cardigan because it's cooler here than when we left the station.

We'd waved goodbye to Daddy after a brief encounter in town. Me arriving, him departing. It wasn't supposed to be that way, Mabel. But *he* is booked for a shoot in Kings Cross early tomorrow morning and, with the Shibbles launch to plan with Kim and Bryony, *I* couldn't leave London today until noon. 'I'll miss you,' Craig said, as we walked to the platform.

'Just enough missing us,' I kissed him. 'Be sure to enjoy it too.'

I did, Mabel. A few days ago, I left you and your father for three nights in a rented studio flat in not quite London but not far off. Craig was right when he'd said it wouldn't work. That there was no way we could keep our house, Dad's place *and* have the money for him to be able to stay over in town as frequently as would be required for him to take the job with Capture.

So we sold. Cash buyers. A couple from Manchester, who talked about turning your nursery into a home gym and putting a hot tub in the shade of the tree. It stung, of course, the knowledge that those seeds might never flower, but I don't doubt we will see bluebells, Mabel, that we will grow them in our own time and in our own way.

Granddad's is now ours. And so is the twenty-nine-point-three square metres in Watford, where Daddy and I will each have the time and space to —

'— to what exactly?' Aunty Pat's face when I tried to explain it to her looked like I'd revealed Craig and I were participating in a mass orgy live-screening on Channel 5. 'I don't understand it, Bea.'

'Craig'll use the Watford studio flat when he's doing freelance stylist work for the magazine, and I've told you about the new Tonight Will Be Fine.'

'Ah, yes. The events business.' I swear even you rolled your two-year-old eyes at her sigh. 'What about Mabel?'

'Mabel will live at Dad's place, which he's very kindly renting to us at a low rate so we can give these new opportunities a go.'

Aunty Pat shook her head. 'What kind of opportunities? What about your teaching? What about job-security? What about —'

'It's really not that complicated.' I took her half-finished cup of tea from the table, rinsed it out and put it in the box with all the other crockery I'd packed for the imminent move. 'Dad's place will be mine and Craig's home. With Mabel, *and* with each other, but Craig and I will come and go.'

Today it was my turn to come.

I ran to you. From the train along the platform, I couldn't hold you fast enough. And, *god*, my lingering kiss with your father too.

'Ours,' you say, plumping yourself down on the front step.

I sit next to you, rummaging in my bag for my keys. You dip your hand in, begin pulling things from it like you did that afternoon with Grandma Alice. 'Tissue,' you say. 'Mirror,' you say. 'Bulb.'

'What's that, Bells?'

You hold it up, like I did in the carpark of B&Q after I'd found you. Here, now, you are proud as punch of your indisputable treasure-hunting skill.

'Bulb!'

'So it is.' I thought I'd lost you then. I thought you'd been taken from me. By kidnappers, Mabel. By karma. By serves-that-stupid-woman-right. The relief when I'd found you, when I'd realised how things might not be perfect, but I wouldn't be without you and how much I *do* want to be your mum. 'You remember, Bells? This is contraband!' A new word for you. 'Smuggled goods,' I say. 'We're pirates. We need to bury our loot.'

'Now!'

There is nothing to stop us. Nothing else on the agenda until bedtime when we will read a book. I bought a new story for you today.

'Yes, now.' I take your hand, and we go around to the back, where I tell you to be careful in the shed because, 'tools, Mabel,' I say, pointing at the various dangerous objects, though there is none so dangerous as me.

I could have hurt you so badly. And maybe I did. But, for the moment at least, for tonight, you are fine.

'We need rain,' I explain, as you whack at the ground with the trowel. It's so hard.

'Clouds, Mummy!' You point at the sky, which is thick, ominous, grey. We have matching goosebumps on our skin.

'In some cultures, Mabel, they think you can summon the rain by dancing.'

It's all the cue you need, chin up, arms raised, feet clomping the solid ground, you stomp around the garden – *our* garden – shouting for the wet to make the earth diggable so we might plant our bulb, which is clutched, an unknowable future, in your palm. I ignore the twitch in my fingers for my phone, its camera, the barrier it puts between us, and come join you. Copy your noises. Your squeals of delight.

Somewhere in the distance, the thunder claps, and you scream, turn to me, your face filled with fear of what is coming.

Spilt Milk

But there is wonder too.
You don't know what pressure the storm might ease.
What clarity it might bring.
You raise the bulb.
Summon the rain.
I love you, Mabel.

ACKNOWLEDGEMENTS

It's common practice to thank your agent in your acknowledgements, and while every other note of gratitude to Hannah Sheppard has been heartfelt, my recognition of her involvement in Spilt Milk warrants a bigger thanks than ever. So…

THANK YOU, Hannah,

for planting the seed, for calming my nerves and for pushing for the ending Bea, Craig and Mabel deserve.

This novel was several years and several submissions in the making. Patience may well be a virtue, but it's not easy to master when the rejections come thick and (not so) fast. That said, the *yes* we had from Genevieve Pegg at Harper North was most definitely worth the wait. I couldn't have asked for a better or more enthusiastic editor. If I thought my dream-reader list was wild, Gen upped the ante when she suggested we send a copy to Uma Thurman. 'She might never read it,' Gen said, 'but you never know.' Uma, if you *are* reading this, thank *you* too. And let's talk soon, yeh, about who you might play in the movie?

To Alice Murphy-Pyle, Megan Jones and the rest of the Harper North team, thank you for the faith you've shown in me and the valiant efforts you're making to get Bea's story into the hands of as many readers as possible. The bold and beautiful cover designed by Emma Rogers will definitely help.

There's a lot of talk these days about finding your tribe, and I've certainly found mine. To all my writer friends, especially Susie Bassett, Sandra Dingwall, Sara Emmerton, Tess James-Mackey, Liz Pike, Ko Porteous, Louisa Reid and Ciara Smyth, thanks for your unwavering encouragement, your WhatsApp plot diagnoses and your continued presence in any writerly – or otherwise – high or low. Writing can so often feel impossible but somehow you all turn what could be a terrible writing day into something enjoyable and good.

Redrafting Spilt Milk several times over meant I had lots of early readers offering invaluable feedback. It takes an enormous amount of time and effort to read an entire manuscript, especially one that isn't yet polished. So big love to Ko, Susie, Sara, Louisa, Tat Effby, Anstey Harris and Charlotte Hartley-Jones.

Additional thanks to Louisa for your especially useful inside take on the finer details of being a teacher, and for your love of profanity that makes me feel better about mine.

Jess Ryn, Elena Wilkes and Stella Duffy. Your early endorsements were an absolute boost. Stella, I hope one day there will be a limited-edition print run with "This is a fucking good book. A fucking good *feminist* book" plastered across its top.

Thanks to Debbie Flint for giving me an insight into how Bea's TV appearance might run and to Jake Flanagan for giving me his name – hopefully you'll feel your bid in the charity auction was money well spent.

Thanks to Ella Spraggan for answering my questions about the administration and procedures around abortion pills and to Ayo Adebiyi for responding so quickly and graciously to my out-of-the-blue message. Good to know my portrayal of Kim isn't utter 'shitcocks'!

Always enormously grateful for Emily Johnson's reading, talking, running and general marvellous friending and to the many other friends who not only listened to me blethering on about Bea but also shared their own experiences of the thorny division of emotional and domestic labour.

And on that note, a special mention for Gemma Hartley, whose fantastic book Fed Up came into my life when both Bea and I most needed it. For anyone interested in better understanding the invisible work of women, please do check it out.

To make the dull domestic tasks more bearable, I listen to podcasts, which often find their way into my writing. In that vein, special thanks to Franki Cookney whose excellent series The Second Circle – 'the podcast that takes sex seriously' – was extremely helpful in writing Kim and Adam's non-monogamous relationship. I'm also extremely grateful for the brilliant Grief Cast hosted by Cariad Lloyd and for the many podcasts I listened to with Alan de Botton, one of which gave me the quote Adam puts in Kim's birthday book.

Thanks to Janie and Mike at Chez Castillon Retreats for the food, wine, company and time time time. I repeat…all that perfect precious time.

As ever, Mum, I love you, and not only because you read whatever I send no matter how rough the draft (though that helps). We joke that the common thread of my books is women finding their own self-worth. I think though that I likely inherited that interest in self-worth from you. Because you have always very clearly and very carefully encouraged me to find and hold onto mine. Thank you!

Phil, I appreciate being married to a writer, especially this writer, isn't always easy. The long nights. The inevitable tears. The cries of 'I just can't do it anymore.' I'd imagine it's even harder when the writer you're married to is writing a book about a couple in which the husband – no matter his good intentions – fails to see the inequity in the relationship. As I'll come onto in a moment, there's a common assumption when women are writing about domestic issues that their work is autobiographical. Spilt Milk is fiction, but there is a kernel of truth in Bea's frustrations with Craig, and you not only recognised and acknowledged that but actively addressed it too. So thank you for reading, for listening and for not just seeing the invisible work but doing it. And special thanks, even though there's no such thing as blue jobs or pink jobs, for doing the bins way more often than I do. And in that vein, I hope you're as excited for this new book from me as you were for the new purple bin from Shropshire Council.

Monty & Dolly, I had my reservations about writing a book in which a mother blogs about regretting having her daughter. Several people suggested that it was a terrible idea because you might think I feel that way about you. I would like to put it here in print that I do not. Though I hope you know that already, that you remember I write stories not memoir and that you feel how ridiculously grateful I am for my brilliant babies every single day. Just as Bea is ultimately grateful for Mabel. Because Bea's regret isn't really about her child. Bea's regret is for the inequality having a child exposes in her relationship with Craig.

You are no strangers to conversations about feminism. We have spoken about women's right to abortion, the pay gap, domestic abuse and many other issues and how they require collective effort that can feel too big for us to tackle as individuals. What Bea struggles with in Spilt Milk is different. The every-day work that falls to women for no other reason than it's always fallen to women. We, *you*, can change that. You can support mine and Daddy's attempts to break stereotypes, and you can support each other in resisting those tempting cliches of what is it to be a boy or a girl.

I was, at one point, scared for you to read this book. But now I really want you to read it* so that you grow into adults aware of the gendered traps we so easily fall into, that marriage is not a fairy tale, and that like everything else in life, love is complicated and can simultaneously be both wonderful *and* hard.

Always remember, you are my marmite on toast and hot chocolate. What I mean is, you make me feel better and happier no matter what.

---

*When you're older. I know we let you watch Task Master, but Spilt Milk is even swearier than Greg Davies and Little Alex Horne.